D0981962

In the Garden of Papa Santuzzu

Also by Tony Ardizzone

In the Garden of Papa Santuzzu

Tony Ardizzone

Picador USA
New York

Picador® is a U.S. registered trademark and is used by
St. Martin's Press under license from Pan Books
Limited.

Book design by Ellen R. Sasahara

Library of Congress Cataloging-in-Publication Data

Ardizzone, Tony.
    In the garden of Papa Santuzzu: a novel / Tony
Ardizzone.—1st Picador USA ed.
        p.   cm.
    ISBN 0-312-20307-1
    1. Italian Americans Fiction   I. Title.
PS3551.R395I58   1999
813'.54—dc21   99-22963
                                                        CIP

First Picador USA Edition: July 1999

10 9 8 7 6 5 4 3 2 1

In memory of my father
𝒞 ANTONIO ARDIZZONE
(March 31, 1921–March 30, 1996)

and my grandparents
𝒞 ROSE MONTALBANA PIZZA
and VITO ARDIZZONE

and all who made the
journey with them

℘ Acknowledgments

The author and publisher gratefully acknowledge the following magazines, which published chapters or sections of *In the Garden of Papa Santuzzu* in slightly different form: *Agni, High Plains Literary Review, Italian Americana, Many Mountains Moving, Ploughshares, River City: A Journal of Contemporary Culture,* and *Voices in Italian Americana.* Song lyrics cited are from "The Internationale," by Eugene Pottier (English translation by Charles H. Kerr); "Solidarity Forever," by Ralph Chaplin; and "Workingmen, Unite!," by E. S. Nelson (*I.W.W. Songs of the Workers: To Fan the Flames of Discontent,* 13th edition, 1917).

I also wish to thank Kit Ward, for her steadiness and faith; Fred Gardaphé and Walter Wetherell, for their friendship and encouragement; the Indiana University Research Office, for a summer fellowship, which enabled me to work on an early draft of this book; Jerre Mangione and Ben Morreale, for their example as well as for writing *La Storia;* Gaetano Cipolla, for *Arba Sicula* and his help with Sicilian words and phrases; my father's sisters, Eva Sanfelippo and Mae Sipiora; Diane Kondrat, my first reader; and my editor, George Witte.

The Negro is not the man farthest down. The condition of the colored farmer in the most backward parts of the Southern States in America, even where he has the least education and the least encouragement, is incomparably better than the condition and opportunities of the agricultural population in Sicily.

℘ Booker T. Washington

In all human history no country and no people have suffered such terrible slavery, conquest and foreign oppression, and no country and no people have struggled so strenuously for their emancipation as Sicily and the Sicilians.

℘ Karl Marx

Almost all Sicilians have an instinctive fear of life, and so they withdraw, secluded, happy with little, provided it gives them security. . . . It is the sea that isolates them, that is, that cuts them out and makes them alone, and everyone is and makes an island of himself, and, by himself, he enjoys his little bit of joy—but barely, if he has any. By himself, silently, without seeking comfort, often desperately, he suffers pain. But there are those who manage to escape.

℘ Luigi Pirandello

Cu nesci arrinesci. He who leaves succeeds.

℘ Sicilian proverb

Contents

Field of Stone

 Rosa Dolci

NCE THERE WAS a poor but honest
man, *un'omu d'onuri,* a man of honor, who worked the whole day—
day after day—in the unrelenting heat of the blazing sun, scratching the pitiful dirt at his feet with a wooden hoe, coaxing the useless
dust first this way and then that way, like a mother combing her feverish child's thin, dulled hair, urging the earth to release something
he and his children and wife might eat, so that they might live to
work beneath the scorching sun another day, and not starve. Thank
God, *figghiu miu,* that even in these hard times you're a stranger to
real hunger. Do my arms squeeze you too tight? Ha! Imagine the
slow and suffocating stranglehold of true starvation, like a snake
slowly coiling itself around your belly and ribs, squeezing all breath
and vitality from you. Each passing day you grow more weak. In the
shadow of your hut you squat and chew straw.

The man's name was Papa Santuzzu. He was your *nonnu,*
father of your father. This is his story and the story of his children.
It's also the story of people like me, whose destiny it was to marry
into the Girgenti family. God willing, one day you'll pick up the
thread and tell these stories to children of your own. May you be
blessed, *figghiu miu,* with a fair wife and many children! May you
have a clear gaze and a strong back!

Papa Santuzzu's story starts back in Sicilia, in another world, the land that time forgot, where those who stayed behind sometimes gathered against the long night around a blazing fire, talking about themselves and all those who'd left. Everyone was expected to bring some wood. As we squatted around the fire someone would beat out a tune or hum until a second would sing or take up some instrument and play, and as the moon slid higher in the sky toward the promise of the coming day, a third would start a tale and, like a weaver with her yarn, stretch it out and let it spin

> *and end her story with a rhyme,*
> *and so the next soul with a tale would begin*
> *and all would pass the time*

bringing fresh wood to the fire, telling one story after the next, until we'd gone full circle and everyone who had wanted to had given breath to a song or story. Then the one who started the first tale would tell another so as to knot the thread, as the moon grew pale and thin and the fire low, and the village cocks stretched their wings and scratched the rust of sleep from deep inside their throats, and from the waiting fields you could hear the songbirds' sweet singing.

WHAT DID PAPA SANTUZZU look like? Well, his skin was as dark as an olive soaked in brine. His nose was long and sharp, like the beak of a great bird. He had a big black moustache that drooped nearly to his chin. He wore a gray cap to protect his head from the sun. You could see at once in his brown eyes that he was gentle. When he laughed, your mouth had no choice but to laugh, too.

For a poor man Papa Santuzzu was no stranger to laughter. During a game of tresette one lazy evening in the village, Papa Santuzzu was dealt a perfect hand. He couldn't keep a straight face and so infuriated his opponent that the man wagered an old donkey which Papa Santuzzu's subsequent run of absolutely perfect cards won. When asked by the man why he had laughed in the face of such fortune, Papa Santuzzu replied that luck is like a person's shadow, it chases best those who flee from it.

Lu muttu di l'anticu mai mintìu. The proverbs of the ancients never lie.

The old donkey was known as Gabriella because her bray was like the loud trumpet call of Angel Gabriel's horn. This was a donkey whose song was stronger than her pull. Papa Santuzzu had secret names for Gabriella, names he'd whisper into her long ears while the pair labored together for long hours each day in the fields. She too wore a hat to protect her head from the sun, though her hat was floppy and wide brimmed and made of straw.

One day Gabriella flat out refused to work. Papa Santuzzu took a deep breath, then tried to reason with her. No good. Gabriella wouldn't move. Papa Santuzzu tried rubbing her legs, hoping that by massaging her strength he might rouse it. The stubborn donkey remained motionless. He tickled the sweet spot behind her ears. Gabriella refused to budge. He whispered promises in a tongue believed to be irresistible to donkeys. Gabriella whickered and shook her head.

Papa Santuzzu then gave up and called her the name of every lazy no-good-for-nothing thing in existence. It was midday, sweltering hot, so Papa Santuzzu sat down in the shade of an almond tree. Gabriella lay down beside him, and while the pair snoozed, a drunken soldier from the mainland ambled by and took a sudden liking to Gabriella's straw hat, exchanging it for his own. When Papa Santuzzu woke up, he looked at the donkey and saw that she now wore the cap of an Italian soldier.

"Gabriella, Gabriella," Papa Santuzzu shouted in great distress. Tears sprang from his eyes. "I know I yelled at you and hurt your feelings, but you didn't have to go and join the army!"

·   ·   ·

EVERY DAY PAPA SANTUZZU broke his back in the fields. He who does not work, dies. The land was parched and ancient—in places it was as dry and useless as bone—and sprinkled over with a powdery coat of dust so tired that the particles just wanted to blow away someplace where they could sleep for a century and not be bothered.

Now, a piece of land is like any living thing. For it to prosper, it has to be both fed and loved. This was land that was starving, owned by a wealthy baron and ruled by a cruel *gabbillotu,* or overseer. Both wanted to take as much from the land as they could. The pair allowed Papa Santuzzu to tend it in exchange for the bulk of his harvest, so great a share that Papa Santuzzu knew that he worked for himself in name only and was in truth another man's slave. Gabriella was the only thing Papa Santuzzu truly owned. The baron owned even the house Papa Santuzzu lived in with Mamma Adriana, their seven children, a scrawny pair of goats, an occasional hen, and far too many flies and fleas to count.

Gabriella lived in the house, too. The house was just a simple hut. One room, a dirt floor, a wooden chair or two, a ladder sprinkled with chicken droppings leading up to the loft where at night the people and their fleas and flies slept.

The poor land, I believe, was trying to sleep, too. For thousands of years, since the beginning of time, Sicilia had been forced to feed a thousand and one mouths, her own true children as well as all of the invaders from the south and east, the north and west. Every nation mighty enough to stretch canvas across a beam set sail for Sicilia and landed on her shores. She was once the bread-basket for the known world.

Back when we all were the great-grandchildren of Adam and Eve, Sicilia was a young, ripe fig. Her fields burst with wheat, rice, olives, sugar, every kind of fruit. It's said that the most delicious sausages hung from her trees. Anchovies leapt from the sea right onto your plate. Herbs furred the forest floor. In the forests loped antelopes whose antlers were so strong they could saw the hardest wood. Elephants with little houses on their backs sauntered freely throughout the countryside. Each tree in the forest dripped with syrup and honey. In the branches above, silkworms wove the finest cloth. Partridges laid so many eggs that you couldn't take two steps without stumbling upon a nest. Goats were so full that each morning they pleaded to be milked. Sicilia was a garden paradise, and her grateful people ate of her and replenished her in return. Even today someone drinking a glass of wine will toss the last mouthful back onto the earth out of respect and gratitude.

But over time the mouths multiplied, and the first flotilla of invading sails landed. These pirates recognized no law. They took whatever they desired. Soon the native people built their villages in twisting mazes, known only to those born there, as a means of protection against the thieves. The *cristiani* shut their eyes and ears to everyone strange. They made a maze of their language, too. Only a fool gives clear directions to his house or his daughters' whereabouts.

The land was also misused. Sicilia's mighty forests were cut down. Her richest fields were gutted and left empty. The earth wasn't given back a tenth as much as was taken from her, and over time too many new hands reached out for her, too many new mouths ate of her, too many hungry stomachs were born bawling out their complaints, until the island erupted and belched smoke and fire, crying out that she needed to rest, and the *genti di campagna* shouted no, not yet, we're starving, feed us, you can't go to sleep yet.

Every day Papa Santuzzu and Gabriella worked to keep the tired earth awake. The ground was tough and stingy, like the meat of an old goat, like the petrified heart of someone ignored, mean and hard and sad enough to shatter Papa Santuzzu's hoe into splinters. Worse, the earth was choked with so many rocks that there wasn't sufficient space on which to pile them all. Some rocks were so big that even with Gabriella's help Papa Santuzzu couldn't roll them from the fields. The soil was so poor that even weeds snubbed it. The dandelion likes to set down his long claw just about anywhere, but he'd scamper past this inferior dirt. We'd eat dandelion, *cicoria*, borage, thistle—nearly every green thing— whenever we could find them. Greens swell the belly, though after too many days of eating them the *culu* cracks and the mouth desperately craves something else.

Once, the only thing to grow in Papa Santuzzu's plot of earth was a nasty bush of thorns. These were vicious and stubborn thorns, as is the nature of things that are thorny. Whenever Papa Santuzzu tried to cut them back or pull them out they leapt at his eyes and sliced his legs and hands and arms, eager for the blood that would nourish them. The thorns spread so far and wide across the ground that the insects crawling the dry earth imagined that the sun had been swallowed up entirely. Even Gabriella be- came lost in the snarl of thorns! Only her long ears and the crown of her army hat could be seen.

Papa Santuzzu stood in the field, listening to Gabriella's plain- tive trumpet. He too became lost in the vicious maze of thorns, which pierced his skin and eagerly drank his blood.

Now, instead of feeling sorry for himself, as some would, Papa Santuzzu thought of how he really was quite fortunate. That took some imagination, for the thorns had grown so thick around him that he could hardly move.

The thorns haven't pierced my hands and feet, Papa Santuzzu told the sky. I am thankful to the Lord for that. They haven't pierced my side. They haven't crowned my head, as they did the Savior, Jesù Cristu. For these blessings I am thankful.

Just then Papa Santuzzu noticed a melon trapped in the tangle of thorns. It was a small and modest melon, hardly worth eating. Still, Papa Santuzzu worked a hand free, tore the melon from its vine, then managed with his knife to slit the fruit open. Inside the slit crouched a tiny spirit. The spirit tried to escape, but Papa Santuzzu caught it and held it fast in his hand.

"Let me go!" the spirit cried. "Let me go!"

"Not until you've helped me," Papa Santuzzu said.

So the spirit stopped squirming and told Papa Santuzzu he could have three wishes.

First Papa Santuzzu wished that Gabriella would be free.

"Done!" the spirit said. And the donkey stood free of the thorns.

"Now clear this field entirely," Papa Santuzzu said.

"Done!" And the field was clear.

With his last wish Papa Santuzzu was tempted to ask that the field be filled with grain. But instead, maybe for the first time in his life, your father's father stopped thinking like a wretched laborer whose sole purpose was to put coins into another man's pocket. Papa Santuzzu took a gulp and wished for a house as big as the baron's.

"Hey," the spirit cried, "do you think that if I had a house as big as the *baruni*'s I'd be living in this scrawny melon?"

With that the spirit scampered away. Papa Santuzzu stood alone with Gabriella in the middle of the barren field. But at that moment an exciting new idea dawned inside Papa Santuzzu's brain. Just like when he'd won Gabriella in the game of tresette, Papa Santuzzu had a glimmer of inspiration. He imagined that someday he, rather than the gods that ruled, might be able to alter his destiny.

UP UNTIL THEN he had worked long, unimaginably hard hours without question or protest. At the end of each day, when the sun blazed like a red coal in the sky, he had only the hardened calluses on his hands and a thousand and one aches in his back to show for all his labors. Each day he'd stand, glance at the uncaring sun, mumble a prayer to a mostly silent God, and mop the sweat from his face with his big kerchief. While the *baruni* in his mansion grew fat on meat, Papa Santuzzu and his family ate slugs, *babbaluci,* and boiled weeds.

One night after the air grew quiet and cool, Papa Santuzzu

stared through the gap in his roof. As was his habit he pondered the stars. He was just like the stars, he told himself. He and the slowly shifting flecks of light had no choice but to hang in the sky in their fixed, ancient, preordained positions.

Gabriella had limped all that afternoon, he considered as he gazed at the sky. His daughter and three sons again had mewed with hunger after they'd licked the supper bowl clean. Again Adriana had gone without so that the children might have more to eat. There were new taxes to pay to the thief of a government. Papa Santuzzu thought of the government in Roma as just another absentee landlord, only bigger and more greedy! It even had a tax on Gabriella! Worse was the conscription law that required of young men seven years of armed service. Seven years might as well be seventy since the boys almost never returned. Every autumn soldiers from the mainland marched through the province and took away its sons. These cruelties were, are, and always would be, Papa Santuzzu considered. He stared at the bits of light dotting the deep and endless sky, and just then a shooting star arced westward across the heavens.

He dreamed then of possibilities even more fantastic than the perfect run of cards that had brought him Gabriella, or the spirit that had nearly granted him the *baruni*'s house. Papa Santuzzu dreamed of something he'd heard men discussing in the village. This dream was about a wonderful, faraway land.

The marvelous new land was called *La Merica*. This place was said to have such vast, fertile fields that all you had to do was to push a seed into the ground and it would grow! You had to step back fast, claimed the men, or the plant's stalk would knock you right down! In *La Merica* there were rivers and seas leaping with fish. There were vast mountain ranges filled with so much gold that roads were actually paved with it! No one went to sleep hungry. In *La Merica* there were three villages where a working man could earn a real bundle. Like conspirators the men cupped their fingers beside their mouths as they whispered the villages' names. "New York," they whispered. "Brazil. Argentina."

Papa Santuzzu gazed up at the glowing stars in the sky, his lips whispering the magical names of the three golden villages of *La Merica*. "New York. Brazil. Argentina."

Mamma Adriana lay beside him in the straw, wheezing, her belly already beginning to swell with your saintly twin aunts. The firstborn child, Carla, lay at her side. The three boys—Gaetanu, Luigi, and Salvatore—slept near her feet, mouths open, drooling, their legs twined together like the strings of a single rope. From the straw on the ground floor of the hut came the resonant snores and sporadic grunts and various intestinal discharges of Gabriella.

If he could win a donkey, Papa Santuzzu thought, if a spirit could clear an entire field of thorns, if a star could wrestle itself out of its fixed hole and leap like a rabbit westward across the sky, then maybe, just maybe, his children could live in a generous and more forgiving land.

Papa Santuzzu pulled himself up from the straw, crossed himself, then thrust his head and shoulders out the gap in the roof. "New York!" he shouted as loud as he could up to the stars. "Brazil!" he shouted. "Argentina!"

See, all the talk in the village had dropped the bean of an idea into Santuzzu's brain. Once it grew into a tall beanstalk, there was no stopping him from climbing it. His old thoughts and old ways hardly had time to step back before the force of the new idea knocked them right down.

Don't think it didn't take some doing. And don't think it didn't shatter Papa Santuzzu's heart. For a parent there are few pains worse than to see a child wanting. Papa Santuzzu knew that his children were hardly better off than Gabriella. Said simply, they were slaves. Adriana knew this, too, and over the next years with the birth of the twins and her last child, Assunta, Adriana felt joy edged with the most unbearable grief. She too understood that the chains of *miseria* had to be broken.

Figghiu miu, it would have been so easy for Santuzzu and

Adriana to say, let our children be the ones to break the chain. After all, just look at us, we're old. We've worked, we've suffered, we have such pains. Certainly now we deserve to sit in the shade of our years and allow our cloudy gaze to fall on the heads of our grand-children! Let them be the ones to decide to send their kids to the New Land. Besides, who will close our eyes when we die? Who will wash us? Who will cover our bodies with stones and grieve?

I tell you, after a woman gives birth she labors for a while longer until she delivers the broken sack that only moments ago held the infant she now cradles in her arms. The ruptured sack is a lovely, shimmering thing. It emerges inside out, rippling with veins, multi-colored and shiny, like a muscle. You nearly believe it is alive. As the woman delivers it, out pours a fluid the color of fine red wine. There is so much of this birth wine the midwife has to hold a bowl beneath the mother to receive it all. You can hold the sack in your hands and imagine how the newborn fit inside it, how it swaddled the child, how its smooth and perfect surface kissed the babe's cheeks and face, every part of its miraculous body.

Mischinu! Listen to me! How I go on. But whenever I think of the pain Adriana and Santuzzu must have felt as they said farewell to their seven children, the image that comes to my mind is a ruptured and shimmering birth sack.

IN THE END I believe it was Mamma Adriana's decision. If the man is the head of *la famigghia,* the woman is surely its center. She is the family's heart and womb, you understand? She is the source from which the strength and vibrant urgency of *la famig-ghia* flows.

So Adriana and Santuzzu called Gaetanu to them and, for his own good, ordered him to leave. And the earth overheard them and opened her eyes and wept such salty tears that fish leapt into the air three times filling the baskets of the *campagnoli,* and that night in the village there was a great feast.

The people of the countryside ate, then made music and

danced. Even Gabriella feasted and brayed along with the music.

The next morning Gaetanu made ready to depart. He kissed Papa Santuzzu for the last time. He kissed Mamma Adriana for the last time. I watched the three of them, standing beside the road in the sun. I was just a girl, barely bigger than you are now, the daughter of Gnaziu and Francesca. Mamma Adriana pulled on her hair and said, "Tannu, my son, Tannu, Tannu. May the Madonna be with you always and keep you safe." She handed him a basket of bread and leftover fish.

Papa Santuzzu was unable to utter a word. All he could do was to stand in the sun beside Gabriella, his face shaded by the bill of his cap, wiping away his tears with the backs of his hands.

Above them the sun shone down stupidly, as if nothing important was taking place on the spinning world below.

So GAETANU BEGAN his long journey, walking the whole way from Girgenti to the city of Palermu, then sailing across the blue water to Napuli, where he would meet the steamship that would tumble him across the mad ocean to *La Merica*. No sooner had he left the village than deep in the forest he heard some talking. He stopped. Three old women stood in a clearing.

The first woman said, "We're hungry, stranger."

"Wake up," said the second woman. *"Cu dormi nun pigghia pisci."* He who slumbers doesn't catch fish.

The third woman said, "Have mercy on us, in the name of your dear mother and her mother before her and so on and so on until the birth of time."

Gaetanu considered the three women. They were ugly and old and as skinny and gnarled as twigs. But Gaetanu had a generous soul, and so he opened wide his basket and gave the women all he had: three leftover fishes and some scraps of bread.

In the bottom of the basket he saw a piece of thread that had fallen from Mamma Adriana's sleeve. The thread was all he had left in the world. He held it to his heart. Then something strange took place. The more dearly he held it, the longer and thicker it grew! Soon it was as fat as a fat piece of rope. Gaetanu held the thick rope in his hands.

The old women chewed carefully, as those with only a few teeth do. One enters the world with a cry and no hair and teeth, one leaves the world the same way. Then the old women shriveled one by one into gold coins that fell softly to the forest floor.

Gaetanu smiled and put the coins in his pocket. With them he purchased passage on a steamship to *La Merica* after borrowing many more coins at an incomprehensibly high rate of interest from a *struzzeri* who hung upside-down by his feet from the ceiling, and with his long fingernails scooped the marrow from Gaetanu's bones while sipping a cup of his hot, terrified blood.

THE NEXT DAY Luigi and Salvatore saw a fish flying in the air.

I saw it too from where I worked in the fields. You don't often see such a thing, so we leaned on our tools for a moment and stared up at it. We were threshing grain that day, singing as we threshed. I was helping with the gleaning. You know that my mamma died when I was only a little girl, and my papa was so lame he could no longer walk the distance from our hut to the fields. And these were two whose hands were never seen in their pockets! The fields we tended were more than a league away from the hut where Papa Gnaziu and I lived.

I worked with the other village girls. Already your father had taken notice of me. Sometimes our eyes would meet across the bobbing heads of grain, and for a moment or two we'd lock gazes. I didn't have the prettiest smile or anything bright to wear, so I imagined there was a brightness inside me—something silver or red—so he'd see that I'd noticed him, too. I'd let a little of the brightness shine out through my eyes, then cast them down quickly so he'd think well of me.

On the day of the flying fish he was standing alongside Luigi, who pointed and shouted and waved at the sky. The tuna saw

Luigi's wave and dropped, landing at Luigi's feet. In its mouth the tuna had a message from Gaetanu.

"Dear Luigi," spoke the tuna, "I'm in *La Merica,* the Golden Land, in the city of Lawrence, state of Massachusetts. I've just completed the arduous task of paying off my debt. Also, I took in marriage a marvelous woman known by the name Teresa Pantaluna. While we speak of names, the authorities on the Island of Tears gave me a second one, the name of our province, so I am now Gaetanu Girgenti! That's a lot of nice sound to come out of a mouth all at once! Anyway, here's a basket of food and a piece of rope. May the food ease the hungers of your journey. The rope is so that you'll be able to find Teresa and me. Inform the men on the Island that you're my brother. Hold onto the rope tight. No matter what, don't let the rope go! With it, my brother, Teresa and I will pull you across the sea."

Then the tuna opened wide its mouth and out popped the rope and the basket of fish and bread. So Luigi, the second brother, set out with his older sister, Carla.

The earth again wept, and all the people feasted, and the donkeys sang and danced.

The next day in the forest Luigi and Carla met the three old women, the bones of their arms and legs so thin they resembled sticks.

"We're starving," they said. "We're so hungry we've gnawed even our most bitter memories. All of time has collapsed into an unbearable gnawing pain."

Of course Carla gave them the basket of bread and fish. Who could say no in the face of such need? The women gobbled the scraps in an instant, then begged for the piece of rope. "To keep our skirts up," they said. "See, we're so skinny, our skirts keep falling right off."

Luigi put a finger to his forehead, thinking. He remembered the fish's warning. "No," he said, "no matter what, I'd better not let go of this rope."

In the light of the women's disappointment Carla said, "It's a lot for a woman to lose her skirt, Luigi. Look at the rope, it's plenty big. It's long enough for us all."

She offered the women one end, all the while holding tight to the middle. The women blessed her as they wrapped the rope around their waists. By the time they were through all five were tied together, like a bundle of sticks, with Carla and Luigi in the middle.

Then the women turned into three gold coins, and the end of the rope fell to the ground and transformed itself into an eel, and the eel said, "Don't worry, just follow me." All the while Luigi and Carla held on tight. Hold tight onto my finger, just like Zia Carla and Ziu Luigi. Yes, that's it. Tighter. Yes!

So Carla and Luigi followed the eel through the forest. Along the way they stopped for Ciccina Agneddina, who was to be Luigi's wife, and Gerlando Cavadduzzo, the famous baker, who married Carla. Together the quartet found the ship and with the gold coins paid for their passage, and the eel pulled the boat across the blue-green ocean to the Promised Land where Gaetanu and Teresa were waiting.

THE NEXT DAY in the fields there worked only Santuzzu, Salvatore, and blind, old Gabriella. By now Salvatore did the labor of three grown men. He was very handsome and unbelievably strong. Like a hard, hot iron his body was! I can't even begin to tell you. Your papa was a tree the wind couldn't bend, a mighty rock on the seashore, *un pileri,* a fine specimen of a man. As he labored in the fields he again saw the flying tuna. In the tuna's mouth was a message from Gaetanu and Luigi.

"Brother," the letter said, "it's time that you joined us. Here are coins for five, the rope, and a basket of food. Don't let go of the rope, no matter what. Bring Papa and the twins, Rosaria and Livicedda, as well as the infant Assunta. Tell everyone we miss and love them. Say a prayer on behalf of each of us on the ground beside our dearest mother's grave."

I accompanied your father to the village, where we found the man who could read and write. Before touching our letter he washed and dried his hands, then drew his spectacles ceremoniously out of a box lined with green velvet and held the twin circles of glass up to the sun, then strapped their glistening hooks behind his ears.

By then Gnaziu, my father, had passed from this world. No one from my family remained in the village. My brothers and sisters had all drifted away, like winged seeds in the spring wind. The wind blew a few of my brothers to Brazil. The wind carried the others along with my sisters to Argentina. To the shores of New York, the wind blew only me.

Sometimes late at night I still can hear the songs my mother sang while I fed at her breast. Sometimes just before it rains, when the wind is high and the light is dying, my nose fills with her smell. Her smell is a mix of almond blossoms and souring milk tinged sweetly with sweat. I close my eyes and hold a soft piece of cloth against my cheek. Sometimes I can feel her standing beside me. I feel her trying to take my hands in hers. Sometimes her fingertips brush against my face or hair. Sometimes I think that if I call to my sisters in the other *La Merica* that lies far away to the south they might hear me and answer back. I try calling to them with my mind. Then I make my mind very still, and I close my eyes and listen.

So the day that the letter was brought to us was extremely sad, you understand, because I knew even before the penman had time to clear his throat what words were inked on that paper, and what those words might mean.

TOGETHER SALVATORE AND I carried the words to Papa Santuzzu. He was waiting for us, sitting silently in the shade of a gnarled olive tree. By then he was so old that his eyes were no longer black. They'd turned white, dusted with chalk. He couldn't

see much more than our shadows, but he was like an old owl, he
didn't miss much.

"Regard me," he said. He took off his gray cap. His hair was
as light as lemon blossoms. His eyes were bowls of cream. Alongside him in the dappled shade sat Gabriella, front legs curled beneath her body, which had turned the color of snow.

"Do you remember that rock we found five springs ago," Papa
Santuzzu said as he pointed toward a distant field, "or was it
seven, eight, nine, ten?" For a while he counted on his fingers.
He knew how to count from one to ten. "The one that at first
seemed so easy that Tannu said he'd take care of it all by himself?"
Papa Santuzzu laughed. "Yet as Tannu dug, it grew bigger and
then even bigger?"

Who could remember one rock, I thought, when there had
been so many.

"I remember it well, Papa," Salvatore said.

"We worked on it for weeks," Papa Santuzzu said.

Why were they talking of rocks? I wondered.

"The weeks stretched into months, Papa," said Salvatore. "The
months grew into years. For years every spring we tried to dig it up."

"You remember that in the end," Papa Santuzzu said, "we
decided that it wasn't a rock at all. It was a hard edge of the
world."

"You said it was an edge of the bedrock, Papa. It was a part
of the island of Sicilia herself."

"A living edge of the world itself," Papa Santuzzu said. "I
climbed down into the hole around it and could hear the earth
breathe."

"I remember all the trouble we had pulling you back out,"
Salvatore said.

"I didn't want to leave there," said Papa Santuzzu. "The rock's
breathing seemed to match my own."

"Tannu had to climb down and tie you in a harness," Salvatore
said.

"Pieces of rock that have broken off," Papa Santuzzu said, "even very big pieces, in time you can drag them or break them apart and carry them from the fields. But you can't move the earth itself." For several moments he patted Gabriella's side. "You know, when I started all this years ago, I think at first I meant to move only one rock. Or maybe three. I should have remembered that once you begin clearing a field of stone, you're tempted to clear it all." He gave us a hard stare. "Don't leave anyone behind, you two, you understand? Not Livicedda and Rosaria, or even Assunta. Do I have your promise on that?" Salvatore nodded. "But don't be fools and try to move the world itself."

"I understand, Papa," Salvatore said.

"Don't cry," Papa Santuzzu said. You could see he had only two or three teeth left in his head. "Hey, you didn't think I could ever leave my Adriana?"

"She will always be here, too," Salvatore said, pointing to his heart. "There will never be a day that I won't think of her with love and pray to her."

Papa Santuzzu nodded, pressing both of his palms against his heart. Gabriella brayed softly and shed a big tear.

Then Papa Santuzzu opened his arms, and his third and youngest son embraced him. Then I embraced him and covered his face with my kisses and tears. By then I was one of his children, too.

I didn't know how to tell him good-bye. There were no words to say.

AND THE EARTH wept the most salty of all oceans, and the *campagnoli* feasted and prayed to the Madonna and the special saints, and the donkeys spun in circles, dancing with the goats and chickens.

We entered the forest. Your papa told me and his sisters, "Hold tightly onto this rope." Even though it was day, we could hear the howls of wolves. Then we came to a clearing and saw the three old women.

"Feed us," they said, "we're very hungry."

"Clothe us," they said, "for the bright light is cruel, and the winter air is very cold."

"Stay with us, all of you, today and for all days, because we're old and lonelier than the grave of Pontius Pilate, condemned to eternally wash his hands with flame."

Your papa opened the basket and gave them all that was inside, three fish and a few scraps of bread. The women ate. Then Salvatore gave one of the old women his jacket, the second his shirt, and the third his only pair of shoes, saying, "Please, don't request my pants, too!" He introduced Rosaria and Livicedda, and then Assunta, who still sucked her thumb and carried everywhere with her a piece of an old rag. "And this girl"—he motioned to me— "her name is Rosa the Sweet. She's my wife of only a few months, and she's barely had time to sew!"

The first old woman cackled and answered, "If she's your wife of only a few months, you don't have much need of pants!"

"We hope you've shown her how well the needle can stick the cloth!" laughed the second old woman.

"You'll be blessed if in darkness the bride comes to enjoy your threading the eye!" the third old woman cried.

I didn't appreciate such joking, but in the forest strange things are known to occur. One learns that it's wiser to hold one's tongue than to chase after one's head. So Salvatore gave them all he owned. Then they asked him for the rope.

"Here," I said, quickly offering them the skinnier end of the rope. "Remember, a free bowl of soup never lacks for salt." I tell you, I didn't like them taking all of your father's clothes.

The moment the old women touched the rope they turned into three pieces of gold, and the eel led us to Palermu. As we rode in the back of a wagon toward the sea, we thumbed our noses at the moneylenders.

The boat leapt away from the shore. We looked back at the

land as it began to grow smaller, then even smaller. To Sicilia we cried, "I cannot live with you, nor can I live without you!"

THE SEA BEYOND was beautiful, very lively and green, like a fine field after a week of rain. Then the ocean turned angry and gray for nearly a month. It seemed as if the voyage to *La Merica* would never end.

Some on board the ship became so sick and nauseated they prayed to the saints to die. Some made vows so extreme not even Jesù Cristu could keep them. The men in Palermu packed us into the steerage hole like plugs of tobacco in a pipe. The air down there—whew, what a stench! It could turn sweet milk to cheese. We had to take turns going up on deck, and if you weren't careful the smokestacks above blew cinders into your eyes. We shared the space above with cattle and pigs. Their mess ran all over the deck every time it rained. You couldn't help but step in it, or where someone had been nauseous. Then up the ship would roll, then sharply down, down, down and over to one side, then back to the other side and again up, riding the dizzy, never-ending waves.

We held onto the rope so tightly you'd think we'd squeeze off our fingers. On the other end Gaetanu and Teresa Pantaluna, Luigi and Ciccina Agneddina, Carla and Gerlando Cavadduzzo were pulling. Here, help them. Give the rope a pull. "Unh, unh," they pulled. That's it, *figghiu miu.*

Then we glimpsed the incredible city and the massive statue of the lady. The sky above our heads was so full of smoke we thought for sure the city was on fire. No, said a man on board, who had made the trip once before, that's how the sky of the New Land looks every day. They took us on a second boat to the Island of Tears.

Ellis Island—*mischinu!*—it was itself a whole village. They brought us into a great hall, where we were told to sit on wooden benches and wait. You wouldn't believe the noise in the huge room. A thousand voices, all going at once in a thousand different directions! Even now just to think of it I want to cover my ears. When they separated me from Salvatore and then from Livicedda and Rosaria and Assunta, I felt as if I'd fallen into a bottomless well. Aboard ship I'd heard stories of husbands taken from their wives, children taken from their mothers, brothers from sisters, never to see the other again. I had only a shawl and my dress and a pair of shoes. I held the empty basket on my lap. All around me was moaning madness. Waiting on the bench by myself, I thought perhaps I had disappeared or had died. I worried that I'd never see a familiar face again.

The doctors counted my teeth, pulled the lids of my eyes inside out with a hook, poked my ears, smelled my skin, listened to my lungs. I told each doctor I was Rosa, daughter of Gnaziu and Francesca, may they rest, *spusa* of Salvatore, brother to the twinned Rosaria and Livicedda, as well as Assunta and Carla, Luigi and Gaetanu of Girgenti, our province in beloved Sicilia, and had they seen any of these fine women and men?

The doctors searched my hair for lice, thumped up and down my spine, twisted my hands and feet, listened to the terrified drumbeat of my heart. Some women were sent back. The doctors cursed them with signs and symbols in chalk on their backs. I prayed that they would not put their chalk on me! I could see the New Land in the magnificent sunlight beyond the tall windows. Some women were separated from their daughters. Some women could not hold their fright inside themselves any longer, and they wept and moaned with great sorrow and fear.

"All right," a man said to me in English. "You can go on now. Do you understand? You're free to go."

"Free to go," I answered.

I knew enough to know what those words meant. Repeating the words out loud in my mouth made me feel different, like something born, as if I were brand-new.

· · ·

WHEN I SAW your father he was smiling so hard that I thought his face would crack. He stood waiting for me with his three sisters.

We took a steamer from the island with the others. Now I didn't mind the rolling waves. The Golden Land's greatest city stood proudly on the approaching shore, thrusting itself up happily into the warm sun.

Several paces from us on the steamer, a dark-faced man scolded his young wife, then seized his son's blue straw hat and roughly threw it into the sea. I could guess by his somber clothing that the father had spent some time in *La Merica*. A pair of ribbons covered with polka dots fluttered from the back of the boy's blue hat as it fell. It was as if this hat from the old world wasn't fine enough to be brought to the shores of the New Land.

All at once I feared that there was something in me, in Salvatore, in all of us, that would have to be thrown into the sea, too.

THE THREE OLD women? My child, listen and I'll tell you a secret. The three old women shrunk yet again and grew very small, smaller than you, smaller than your belly button, smaller than even the little fingernail on your little finger, and then they hid inside the pocket on Zi'Assunta's skirt. Now they live here in *La Merica,* deep in the forest or somewhere out on the street, testing the hearts of those they meet.

They came along with us, see? We brought many of the old things—the old ways—along with us.

Remember, anything you can imagine can happen to you once. Twice, it's coincidence. But three times and you'd better watch out. The three sisters are giving you a test. So when they ask you, you'd better answer right.

They're outside, waiting. Perhaps someday they'll meet you, too. Have a generous heart, give them anything they want, but whatever you do, don't ever let go of the rope! You may share it with them if you'd like, let them hold one end, allow them to wrap it around themselves, whatever. But never let it completely out of your hand.

The rope is *la famigghia,* see? Each of us is a thread, wound up in it. Before you were born, a rope connected me to you.

One still does, *figghiu miu.*

> *Stronger than twine or the truest of leather,*
> *Family binds us forever together.*

> *Now Gaetanu, the oldest, leans forward to speak*
> *His tale of journey and strike by God's weak.*

Giufà's Hole

❦ Gaetanu Girgenti

HOLD YOUR HEADS HIGH, children, when you get to New York City. That's right, set straight your caps. Wipe your tears and snot. What we're doing is no disgrace, at least not to you or your poor parents. It's a disgrace to the bosses and owners—may they suffer forever in Hell—who starve and deform you. The worst thief is he who steals the playtime of children! Stand proud in New York City and tell them that! Shout to everyone who will listen that the strikers in Lawrence, Massachusetts, were so desperate that they were forced to send their children away. Tell everyone about the condition of the mills, the short pay, the high rents, the water hoses and clubs used by the police. Describe the hot tears in your mother's eyes as she bid you good-bye. Tell them your stories, my children, so you become alive inside their hearts, and so that all the workers here may be saved.

Ahh, don't look at me and shiver. It's not so cold. Don't even think about it. Hop around a little on your feet. That's it, get your blood moving. Today, the tenth day of February, in the year of our Lord nineteen hundred and twelve, could be the beginning of spring. Maybe if we all pretend hard enough that it's summertime, in a minute or two it will get hot. Pretend we're all sitting around a blazing fire and I'm telling you a story. Don't tense your muscles or you'll use up all your heat. Just relax, and every now and then blow into your hands like this, see? Make your breath like an oven. That's it. Don't cry. Think of a big fire burning in the midst of us. Stand closer together and I'll try to block the wind. There. The train will be here any minute. Soon you'll be warm, and I'll go back to the picket line. You can hear the strikers, can't you? They're singing to keep warm.

> *Arise, ye prisoners of starvation!*
> *Arise, ye wretched of the earth,*
> *For justice thunders condemnation,*
> *A better world's in birth.*
> *No more tradition's chains shall bind us,*
> *Arise, ye slaves! no more in thrall!*
> *The earth shall rise on new foundations,*
> *We have been naught, we shall be all.*

In New York, hey, I bet they'll feed you good. Sure! Who thinks they'll eat a big feast when they get to New York City? Yes, wave your hands. Everybody's going to eat! They're cooking that feast for you right now!

Hot soup. Potatoes. Bread. Believe me, I saw it all last night in a dream. There'll even be meat! Sure, some fine turkey and goose! They'll feed you till you're fat as kettles. Warm your mind with that thought. We've lived through colder days.

Hey, remember the story of the princess who would never laugh? All of you, you look just like her.

You don't know the story? Well, once there was a princess who lived in a warm castle and had just about everything you could ever imagine. She had a big pot of beans that never grew empty. She had a big silver platter of meat that could never be licked clean. She had a bee's nest full of honey so sweet that one taste nearly made you die. You would think she was happy and content, wouldn't you? But you forget that she was the daughter of the king, the biggest labor boss of all, the worst of all thieves, and so she was just like him, selfish and vain, and even though she was a child just like each of you, she never laughed.

This princess had everything, so of course nothing pleased her. The king declared that anyone who could make her laugh could have half of his kingdom as well as her hand in marriage, if he wanted it. But this princess was a terribly nasty child. She said that anyone who tried to amuse her and failed would have his head lopped off and then displayed on a tall pole outside the castle walls.

Now, hunger is a harsh master. Soon all the actors and jugglers and acrobats and fools of the village filed into the castle with the hope of making the selfish princess laugh. They tumbled through the air and sang silly songs and recited jokes and puns and juggled dozens of golden balls, not dropping a single one. They performed pratfalls and belly bounces, backflips and swan dives. They painted faces on their stomachs and made their belly creases puff cigars. They hit one another with bats and clubs. They made loud farts with their armpits. They walked backward on their hands, their fat *culi* sticking out of their collars as if they were heads. They twisted their bodies into knots and rolled on the ground like balls. The women dressed like men, the men dressed like women, the adults like children, the children like adults. They danced naked, like Nubian slaves. They swallowed fire and sharp swords and lay down on beds of nails. They ate bowls of air and pretended to be sated. They made marionettes act out the Arabian Nights. They imitated the cock and his chickens, squeezing until they really could lay eggs. They stuck firecrackers up the lawyer's ass. They filled the poet's pen with mud. They put the scribe's eyeglasses on each of their donkeys until one of the beasts really could read Latin. They stuffed the dress of the village's skinniest old woman with so many rags everyone grew convinced she'd birth triplets. They fooled the pompous doctor into drinking a frothy glass of goat piss. They tricked the blind old judge into biting into a pie made of fresh, steaming dung. That chocolate must have been bittersweet! They pulled so hard on their tongues that they turned their guts inside-out, then unbuttoned their belly buttons and stepped out of their skins, and then their skeletons joined hands and danced. In short, the people resorted to every excess and variation known to the imagination, and all the while the princess didn't even crack a grin. Soon the castle's walls were decorated by a thousand and one poles bearing a thousand and one heads, and only the crows and ravens feasting on the fools' sad eyeballs were happy.

> *We want no condescending saviors,*
> *To rule us from a judgment hall;*
> *We workers ask not for their favors;*
> *Let us consult for all.*
> *To make the thief disgorge his booty*
> *To free the spirit from its cell,*
> *We must ourselves decide our duty,*
> *We must decide and do it well.*

NOW PERHAPS YOU'VE heard some of the many stories about Giufà, a thin, dark-haired boy with a plain and empty face, who was so simple and poor, so foolish and literal, that events had no other alternative but to go haywire at the beginning of each of his adventures. Well, one evening as usual Giufà wasn't looking where he was walking, and so he bumped into his mamma's arm as she was carrying to the table their supper's pot of soup. The earth drank it as a result. Giufà's mother scolded him, shouting, "Use your head!"

The next morning Giufà lay in bed, not moving, even after his mamma called to him repeatedly to rise. "What's the matter with you?" she shouted as she roused him. "Are your legs broken?"

Giufà sat up and felt his legs. "No," he responded.

"Then use them and get up," said Giufà's mother.

"Oh," said Giufà. "I wish you would make up your mind. I thought you told me to use my head."

Later that day Giufà again wasn't looking where his feet carried him, and so he fell down a deep, deep hole. Giufà remembered his mother's advice and tried to climb out using his legs. Of course, since his arms hung still at his sides, he fell backward in a heap and after a thousand tries sat down muttering and spent the remainder of the day scratching and pulling his ears, wondering why the bright patch of sky above his head had grown so dark.

The next week the baron's daughter was out in the field riding her horse. The horse, who overheard Giufà talking to himself beneath the ground, spooked and threw its rider. The baron's daughter flew in an arc through the air and down the hole. Giufà stood, remembering his mother's advice, and used his head to break her descent. The girl landed on his shoulders, her pearl-white neck saved. At her insistence, after Giufà used his legs to stand, which allowed her sufficient height so as to be able to climb out, the landlord rewarded Giufà with a big bag of gold. Giufà continued on his way, until he met an old woman in the forest.

"What's in your bag?" the old woman said.

"Gold," Giufà told her.

Now this old woman was very shrewd. She pretended to doubt him. "Where would a simpleton like you get gold?"

"From a beautiful girl who fell from the sky," said Giufà, "as I sat scratching my ears in the darkness of a deep hole."

The old woman laughed at his foolishness. "Your bag's not full of gold at all. Your bag is full of shells from the sea."

"It is not," Giufà said, insulted. He spilled his treasure out onto the old woman's open apron. "See, it's real gold."

"Sold!" cried the old woman, and in the blink of an eye she handed Giufà a white goose whose incessant honking was so loud and annoying that the earth itself got such a splitting headache that fissures the length and width of tree trunks cracked open on the ground.

Giufà tried to give the goose back, but he couldn't do so. The bird's feathers were so sticky that they stuck to his hand and side.

"*Hannk!*" the goose honked at Giufà, as the earth splintered around him. "*Hannk! hannk!*"

Everything that touched the goose stuck to it, or so Giufà thought, until by accident he discovered the secret word of release. Unhappily he muttered to himself the old woman's words. "Your bag's not full of gold at all. Your bag is full of shells from the sea."

> "*If truth be told,*" *the goose replied,*
> "*The master's bag is full of gold.*"
> "*Sold,*" *cried Giufà, so on hand and side*
> *The sticky bird released its hold.*

THAT NIGHT GIUFÀ sought shelter in a farmhouse. The farmer agreed to allow Giufà and his goose to sleep in the barn with the other animals just as long as the farmer's three young daughters were not disturbed. Well, you can imagine how excited the three girls were to see a stranger with a noisy goose beneath his arm talking with their father. As soon as night pulled her window shade down over the sun, the three girls slipped from their beds to the barn.

There Giufà lay, snoring in the straw, and there on his stomach sat his white goose, its feathers glowing in the bright moonlight. The girls could not resist tiptoeing toward the sleeping pair, then kneeling down beside them. They'd never seen such a goose up close before. They marveled at its long curved neck, thick and pulsing in the moonlight. First the eldest daughter stroked it, then the middle girl, and then the youngest, their fingers sticking fast.

Meanwhile, their father had risen for his nightly constitution. Squatting contentedly beside his field, he overheard his three daughters' excited whispers seeping from the barn. Without pausing even to button up his trousers he raced to the barn door where he grabbed his pitchfork, eager to skewer the traitorous Giufà.

But at the moment the girls' papa entered the barn, the rooster crowed loudly, mistaking the farmer's ass for the morning sun.

The three daughters gasped and pulled back their naughty hands, which were now stuck hard to the dangling goose neck, attached to the goose that was stuck to the belly of our hero, Giufà, who saw the raging madman advancing toward him with the pitchfork, ready to make him into shish kebab. Giufà shrieked like a colt about to be gelded. Remembering his mother's advice to use his legs, Giufà bolted from the barn dragging the three young girls along with him, as it so happened directly into the path of the half-sleeping rooster, who flew into the air with alarm and stuck fast to the goose, who began to honk—*hannk! hannk! hannk!*—as the irate farmer pursued them.

This assemblage ran all the way toward the castle. The nasty princess was eating her morning bowl of porridge when a peculiar shape hazily took form on the horizon. Imagine the sight of Giufà, the raucously honking goose, the three curious daughters, the confused crowing cock, and the raging bare-assed farmer brandishing his pitchfork emerging suddenly into view as you sit down with spoon to eat. Well, without thinking the princess laughed right out loud.

Yes, the train's nearing. But first let's pick up the thread of the strikers' song.

> *The law oppresses us and tricks us,*
> *Wage systems drain our blood;*
> *The rich are free from obligations,*
> *The laws the poor delude.*
> *Too long we've languished in subjection,*
> *Equality has other laws;*
> *"No rights," says she, "without their duties,*
> *No claim on equals without cause."*

You're thinking that maybe Giufà took half the kingdom and married the sour princess, then lived happily ever after in the castle surrounded by the thousand and one rotting heads of his comrades?

Would you choose that? Would you, or you, or you?

No, remember I told you that our hero was simple, not stupid. He realized that heads were useless if they weren't connected to bodies, so he had the skulls taken down and restored to the graves where they rightfully belonged, and then he demanded that the king share his profits with his workers, and he told the princess to gather her pot of beans that never grew empty, her platter of meat that could never be licked clean, and her bee's nest of honey that was so sweet it made you nearly want to die and ordered her to go out into the countryside and feed the starving people of the fields until they were satisfied, and thus she came to know hunger and destitution through them.

Shall I give you a real children's tale?

Then the king and the farmer became good friends, and the farmer ruled the *campagnoli* until they could govern themselves, and everyone lived with honor, dignity, and peace.

And the farmer's daughters?

Well, of course Giufà married all three of them, but since this is a Christian country I'll say he did so one by one by one, in full accordance with the rules of the Holy Church. On second thought, hey, maybe each month there were a couple of nights when, like you and your brothers and sisters, they all slept together in the same bed.

There's the train, my children. That's right, all aboard! *Addiu!* May God be with you! May God always be with you and keep you safe!

> *Behold them seated in their glory,*
> *The kings of mine and rail and soil!*
> *What have you read in all their story,*
> *But how they plundered toil?*
> *Fruits of the people's work are buried*
> *In the strong coffers of a few;*
> *In working for their restitution*
> *The men will only ask their due.*

• • •

I'LL ASK AGAIN for mine in just a minute. I want to stand here a moment longer waving as the train pulls away.

How ironic it is that we who left our parents to journey here must now bid our own children good-bye. I've come to hate good-byes. They grievously pain my heart. In each good-bye there is a death. *Matruzza mia!* Forgive me for having abandoned you.

To come here to this God-forsaken place, for what? To meet Teresa? To watch the factory burn? To hold Antuninu in my arms?

I think of the women of the Everett cotton mill running from loom to loom shouting, "Strike! Short pay! All out! All out! Come on! Strike! Short pay! Let's go!" The *Siciliani* beside them shouted a translation. The women from Everett were from Poland, though in labor we're all part of one body even though we don't share a common tongue. The women waved the flag of *La Merica* as they raced through the mills, encouraging the other workers to shut down their machines and join them.

See, we would work fifty-six long hours a week. You wouldn't want to work a donkey that long, let alone a pregnant woman or a hungry child. The mills are a noisy, dusty hell. Inside, it's hard to see or hear or even to breathe, and the racket goes on pounding forever, even in your sleep. Everyone's always coughing, and the work never stops, not for a single moment, no matter what. And if you let your mind wander, the machine can swallow your hand and turn it to a sack of gravel, or grab your hair and in a half a heartbeat rip off your scalp.

That happened to my *amicu* Antuninu, from Campufiuritu. He was quite handsome, with a full head of beautiful, dark and wavy hair! Oh, the girls in the shop all loved him! He always had a smile for everybody.

Until one day he turned to me suddenly from his machine, his eyes wild, the top of his head wearing only a glistening red cap. He opened wide his mouth. No sound came out. For a few moments he panted, trying to catch his breath. I didn't know what to think until I saw his dark hair snagged like something dead in the gears. He sank to his knees, his mouth still open. I knelt beside him and held him in my arms. He told me he felt no pain, only a bizarre sensation of wetness.

"Tannu," he whispered, "what's going on? Why does my head feel so wet? Did I fall into the sea?"

"I'm with you," I said. "You're not drowning."

His teeth began to chatter. "Tannu," he said, "I'm so cold. Tell me, is it winter again already?" He pointed into the air. "Is that snow?"

Inside the mills it always looks as if it's snowing. It's really cotton and dust and filth filling the air. But I told Antuninu that the angels lifting his soul up to Heaven must have hitched a ride down to earth on the back of an ice wagon. What he felt was their wet, icy fingers. Soon he'd be warm, I said.

He smiled at me, then took his last gasp.

> *Toilers from shops and fields united,*
> *The union we of all who work;*
> *The earth belongs to us, the people,*
> *No room here for the shirk.*
> *How many on our flesh have fattened!*
> *But if the noisome birds of prey*
> *Shall vanish from the sky some morning,*
> *The blessed sunlight still will stay.*

I T   A L L   S T A R T E D with the state passing a law against women and children working more than fifty-four hours each week.

The owners still wanted to drink the fifty-six drops of our blood they'd grown used to. So they ordered the mills to speed up. They'd get their fifty-six hours of work, but in only fifty-four! And if a *sceccu* named Antuninu died in a bloody puddle beside his machine, they'd just hire another off the next boat. The owners hammered to the walls of the mills signs saying that from now on everybody—children, women, and men, too—would work only fifty-four hours a week in accordance with the new law. They then bled us of the same production as before and tried to get away with putting fewer coins in our envelopes, paying us for only fifty-four hours while we were still doing the work of fifty-six!

You can whip the donkey once or twice, perhaps every week, or even every day, but inevitably there will come a moment when the beast decides to kick you back with all its might. That's what happened when the women of the Everett mill received their envelopes and counted their short pay.

"Strike!" they shouted. "Short pay! All out! Strike!"

The workers armed themselves with picker sticks and halted the pounding looms. My Teresa stood among them, shouting out a translation to the Sicilian workers. I grabbed a picker stick, too. We ripped weaves and smashed machines as we ran. We raced across the Union Street bridge and burst through the doors of the Wood mill, into Washington, Arlington, Ayer, freeing the mill workers from their machines.

We freed the weavers and spinners, the doffers and lappers and grinders, the strippers and speeder tenders, the carders and loom fixers, the slasher tenders and drawing tenders, oilers and sweepers and roving tenders, the picker-room workers, the slubber tenders, the jack-frame section hands, the warping-mill section hands, banding hands and roving hands, the beamers, clerks, warp counters, engineers, firemen, teamsters, railway-head tenders, the oiling and shafting hands, the dye workers and print workers, bleachery workers, garment workers, the custom-clothing makers, hatters, and cap makers.

Women and men and children, mostly girls aged fourteen to eighteen. Polish and Sicilian, Syrian and Irish, complexion and hair of every color, all surging together out into the cold, icy streets shouting, "Strike! Strike! All out! Strike!"

With balls of snow and ice we smashed every pane of glass in Kuhnhardt and Duck. The snow flew around us just like inside the mills, but this time it was real snow. You could hear the young girls' jubilant laughter. The women had a wet sparkle in their eyes. I looked into my Teresa's eyes, and I just wanted to hold her waist and kiss her!

Here and there men bellowed speeches from atop one another's shoulders, denouncing the short pay and the conditions of the mills. They said that if we all stood together, all twenty-five thousand of us, we could remake the world! One by one we were nothing, they shouted, but united we could be a powerful union! They thrust their fingers into the snowflakes that swirled furiously about their heads as they encouraged us to be steadfast and strong. Then some of the crowd broke out into song, and soon everyone learned the words and was singing.

> *Arise, ye prisoners of starvation!*
> *Arise, ye wretched of the earth,*
> *For justice thunders condemnation,*
> *A better world's in birth.*

By the next morning, Wood and Washington joined Everett and Arlington in the walkout. The bells of city hall rang out in alarm. *Bonnng! Bonnng! Bonnng!* The strike was underway!

Then the state militia arrived and fought us. A line of policemen would charge our picket lines, swinging their clubs at anything in their way. Then a second wave of militia would attack us, bayonets drawn, causing us to scatter until we could join again in line and march again.

Joseph Ettor arrived and gave several speeches. He was a big man with a hearty laugh that made you laugh along with him, and also a Wobbly, from the Industrial Workers of the World. He said his family was from Italy. He stood high on a wooden box, punching the sky with his fist. Then he'd strike the palm of his other hand as the bitter snow blew around him.

Arturo Giovannitti arrived soon after. His words were so fresh they formed images in your mind that haunted you the whole day. I felt proud to hear such glory expressed in my own tongue. Giovannitti wore a fine black suit and a soft dark cloth bunched at the neck. The girls were so still when he spoke that you could hear the throbbing of their hearts. Everywhere workers were listening and nodding their heads. Giovannitti told us that we were human beings, not slaves or animals. He said our work was noble and worthy of dignity and pride. In return, he roared, even the least among us should be respected!

We picketed and marched and fought the scab workers trying to enter the mills and break our strike. Many strikers were injured by the militia's clubs and bayonets. A boy from Palazzolu had his guts slashed open so bad he nearly died. Many strikers ended up with broken heads. Several got cracked ribs as well. The police liked to swing their clubs at our heads. If you blocked a club to your ribs with your arm, the arm bone snapped, too. Despite this, in every speech Giovannitti and Ettor told us to remain peaceful.

One night the police shot one of the young mill workers, Anna Lo Pizzo. She slumped to the ground, then made a bird's nest of her thin, white fingers and with them covered her wound. "Mamma!" she cried out, as if suddenly recognizing before her a face. *"È ura?"* The girl wanted to know the hour. Her bright blood spilled through her fingers and made a wide pool around her on the dark street. You had to step back from it. I couldn't believe that such a small body could hold so much blood.

I couldn't hear all of her conversation. *"Non mi scantu,"* —I'm not afraid—she told the face before her as she died.

Then, even though they were several leagues away talking to other workers, Ettor and Giovannitti were arrested and imprisoned for her murder.

> *No more tradition's chains shall bind us,*
> *Arise, ye slaves! no more in thrall!*
> *The earth shall rise on new foundations,*
> *We have been naught, we shall be all.*

•   •   •

ALL WE WANT is a fair wage. A union of workers. That's the goal.

We earn on average six dollars a week, sometimes as high as eight or nine, depending. You never know what's in your pay envelope until you hold it in your hands. But nearly all of it goes to rent and food. A room for one week costs my Teresa and me five whole dollars, and through winter the place is so cold that our breaths make clouds that hang visibly in the air. So we buy a little wood and some coal for the stove, just enough so our bones don't freeze.

We even have to pay for water to drink when we get thirsty in the mills. All the dust in your nose and throat makes a glue that's not easy to swallow. Everybody here is always coughing, some with such ferocity that they hack up blood and tiny pieces of their lungs. So far the cough has escaped me.

Each day we eat *pani e favi*—bread and beans—and never enough, just enough to live to be hungry another day. Once a month after her time Teresa goes to the bathhouse. I go to the bathhouse four times a year, with the change of each season, but whenever there's a good hard rain I wash down on the street with the other men and boys for free.

Most of the time I stink worse than a goat. My hide's far from a stranger to lice or fleas. I keep my hair short—nearly shaved—to give the lice as little as possible to lay their eggs on. My smell sometimes is so high it could make a dead man without a nose roll over three times in his grave.

Every dime saved brings me a dime closer to Papa Santuzzu. Teresa keeps count. I'd rather stink and give her the coins in my envelope than be clean and not be able to return to Sicilia or to bring the others—my two brothers, Papa and Mamma, my four sisters—over now that I've paid off the debt that brought me to this cursed and magnificent land.

•   •   •

I MET TERESA ON the boat coming over. Teresa had—how else can I say it?—deliberately taken on a disguise. She traveled to *La Merica* not as the woman she is but in the manner and clothing of a nobleman. In truth it took me more than a full year to peel away the various layers of her deception. But that's another story for another time.

If truth be told, I came to *La Merica* in disguise, too.

Who didn't? Even Columbus told the Indians he just wanted some spice for his soup.

See, after I hiked all the way from Girgenti to Palermu I discovered that it could easily be a dozen or more years before I could earn enough money for my passage to the Golden Land. The streets and narrow alleyways of Palermu were jammed with men like me, the strong, restless sons of impoverished families, trying to piece together the thirty-five dollars required for passage by the steamship company. That was more than a full year's work, assuming that you could find work and keep it and that you slept out on the street and ate and drank nothing more substantial than God's free air.

There were taxes on everything. The thief of a government was stealing everything. Soldiers from the mainland roamed everywhere, rounding the young men up, marching us off to seven years of service to Italia, the country rumored to lie somewhere north of Napuli. I didn't think I owed this Italia seven years of my life. Italia seemed like just another absentee landlord to me, the soldiers her uniformed *gabbilloti*.

I knew the history of my land. Since the beginning of time Sicilia has been dominated by many, conquered by none.

Sure, in my village there were men still singing the praises of Garibaldi, but sometimes you kiss the hand you'd like to cut off. As for me, Garibaldi never put an onion on my mother's table. Garibaldi never labored alongside my father, brothers, and sisters in the fields. The land was generous, but the master's share was vast. Did Garibaldi ever clear a field of rock? Did his palms know the feel of a hoe? Had his fingers ever traced the curve of a sickle, for which they say *bedda Sicilia* was named?

I am a *cristianu,* a *Sicilianu* from a province they call Girgenti, loyal only to my family and to myself.

All I hoped for was a chance to labor in the New Land for a year or two, fill my empty pockets with a few bags of gold, then return home with enough money to ease my family's *miseria* or fashion a rope of my earnings and pull them all to me across the wide sea.

In Palermu three roads lay before me. I could work and save my earnings until I could afford steerage passage, I could borrow a sum of money from one of the many *struzzeri,* or I could walk back to Girgenti, defeated.

The second alternative was unthinkable to me. It would be tantamount to admitting that *miseria* for my family would be a permanent way of life. So I followed the first option and sought work, doing anything offered me, at any wage. After a full year of working in Palermu I was nearly as penniless as the day I'd arrived. That left me only one path.

They say that when Jesù Cristu was just about my age, the devil appeared to him and promised all the earth's riches if only Jesù would kneel for a few moments and worship at Satan's feet. Don't let your eyes look past an offer until your ears hear it made. I didn't get a close look at the *patruni*'s feet, but I'm confident they were cloven, too. I know his tongue was split and rolled in oil.

"I've met many young men just like you," the *patruni* said, lighting a thin, twisted cigar. "I've helped them all go to *La Merica,* where any man willing to work can become rich."

"I'm willing to work," I said.

"Willing?" he said in a puff of smoke.

"I'm more than willing," I said. "Look at these hands." I stretched my hands forward. "I wouldn't know what to do without work before me."

"That's a lullaby to my ears," the *patruni* said and smiled. He then described a land where the world's sweetest fruit grew in such abundance that it fell from trees unpicked, where everyone ate meat every day, where there were magnificent mountains full of nuggets of gold. All you had to do was bend down and pick up the gold. All you had to do was reach up to the next branch for the fruit. A lovely girl would carry the meat to you on a golden platter. In her other hand would be a glass of fine wine. He smiled again and sipped from his glass of fine wine. All I had to do was to put my mark on his papers.

And to prove his words, he then introduced a man who informed me that he'd just returned from *La Merica*. Word for word the man repeated everything the *patruni* had just said! All I had to do was mark the papers and I'd be guaranteed passage over and a job in the Golden Land! So I borrowed money from the *patruni's* partner, the *struzzeri,* not realizing until later that I was only exchanging the slavery my family endured under the *baruni* for slavery beneath this moneylender.

The *struzzeri* didn't mention that for the next several years I'd be paying him a king's fortune in interest. What did I know of interest? I barely knew two plus two. I knew that he had my mark on his contract, and if ever I were to break my promise to him he knew where he could find my family.

Don't make a mistake, he told me. The world is a place where unthinkable accidents can happen. A hut can catch fire while everyone is sleeping. A stray bullet or two can pierce the heart of a younger brother working in the middle of a field. I'd keep my side of the deal, yes? On my mother's life, I told him. My promise was to work in one of Satan's fiery pits, a factory in a place called Albany, until my debt was paid. Then the *patruni's* men instructed me what words to say when I arrived at Ellis Island.

Yes, I have a few dollars in my pocket.

No, nobody loaned money to me or paid for my passage.

No, I do not already have a job.

Above all I was to say that I signed nothing. Nothing. *Niente!* I was without papers. Without papers!

Then I enthusiastically thanked these leeches. I think I even bowed and kissed the *patruni's* outstretched hand.

• • •

AT ELLIS ISLAND the authorities were very clever, phrasing their questions in different ways so as to lure the truths I was hiding out into the light.

"Who paid for your passage and loaned you the money in your pocket?" they asked me.

"Nobody," I replied.

"You can't expect us to believe that," they said. "Do you think we're fools?"

"If I did," I answered, "I'd be the fool to tell you so."

"Where did the money come from?" they asked. "Did it fall from the air?"

"If money fell from the Sicilian air," I said, "God knows I'd still be breathing it."

"Did they say whether you'll work in New York or Brooklyn?"

"I'll work wherever I find a job," I said.

"But you already have a job," they said. "You signed a contract."

"I do not already have a job."

"But you were paid some money when you signed the contract, weren't you?" they said.

"I didn't sign any contract," I said.

"We're only trying to help you," they said. "You have no idea what difficulty you're in. You'll thank us later. Admit to us that you're contract labor."

"I didn't sign anything," I said.

"Of course not," they said, "but in Naples, or perhaps it was back in Palermo, you put your mark on some papers, didn't you?"

"No," I insisted, "no papers."

"Don't lie," they said. "We know that you signed papers. Isn't this your mark?" One of the men then drew a piece of paper out from his desk and upon it wrote a large *X*.

My heart thumped so loud that I was sure they could hear it. On the paper was precisely my *X*! "I have no mark," I answered, taking a deep breath.

"Isn't this the mark you made?" they said again.

"I signed nothing," I cried. "I am without papers, in the name of God!"

They sat back in their chairs and stared into my eyes then.

I said a silent prayer to the Madonna and turned my eyes into two stones.

After a long silence they took my forms and printed on them a *W* and an *O* and a *P,* for the words "without papers."

"Here you go, wop," the authorities told me.

"Grazie," I said, dropping down to one knee. If they hadn't turned away from me, I would have kissed their shoes.

I didn't know it then but just like Giufà I'd fallen into a deep hole.

I WAS SO GREEN, if asked I might have kissed the Lord's cheek. I did anything anybody in authority asked of me. "Sure, sure," I said to any request. "OK, right away, OK." In Albany I worked ten, twelve, sometimes fourteen hours a day. My job was to push wheelbarrows of machine parts around the factory, delivering them here then there, then shoveling finished parts into huge bins. My wheelbarrow was a rusty blur of motion that never slowed. I was like a miner working inside a vast, noisy cave of greasy bolts and nuts and gears.

Sometimes it seemed as if the bins and machines were living things. Sometimes they whispered to me, in the dialect of my province, telling me to work faster. Some bins were mouths that wanted to swallow me up. I'd feed them several shovelfuls of fresh parts, whispering a prayer to the Madonna to keep me safe. In my pocket I kept a string of rosary beads my mother had given me for protection.

Sometimes through the thunderous din of the factory the Blessed Virgin herself spoke to me. She never showed her face, but I could hear her words as plain as day. She sounded just like my mamma saying all the sweet things she'd told me back when

I was a small child. She'd count my fingers and toes, my ears and eyes and nose. She'd remind me that I was her firstborn son. To pass the time we sang old songs together. We'd sing the song of the threshers and then the song of the reapers. We sang the song all the villagers sang after a night of stories and rhymes around a blazing fire. The machines in the factory wouldn't want to swallow me up then, not with those holy beads in my pocket and my mouth full of sweet song!

Sometimes the Madonna would have important business elsewhere and ask me to mind the infant Jesù. Jesù was just a wide-eyed kid, sort of like a boy with the face of a very wise and holy owl. He was never much trouble though he was always strangely quiet; I believe it was because he could already feel pressing down upon his frail shoulders the weight of being the son of God. He'd gaze up at me with his huge brown eyes and straddle the wheelbarrow's backside like a little porcelain doll, his sandaled feet and the hem of his cloak carefully positioned out of the way of my greasy machine parts. I'd push my wheelbarrow real easy on the days he was with me so as not to give him too bumpy a ride. I knew he had a difficult enough life ahead of him without me adding to it! I'd whisper to him all day long, but unlike his mamma he didn't like to carry on a conversation.

The first year passed, then the second and third years. I lived with Teresa in a company-owned house with eight or nine other families. This house was so small that when everybody was there someone had to be outside. If you had an itch, you'd have to ask another to scratch it. We slept men with men, women with women, like matchsticks in two boxes.

Even at night in my dreams I pushed a wheelbarrow, straining to go faster, to keep up, to speed up, because my boss shouted to me that I was always behind. In my dream the factory floor would turn to sand and my front wheel would melt, and I'd push and push and push, braying sadly like an old donkey. Sometimes in my dream I would start to sob. Then the others would knock on my back and shout to me to shut up and be done once and for all with my noisy nightmare.

One day the boss ordered me to run one of the machines. Jesù waved his little hand from the front of my barrow and said *addiu*. When the boss yelled at me to make the machine go faster, I made it go so fast that my mind could hardly keep up. I knew that only through more work could I ever outrace the *struzzeri* and the mounting interest of my debt. With this machine there was no time for conversation or even thought. It demanded that every instant I attend to it. It demanded that I do its bidding and become its slave. The machine was all I thought about, how to make it run faster. Once my hands wrapped themselves around its handles, I couldn't let it go.

I'd stand outside the factory gates, staring at its fiery bowels and towering smokestacks, before dawn could crack the crust of night's darkness. I worked morning, afternoon, evening. I was the first to start, the last to leave. I wouldn't quit until the foreman put out the section lights and everybody had trudged home. Then I'd go home, too, back to my matchbox.

Even in my dreams I ran my machine, producing more and more machine parts, which grew in a mound at my feet and then fused together into more machines, which I then operated, caressing their levers, oiling their joints, staining their handles ebony with the sweat of my hands, never quite able to keep up as the machines produced more and even more machine parts, which grew in even bigger mounds at my feet and then fused together into even more machines, which I then operated, caressing their levers, oiling their joints, staining their handles ebony with the sweat of my hands, never able to keep up as my machines produced more and even more machine parts, which grew in even more imposing mounds at my feet, never able to keep up as the almighty machines produced even more machine parts which grew in even more towering mounds beside me and then fused together and rose up into more machines, which I furiously operated, caressing the levers, oiling the groaning and terrible joints, staining the rough handles ebony with the sweat of my hands, impossible to keep up as the machines created still more machine parts, which rose up massively in a mountain alongside me, a fiercely smoldering volcano darkening the sky, suddenly spewing smoke and ash like a perverse snow, spitting rock and molten lava and scoria, rising like Sicilia's mighty Mungibeddu, this ominous maze of terrifying whirling metal, demanding that I caress its flaming levers, oil its molten joints, stain its burning handles ebony with the sweat of my hands, never quite able to keep up, always falling behind as my legs and feet and now my arms and hands turn to sand and I can't move I stumble, no—

yes, headfirst I stumble into the flames of the inferno, my mouth open trying to scream to make a sound just any sound to stop it but unable oh, *matri di Diu,* help me! *Jesù e Mari,* help me! *O Madonnuzza!* oh, oh, *povira matri mia!* help! then screaming, screaming!

God's blood, the factory burned to the ground that night, the night that my nightmare awakened the house. Already sparks from the blaze had reached our roof. No sooner had we all run out the door than the house went up like tinder—*poof!*—like a basket of the driest leaves. One moment there was darkness, the next a blinding and explosive flame.

We ran from one house of sleeping workers to the next, rousing everyone from their nightmares and dreams. We outran the flames and in no time got everybody out onto the street.

"Thank God for your nightmare!" Teresa shouted as we stood in the street. Around us everything was embraced by flame, even the last few trees struggling toward the sky above the blazing factory.

"Look," someone cried, "everything here is burning!"

The deep golden color of the flames hopped across our faces and hands and made the crushed rock on the roadway on which we stood appear golden.

"It's finally true," another shouted. "Back in Naples they said I'd be sure to see it! They said the streets of *La Merica* were paved with gold!"

"Yes," another answered, "but as soon as we stepped off the boat we saw that not only were the streets not paved with gold, they weren't even paved! And what's more, we were the ones who'd been brought over to pave them!"

"And dig the ditches, lay the sewer pipe, mix the mortar, line up the bricks, hoist the girders, pound the rivets, toil in the sweatshops, the mines, the endless factories!"

"Mannaggia la miseria!"

"The only true gold here is in our hands."

"What flames! If they go any higher they'll singe the sky!"

"Everything's burning!"

"Yes, everything's burning," someone yelled, "even the office with its wooden cabinets full of our papers and the totals we owe, the pittances we've paid the *patruni* against our debts."

"Then that means we're free!" someone screamed.

Imagine a crowd one winter's night standing out in their bedclothes in the midst of a huge bonfire, cheering.

"We're without papers!" I told Teresa. "Now we're really wops!"

The crowd laughed and chanted. "We're really wops! We're free! We're without papers! We're no longer slaves! We've become wops!"

In a few moments the fire brigade arrived, but it was far too late for them or anyone to put out these blazing freedoms.

WELL, SO MUCH for my story. There's a picket line to march. Giovannitti and Ettor are still in prison. The children make their way to New York City, where they'll be fed and given warm beds. Soon all of *La Merica* will hear about the strikers and their starving kids. Their stories and songs will shame the selfish bosses into giving us workers our just due.

Then the masters of this New World will be made to feed us from their big pot of beans that never grows empty, their big silver platter of meat that can never be licked clean, their bee's nest full

of honey so smooth and sweet that one taste nearly makes you
want to die.

> *Though the fool fell in a hole, he kept his head*
> *While others from poles looked on quite dead.*

> *So goes lucky Giufà and the bold workers' tale.*
> *Now it's my fair Teresa's turn to regale.*

The Fisherman's Son

ℒ Teresa Pantaluna

ONCE THERE WAS a poor but honest man, what we call *un'omu di pazienza,* a man of patience, who worked the whole day—day after day—in the unrelenting heat of the scorching sun, casting his nets out into the blue sea, then rowing his little boat wide and far so as to make the nets stretch, then pulling them back, hand over hand, up through the dazzling water, each drop a blinding turquoise jewel, snagging barely enough fish to feed a kitten let alone a wife and a house overflowing with daughters. The man's name was Placidu. As the father of a hundred daughters, he was most ironically named.

Did I say a hundred daughters? I meant a thousand. Hey, twenty thousand is more like it. There were so many of them it was impossible for me to keep count! I have only so many fingers and toes!

As a young man Placidu was exactly as his name suggests, as calm and unfettered as water in a stream. If there was a rock in his path, he flowed around it. When he had to row his boat against a strong tide, he apologized to each wave for upsetting its wake. He smiled at nearly everything, especially the fruit of the sea that he lifted up into his boat, until both his cheeks became creased with the dimples that all of his grandchildren inherited.

One day Placidu fell beneath a spell that couldn't be broken by prayer or potion. He discovered a secret island. On this island was a pathway twisting darkly through a thicket. The path led him through nettle and bramble, down valley and up hill, to a secret nook hidden away deep in the forest, where there was a small pond that each evening at twilight filled with the glimmering figures of scores of girls bathing.

The girls frolicked in the water, shoulders glistening, long legs fluttering just below the water's surface, bottoms bobbing delightfully in the gently lapping waves. At the pond's far end, several girls washed their long dark hair beneath a cascading curtain of water. Then they dove into the pond, knifing the surface with their hands.

Each evening Placidu spied on them, squatting beside a fig tree. After a while his appetites grew so inflamed that he grabbed one of the nearby figs and squeezed it until all of its seeds spurted out onto the ground. He did this night after night, again and again, until the tree was nearly bare of fruit.

One evening as Placidu watched the swimmers, he grabbed the tree's last fig. As usual, in his excitement he squeezed it until it burst, but now instead of seeds the spirit of the pond leapt from his clenched hand. Placidu fell back, amazed and frightened.

The spirit was about as high as a woman's thumb. Hey, it only makes sense that you can't be too tall if you live inside a fig! But even if you're small, you can still be powerful! Young Placidu had the wits to grab the spirit and command three wishes, but the clever thing twirled like a *trich-trach* until Placidu's palm throbbed with pain. This female spirit accepted no rough treatment or disrespect.

She stood on Placidu's burning palm, one hand on her hip, the other raised, like a sensible mother correcting an errant child. "You say you demand three wishes? Well, first I'll ask three questions! Where do you come from? Where are you going? What do you want?"

Placidu's head spun. He wanted only to tumble in the water

with the girls, but his tongue couldn't catch the words to express his desire. As to where he was from and where he was going, he'd never given either concern much thought. So he just pointed to the pool and grinned.

Now, spirits generally aren't known for their good tempers. This spirit was particularly testy. "Silly boy," she proclaimed, "you want to frolic with these girls, and yet each night you come here and steal my fruit. Instead of splashing in the water with them, you splash the ground with my seed. All right, I'll give you something to remember me by! From this day on, from now until the day you die, I say that each seed you spill will become a girl just like one of these girls, and I command that you feed and clothe them and give them a place to live, a house with a tight roof and strong, thick walls and narrow windows covered with jalousies so that sneaky, empty-headed boys like you can't spy on them each evening when they're naked and at play."

Then the spirit and the girls in the pond disappeared. Placidu made his way back to his rowboat, thinking the spirit had been only one of the sea's occasional hallucinations. But the next day when he walked the twisting trail and returned to the pond he found no one there, and the day after that he saw that the pool of water had nearly dried up, and within a week there was only mud and some tender *basilicu,* which Placidu picked and chewed sadly.

The poor fisherman sorely missed his twilight adventures. One evening as he ambled back to his rowboat he saw standing in a nearby field a ewe with the eyes of a woman. Since no one else was about, he coaxed the animal toward him, offering her some of the fresh *basilicu,* and then he grabbed her and rode her back. Within minutes her sides puffed up as if she were about to explode. Then the field filled with a hundred and one baby girls, each mewing hungrily for milk.

It took him all night to get them into his boat, all the next day to take them home and feed them, all night to clean them and put them to sleep, and all the next day to feed them again. The cycle spun like a whirlpool that knows no end. Soon Placidu had no time for anything else. There was always some task to do: some crying mouth to feed, some soiled face to wash, the next meal to cook, a stack of bowls to clean, some child's stinking bottom that needed wiping.

"*Semu tutti matti!*" Placidu roared, then gnashed his teeth and foamed profusely at the mouth, all the while rolling about on the floor. It was all he could say. We're all crazy. All crazy. "*Tutti matti!*" All crazy.

In short, the clever pond spirit had cursed him with a woman's outlook and life.

THE GIRLS GREW, as all living things do, and Placidu's appetites swelled, as all appetites will over time, and soon the house was bursting with daughters.

"This can't go on. This has to stop," said the ewe with the eyes of a woman. "Do something, now, before I go mad." She handed Placidu a cleaver. "Here, cut it off."

Placidu took his *cosa* in his hand and stretched it on the wooden table, then raised the cleaver high over his head. Three times his arm started down, each instance halting the blade just before it could strike flesh or wood. Finally he dropped the knife on the table and went out to visit the village priest to inquire how in the world one can both be a man and at the same time remain pure.

"Why, whenever it begins to expand," the priest said, "sprinkle it with some holy water."

"Holy water?" Placidu said.

The priest nodded. "The coldest you can find."

That night Placidu carried home a jug of holy water. With each twinge of desire he sprinkled and doused himself, and though his *cosa* became as clean as Saint Joseph's lily, it still raised its head and expanded. So Placidu went back to the priest. "I did just as you said," Placidu told him.

"Just as I said?" asked the priest. "Did you kneel on a pile of acorns and beans?"

"No," Placidu said, "you said nothing about acorns and beans."

"You didn't listen," said the priest. "Before sprinkling it with holy water, you have to kneel on a pile of hard, uncooked beans and acorns."

So Placidu tried kneeling on a mound of uncooked nuts and beans, going so far as to try baskets of broken almond shells and cups of dried peas, but his efforts met with little success. Again he went back to the priest. "I did just as you said," Placidu told him.

"Did you hold out your arms as if you were being crucified?"

"No," Placidu said.

"Well," the priest said, "you have to hold out your arms for at least three hours, until they become as heavy as lead, so heavy you can hardly hold them up any longer."

"But how can I possibly splash on the holy water if I hold my arms out?" Placidu asked.

"Trust in God," said the priest. He pointed to the straw roof of his hut. "Put your faith in God and he'll help you find a way."

Placidu obeyed for several weeks until he finally understood that there was no way to do what the priest proposed. The sheer impossibility of purity was supposed to curb his desires. So Placidu let out a long sigh and slipped his head back into its halter. He resigned himself to his expanding household. *"Tutti matti!"* was all he could say.

I WAS ONE OF Placidu's many daughters, number eighty-nine thousand seven hundred and twenty-six. I was the stick in the bundle that snapped my papa's back. Just before the ewe with the eyes of a woman gave birth to me, Placidu proclaimed to the sun and sky and sea and earth that the very next baby to pop out from between my mamma's legs would be a boy no matter what.

The ewe dressed me in men's clothing. Everyone from leagues

around came to see me, the firstborn boy of eighty-nine thousand seven hundred and twenty-six.

"He's a beautiful baby, God bless him," they all said. To ward off the evil their compliments invited, Placidu put around my neck a coral horn.

Even though the ewe bathed me herself, she noticed only what her big sad eyes had been told by her husband to see. Placidu wanted a son, so she saw me as her son. Soon I worked beside my father on the sea, even though I had a pair of rosebuds on my chest and I squatted over the baron jar whenever I peed.

"Papa," I said to him one day as we let out the nets, "would your life have been any easier if you and Mamma had sons instead of daughters?"

"Tutti matti!" he answered, and by this he meant yes, what did I think, with so many extra hands to help him he would have been extraordinarily wealthy.

"Papa," I said, "do you admit that my work is satisfactory and good?"

"Tutti matti!" And by this he meant that only an idle boat blows wind into its own sails.

"Papa," I said, "then why don't we have a few thousand of my sisters out here helping, too?"

"Tutti matti! Tutti matti!" Meaning that a girl's place is inside the house beneath her mother's gaze.

"And why is that?" I asked. "Does a daughter not have two hands, just like a son? Two arms? Two legs? Two eyes, just like you and me?"

"Tutti matti!"

"What makes me a boy?" I asked. "Is it that Mamma cuts my hair? That I wear these pantaloons? That I work in the boat beside you?"

"Tutti matti!"

"Look at my hairless chin. My round hips. These apples bursting forth on my chest. Papa, am I defined by my essence or my function?"

"Tutti matti!"

"And if you're concerned that a girl allowed outside the house cannot be adequately protected," I asked, "what possible harm might befall her out here with you, in the middle of the vast and lonely sea?"

"Tutti matti! Tutti matti!" he replied, looking frantically about, and by this he meant that danger lurked everywhere, and my naive and rash words risked inviting it.

"Do you mean that some octopus or eel or stingray might swim by and spy on her?" I asked.

"Tutti matti!" Meaning that any man's gaze might fall on her and by seeing her the man might come to crave her, and his desires might do her irreparable harm and evil, that a daughter's place was to be hidden away, to be kept inside and out of sight, locked up and away, screened, cloaked, veiled, shrouded, made secret, invisible, unseen.

"It sounds to me as if the boys rather than the girls are the trouble," I said.

"Tutti matti!" The thickest vein on his neck throbbed wildly and appeared ready to pop.

"And yet the girls are punished and made to stay inside."

"Tutti matti!" Meaning that we would be wise to remember that he didn't create the world.

"So all of this is God's fault," I said, pointing up to the sky.

"Tutti matti!" Meaning that the gnat struggling in the web is in no position to criticize the spider.

"Particularly when the spider's a man," I declared.

"Tutti matti! Tutti matti!" he exclaimed, falling to his knees and beating his chest and repeatedly making the sign of the Cross.

Of course we'd gone around in too narrow a circle that day to catch much more than seaweed in our nets, but I saw then how the whole system worked and how truly bad it stunk. God's will or not, this boy-girl business simply wasn't a productive or intelligent plan.

I understood that rules come from community and serve the community's overall needs. To make good soup, you can't have everybody drawing water from the well. Someone's needed to chop the zucchini. But this idea of keeping my eighty-nine thousand seven hundred and twenty-five sisters locked inside the house every day seemed to me utter folly and waste.

I reminded Papa that God had originally wanted the Virgin Mary to be a *Siciliana*. God had little trouble finding an appropriate candidate—there were virgins in Sicily of every size and age—but the Almighty was unable to find a single Sicilian household where he could send in his pigeon without the bird being attacked by the girl's mother and a gang of her aunts.

"Who gave you permission to sneak in here and talk to her?" the women would shout at the bird, whacking the terrified thing to death with their brooms.

So God searched for a land with looser morals, where his feathered messenger wouldn't end up in the stewpot.

Cu nesci arrinesci. He who leaves succeeds.

Departure was my only option, disguise my only way out. A girl traveling alone was viewed as damaged goods, a cracked or broken vessel, abandoned and deserving of shame. She was prey to every vulture gliding the air above her. It was unthinkable for an unmarried girl to live apart from her family. A girl without family was considered as having no value or worth. Where was her father, her brothers, her uncles? Without men to safeguard her, the vultures would conclude that she'd done something horrible to cast dishonor on her family. Put crudely, she was a *buttana,* little more than the devil's own dirty slut.

I was the eighty-nine-thousandth seven-hundred-and-twenty-sixth daughter of a sheep whose wretched existence centered around nurturing the endless procession of bawling lambs that slipped from her womb. My mother lacked the time even to wipe her own pee. There were always three or four dozen infants suckling her teats, always a few hundred more baaing something in her ear, another thousand crying for water, more thousands squalling for something to eat, still more thousands arguing over a piece of lint or the hint of shadow flitting suddenly across a wall, something so insignificant as to hardly deserve notice but that they felt required her immediate and undivided attention, so that all you could hear inside our house was the calling of "Ma! maa! maa! Baa! baa! baa-aa!" rising to such deafening crescendos that only a saint or someone truly insane could be unaffected by the din.

Sometimes, very late at night, I'd crawl to her on the straw across all the other bodies. I'd pick fattened ticks from behind her ears and with my curled fingers comb out her matted hair. There were three or four seconds every night when everyone was silent and she could sleep. I'd pretend she was my lamb and that I was the ewe.

One night in her sleep she whispered, "I'm drowning in a sea of children," so low that I nearly thought the sound was only her breath.

"Mamma," I said, "please forgive me when I run away."

Then a few thousand of the newborns awoke and whimpered and began sucking her raw and dry, and another couple thousand had nightmares and called for her soothing touch, and over here a flock started scratching its fleas, and within a few moments it was a madhouse all over again.

No wonder Papa worked the sea! To be by oneself, in a boat out on the gray water, seemed beyond heaven! The very thought of being alone somewhere was thrilling beyond name.

The first time that my father took me out to sea, the silence was so loud I had to cover my ears. I put a metal pail over my head and beat it with two sticks to match the song in the house I had grown used to hearing! After a while Papa lifted the bucket from my face. We were alone in his little boat, way out on a rolling sheet of slate-gray water. Papa was explaining that this part of the Mediterranean between Sicilia and Africa was known as the African Sea. I pulled my first breath of truly fresh air into my lungs.

"Lu Mari Africanu," Papa repeated, gesturing widely with his arms. He cast out the nets and began to row.

Then all at once I heard the most terrifying pounding. I clutched my ears and then my chest. My mind raced. The pounding was horrifying. I was certain I'd die.

Papa held me until I calmed down. He explained that the sound was merely the beating of my own heart.

"My own heart?" I said. I'd never heard it before. I thought he must be joking. "Papa, are you saying that I have my own heart?"

"Yes, my son," he said.

"Not my sisters' or Mamma's?"

He shook his head no.

"All my own? No one else's?"

"Entirely yours, *figghiu miu.*"

I couldn't get over it. "My own heart!" I cried.

So in my jacket, pantaloons, and boots I set off for the Golden Land, where it was rumored that families didn't have eighty-nine thousand seven hundred and twenty-six daughters. As I began to hike the rocky road through the mountains to Palermu, I listened to my heart. Its steady thumping told me there was nothing I would be unable to do. I had the best of both sexes: the guile and wit of a woman, and the appearance and freedom of a man.

Understand that people see less with their eyes than with their minds. If they are told that a thing is true, they tend to adapt their vision so as to see it as such. I didn't so much pretend to be a man as forget that I was a woman. On my back were a poor villager's rough clothes. That's mainly all that people saw. I stuffed a folded handkerchief into my pantaloons to give them a better fit, but that was it for costume. My hair was short, my face tanned dark from the sea. If I pretended anything, it was that I was rich.

I realized that becoming a man isn't so much a shift in gender as it is a change in class or social standing. So I pretended to be the son of a wealthy baron, attacked by thieves on my way north and stripped of every valuable I owned. I lay flat on my back in a ditch beside the roadway waiting for some peasants to come along and give me aid. I filled the air with angry curses for my miserable robbers, who in their greed took my horse and plucked me bare, leaving me only their insulting rags. I gave my jacket an extra tear or two for show. I smeared a stripe of mud on my face. Finally I heard a gang of peasants tromping up the road. I let loose a low moan and shouted loud my sad story.

As the *genti di campagna* rushed to my aid, I did as the son of a wealthy baron would and chastised them for not arriving more quickly. I called them lazy and useless and unworthy of even the air their filthy snouts breathed. Immediately I ordered them to give me water and food.

They stood about apologizing, their eyes downcast, while I ate. I made a show of tossing the crusts of their crude bread into the weeds and then had the peasants line up in a row and recite their names, villages, and occupations. Then I told them that I wished to be entertained. By now they were asking if they might carry me along the road on their broad shoulders. It's still amazing to me how easily they allowed their necks to slip into the yoke my act provided.

One man pulled a concertina from beneath his cloak. A second beat time on a tambourine. The sun shone with happy fierceness as the peasants sang.

> *The weather this day is so sharp and alive!*
> *Lord, lead me the way back to the bed of my wife,*
> *Whose fat arms and thighs give me such sweet tumbles*
> *As I shut my eyes on my life's trials and stumbles.*
> *Lord, before I'm old, return me to my family!*
> *Pockets bulging with gold after I've crossed the sea!*
> *While I still have hair and teeth!*
> *May her legs wrap me in their wreath!*
> *May her arms hold me tight!*
> *Now and through the long night!*

• • •

IN PALERMU I ALLOWED the singing peasants to tell my tale to the wealthy *baruni* who crowded around us. They knew that *banditi* ruled the hills, particularly in the south. Girgenti was known as a place where a man didn't allow even a fly to land on his nose!

How fortunate I was to have lived, the barons' sons exclaimed, attributing my luck to my slight build, which they surmised must have posed a minimum of threat to my robbers.

I remembered to act unimpressed, pretending I was as rich as any one of these unbelievably wealthy young men. I requested nothing of them, not even a sip of cool water. I merely answered questions put to me and described my situation. When asked if I was tired from my journey, I sighed and said, "No more than one would expect." They then implored me to rest in someone's spacious room, where a servant brought me bread, *minestra,* meat, cheese, and wine.

I picked at the food as if its opulence didn't faze me. I sipped some soup and nibbled a piece of the cheese. Afterwards, over cigars, I told the rich sons the story of Placidu's secret island and pool and the ewe with the eyes of a woman, attributing the tale to my peasant companions. The *baruni* met my wit with laughter and applause.

They insisted that while I was in Palermu I make use of their carriages and drivers. They argued over which tailor's stitches were fine enough to fashion for me a new and proper suit of clothes. They gave me boxes of cigars and *frutta candita.* Several of the young men suggested that I contact their bankers, who were instructed to advance me any sum I required. When I just so happened to mention that I'd intended to visit *La Merica,* the son of an owner of one of the steamship companies gave me the name of his first captain, whom I called on the following day and who politely shook my hand and bowed before placing me *gratis* in a cabin of the finest class.

• • •

IN MY NEW CLOTHES, in my shiny cabin, I made my way across the wide, seemingly endless sea. One morning as I strolled the rolling deck, rocked forth and back by the powerfully swelling ocean, my eyes fell on a lonely peasant, skin as dark as an olive soaked in brine, nose like the beak of a hawk, and beneath it a drooping moustache, my husband-to-be, the firstborn son Gaetanu from the southwestern province of Girgenti.

He was over in steerage walking dizzily among the cattle, clearly every bit as sick as a poisoned dog. I stared at him until his eyes caught mine. He nodded absently and out of habit, like a peasant to any *baruni,* with a sorry look on his mouth as if he were about to spit.

Perhaps it was the soot that blew in his face from the filthy smokestacks or the stench of the animals around him or his nausea from the sea. But there was something about him that gave me pause. Something about him arrested me. I felt somehow as if I were looking at another version of myself. If I'd been born a boy, I thought, I would be exactly like him, not so much in appearance but in attitude. He was like my own brother, I thought, the mirror image of my soul. He was everything that I was, only undisguised and in reverse.

He wore his cap low, nearly concealing his eyes, like I'd worn mine when I fished the sea with my father. He slouched his shoulders, kept his hands in his pockets, and kicked whatever lay on the ground ahead of him, exactly in the way that I'd walked when I was waiting for something in life to happen, when I felt that nothing but more of the same boring sameness lay in wait for me, when I desired sluggish fate to advance and ride on the crest of some wind of change.

Then the smoke cleared and he looked up at me, his solitary stare piercing the linen of my suit. His eyes were bright and clear. For a full moment I felt that he could see me exactly as I was, the disguised, desperate daughter of a cursed yet stubborn *piscaturi* and a wide-eyed, flea-infested, absurdly fertile ewe.

Every morning the peasant and I walked the deck trading

glances until one day he paused within shouting distance and asked me what village was I from. The sea raged wildly beneath us. The remaining cattle lowed continually in complaint.

My heart beat so rapidly that I could barely yell my village's name. He said he could tell I was from the southern coast by the sure-footed way that I paced the deck. I told him that my father and I had fished the African Sea for tuna and sardines.

Ahh, he said with a wistful smile. He'd never eaten sardines but he'd heard from those who had that they were delicious.

I told him the flavor of sardines held no romance, that after a few months sardines came to taste like paste. He laughed and recited the proverb, *"Lu pani di la casa stuffa."* Homemade bread grows tiresome. Then he added, "But to a mouth used to eating slugs and straw, even unromantic paste would be a feast." He tipped his cap and disappeared among the livestock.

We had a few other conversations, none long, all of them across the distance separating the ship's classes. Soon I was able to convince him to accept some of the food brought each day to my cabin. I told him that on my side of the ship food was going to waste, and perhaps he could help me distribute it. I don't know if he ate what I gave him or if in turn he offered it to those more needy. Talking to him during the stormy passage tempted me to forget my pretense. My insides softened and grew mutable as wax.

PEOPLE THINK THE immigrant ships went directly to Ellis Island, but in fact they stopped first at New York's Hudson River Pier, where the *Americani* and first-class passengers departed. The immigration officials inspected me on board ship the afternoon the ship docked.

Remember I told you that people see what their minds tell them to expect. The doctor expected to see a young Sicilian nobleman, so when he entered my cabin that's precisely what he found. For the occasion I wore a silk scarf over my vest, and I puffed a fine cigar.

The doctor apologized for the interruption and inspected my eyes and ears and felt and measured the strength of my pulse. I offered him my box of *frutta candita*. With a nod he gobbled several of the sugared fruits, then looked into my mouth and felt my neck and throat.

I asked him where in the harbor I might find a good bootblack. When we realized we didn't speak the same dialect, I mimed my question until he laughed and understood. I laughed, too, then offered him my cigars. He happily stuffed his pockets until I insisted that he keep the whole box.

I had only to unbutton my vest and pull up the back of my shirt so that he could listen to my lungs as I breathed and I was through.

"OK," he said.

It was my first real American word. I liked the clean sound of it. "OK," I replied. "OK. *Grazie*."

LATER I TOOK the barge to Ellis Island, where I searched for the peasant mirror of my soul. As Gaetanu stepped from the island's tempestuous Great Hall, gazing about at every new thing with obvious fear and wonder, I hailed him and inquired where he was headed.

"Albany!" he replied, smiling so immensely you'd think Saint Peter had just allowed him inside the gates.

"What a coincidence!" I exclaimed. "I too am journeying to this Albany! Let's travel there together, OK?"

He and a dozen other unfortunates were accompanied by a pair of the *patruni*'s agents, well-fed men stuffed in *Americani* clothes. "I go with my friend, OK?" I told them. "Sure," they said, smiling at each other with their shiny gold teeth. "There's always a place for one more." They led us through a dark passageway that opened into a high-ceilinged room, inside of which stood some sort of narrow house cluttered with wide chairs and walls lined with glass windows. Gaetanu and I sat cautiously on a chair inside the house until the floor jerked forward beneath our feet. Suddenly the entire house began to move!

"May God have mercy on our souls!" Gaetanu shouted. "It's the end of the world!"

Beneath us I felt a great series of rumbling explosions, then a pair of screams or high whistles from above. Outside the glass windows, the air grew thick with smoke. I feared that a volcano had erupted. The screams must be from those trapped in its burning lava. "We'd better prepare our souls to die!" I shouted to my new friend.

We'd both fallen forward onto the back of the wide chair in front of us. I sat up and quickly raised my feet from the floor, fearing the lava that would soon pour through the moving house. Then the room filled suddenly with light and a rocky field flew past the windows, and then the field turned green with splendid grasses, and the rumbling floor beneath us clattered more evenly and quietly, rocking us now from side to side. Another pair of whistles pierced the air.

"We're in a flying house!" Gaetanu shouted.

"Perhaps," I declared, "though it may be more a roofed wagon." I decided I had to act like a baron again. "Be calm," I said in a reassuring tone. "I'm quite sure we're safe just as long as the stupid driver doesn't hit a tree."

For several minutes then we gazed out the windows, furiously watching out for oncoming trees.

The others in the wagon with us seemed unconcerned with the danger. Gaetanu imitated them and then sat back, relaxed.

He stared out the windows at the houses and fields. After a while he said, "Look how the flowers grow gracefully beside the other flowers, the thorns and weeds in the ditch beside the other thorns and weeds."

"Yes," I said. "I see."

"Likes with likes. The same with the same." He knocked the first fingers of his hands together. "See, they don't mix, like you and me."

"A *piscaturi* such as me knows nothing of flowers," I replied.
"Yet the fisherman's son travels across the sea in a cabin of the highest class."

"Only a fool judges wine by its bottle," I said. I showed him the calluses on my hands. "Feel," I said. "My hands are every bit as hard as yours. Would a stranger to labor have hands like these?"

As he traced his fingertips across my palms I grunted and pulled my hands away, as one man would with another, yet inside I felt a hot blush rise in my throat and cheeks, and a line of fire sear deep to my core. I slapped his shoulder and laughed. "Trust me, my friend," I said heartily.

"My friend," he said, eyes twinkling, nodding and slapping my shoulder hard in return.

Still he continued to test me, asking me if I rode and if so how I sat on the horse's back, whether I held the reins with one or both hands, and with which hand I used the whip. I straddled the seat, knees apart, my right hand holding imaginary reins, my left threatening with the whip. He asked me the proper direction to pull a razor over one's whiskers, whether it's preferable to go with the grain of the beard or against it. I said that for the best shave one draws the razor against the beard's grain after first wetting the hairs with scented water. Then he asked me why, if in truth I were as rich as my clothes, its pockets were even more empty than his.

I squeezed the cloth that I'd stuffed in my pantaloons and laughed and said, "A dozen maidens between the coast and Palermu would swear that my pockets weren't empty."

"Only a dozen?" he said with a laugh. "On my walk to Palermu I'm sure I had three times more." He gave the prominent thickness in his pants a slight squeeze, then elbowed me sharply in the ribs. "Tell me, my friend, what does a man of your class whisper to the girls before you lay with them?"

"Of course I tell them that I love them, the same as you say to the girls whom you meet, only three times less often," I replied.

He nodded. "And what do they say to you in return?"

"Why, of course they echo the same words, only three times less loud."

He nodded a second time. "And afterwards, what words do you utter as you depart?"

"Of course I say that someday I'll return, just as you tell all those whom you meet and who love you, only three times less sadly."

His mood grew serious then. "In truth," he said, "on the road to Palermu I lay with nothing more gentle than the jagged tips of rocks, nothing more generous than hardship."

"May both mistresses be stingy to us," I said, "now and forever."

"So be it." He nodded a third time. "After all, we're on our way to Albany!"

"Paradise," I said. "The New Eden. The Golden Land."

"*La Merica!*" Gaetanu exclaimed to all seated on the train.

GOD'S BLOOD, the factory in Albany where my Tannu was to work off his debt to the *patruni* was more like Hell.

Blinding fires taller than a house crackled and blazed within endless rows of yawning ovens. The golden flames twisted and writhed in insatiable hunger as the workers scrambled in subservience, like ants on a log. Everywhere huge machines roared in an eternally thumping, pounding, ear-splitting din that knew no end. All of this chaos was contained by the factory's dark, unbroken walls, held down by the ceiling that blocked any breeze or sunlight, so that all the air we pulled into our lungs was stifled and suffocating, wrung dry of any goodness or freshness, tainted by smoke and soot and the fetid smell of grease and metal mixed with oil.

How can people go from working their entire lives out in God's air and sunlight, in his heat and cold, his clear and rain, his bright and cloudy, his calm and windy, to being cut off from all sense of the day's nature?

Oh, how I missed the forgiving openness of the African Sea! To be laboring alongside my father, letting out the day's nets while reciting our prayers for the Lord's bounty, now seemed a faint dream to me. What mistake had I made coming to this tortured land?

For the first months Gaetanu and I shared a tiny room, living as two men. We slept on the same bed, like monks, feet to head, collapsing on the narrow cot nearly the moment we came in from our day's labors. Then after an hour or so we'd rise and eat, mainly *pani e favi,* a piece of bread big as my fist and a small bowl of beans, along with whatever greens we could find and afford. I washed on the sly after he was asleep, in the women's bathhouse, avoiding all the various traps that might reveal me. Each month I was careful to hide the bright evidence that I was daughter number eighty-nine thousand seven hundred and twenty-six.

Gaetanu worried constantly about his debt. He was smart in the way of all *campagnoli* but was absolutely witless and thick when it came to numbers. Pencils and tablets of paper terrified him. I tried teaching him how to count on his fingers, but he frequently confused directions and in the midst of calculation would end up taking away part of what he'd intended to add, or adding half of what he was supposed to take away, so that by the time his reckonings were finished he was usually exactly where he had started. Then he would argue with me that his wrong answer was correct and that all calculation and mathematical processes were absurd and meaningless.

He'd spend endless hours trying to convince me that one plus zero equaled zero. He would start with one finger raised on his hand, then transfer it to the other, making his first hand into a fist, juggling the one raised finger back and forth, all the while asking me if his addition was correct, until he'd use the one raised finger to count the number remaining on his other hand, which of course always was zero.

Gaetanu was extraordinarily fond of zero. He said it was the most fascinating number because it was so unlike the others, something and yet not something all at the same time. He said that here in the New Land very often he felt the same way.

"In Sicilia I used to be something," he'd say, raising a finger, "but here I feel just like this," pointing the finger at his other, empty fist.

He liked to hold up one fist and ask me how much.

"Zero," I'd answer.

"No," he'd say, "one," and shake his head and point to his fist.

And if I answered one, he'd point to his absence of raised fingers and say zero. Then we'd argue.

To silence his senselessness I'd start counting. Daughter of a most prolific mother, I was born with an appreciation for numbers! I'd grown up literally counting sheep! I knew just how high numbers were able to climb!

But Gaetanu would refuse to listen to me. He'd repeat the contradiction of his raised fist and his justification that one plus zero equaled zero, claiming that these additions explained how he had journeyed all this way and had still gotten nowhere and was in fact even more poor now than he'd been before.

No one could argue against that conclusion. In truth, after the first year he was in an even deeper hole of debt to the *patruni*.

ONE HOT SUMMER night as we lay in bed discussing these arithmetics, the air grew so thick and heavy it was a great labor just to take the next breath. Neither of us could sleep. The humid night stretched endlessly before us.

We tossed on the mattress until his hands happened to brush against my hips. He was arguing with me about the number ten, claiming that all sensible arithmetic must stop there, that no number could ascend higher than ten because ten tumbled back to zero before it could possibly reach the height of elevenness and as a result might as well be merely one, so that at the second he touched my hips the fingers of both his hands were stretched forward.

Then a bolt of lightning shot through the sky, transforming the inky darkness into a clear moment of day. A cool wind surged through the room. A curtain of rain smacked the street below our window with a steady *shhhhhhh,* and darkness mercifully fell again over us as his ten fingers drifted from my hips toward the front of my pantaloons.

"Tell me your name," he whispered in the darkness. I could barely hear him, the rain was pounding the roof with such force.

"Your name," he said in a deeper voice. "Tell me your true and real woman's name."

The lightning bolt had transformed him into a bull. I stroked his thick shoulders and then his forehead, careful not to hurt my hands against his sharp, upturned horns.

He scrambled from the bed and stood, pawing the floor with his front hoof, then stretched back the bulk of his powerful neck and bellowed loudly in the night.

As I changed myself back into a woman, I told him all he needed to know.

STILL, I DIDN'T like wearing dresses one bit. During the textile strike in Lawrence, when Elizabeth Gurley Flynn arrived to give speeches to the Irish workers, I told her how much more comfortable it was for a woman to wear pantaloons. Elizabeth Gurley Flynn was a healthy woman who wore thick cotton blouses buttoned all the way up, with a dark triangle of a necktie and a heavy woolen skirt. She'd pinned her hair up on top of her head. I also meant to tell her how much more cool she'd be if she cut her hair short. But she reached across the crowd to me with her eyes and voice and said that a woman needs to be able to afford trousers before she can wear them, and the crowd cheered loudly. I understood her point. Can you believe that after I showed up to work as a woman in the factory they cut my pay in half?

Gaetanu had considerable fun applying his warped comprehension of mathematics to explain that.

Later the government sent me a draft notice, even before they conscripted Gaetanu and took him to fight in the Great War. This was after we'd moved to New York. We carried the letter to a scribe, who for ten cents agreed to read and translate it. The penman explained when and where I was required to report.

"But it says here you're a man," the draft officials at the center insisted.

I rested my hands on the bulge of my abdomen and smiled. By then the first of my many *cucciddati* was already six months on the way.

DISGUISE WEARS MANY masks. They made Tannu wear a costume, too. They dressed him in a thick jacket and pants, then put a soup bowl on his head and issued him a rifle and a bayonet.

They put bowls on the heads of all of the *cumpari*: on Luigi, Salvatore, Gerlando Cavadduzzo, all of the others. Just as the old one in Rome had threatened, this new government marched all the young *Siciliani* off to war.

I'll tell you one last story. I grew up not too far from a village known for its wars. As you walk inland from the African Sea, you can count the graves. The local men would point to the ground and say, here lies a real fighter! And here! One here! Another here! You look and all you can see are dandelions gone to seed, their tops white and nodding like the bent heads of the old men the dead warriors never had the chance to become.

One day in this village the women grew sick of it, sick of washing the dead bodies as they stiffened, sick of wrapping the dead in white sheets, sick of covering them with dirt and stones, sick of letting loose their wails. Sometimes I'd trail after the women to these funerals, and one bright night I followed them to the cemetery, where I hid behind a tree watching them as they squatted on the graves of their dead men.

Everyone discussed the constant fighting, and the full moon looked down on the women and gave them an idea. Just as the moon's face changes and disappears each month, the women imagined that they could change and disappear into the darkness, too. The women could band together and strike. They didn't have that word then—strike—but that was the general idea. At once the women decided that from that moment on they'd have no more baby boys.

No more baby boys! What a delicious idea! You should have seen the women's smiles. Surely, they thought, that would put an end to the fighting! But no sooner had everyone agreed than one woman—I believe her name was Ducella—dropped a baby boy right on top of his grandfather's grave.

The women cursed the moon. Then they realized that since nobody but they and the moon had witnessed Ducella give birth, perhaps they could keep it a secret. So they hid Ducella's baby inside a cave. And to give Ducella an alibi, the women gave her a newborn lamb. Then they returned to the village with Ducella and her baby lamb.

Whenever one of the women was ready to drop a baby, the others got the men out of the house fast and one of the women had a baby lamb ready, just in case. If it was a girl, the women celebrated. If it was a boy, they got out the lamb. Another woman hurried the baby to the cave. And soon the war and fighting stopped, and soon the village became famous, known all across Sicily as the peaceful village of cursed women who gave birth to girls and baby lambs.

Doctors came from as far away as Messina. A merry band of priests arrived from Rome, holding perfumed hankies up to their noses, their buckled shoes carefully stepping around the sheep droppings. With their soft hands the priests made many signs in the air. Their dialect was so weak and thin that when they spoke no one could understand them. They blamed the villagers for their failings and sprinkled holy water on everybody and everything.

Soon I was asked to take a baby to the cave. It was filling up fast, let me tell you. In no time that cave was crowded with boys of all ages and sizes: boys wrestling on the ground, boys betting on which one had the strongest flow of pee, boys sucking their thumbs, boys kicking round stones, unhappy boys, boys playing finger games, singing boys, boys doing somersaults, boys fencing with sticks, boys torturing smaller boys, boys spitting high into the air and then catching their spittle in their mouths, sleeping boys, boys walking with their hands out and eyes closed, boys making faces, boys screaming at the top of their lungs, boys hopping on one leg, boys drawing pictures on the walls, boys playing buck buck how many fingers up, boys making farts with their armpits, boys imitating toads, boys pretending to row boats, bored boys, hungry boys, boys pretending to catch eels, boys becoming so filthy you couldn't see the pink of their mouths, boys standing on their heads, boys sucking their fingers, boys picking their noses and teeth and ears, boys scuttling sideways like crabs, boys attempting to remember their prayers, dreaming boys, boys eating dirt and clay, boys chanting over and over the song of the ricotta seller, boys dancing the *tarascuni,* boys flapping their arms like eagles, boys punching everything near them, boys hanging by their toes from the ceiling like bats, dazed boys, drooling boys, boys crying sadly in the darkest corners, boys reaching into the darkness for the arms of their mammas.

I rolled shut the rock at the mouth of the cave fast!

Some time later there was an earthquake so mighty that everybody fell and rolled around on the ground. We were sure it was doomsday. But when we looked up at the horizon, instead of the archangels we saw an army of filthy boys, boys waving jagged branches of trees, boys wielding clubs, sickles, pitchforks.

They'd just attacked the village we used to fight with, and now they sang ancient war songs as they marched victoriously home. In their hands several held what looked to me like melons. Only as they neared could I see that they were really the cut-off heads of the dead.

The men of our village shouted gleefully and rushed forward to meet their sons. Then the earth shuddered again, and out of a yawning crack in the ground came a plume of twisting smoke and an angel.

He couldn't have been a very high angel because his face wasn't very bright. He didn't have golden hair or even a small halo. But he was distinguished enough to have thick, intricate wings that brushed the ground behind him as he walked, stirring the dust until it scurried with scores of spiders and scorpions.

The young warriors on the horizon gazed lovingly at him and hailed him, calling him their Angel of Victory. He nodded to them and then flew around their heads in little circles for a while—a real peacock, all the women thought—and then he landed on his feet and simultaneously crossed his arms and closed his wings.

The women had interfered with nature, the angel told us, and the Highest Power was most displeased. But now that our sons were free, the balance of things was restored and all things on earth could be put back in order. Yet as punishment, the angel said, from that day forward men would die before women. This would give women time to think about how lonely and terrible a place the world would be without men. It would give the women great and untold pain and suffering as they hobbled slowly and alone to their graves. From the crack in the ground behind him, a bolt of lightning leapt suddenly into the sky.

The priests crossed themselves and proclaimed it a great miracle. The doctors applauded and declared it scientific fact. The men of our village stared at the women, the dim awareness of their betrayal beginning to burn inside their eyes. Then the angel stepped back into his crack. As the frightened women turned and began the walk back to the village, I looked to the north toward Palermu, toward the promise of the New World, and fled.

Tell me, how should we read this last tale? The angel confuses me. I have no doubts that he existed since I saw him with my own eyes, but I can't help but wonder about that angel.

Was he sent by God to punish the women, as he claimed, because they'd tried to trick nature? Or was he really punishing the men, since their follies so often invited death and led to the horrible slaughter of war? Or was the angel really a devil since he stepped from a crack in the earth? Aren't angels supposed to descend in glowing light from the sky above?

When Tannu came back from the Great War, he wanted to wear his uniform everywhere. He wouldn't take it off he was so proud. He raised his first finger and poked it into his chest, saying the uniform made him and all the others *Americani* one hundred percent!

I shouted at him to throw the damn thing away. I tell you, I could smell blood on it. But he wore it anyway. Wrapped in its disguise, he wasn't the same man.

> *I know the true weight and strength of disguise,*
> *How it transformed my fate by deceiving the eyes.*
>
> *Now the wolf of Girgenti wants to let loose his song*
> *And tell you his story about right and wrong.*

The Wolf of Girgenti

Luigi Girgenti

Hell's a lonely place. You don't have to ask me how I know. I know. I know because one bright night, when I wasn't much older than the youngest one here, I became restless, and the soft Sicilian air smelled so sweetly of lemons that I couldn't breathe, and the stars in the gap of the roof were so bright that they kept me awake, and if I listened with all my might I could hear the wolves. The wolves were up in the hills, deep in the forest, calling to one another. I thought that they called to me, too. So, more quietly than the shadow of a mouse's tail, I pulled myself up and out of the pile of dusty straw that made up my bed. Don't ask me why. I was a foolish kid, a real peacock. The empty squash of my head was full of a thousand and one big ideas back then.

I pulled myself out from the warm straw and the clutches of my sleeping brothers up in the loft where the three of us slept, trying not to rouse the goats or Gabriella, my father's donkey. The animals slept beneath us, on the ground floor. In truth, the place was less ours than it was theirs. Anyway, like three old chaperones, Gabriella and the two goats guarded the door. To get out I'd have to sneak past them.

Now, a sleeping goat isn't something you want to disturb.

Goats are tense, uneasy creatures, as high-strung as the tendons in their lank and scrawny legs, able to erupt in incredible noise and motion if even an unexpected mote of dust dares to land on their nose. Goats fear nearly everything, particularly that which is invisible. That's why you often see them leaping about. They're jumping out of the way of invisible demons.

And that's why the Almighty gave goats a pair of horns, to repel evil, which more times than not can't be immediately seen. Evil has a hard time penetrating horn. Also coral. Evil shoots out like an invisible beam of light from the yellow slits in the demon's eyes, hits one of the beast's horns, slides down to the horny base protecting the skull, then bounces up and off the other horn as the animal cleverly hops away.

Frightened, a goat will bleat with such shrill consternation that you'd think someone's skinning the poor beast alive. That's the goat's second manner of defending itself: terrifying the wits out of anyone in earshot. One strident bleat and Mamma Adriana would jump up and shout what in God's name was I doing down there agitating the poor animals, or Papa would curse and throw a shoe at me, and when I say throw a shoe I mean he'd throw a shoe! Shoes were made of wood back then. Want to see my scars?

To escape I had to tiptoe past these guards. Let me tell you, with her long nose that Gabriella could really snore! Even when asleep her tall left ear would twitch and dance as if it were a living thing possessing a mind all its own.

"Shhh," I whispered that night to Gabriella's quivering ear. "Shhh," I whispered to the mangy, ragged goats, whose limp sacks never held enough milk for all of us. I pretended I was midsummer's wind caressing my favorite grove of trees. With my palms I made calm circles in the air. "Shhh, shhh," I said as I tiptoed across the straw toward the door.

The goats answered with a shudder of their curled-up tails and a sharp pair of farts.

"Brrrp! Brrrp!" Wrapped in the cloud of their nauseating odor, I slipped out a crack in the door.

When I got to the edge of the forest I shouted with joy, then cupped my hands beside my mouth and called:

> "*Hey wolves, why don't you come out and play*
> *Or else shut up so I can sleep!*
> *I'm a village boy who's roamed this way*
> *To romp and frolic, gambol and leap.*"

And the owls in the trees cried, "Who? Who?" and I shouted, "Clean the wax from your ears, you bags of feathers, I just told you, it's me, the second-born son of Santuzzu and Adriana, the ambitious, handsome, sly, and ever-hungry Luigi!"

Well, you can guess what happened next. The owls, being wise and thinking they knew what was best for me, tried to trick me by leading me away from the wolves' camp. After tailing them for several leagues I caught a whiff of the smoke from the wolves' campfire and doubled back, walking higher up in the hills, deeper and ever deeper into the forest.

Their fire was still flickering brightly enough that I could make out their tents and the spot where they'd tethered their horses. I saw their makeshift pen full of lambs, likely stolen from the *baruni*, several fat goats, teats bulging with milk, some chickens and pheasants, even a couple of cows! No wolves had stayed behind. I figured they were all out on a raid.

Then I saw a big sack of coins and an inviting pile of leftover bones. Now, an empty stomach presents the moral mind with a most compelling argument. While my mind knew the hand was wrong to take something that hadn't been offered, my stomach reminded my brain that I was created to give due honor and glory to Diu, Jesù, and Mari, which I could hardly do if I starved to death. Besides, when the cat is not home the mice dance.

So I grabbed the smallest rib from the heap and gnawed it. There was enough meat and gristle clinging to the bone to make it worth my while. Soon I'd picked the pile clean. Then I broke each bone in half and sucked out the sweet marrow, then ate the bones themselves, chewing slowly with my back teeth, grinding the bones down to a scrumptious and satisfying grit, until the entire pile disappeared.

What a feast! It was the first time in my life I'd ever eaten until I was full! Was my belly content!

I was pretty thirsty then, so I looked around until I found a bag of water. I drank the bag dry. Ahh! For the next hour or so I strummed my taut belly and happily sucked my teeth. Then I saw that my fingers were edging gradually nearer and nearer to the bag of gold, and after a while my fingertips innocently untied the string at the bag's neck, just for a peek inside. Then, just to keep my idle hands busy, I fingered a couple of the shiny coins that had spilled out on the ground.

There were so many gold coins in the bag! Who could know exactly how many? Not even God could know, I thought. In the blink of an eye, one coin hopped its way into my empty pocket. Then a second coin joined the first, then a third.

That did it! A streak of lightning shot up from a fissure in the ground, right through the crack of my *culu*. You should have heard me holler! Then thick tufts of hair sprouted from every pore of my body. My back constricted and bucked and twisted me so fiercely that I fell down on all fours. My hands and feet shriveled into paws. A bushy tail sprang out just above the spot where the lightning had got me. My skull collapsed and warped in shape. My ears stretched up and out, gravitating to the top of my skull. My nose grew so keen and pointed that I could smell the colors in the air. My eyes shrunk to the size of *ceci* beans. Teeth long as nails protruded wildly from my muzzle. I gave mother moon a howl.

I'd transformed into a wolf!

So I RAN with the wolf pack, feeling one with mother earth, as if I were her son and she were truly family to me. There was nothing in the hills or valleys—perhaps in all of Girgenti—as wonderful as our pack of wolves. There was nothing as strong or as just. The wolf pack settled all disputes with the thieving *baruni* and their *gabbilloti* henchmen who threatened to hunt us down and kill us one by one.

But they couldn't touch us, at least back then! Whatever we wolves wanted took place. Whatever we wolves decided became law. Soon we were rulers of all that our senses fell on. The *campagnoli* came to depend on us for order and some semblance of justice. In truth most of us who'd taken to the hills were merely the sons of tenant farmers, upholding the honor of our fathers, who were too old and weak to defend themselves against the *baruni* and their overseers. Yet some nights when we thundered down from the hills on our horses it felt as if we were the actual fingers on the hands of God! Let me tell you, it's quite intoxicating for a man to feel that he's a warrior! Perhaps there's nothing sweeter in a man's life than to feel strong within himself and at the same time part of something truly mighty.

And how we ate! Let me tell you, we ate good! Look at my belly and you know I mean what I say! We had something to eat every night: eggplant, peppers, zucchini, *braciola,* partridge, sometimes lamb so rare the blood was still warm and throbbing. Sometimes eel, anchovies, tuna, *calamari,* mussels, and on special occasions my favorite: sardine and macaroni pie. Many nights we ate *cùscusu* with fish. You have to be careful steaming couscous so that you don't allow the boiling water to splash into the grain. The wolves made me into a cook since I didn't really have the stomach for fighting and since my eye liked to keep itself trained on whatever in God's bountiful world might become my next meal. Whenever I saw something I wondered how nice it would be if I could eat it! I grew right into my pants.

I should explain that back then most of the people of the province were being worked or starved to death. The *campagnoli* would labor all day in the fields, or deep inside the dusty bowels of the sulphur mines, or out on their fragile boats fishing the raw sea, and each night they'd fall exhausted onto their miserable piles of straw, like old donkeys, one day closer to death, with little more than their continued existence to show for their efforts.

Say a man owned a modest piece of land, which he farmed with his sons or brothers. He labored first against mother earth, which in most places was made up of sterile clay marbled with rock. He had to labor beneath the broiling sun, which in summer was like a hot hammer in a sadistic giant's fist. He labored against drought and the scorching sirocco blown in from the furnace of North Africa. He labored against the perpetual rains of winter, which annually flooded nearly all of the previous season's work away. He also had to work against the thief of a government in distant Rome, which taxed him so severely that there were tariffs even on donkeys and mules, though none on the horses and cows owned by the *gabbilloti* and their fat-assed bosses, the rich estate owners or *baruni*. No, the *baruni* had their friends in Rome, where the laws for this distant land were set. So the *genti di campagna* paid nearly all of Sicily's taxes, which blew along with the hot winds to the north, vanishing along with the common man's dreams and hopes.

In time, the average farmer owed more taxes than he could possibly pay. So he sold his modest piece of land to the *baruni*, who in turn most likely leased it back to him. The price for this second arrangement was fixed: so many bushels per hectare, usually two-thirds of what the baron imagined very good land could yield in a perfect year. Of course, in most years the rented lands produced half the ideal amount. Then not only did everything go to the landlord but the man found himself having to borrow against the following year, falling even deeper in debt if the yield again disappointed, falling still deeper in debt the year after that.

Nearly every year the *gabbilloti* relocated the people's fields. My father, Santuzzu, would work a poor piece of land, clear it of rock, till it, put down manure, plant good seed in the right proportions, and the next year the landlord would take the much-improved field and lease it to his good-for-nothing nephew or lazy dolt of a cousin. In its place the *gabbilloti* would issue Papa Santuzzu and my brothers another worthless plot studded with rock, covered with nearly impenetrable bramble, land hardly fit for goat's pasture. This my holy saint of a father would again be asked to turn into a garden.

Tell me, any of you who dare to judge, what other alternative existed?

Tell me, how can a man do nothing while his brothers and sisters starve? How can he remain a man? In the event that you've been so blessed never to have observed or experienced starvation, let me tell you that there's nothing romantic or dignified about it. What do you imagine it was like watching my mother and brothers and sisters go without every day, day after day? If you judge me, in the end God will judge your judgment. Pray that he's less harsh with you than you are with me.

Thus wolf packs formed in the Sicilian forests and hills and commenced to rob the robbers, taking back a small portion of what was rightfully ours. Intelligence suggests this was inevitable. When a tree puts out a branch on its left, in balance another begins growing on the right. Some force on the people's part was necessary to correct the unjust forces working against them. The wolf packs were only fitting. They were only natural and just.

So THE WOLVES rescued some of the riches the vultures had stolen, and if an honest man had an honest debt, we helped him pay it off. If someone fell into a hole of trouble and had to get away fast, coins from our bag of gold sped his way. Whenever a man of honor retaliated against the *gabbilloti* and was killed, his widow woke up the next morning to find a fistful of coins beside her shoes, a couple of nice fat chickens clucking outside her hut, a goat or perhaps even a lamb tethered to her door. The modest gifts enabled her to hold her head a bit higher as she lowered her husband's body into his grave. Moreover, the gifts showed the landlords and overseers that the ordinary people of the earth could take care of their own.

Then after a few days, or sometimes a few months or even years later, someone from the village would discover the man's murderers dangling from a tree by their broken necks. Sometimes the murderers would be found in a field, lying upside down on a pile of rocks, hands and feet bound, throats slit, an offering to the flies. A fitting outcome for a vulture, no? Our retaliation matched their crimes. *Gabbilloti* overly generous with the whip would receive a good taste of the lash's bite. Greedy *gabbilloti* would be found with their hands and pockets cut off. Informers, with a mouth empty of tongue. Oh, I could tell you stories that would turn your hair!

Sometimes we only captured one of the landlords and held him in a cave up in the hills. We tied his hands behind his back so that they couldn't steal. We pulled a grain sack over his eyes to make him blind. We hobbled him like a horse. We fed him what our families in the village ate: weeds and water, an occasional snail or teeming ball of grubs, every other Sunday perhaps a crust of bread. If his family paid the ransom we requested, the landlord again saw the sky and trees. If not, how could we possibly let him go?

There's nothing pretty about any of this. As they say, truth and beauty rarely dance to the same tune. You can't clean something covered with shit without getting some shit on you.

Even though I was mainly a cook and occasional stableboy, I'll admit that I'm as responsible as anybody for all that was done. If I wish to accept any credit I must also accept any and all blame. As for apologies, I'll save them for Jesù Cristu, for the day I die, for the moment when he judges me and I see him face to face.

Sure, the gentle people in the villages and countryside were afraid of us, but that was part of our purpose, to become something that was feared. Those who punish one person threaten a hundred others.

This force was entirely necessary. If a few of us, say, were being pursued and needed to hide in a man's hut, the man who feared us didn't waste valuable time asking foolish questions but instead and without hesitation covered us with straw. If we needed to water our horses, we were welcome at his well. He'd invite us to join his table. Later, if the authorities asked him whether he knew our faces or names, the man's memory would turn into a field gleaned bare of every stalk. He'd do an imitation of the wide-eyed owls in the forest. "Who?" he'd answer. "Who?"

Who knows how often the *gabbilloti* were less unfair or brutal because of our footsteps and shadows? Who can say how much misery and deprivation were prevented by our presence in the hills? Who knows how many regrets the overseers whispered to the darkness as they tried to sleep on their goose-feather pillows and heard us deep in the forest howling? Don't judge me before you walk in my shoes.

Besides, what's a starving boy to do? Especially after he sees that there's only so much food in the family's bowl? Should he take from his brothers and infant sisters? His dying mother?

I tell you, none of my mother's children loved her more than I did!

Does the boy not help them all by leaving them one less needy mouth? In the natural world there are animals who leave the den and go off by themselves hungry so that those who remain in the den may live.

You're listening to one of those animals.

Allow me to turn my snout to the moon and howl!

Damn the poverty! *Mannaggia la miseria!*

You know, when I first came to *La Merica* I thought, what a foreign place! It was so different from Sicily that I didn't know how I could possibly remain. For several months I felt lonely and strange until a friend of Tannu's took me to the theater. The friend was a pal of the doorman, who slipped us through the side door just as the magnificent chandeliers above the audience dimmed. There up on a huge white wall was the most Sicilian thing I'd seen in *La Merica*: a cowboy movie!

I couldn't get over it. A baby's sneeze could have knocked me down. The movie showed nearly every Sicilian thing! There were hills just like the ones back in Girgenti, a forest where the outlaws could hide, and in the valley below fields pocked with rocks— hardly good for farming. The village square was filled with poor people terrified of the crooked *gabbillotu* sheriff and his gang.

Then the bad sheriff and his men showed disrespect to the poor farmer's daughter, a young and rather pretty girl. No mother to raise her. Her sad father was humbled by a heavy collar of debt. The *gabbillotu* told the girl that he'd put her father in debtors' prison if she refused to marry him. The girl walked home, confusion tearing her in two, and threw herself onto her bed and wept.

Meanwhile, a pack of good outlaws, whose camp was hidden up in the hills, deep in the forest where the *gabbillotu* couldn't find them, met around their campfire one night to plot how they would fight for the girl's honor.

I sat in the darkened theater amazed. "I know this story," I whispered.

"Yes, of course," my friend said, patting my hand. "They call this an American western, and yet everything in it is Sicilian."

I admired the outlaws' clean shirts, their shaven faces, the wide, curled brims on their big hats. Back in Girgenti we had nothing like their fine hats. We had little time for washing our clothes or scraping the whiskers off our chins.

"But how come they don't speak Sicilian?" I whispered, pointing up at the dancing images on the screen.

"Because of the *Americani*," my friend said with a nod. He was no greenhorn, fresh off the boat, like me. He was a fox, able to make sense of even the most foreign of things. "See," he whispered, "if they spoke with their Sicilian tongues, how could these *Americani* all around us understand?"

In the end the outlaws discovered that for years the sheriff had been stealing the poor farmer's gold. In a hill at the edge of the poor man's field was an old gold mine thought to be empty. The *gabbillotu* had been secretly mining it for years. Exactly like Girgenti! I thought, though Girgenti's gold was her grain and sulphur. After the shrewd girl made the discovery, she informed the handsome outlaw leader.

Then the outlaws fought the *gabbillotu* and his men. The *banditi* shot every last one, very clean, and every time with the very first bullet! What excellent marksmen! And there was never even the slightest drop of blood!

Then the young woman married the outlaw leader, and everyone in her village came to her father's house for a big celebration and feast.

The full moon rose in a cloudless sky. An old man with a mandolin sang sweetly to his horse. Couples locked arms and danced to the music in the light of a blazing campfire just outside the farmer's front porch. The farmer even had a big pair of bull horns hanging over the door, like any smart Sicilian, protecting his house from *il mal'occhiu,* the evil eye.

I WON'T CONFESS ALL that I did during my days as a *banditu.* It wasn't at all like these cowboy movies. In the movies, a man strikes another's face and there are no screams or shattered bones. One or two punches and the fight is over. A man is shot, and there's no wound or hours of wailing in pain. He drops to the dust as clean and silent as a stone.

Life's a lot more messy.

We had two shotguns, but only one worked well enough to trust it. We had pitchforks, knives, clubs, our fists. Some would drive a nail or spike through a length of wood so that the point stuck out the other side. You hear sometimes that a man fights tooth and nail. I've often seen these weapons used.

A strong jaw can be a very potent weapon. A wolf bites down hard, then violently twists its head back and forth, ripping the flesh of its prey before letting go. We also fought in that manner.

There were times when I saw *gabbilloti* turn pale and drop to the ground in horror, bellowing as they searched the dust for a lobe of their ear or the tip of their nose or a chunk torn from their cheek, a missing finger, a jagged crescent of flesh no longer part of their neck or arm. Tearing a piece off a man's body and spitting the piece out on the ground gains the other's attention real fast. There's a force within the body that makes it want to keep all of its parts together.

YOU SHOULD UNDERSTAND what kind of place the world really is, as opposed to the fantasies taught in school, and especially what the robed cowards preach each Sunday in church. Of teachers and preachers I have no use. These priests, how can they possibly instruct others how to live when they devote most of their lives to avoiding living? Think about it. The vows they take—to poverty, chastity, and obedience—I'd ask only of a two-legged dog, an idiot, or a mule. You want to learn about life, ask a man or woman who's spent a few days alive! Talk not to the saint but to the sinner!

The outlaw is always wiser than the sheriff.

See, way back in the beginning of everything there wasn't much in existence other than Almighty God. Way back in the beginning there was only Possibility and Chaos bumping up against each other in a void of swirling darkness. This was so for a nearly endless stretch of time, until the Father separated the void with his hands, as you would a mound of bread. He created two loaves: the worlds of the seen and the unseen.

In the seen world, of course, there exists everything observable. Now, it only makes common sense that in order for a thing to be observed it must stand in light. So God created light. The seen world is the world of light.

You can try to make a life entirely in the world of light. You can close your eyes and hope to sleep through the long hours of darkness, with a bar across your door and a prayer on your lips, a cross and horns hanging around your neck, your hands folded, fingers furiously beating the beads. Like a solitary monk or a new-born goat, you can pass the night shivering and fearful. But as even the most naive priest learns from hearing confession, the earth's sweetest delights take place in darkness, in the unseen world, in the world of spirits and passion.

To be whole, a complete woman or man, one learns to move through both of these worlds. You teach your feet to walk the path in between light and darkness.

ALLOW ME TO explain how life as we know it began.

After the Father formed the worlds of darkness and light, he made the path of shadows that lies in between so that the creatures from both of his worlds would have ground on which to meet. Then he created the nine orders of angels as well as various other spirits to populate the unseen world. To fill the seen world he made man and woman—Adam and Eve—and all the animals of earth, water, and air, along with the plants and insects. He intended everything to exist in harmony. Each creature he made was a separate note of the melody only he in his eternal wisdom could sing.

Now, like any other old man, the Father wanted a little peace and quiet after having survived all those centuries of Possibility and Chaos bumping noisily together in the void inside his brain. He wanted to sit back in his most comfortable chair and listen to Verdi on the radio while his grandchildren played peacefully outside in the backyard. He'd leave the actual running of things to his two children, Jesus and Mary. But before the old man could even get around to making his kids, the spirits and the angels in the unseen world began to argue.

The strongest of the spirits, Satan, was the Almighty's own dark reflection. Satan challenged the others in the unseen world to a fight and defeated every specter and angel foolish enough to take him on. This made the Father so upset that he hurled Satan into the deepest pit in chaos, then poured the pit full of fire and burning rock and plugged it shut with a thousand and one tons of the earth's hardest stone, sealing the demon forever in a fiery grave. Of course this grave is known today as Hell.

To make the punishment even worse, the Father denied Satan and his followers the dignity and mercy of death. The disloyal spirits would have to endure the sweltering pit of fire with their senses eternally open, fully awake for the remainder of all of time. So Satan and his gang writhed in their grave of agony and endless torment.

One thing to keep in mind about demons: the personality of the best of them is such that they never quit. As the others around Satan screamed and wept in despair, he suggested that they shut up and try to keep a cool head. He organized his men, passing out shovels, picks, axes, clubs, pitchforks, and ordered everybody to work. The spirits labored for a thousand and one years with no success until one day Satan managed to make the tiniest of cracks in the rock above his head.

"Ahh!" all the devils said in admiration of the crack, so minuscule that it was thinner than the faintest shadow of the least hair on the leg of the smallest flea.

Still, a crack's a crack. An opening's an opening. The demons set to work on it, patiently chipping away, bit by bit, never quitting, splitting the rock a bit more, particle by particle, grain by grain, sliver by sliver, forcing the gap to yawn wider, then a bit wider, then even wider. Soon they were taking out stone piece by piece, then chunk by chunk. This is the way true evil operates. Evil mimics the manner of success. Each advances incrementally and never quits.

One gap in the rock led to the next, until the devils were able to slide their entire beings up inside the opening chasm, all the way up to the roots of the apple tree in the garden of Adam and Eve. By then the Father had formed Adam and Eve from a slab of dark clay.

Now, whenever demons slither across the path of shadows up and toward the world of light, they have to put on some kind of disguise. This is so they can take form and be seen. Remember, spirits come from the world of the unseen. Always keep this in mind. Evil always puts on a disguise, pretending to be something it's not. Another thing to remember is that after all those centuries in the smoldering lava pit, those devils grew used to, even fond of, that hot fire. After a while it's a great pain to them if the temperature isn't at least a thousand degrees. So demons like to keep their bellies down close to the ground, way down as close as they can get to their comforting, blistering inferno. That's why the devil is usually depicted as a snake or some lowly, slinking animal. Five times out of ten when you see a snake or a rat scurrying about on the ground it's really a demon.

As to how I came to know these things, I'll tell you a tale.

Once there was a poor but honest man, *un'omu di panza,* a man of belly, who through no real fault of his own gradually became a great sinner. He'd never intended to choose sin as his vocation, but one sin led him to the next. It was like offering a man a great platter of sweet grapes. First he eats one, then another. After a while he realizes that he's eaten so many he might as well consume them all. This the man tried, at least until he grew sick. He had second thoughts. So he decided he'd turn his talents and appetites toward being good.

He wanted a fresh start but feared that God wouldn't forgive his past, so he went to a priest to find out what God might do. The priest told the man that of course God would forgive any sin, no matter how great.

"Any sin?" asked the sinner.

"Any sin," assured the priest.

"In all amounts?" the sinner said, unconvinced.

"From the greatest," said the priest, "down to the least."

So the man began the recitation of his transgressions. As the minutes advanced into hours, the hours into days, the days into weeks, the priest was first amazed, then shocked, then repulsed, then angry, then finally so exasperated that he made the sign of the Cross, kissed his thumb, and clapped his hands over his ears shouting, "Not even the Father, Jesù, and Mari together could forgive this endless litany of horrors!"

The sinner smiled weakly and admitted that he'd hardly begun peeling the onion.

The robed pantywaist held a finger over the sinner's lips. "Utter not another word," the priest said. Before sending the unforgiven man away, the priest advised the man to prepare in the best way he could imagine for Hell's everlasting fires and God's stern judgment.

The sinner took the priest's words to heart. He found a job working as a cook. Soon he was put in charge of butchering and roasting the day's meat. The sinner made some of the finest roasts in the world, quite a few of which I myself have tasted.

The sinner stood beside his oven while he cooked the meat. After a while he forced himself to take the roasts from the oven with his bare hands. Then he stretched his entire arms into the hot oven. Soon he was crawling half-naked into the oven so as to watch the meat cook. After a while he started living entirely inside the hot furnace. He had his friends heap the fires with wood and coal to make the oven even hotter. See, he'd taken the priest's advice. He was preparing himself for God's judgment and the hot fires of Hell!

After the cook died, he woke up in a room of fiery and intense anguish where the miserable souls about to be damned await their final sentence. Around him other newly dead souls thrashed in horrible agony, writhing and screaming in unspeakable pain. The sinner took a chair in the corner, hardly breaking a sweat. When Satan entered the room and surveyed his charges, the sinner shouted, "Hey, you with the pitchfork, shut the door! The draft is freezing my ass!"

One can grow used to anything.

• • •

DON'T THINK I'M making Satan out to be some kind of hero. If he were to crawl near my boot I'd step on him in an instant. It's just that God the Father isn't as perfect and holy as a lot of people make him out to be.

God is like marzipan. A little goes a long way. You can eat only so much before your stomach starts to turn and you get sick.

The world's a complicated place.

Satan didn't stop working once his system of tunnels connected Hell to the surface of the seen world. Like a master architect, he then designed a pattern of passageways linking Hell to nearly every hectare of land known to man. He explored every fissure and crease on the planet, every cave and burrow, dimple and crater, grotto and pit. He has the power to dwell in and crawl up through them all!

Satan also learned how to slip up through the earth's eyes, up through her wells and springs, to the ponds, rivers, and lakes— to any body of water. That's why children are cautioned never to stand over a body of water staring down at their reflection. The image they see shimmering before them may not be their own. Really, they may be staring straight at the devil!

To ward him off you need a weapon, a sure sign of strength. Children are like slugs they are so helpless. So children are given to wear around their necks a claw or tooth, or more often the horns, or *cornicelli*. See? I wear mine on a chain around my neck. And in a pinch if for some reason you've taken off your *cornicelli* and you suspect that someone is giving you the evil eye or that a devil is about to leap into your body and take a grab at your soul, you can make horns of your first and little fingers, like this, see, to repel the evil.

That's it, make the horns with your first and little fingers. Point it at the ground, not at me, unless your intention is to insult.

The devil leaps up at you, hits the tip of one horn and then shoots down and around, bouncing right off and straight back into Hell! Some of the old people like me like to spit between the horns so as to spit right into Satan's ugly, pitted face as he makes his leap. The spit also acts as a lubricant, helping him to slide even faster back down to Hell where he belongs!

Listen to me good. In the same way that Satan discovered how to sneak out of Hell, he learned how to trick his way into our bodies. He can do it as easily as we slip an arm through a sleeve. Hey, he can do it more easily than that! This is no joke. Satan is constantly searching for cracks in us, too.

He can slide in through any crack or hole in the body. Most often he tries to enter us through our eyes. One image can do it. A man can lead a pure life and for thirty years never stray, and then he can look on a voluptuous woman and something about her spirit can inflame his, and all those years of virtue can be shot!

A woman can walk down a road knowing inside that she's happy, and in all ways she can be truly content and at peace with herself and her world, and then she can see something that she doesn't own, and the idea of possessing it can fill her mind with such desire that her attitude of bliss will be broken.

Every thief understands that the eye steals before the hand.

Satan can enter through our ears, by something we hear said. Isn't idle conversation the source of much of our jealousy and discontent? Satan can lead us toward evil through provocative odors, inviting us to chase the forbidden through the dim shadows with our snouts raised in the air like eager dogs.

The mouth is yet another passageway. Consider sins of appetite, several of which I myself am guilty!

I didn't get this stomach eating Communion.

Think of the poor souls cursed with a thirst for alcohol. Every time they empty another bottle of booze, what they really empty is themselves! Each drink snatches away another piece of their soul. Like spirits in the old stories trapped in pumpkins, each piece of soul ends up trapped in an emptied bottle. Think of all the empty whiskey and gin bottles filled with pieces of lost soul!

And now Satan has discovered a way to get into our blood, into our veins and arteries and the very center of our heart, with a needle full of dope!

What a woodpecker! That clever Satan never quits pecking away, inventing new tunnels and passageways! Now he uses even the hollowed nose of the doctor's needle to crack open the skin. What will he think of next?

In Sicily, daughters are made to wear a long dress and a scarf over their hair, and their fathers keep them close to home, preferably safely inside the walls of the house with their mammas, so that the young girls see and hear nothing, and so that nothing will see or hear and thereby come to covet them.

Even a woman's most private and sacred part is a passageway through which the most horrible evil can enter. The same is true of man's most private part.

Any fissure or crack, even in idea or resolve, can be a mode of passage. A confident man is able to roll a heavy rock up a hillside, while the man cracked by doubt is crushed by it.

SO PERHAPS NOW you can understand what happened to me that night when I heard them howling in the woods, when I smelled their campfire, saw their stolen lambs, gnawed their discarded bones, fingered their gold coins, drank their water. These things opened in my mind cracks through which the desire for riches beyond my imagination spread. From those hungers sprang several actions for which I am still repentant. But when I tried to repent, our village priest would have none of it.

When he interrupted my confession, telling me that my sins were too numerous for Almighty God to forgive and that I should prepare myself for an eternity of suffering, I slapped his face. I grabbed the fool by his collar, raised him from his soft chair, then shook him like a child shakes a doll made of rags. At that moment the priest seemed to stand between me and any chance I had of salvation. I wanted to crush his pious bones with my bare hands.

"Who are you to deny me God's forgiveness?" I shouted.

He turned his face from mine and mumbled something and smiled, as if he were grateful to me for my anger.

I raised my hand to slap him to the ground, but then I noticed that stuck in the gaps between his teeth were clumps of food from the table of the *gabbillotu,* and I smelled on his breath the landlord's wine, and I saw on the front of his soiled cassock flakes of the dainty pastries the *gabbilloti* were fond of eating after they had gorged themselves with meat, while the *cuntadini* starved on their soup made of tree bark and stones. I pushed my palm against the man's slack belly. I inspected the hypocrite's soft, perfumed hands.

"You're not a man of God!" I shouted. "If Jesù himself were here, he'd spit into your face!"

"As someday he'll spit into yours," muttered the priest.

Go on, you who sit with me this night, listening to my confession. Judge me. In this story, who is the worse sinner?

AFTER THIS CONFRONTATION, that night at the edge of the forest along the secret trail back to camp, I paused and shed my wolf skin. The skin fell from my shoulders in pieces, a ragged coat that no longer hung together or fit.

As I walked deeper into the woods I could hear the pack's happy cries. They were preparing for another raid, running in wide loops around the fire, snouts raised, howling, jaws eagerly snapping the air. The horses stood saddled, ready for the ride, pawing the ground.

I had no stomach left for being a *banditu.* Even the horses could sense it. They announced my approach with neighs of fear. I admitted to the others that I'd passed the evening talking to a village priest who must have put a spell on me and somehow turned me back into my dear mother's son. Indeed, as I looked down at my body I saw that it had transformed back into the shape of a peasant boy.

"He's been cursed," the wolves said after they inspected me.

"True, true," others agreed. "It must not have been a priest he spoke to." They asked me if I'd noticed the person's feet, if they were cloven.

I told them I couldn't see them beneath his black dress but that the man's hands were tender and perfumed.

"Perfumed hands!" they shouted. "And did you allow this witch to stare into your eyes? Did she stand so close that you inhaled the scent of her breath?"

I nodded. "I held the demon by the collar directly up to my face," I said. "The spirit's breath smelled like fine wine."

"He's lost to us now," they howled. "Lost, lost, lost! Oh, who will make our sardine and macaroni pie? Who will fry our peppers and onions and eggplant? Who will steam our couscous?"

"Someone else will have to learn," I said, "just as I learned."

"*Cùscusu!*" they howled at the moon. "*Cùs-cu-su!*"

GETTING BACK TO my parents' house and my bed of straw wasn't nearly as easy. In truth I somehow hoped that no one had noticed that I'd been gone. As I approached the village, I saw our hut standing as white as a shroud washed in the moonlight beside the other huts. I listened hard and made out old Gabriella's rhythmic snores. I think I would have been able to sneak back undetected if it hadn't been for those damn goats.

As I was slipping past the sleeping animals, the goats bleated and betrayed me. Their screams frightened Gabriella, who raised her long nose to the roof and sounded her harsh trumpet. Within a moment Mamma Adriana was upon me, slapping me first with her open palms, then beating me fiercely with a broom.

"Mamma," I shouted, "it's me, your second-born son, Luigi!" I thought that perhaps in the dim starlight she had failed to recognize me and took me for a stranger or a thief. But the mere mention of my given name only made her beat me all the more.

The beating lasted throughout the night and went on through the next day and night, until sunrise on the morning of the third day. By then she'd broken over my back the broom, the shovel, and the pitchfork. It was Sunday, Easter morning. The cock was crowing. The village air was full of the smell of baking bread.

Mamma Adriana beat all of my sins right out of me. She beat me so well that two of God's best archangels ringed by a host of cherubim came down from the clouds with a golden halo, never used, ready to make me a saint.

Me! San Luigi!

You don't believe me? Want to see the welts?

On your ears before your eyes I sing these words.

> *Listen to me and learn these lessons well*
> *So you don't burn for all eternity in Hell.*
>
> *Now the wolf hands the thread of his true tale*
> *To the lamb fated to wed the most despised male.*

Caesura

℘ *Rosa Dolci*

THESE SONGS AND stories, they go on all through the long night. We pass the role of speaker as we would a ladle of water, moving around the fire from one soul to the next, to whoever has the thirst to lend a tale or two voice. We circle the fire like the moon with her many faces making her steady passage around the earth. The waxing moon shimmers on the water inside the ladle. We tip the ladle slowly so that we swallow the moon along with the cool water. Meanwhile, the fire in our midst burns. There's no hurry to what we do. We have all the permission that night allows. An occasional pause or silence is not something to be feared. All are welcome to stay or go as they please.

Sometimes, like now, everyone pauses to gaze at the flames that blaze here in the center that holds us together. There is something about a fire that grabs the eye and stills the tongue. The fire cares nothing about us—certainly not that we observe it—and demands only that it be fed. Hunger requires no witness. The wood hisses like a snake caught in some great bird's talons and then chitters and snaps like a nest of shelled insects as it is consumed. Embers throb like the thickest veins on workers' necks. Sparks compete with one another, leaping into the night sky to see if for a moment they can outshine the stars. After blazing brilliantly for an instant, the sparks fall back down to the earth, ash.

Some *campagnoli* stand, stretch their arms and legs, and wander across the hills. The practical walk to the edge of the forest in search of more wood. Some wander among the nearby ruins and touch the ancient stones. At night the columns glow white, as if they hold some inner light. Some souls look for a soft spot on the ground between the stones where they might rest their weary bones for a while. Some bend and begin clearing a field of rocks. Some look for a place to make water. The young sometimes look for a spot unseen by the chaperones. Some souls chase their shadows up the hills in the moonlight. Some search for something forgotten or lost, here in this land that time forgot.

Some call out a name, over and over, like a lamb that has lost its mother or has just learned to bleat. Some gawk up at the sky, even though it's the dead of night, hoping to see a flying fish. Some pretend to come across the *gabbillotu* fallen from his horse, and beat and beat him with their fists. Some dance to a music no one else hears. Some breathe the air deeply, as if the smell of lemons were a food they cannot get enough of. Some sing the same tune over and over until you want to sing it, too. Some count the stars until they run out of numbers. Some look for the three old women in the forest. Some scour the ground for the hole that Giufà fell into. Some tramp into the forest and ask questions of the owls. Some look for Placidu's island. Some search for Ducella's cave.

My, how you've grown. My eyes hardly believe it.

Stay here, beside me, by this fire, for as long as it pleases you.

Lamb Soup

Ciccina Agneddina

EVER SINCE NONNA Nedda, the toothless, blind old grandma who could foretell your marital future after you prepared for her a bowl of soup, informed my dear mamma that I was destined by age eighteen to marry a man riding a dappled horse, I feared that I'd end up with the disgusting *gabbillotu*.

You had to stir the soup with your little finger after the broth was poured into a bowl. This was after you invited the old woman to your house. You had to sweep the floor and shoo out all your brothers and sisters as well as any animals. Even though she could see less well than a moss-covered rock, if you had a rack of candles Nonna Nedda expected them to be lit. She sat on your best chair, and for an hour you were supposed to engage her in gossip while the soup that was about to reveal your fate simmered over the fire. Mamma had me tend the pot. In it she'd put a whole onion and some herbs and three handfuls of beans. Nonna Nedda was said to prefer bean soup over broth made with only a bit of onion and greens. That's what we usually ate: soup made of boiled onion and greens.

The women chatted about one of the village's farmers, Don Ricci, who owned a piece of extremely good land and whose goats that past spring were said to have had seven babies.

"Seven goats!" Mamma announced brightly, as if she'd given birth to them herself.

"Humph," Nonna Nedda said, perched on our three-legged stool. The black dress she perpetually wore clung to her rolls of fat like a shadow. Stuffed in their black stockings, her legs hung down to the ground like a pair of dark sticks. "You've seen these goats with your own eyes?"

"No, Nonna," Mamma said, "but he's shown all seven to others I know in the village."

"His goats had ten or more," said Nonna Nedda. She rolled her head wildly, then sniffed the air like a hound. "At least three real strong ones, which he keeps out of sight."

"Ahh," my mamma said, nodding. "The hen's unseen eggs are never stolen."

"He throws the stone," Nonna Nedda said, "yet hides his hand." She fluttered her dead eyes. A finger stretched out across the room and pointed out at me. "The beans are nearly soft enough. Bring me your little lamb."

Agneddina, Little Lamb, was my nickname, an endearment my father bestowed on me when I was still on all fours. He gave each of my brothers and sisters nicknames of animals, too. In our family there was Little Monkey, Little Butterfly, Little Parrot, Little Owl Eyes, Little Weevil, Little Bat, Little Turkey, Little Red Fox, Little Gray Mouse. Sometimes when he called all of us into the house you'd think he was wise Noah loading the ark. If ever I tarried or came near to disobeying him he'd put on a serious face, point to my hair, and ask if I wished to be fleeced.

"Shall I pour Nonna the bowl of soup now, Mamma?" I called.

She didn't answer. Instead the fat old crow on the stool wagged her head no, then curled her gnarled fingers in the air. Her fingers were the tips of branches of trees that were too ancient and dry to bear any more leaves. Her arms were rotting tree trunks that wanted to leap out of the forest and fall on top of you. I stood before the old sausage, trying not to stare at the straggly dark

whiskers sprouting on her chin and the thick tufts of hair generously protruding from her ears as well as the gaping nostrils of
her immense nose.

She ran her claws up my arms, over my shoulders and across
my chest, down my back and rump, over my hips, then between
the middle of my legs, all the time saying, "My, my, my." Believe
me, I don't think the old woman had ever known a washtub.
Behind me Mamma smiled with approval as she spooned all the
beans she could gather into the woman's bowl.

"She's fine," announced Nonna Nedda, "though quite far from
perfect. She's too skinny, though she's getting nice and firm on
top here where you want a young girl to be round. But these
hips—" She stuck her tongue forward and smacked her gums.
"These hips should be a bit broader. Warn the midwife. She'll be
in for a hard time with the first baby." Again she clawed my arms.
"She's fourteen years, you say? She'll be plucked and gone from
your tree in four more. Already I can tell her plum's ripe and
sweet." The old thing's talons patted me between my legs, then
gave my cheek a fierce pinch.

"I was skinny at her age, too," my mamma said.

"She's skin and bones," Nonna Nedda sneered.

"She never goes without. We feed her all we can."

"And what do you do when all is not enough?" The old
woman paused. "Tell me, does she eat dirt at night?"

"Never," I said.

"A spoonful every now and then would help her bones." She
pointed around the room, then patted my shoulders. "Look for a
nice soft spot in the wall. You don't have to eat a lot. A mouthful
twice a week will be enough. With it, drink fresh water until you
feel your belly swell."

The thought of eating the walls of the house was so ridiculous
I put my hand to my mouth and laughed.

By this time Mamma had ladled out the bowl of soup. I stirred
it with my little finger before handing it to the old witch, praying
that she would say I was destined to marry someone gentle and

handsome, with kind eyes, like my papa, whose skin was as clear as the inside of an almond shell, and whose drooping moustache tickled whenever he kissed me, and who at night sometimes would comb out my long hair and not hurt me by pulling the comb's teeth too quickly down through the thousand and one snarls in my hair. As the old woman took the first sip of soup, I prayed that she'd predict that the man would be from a village nearby rather than from somewhere far away so that I could visit my family as often as I wanted and care for my parents when they were old or if ever one of them were to be alone.

Instead Nonna Nedda said she saw water, and lots of it, so much that it was gathered in great white-tipped waves that rolled and spilled wildly back and forth on top of themselves.

I immediately guessed she meant the African Sea, which my eyes had never actually seen but about which my ears had heard numerous tales. Monsters with eight long arms and a thousand and one mouths were said to live within the sea, along with creatures with wings so huge some men used them as sails. There were fish whose top fins were as sharp as saws, able to cut boats in half. Other fish had swords as snouts. Some fish had such big bellies and mouths they could swallow a whole house. I knew the story about Nick Fish, the famous boy from Messina whose mother's accidental curse transformed him into half fish, half human. Perhaps I'd wed a boy like him, I thought. Perhaps I'd marry a *piscaturi*.

At once Nonna Nedda shook her head no, as if in answer to my thoughts. She opened her eyelids and held the sides of my head, her sightless white eyeballs spinning up and down inside her skull.

"He rides a dappled horse," she said. "He's a man of belly, *un'omu di panza*. There is even more water."

"Blackest of days!" I cried. "A dappled horse!"

My poor mamma gasped, fell back several steps, then crossed herself.

I pictured the only dappled horse in the province, the overseer's dappled gelding. I fell to my knees, at once sobbing. "No!" I cried, "not the *gabbillotu!* No, no, not him! Oh, Nonna Nedda, please say it's anyone but him!"

"*Sali,*" was all she would reply.

All the blind crow would say further was to ask my anguished mother for a pinch of salt for the beans and onion that lay heaped in the bottom of her bowl like the mound of stones topping a grave.

E VEN THE WALLS one is told to eat have ears. Within the day, word of my cursed fortune spread. The fastest animal on one leg is the gossip's tongue.

With the exception of the old baron, the *gabbillotu* was the most evil man in the village. Like a piece of thickly varnished wood, the *gabbillotu* acquired his many layers of evil gradually, coat by coat by coat. It was said that as a boy he had a penchant for inventing torments for the Almighty's most helpless creatures. He captured the happy cricket and pulled off its notched legs. He set fire to the butterfly's wings. He netted the contented cod and chortled as it thrashed and drowned in the horrible air. He cracked the proud, noble shell of the land turtle's house. With a sharpened stick he poked holes in the eggs of songbirds, then filled the shells with ants. He fashioned a whip of thorned vines and tortured the passing mole, field mouse, and hedgehog. Whenever he came across someone younger or smaller, he threw dirt in the child's eyes, then beat the poor thing's face until the child cried.

To become a *gabbillotu* you have to convince the estate owner that you can be vicious enough with the peasants to squeeze them of every last measure of their labor. You have to turn your living heart from flesh to leather, then from leather into the most unfeeling stone. This path begins with mistreating God's most helpless creatures.

Years ago the baron noticed the boy's talents and asked if he ever considered becoming an overseer. The baron invited the boy to take the test each *gabbillotu* apprentice must pass. The boy was ordered to tend a garden of nettles and thorns, in the middle of which lay a gentle tomcat whom the baron commanded to assist the apprentice in whatever ways he could. Each day for a month the apprentice carefully watered the weeds and pulled up the roots of any stray wildflowers that happened to blow in on the edge of summer's hot winds. Then the master denied the apprentice all further use of his well. The weeds immediately began to wither in the sun and constant heat.

"Oh, what shall I do?" cried the apprentice.

From the center of the nettles the cat answered. "Have you any human feelings?"

"Yes," replied the apprentice, looking perhaps for the first time into his soul. "I have sorrow and sorrow's expression, tears." So the boy thought of the dying weeds and wept, and in this way was able to water the baron's garden. The apprentice's tears lasted for three days. But after he'd drained himself empty, the master's weeds again began to wilt.

"Oh, what shall I do?" cried the apprentice.

From the center of the nettles the cat answered. "Have you any human feelings?"

"Yes," replied the boy, looking again into his soul. "I have empathy and its metaphor and expression, blood." So the apprentice thought of the thirsty nettles and cut open his chest and bared his heart, and in this way was able to water the garden. Again this lasted for three days. But after he'd drained himself empty, the master's weeds again began to wilt.

"Oh, what shall I do?" cried the apprentice.

From the center of the nettles the cat answered. "Have you any human feelings?"

"No," replied the apprentice, looking into the now-dark void where once his soul resided. "I have no more sorrow or tears. I have no more empathy or blood. All is dry and withered within me. I am a desert of endless sand. I have no liquid left in me, nothing wet within my soul with which I might be able to water the master's weeds."

"If you have no human feelings, then perhaps you're no longer an apprentice. Perhaps you've become a *gabbillotu,*" said the cat, who lay in the center of the withering weeds proudly licking the shiny coats of his seven kittens.

The apprentice overheard the smallest kitten's gentle mewing. He stepped deliberately through the garden, careful that his boots not fall on any of his master's weeds, until he came to the center where the cat lay. One by one the apprentice took the kittens in his hands, twisting their necks until their little bones snapped, and then he crushed each of the seven limp bodies against the hard earth with his heels.

"Indeed, you have no human feelings," cried the cat, whose copious tears of sorrow watered the master's garden so well that all of the wicked weeds grew tall and immediately bore seed.

"Indeed," said the baron, seeing the seeds of his many foul weeds take wing and fill the air. "Indeed, you've passed the test and become a *gabbillotu.*"

So it was that Don Babbuinu, the *gabbillotu,* came to live in the absentee landlord's extravagant house, more of a mansion really, or now that I've seen one I should say more of a museum, a place where exotic objects from the mainland of Italia were set on display in cabinets made of the finest wood, all of it smothering beneath a thick coating of dust.

But I'm getting ahead of my story. Before my eyes were to view the many treasures the cabinets held, word of Nonna Nedda's prediction reached Don Babbuinu's ears.

"What?" he shouted, hands flying up and over his head.

Don Babbuinu thought the woman's prophecy absurd. The very idea of marrying a poor girl from the village was so ludicrous that even on the far edge of the forest the deaf gatherer of moss and mushrooms could hear the overseer's roaring laughter.

Now, Don Babbuinu was exceptionally vain. It was said that he shaved twice daily and perfumed his thick and matted hair with oils from France, which the old baron sent special from Roma. Don Babbuinu wore white silk shirts with a useless splash of frill at the neck and tight black britches, which he tucked into his boots. He could often be seen scratching himself then holding between his fingernails whatever guilty party—usually a tick or flea—he'd discovered. He carried a whip which he used on the peasants all too frequently. He dwelled in the mansion with the sad old tomcat everyone called Don Gattu out of respect for his advanced age.

Since Don Gattu had belonged to the baron, the old cat had no other alternative but to be Don Babbuinu's companion in the house. Don Gattu wept so copiously over witnessing his seven children killed that his tears cut ridges through the gray fur on his cheeks, which perpetually dripped with sorrow wherever he would go. If he stayed in one place for more than a few moments, Don Gattu soon stood in a puddle of tears. One could always find him by following his brackish trail, in which starfish stretched their arms and frogs and toads laid twisting strings of eggs and a flock of ravens could usually be found bathing.

It is said that the mourning dove acquired its melancholy coat and mournful call by drinking too frequently from Don Gattu's river.

The old cat was tantalized by the idea of a peasant girl whose destiny dared to take her to live in the *baruni*'s house. "Perhaps we should invite the young girl of the prophecy here," Don Gattu said to Don Babbuinu that evening during dinner. "Have you no curiosity? How could you not want to meet her?"

"If I wanted another fly at my table, all I need do is open the door," replied Don Babbuinu, leaning back in his chair and scratching his hairy belly.

"You don't know that the girl's a fly," said the cat. "She might be fair."

"And roses might grow out of your ass!" Don Babbuinu guffawed. "I could invite my horse in here, too, and he could give the little gnat and her whole family a fresh, steamy pile to feast on!"

Don Gattu patiently dripped his sorrow onto the floor. A pair of tadpoles leapt over his tail. "But you can't just sit by idly. You must do something about this prediction. It certainly would be prudent if you at least were to break bread with the girl's father."

"It certainly would be prudent of me if I were to break my thickest strap across her father's lazy, useless back!"

Don Gattu started a new puddle. "You don't know that he's lazy."

"All peasants are lazy," Don Babbuinu said. "It's only logical. That's why they're peasants."

"Your logic's circular," replied Don Gattu.

"Circular?" Don Babbuinu roared. "So's my ass! So what? If my ass was square or triangle, it wouldn't stink any less. If peasants weren't lazy, they wouldn't be peasants! They'd be landowners. Some might even be rich."

"You know that's not true," said Don Gattu. "No amount of work alone can possibly lift their lives out of *miseria*."

"Leave what's true or false to the judges and lawyers," Don Babbuinu said. "All that matters to me is the way a thing is, which as far as my philosophy stretches is the way it's destined to be, for now and for ever and always, until the end of the illusion we call time."

"The way a thing is, you say?" countered the cat. "Well, the thing of this prophecy is that you end up marrying a peasant girl."

"My wise old Ziu Culu has two words for that," replied Don Babbuinu. He lifted one haunch. *"Brrrp! Brrrp!"*

Don Gattu stepped back quickly, one paw waving the air in front of his nose. He stopped in the room's far corner, where he began another puddle. "But everyone knows that the blind woman has never been wrong."

"Brrrp!" Don Babbuinu farted. *"Brrrp! Brrrrrp-ppa-paa!"* Sitting back in his soft chair he strummed his fingers on his full belly and sighed a contented, "Ahh."

"Has the tuba completed its after-dinner recital?" said Don Gattu after the air had cleared.

"Only if you first amuse me with the recitation of rhyme."

"Had I both wit and time," Don Gattu said and bowed, "my words might be more sublime. Tell me, Babbuinu, what will you do if this fortune proves true?"

"Rue the day I heard of the shrew's words." The overseer scratched his armpit, then behind his ear and knee.

"Her reputation," replied Don Gattu, "is regarded highly through the nation."

Don Babbuinu held up to a candle a fat flea. "As mine would be sure to decline, were I to wed swine."

"Or perhaps pearl. The girl's face, if washed, might display charm and grace. Sir, I see no gain by remaining still. What harm lies in greeting the girl? Or consider this. Switch, and meet the witch?"

Don Babbuinu's nails sliced the struggling bug in two. "Perhaps, perhaps. I know not what to do!"

"Glue your doubts to actions! Doesn't this prediction make you curious?"

"Enough!" shouted Don Babbuinu. Furious, he dropped both fractions of the flea into the flame. "God's name, I'll put a gag on this matter!" He gestured for the bold cat to come near. "Call the old hag here! Then all this chatter about my future will be clear!"

So the cat led old Nonna Nedda up the hill to the baron's mansion, where Don Babbuinu prepared his pot of soup. In another room Don Gattu and a newly hired stableboy boiled second and third pots of soup, at Don Babbuinu's instruction, stirring them every now and then with the tips of their little fingers, or, in Don Gattu's case, with the least of his claws.

Bowing nearly to the floor, Don Babbuinu offered Nonna Nedda his finest chair, then pulled at his nose and said, "Let's dispense with the chitchat and proceed straight to the hocus-pocus." He poured out a bowl of soup from the pot he had made, stirring the stock ceremoniously with his little finger.

"This is for you, dear Nonna Nedda," Don Babbuinu said, offering her the bowl.

At that moment there was a loud crash from the next room. "Nobody move!" Don Babbuinu shouted. He whirled and rushed after the noise, carrying his bowl.

A few moments later he returned to the room. "Forgive me, Nonna Nedda, it was nothing, just the wind." In his hands he now carried a bowl of the stableboy's soup.

After Nonna Nedda took the first sip, she smiled and said, "Now here's an untamed, spicy broth! I could drink this soup all day!" Her thick tongue lapped her lips. "This soup tastes of the hills and the forest and its wildest rivers! I sense that like a river the maker of this soup knows when to meander through the meadows and go slow, when to be furious and fast, when to dip, when to bend, when to curve, when to fall, when to rush and be foamy and surging and reckless!"

"Bravu!" cried Don Gattu from the doorway, his tears forming a pair of sudden waterfalls from the twin ruts on his cheeks down to the floor.

Don Babbuinu yanked the bowl from the old woman's hands and threw it against the far wall. "Very well, you old charlatan, you've passed the first test. That soup was made by one of the stableboys."

"Any mare under his care must be most content," the old woman said.

"Now for the second bowl," Don Babbuinu growled.

"Please," said Nonna Nedda, twisting her gnarled arms into a knot, then pointing to her mouth, "bring me a little something to clear the palate."

"What would you like?" cried Don Gattu.

"Only a teeny tiny something."

"Only a teeny tiny something," minced Don Babbuinu.

"Sure," Nonna Nedda said, "whatever you've got."

Well, in the master's mansion when a guest asks for her palate to be cleared it stays clear for a long time. Nonna Nedda ate a plate of roasted chickpeas, a bowl of olives, some peppers, cheese, eggplant, zucchini, a platter of ziti, several boiled eggs, a couple of loaves of bread, a leg of lamb, *braciola*, a bowl of couscous, *calamari*, eel, anchovies, tuna, more ziti, and an entire sardine and macaroni pie, all washed down by glass after glass of red wine and prepared in Don Babbuinu's kitchen by the new stableboy.

The *gabbillotu* again poured the old woman a bowl of soup from the pot he had prepared, stirring the steamy liquid with his little finger. "This is for you, dear Nonna Nedda," Don Babbuinu again said, offering her the bowl.

And again at that moment the sound of a loud crash. "Nobody move!" Don Babbuinu again shouted, whirling and rushing out of the room, carrying his bowl.

When he returned he said, "Forgive me a second time, Nonna Nedda. It was nothing, just the wind." In his hands he carried a bowl of the soup made by Don Gattu.

As Nonna Nedda sipped this bowl, she began to cry. With the next sip she moaned and wept so openly that the room's marble floor soon was covered by her tears, and all of Don Gattu's water creatures had a much bigger pond in which to splash. The sky outside darkened and the air grew strangely cold, and from the distance everyone in the village and out in the fields heard the tolling of church bells even though there were no churches with bells for leagues, and all the *genti di campagna* fell to their knees as if they'd just been informed that someone they dearly cherished had died, and everyone wept and moaned and began reciting the doleful verses of the *rèpitu*. Then the disconsolate sky opened its eyes, and it stormed for seven days and nights in sorrow and pain and the keenest misery.

Don Gattu knelt at Nonna Nedda's feet. "Mother," he cried, placing a paw on her knee, "forgive me for sharing my life's sadness with you."

Nonna Nedda took the cat up into her arms. "Oh, puss puss puss," she said, "how I wish I could lift even an ounce of your heavy pain."

"Take me to live with you," Don Gattu whispered into her ear. "Oh, please, I beg you, I've been waiting for someone like you to rescue me for what seems like a thousand years! Look at him closely! He's not a man! He's a baboon! Demand me as payment for telling him these fortunes."

And so it was that Nonna Nedda came to be the companion of the old gray tomcat, who continued to weep wherever he went until the dawn of the day that his ninth life expired, when his heart filled with the hope that he would again be united with his seven children. And it's said that this pair—Don Gattu and Nonna Nedda—joined the parade of others making their way up the road to Palermu and the New World, and that their tears, combined with the tears of all those leaving and all those left behind, created new rivers and streams that tumbled sorrowfully and swelled the banks of the Tyrrhenian Sea.

After the week of rain stopped and Nonna Nedda again had cleared her palate, this time ordering the new stableboy in the kitchen to fill thirty wheelbarrows with food for the people in the nearby village, and after she'd been granted custody of Don Gattu and momentarily dried the ridges in his cheeks with the hem of her black skirt, she agreed to taste the bitter brew in Don Babbuinu's bowl.

"This is for you, you greedy shrew," hooted Don Babbuinu as he handed her the bowl of soup he himself had spent his life making and in which floated remnants of each of his life's foul deeds.

The old woman lifted the bowl to her lips and took a sip. At once she gave out a terrified shriek and fell to all fours, braying in unimaginable pain and agony. Her long head wagged in exaggerated fashion. She squealed pitiably, mimicking perfectly a donkey trying to kick someone standing behind it, someone doing it a disservice forbidden by both nature and God, the obvious cause of the miserable beast's distress.

After several moments Nonna Nedda's body went still. Then her eyelids fluttered like a pair of beating wings, and her white eyes twitched in rolling spasms of apprehension and terror. Her mouth gaped wide as she vomited out onto the floor a snake and seven scorpions, which scuttled at the baboon's feet and then climbed up the legs of his black britches and beneath his white blouse to the flesh covering what would have been his heart, if he had one.

The snake formed a circle around Don Babbuinu, holding its tail in its mouth and rolling sideways up and down like a fallen ring, preventing the overseer from wringing the necks of the old blind woman and the gray tomcat, who fled out the door into the nearby hills and forest, never to be seen by the people of our village again.

WELL, YOU REMEMBER what I said about walls having ears. From that day on, whenever Don Babbuinu turned his back the peasants brayed like a donkey and made loud kissing sounds.

With so much laughter in the fields during the day, nights in the village became particularly noisy and active. Soon the belly of every woman in the village inflated like a bouquet of balloons. Perhaps Don Babbuinu's humiliation piqued the virility of even the village's most timid. Perhaps it was some scent or seed floating through the night air, a spell Nonna Nedda placed on us before she left.

No matter. But then two events took place.

To replace Don Gattu, the old baron in Roma sent three wild dogs who arrived the next day on sleek Arabians. And then, to regain some small shred of dignity and to disprove Nonna Nedda's prediction that his marital future involved the rape of a donkey, Don Babbuinu began to woo me.

Now, in our village back then this otherwise romantic matter was undertaken by the mothers of the boy and girl. After all, only the fool thinks he knows more than his mother. There is no sense more sound than a woman's. So, in accordance with the rules of this ancient arrangement, a certain ritual would be played out. One of the mothers, usually the boy's, would approach the other, and after the introduction of her child and the proper passage of time, the daughter would be introduced and the match discussed. But, to displace the possibility of rejection, the boy's mother would lay a disguise over the topic of her conversation. Instead of directly discussing the attributes of her son and risking the other mother's rejection of him, the woman requesting the match would ask the other mother if she preferred, say, a comb with sixteen teeth, or was she content using a comb with teeth amounting to nine.

It's the numbers used by the women that are the key to this play. In the Sicilian dialect sixteen is *sìdici,* nine is *nòve,* with the first syllables stressed in these instances to stand for *sì* or *nò,* yes or no.

"Yes, I'm most happy to say I'd very much like a comb with *sì-dici* teeth," the girl's mother might answer, "and I'd be most pleased if you would look at my comb tomorrow afternoon," meaning that the second mother finds the son agreeable and is willing to introduce her daughter to the pair the following day.

Or, "No, I'm so very sorry to say I prefer *nò-ve* teeth on a comb," the mother could answer, meaning that she isn't agreeable to the match.

This drama allows both the women and their children to save face and uphold their honor within the community. Or at least it was how this thing had always been done, which back then was reason enough to do anything.

Now, WITH NO mother to speak for him, Don Babbuinu risked revealing himself even more publicly as a buffoon. Sure enough, early one evening my family heard the sound of approaching hooves outside our hut, then a reckless shout.

"Mother of Agneddina," Don Babbuinu yelled from the saddle

of his dappled horse, "hear me! Hear me, mother of the Little Lamb! The master has sent me several barrels of fine wine, which I wish to share with you and your family. Tell me, do you prefer a barrel made of sixteen wooden slats, or a barrel made of only nine?"

The twelve of us were sitting near the fire, sipping our evening soup of onions and greens. After hearing the overseer's voice, Mamma made a horn of her fingers, spat between them, and pointed the horn at the door. Then all my brothers and sisters, even the one at my mamma's breast, did likewise. The rude overseer got the horns from the Little Parrot, the Little Monkey, the Little Butterfly, Little Owl Eyes, Little Bat, Little Weevil, Little Turkey, Little Gray Mouse, and Little Red Fox. I shot him the horns too as my papa stood, hesitating as if in thought, then put a finger to his lips and leapt out the back window.

"Mother of Agneddina," Don Babbuinu shouted, "speak to me! Is it sixteen or nine?"

We remained as silent as a forgotten aunt.

"Answer me or I'll knock down your door!" the voice again roared. "*Sìdici o nòve?* Sixteen or nine?"

Then we heard Papa's voice, disguising itself as a woman's.

"Kindest sir," Papa called out, falsetto, "I'm right here with my daughter, gentle sir."

We snuck a peek out the door. Papa had borrowed and donned a woman's cap and long apron, and led a neighbor's donkey by its harness. "Permit me to introduce her, gentle sir," he called. "Yes, I like a barrel made of sixteen slats. Sixteen, do you hear me, kind sir?"

The overseer's face contorted with fury as chuckles burst from a nearby hut. Within moments the laughter spread from one hut to the next. The villagers gazed out a window or doorway, giggling, hiding their glee with a hand over their mouths. Soon everyone stood in front of their huts, roaring and pointing alternately at the *gabbillotu* and my papa dressed in women's clothes.

"There's an agreement," shouted one of the villagers from his door. "You heard the fair woman's reply!"

"If that woman be fair," shouted another, "Don Babbuinu's destiny is certainly foul!"

"*Sìdici*, Don Babbuinu! *Sì sì, sìdici!*"

"Hee-haw! Hee-haw!"

"They'll call their firstborn son *lu sceccu-omu!*"

"No, *l'omu-sceccu*, since his father is the bigger ass!"

"Such a long nose on that bride!"

"Every nose has a face to match!"

"Oh, he'll soon have her smiling!"

"Hee-haw! Hee-haw!"

"*Sì, sì, sìdici!*"

From the north a second man appeared dressed in a woman's cap and apron, leading a donkey by its harness, and singing in a high voice, "Don Babbuinu, what about *my* fair daughter?" Then from the south a third man appeared in the same disguise, calling out the same. From the east and west appeared two others, likewise dressed.

"What about *my* daughter?"

"No, kind sir, *my* daughter!"

"*Sìdici*, Don Babbuinu! *Sì, sì!*"

"Choose *my* daughter! Mine!"

"Hee-haw! Hee-haw!"

"The truth is in the soup!"

"The proverbs of the ancients never lie!"

Don Babbuinu slammed his heels into his horse's dappled sides, then jerked the reins sideways and rode away. The villagers stayed where they were, in their doorways, still silly with laughter. I think we wanted the moment never to end.

Night was falling fast. One of the men grabbed his wife's cap and put it on his head, and someone else shouted, "*Sì, sì, sìdici!*" and that made us all laugh all over again. It was good to hear the women and men laugh. Soon one of the peasants was throwing down wood for a fire, and another joined him, and I smiled, knowing it would be one of those nights when all the people sat around a fire together making rhymes and telling stories.

I squeezed Mamma's hand, all at once frightened. Now I knew that the overseer really did want to marry me. And now that we'd ridiculed him, I thought, he'd want me three times more. The thing denied always grows in beauty. Even worse, I feared that it truly was my destiny to be his wife.

I pictured his horse, remembering how roughly he'd kicked its sides. I could still see the animal's wild eye rolling upwards in its skull as the man's rough hands pulled mercilessly on the reins. I didn't want to become something saddled and reined. Something in my soul feared that I wasn't really a girl at all but was instead actually a donkey, as foretold by Nonna Nedda's prediction.

I pushed my head against my mother's belly and filled my nose with her smell. I tried to bury my face inside her. I wanted to crawl back up inside her and suck my thumb and curl up deep in her belly and feel safe again.

I pushed against her so forcefully that I must have caused her pain. Her hands shoved me away and I fell back, tripping over my feet, into the dust. I think that was the first moment the cord between us felt truly cut, when I first felt separate from her, curiously apart, suddenly aware of the air surrounding my isolated and individual body. Looking back I think she already could sense what was going to happen to my father. Though his actions that night spared me from the promise of marriage, his joke strayed beyond humor into insult.

Nearly all the men now were wearing their wives' caps. Mamma's hands pushed me and the other children into the circle around the fire. Already a voice was beginning to give form to the story of my bold papa and Nonna Nedda's prediction and Don Babbuinu.

The fire in our midst surged brightly against the darkness. I sat next to my papa, holding his hand. I wanted the night to last forever. I knew we would not be alone for as long as it was night and the fire remained lit.

•   •   •

THE SOLDIERS ARRIVED on the third morning.

They pushed my father down to the ground, kicking him as he fell, then pulled him back up and punched his face and chest. Then they bound his hands with rope. I wondered why they pushed him down only to pull him back up again. Was it just because they could, as a display of their power? Still, they didn't dare look into our eyes. Mamma hurled curses at them and threatened them with a pitchfork but put it down after they pointed their rifles first at her and then at the heads of my brothers. The soldiers had my papa march between them as they took him away. He kept shouting out his love for us until his voice faded into the wind.

My brothers took up his work in the fields. Two mornings later Mamma found a gold coin inside her apron pocket. The day after that, a fat young chicken scratched the dust outside our door. Every day from then on there was something for us.

Then we heard word that the night that Don Babbuinu came to ask for my hand the old baron's estate had been robbed of all its livestock and gold. According to the rumors, the mansion had been looted of its finery and burned to the ground. It was said that my father had organized the raid. We heard that there were witnesses who had sworn that he was absent from the village that evening. The four others who'd dressed as women and come from east and west and north and south to mock Don Babbuinu were named as my father's accomplices. Knowing the authorities were searching for them, the four fled to the hills. We were told that after the court pronounced my papa guilty, he'd be hanged by the neck until dead.

There was little laughter in the fields during these days.

I lost hunger, then all desire, until I realized that the knife could cut both ways. There was only one path before me, only one road my fate could take. So the next afternoon while my mother worked with the other women and tended to my brothers and sisters, I made ready to leave.

Before departing I gave blessing to the hut's walls—may these good walls remain strong and never again hear the footsteps of soldiers—and to the floor—may this good earth remain clean and never again be asked to drink the tears of my family's sorrow and grief—and to the thatched ceiling—may this good roof keep out the wind and rain and never again look down on my family's hunger or need. I blessed the hearth and pot and pitchfork and the three-legged stool. I gave blessing to our bowls. I ordered any spirits or little demons lurking in the corners of the hut to jump into the fire and take their mischief up with the smoke. I put my finger to my lips and told the house to be quiet and not tell my mamma or brothers or sisters my plan.

Then I set out on the road toward the remains of the baron's mansion, where I would agree to marry Don Babbuinu in exchange for my papa's life.

CONTRARY TO RUMOR, the great house had not been burned. Indeed, it hardly looked touched, although I noticed immediately that the livestock pens stood silent and empty. The estate as well was oddly quiet. There were no chirping insects in the grass. Not even the smallest sparrow sang from the least tree.

At the front door I was met by a dog who introduced himself as Don Cani. He pushed past me and growled in the direction of the village and snapped his teeth for several minutes, then invited me inside, licking his chops.

"Follow me," he said, his nails clicking on the marble floor as he scampered in circles and then, as if he could not contain himself any longer, raced wildly from one room to the next.

The walls of each room were lined with cabinets and wooden shelves stacked with riches and frills. I took my time walking about. There was one room filled completely with magnificent bowls and platters on which were painted various scenes of dance and costume, hunting and horses and dogs so lavish that my mind could barely believe or contain them all. One showed a wolf and a wild dog embracing in a fight to the death. I walked past rows of delicate teacups and saucers and gold-rimmed goblets. The next room displayed shelf after shelf of exquisitely fashioned glass. A third room was devoted to embroideries and velvets. I ran my fingertips across a swath of black velvet whose nap was so deep that my shoulders tingled with delight. When I put my cheek against the cloth I thought I'd faint. In the next room were a thousand and one porcelain dolls dressed as lushly as any king or queen. I swear each painted face held living eyes that could see me. I crossed myself and ran from that room to the next, in which more lions and tigers than I could count stood waiting for me, silent and still, threatening to devour me. Around them the walls were decorated with the heads of all the lower beasts they'd already feasted upon.

"My two brothers will very much enjoy meeting you," Don Cani said as I ran from that room.

I stopped in a marble hallway near the front door. "I'm here to speak to Don Babbuinu," I replied.

"The baboon's gone," snarled a second dog, stepping out from behind the drapery, in all appearance the twin of Don Cani.

Then their triplet emerged behind me. "We haven't the slightest idea when he'll return," the third dog announced, "but we'll be most happy to entertain you while he's gone."

"Extremely happy to entertain you," said the first Don Cani, pacing closer to me.

"Happier than you can imagine," said the second.

"Oh, how I drool just to think about it," said the third, panting so heavily that his breath was like a hot oven against my hand.

They circled me, sniffing my legs, then began pushing their snouts up beneath the hem of my skirt. I slapped their noses away and made the sign of the Cross in the air above their heads, saying, "In the name of Mary, Mother of God, and the all the holy saints, I banish thee to Hell!" Still, the three demons persisted, revolving in an ever-tightening circle around my legs, backing me up against one or the other until I tripped over one of their backs and toppled to the floor.

I kicked and slapped them and tried to claw their eyes. "Hail Mary," I shouted, "blessed are you, among all women born! Keep me chaste and pure, untouched and untorn!"

At that moment I heard a howl so loud and long it made the moon spin. The dogs froze, all wide eyes and twitching ears. No one breathed. Then something sudden and loud and mighty kicked open the mansion's front door. It slammed solidly against the wall, then creaked eerily back on its hinges. There was the distinct smell of lemons on the cool evening breeze.

Into the room stepped a powerful wolf.

The three dogs dropped their heads, ears flattened, and stepped slowly back and away from me. No one moved. Then one by one they bared their teeth and leapt at the wolf, who pulled out from beneath his cloak a twin stick of fire and made it explode once and then twice, stopping in midair the first two dogs who'd charged him. The room grew hazy with smoke. The dogs' bodies flew backward, slamming against the walls where they bled to what I hope were painful deaths.

Don Cani, the first dog, remained, timing his leap for the moment that the wolf dropped his magic stick. The dog and wolf struggled, leg to leg, paw to paw, until the strength of their forces balanced the other so evenly that their motions hardened into the peculiar *tableau vivant* painted on the master's bowls and platters.

Then Don Cani yelped and fell back, his front paws holding his throat. His throat was gashed wide open and red. Don Cani's paws worked against it, furiously moving up and down, back and forth, as if trying to push back together the separate flaps of his skin. His blood surged from between his paws in bright, hardy spurts, then in weaker and ever more feeble arcs in the air.

The wolf put the handle of the bloody knife in the paw of one of the first two dogs, then said to me, "Don't be afraid." He took the shotgun and cradled it in the front legs of Don Cani, whose bloody, still figure no longer resembled anything painted on the master's platter. The wolf grasped my hand and helped me to stand, modestly looking away from my eyes.

"Did they injure you?" he asked me in a soft voice.

I shook my head no. My heart thumped so furiously that I wanted to laugh or scream. He held my hands in his.

"Look at your feet, not at their bodies," he told me as we walked out the door into the cool evening, careful not to step into any of the blood.

The black sky had swallowed the stars and nearly all of the moon. I thought of the velvet that I'd held up to my cheek. It was much too dark to see.

"There's a storm approaching," he said. He led me to his horse, which was tied to a post outside the mansion. Then he washed his paws and muzzle and all the blood from the fur on his chest and legs in the trough from which the horses drank. He moved easily, without hurry, as if we had all the world's time, as if there was nothing to be afraid of.

Around us, as if suddenly awakened, the countless insects of the fields released their cries.

THE SAINTS MUST have been with us, the wolf said as we rode together on the horse back to my village. The shotgun was old, he told me, and old shotguns were known sometimes to explode in the hands of those who fire them. The dog's knife, he said, hovered between their throats for so long that he nearly felt his strength give out. Then a strange thing happened, he told me. In his mind he saw the knife's keen blade slice the dog's throat open, and then the knife leapt from his hand as if it had a will of its own and did precisely as his mind had imagined.

He spoke in long, lively, delirious sentences. At times his voice grew so jittery and shrill that it broke and he had to pause and howl at the moon. At other times he had to stop and gulp down breaths of air as if he couldn't breathe. Then he'd start to shake all over. I sat behind him on the saddle, holding tightly onto his coat. All the while I could feel his body trembling.

"It's hard to believe what I did," he said after a while. "I'm really only a cook and stableboy, and not really much of either, to tell you the truth. A few months ago I was sent to the mansion to spy. Really, we'd planned only on taking the *baruni*'s livestock once it had fattened." He began to wheeze.

"You don't have to talk," I said, stroking his back. I'd never before stroked a wolf's back. It wasn't unpleasant. Once I began to talk I couldn't stop. "May the Mother of God bless you. May Jesù Cristu bless you. May all the saints bless you. Blessings on your mother and father and family."

He wheezed more loudly, then nodded his snout in thanks.

"My family owes you my life," I said. "Those dogs certainly would have killed me."

"They would have done far worse," he said. "Forgive me for saying so but it was foolish of you to go there."

"I wanted to save my father," I said.

The horse pulled up. Now we were just outside my village. "Don't worry about your father," he said. "He'll be just fine."

"But the *gabbillotu*—"

"Don't worry about the *gabbillotu*. Others"—he gestured a paw toward the hills—"have more than taken care of his needs."

"But my father—" I began.

"Listen to me," he said as he helped me down from the horse. "I give you my word. They won't hang your father."

"I pray you're right," I said.

"You have my solemn promise," he said, swinging himself down from the saddle, "in exchange for one thing. Your name."

After I told him Agneddina, he laughed and said it was a name more fit for a child. We stood alongside his horse. It was starting to storm. I could see his features begin to fade from a wolf's back into a man's, as if he'd once been one. I wanted to ask him why I was no longer a child. I wanted to touch his cheek, even to kiss it. As his eyes held mine, then took my measure, he asked my true age and what name had been uttered when I was baptized.

"Remember me, Ciccina," he said just before he changed back to a wolf and rode off on the dappled horse toward the hills and forest.

THE FOLLOWING DAY a few of the villagers scavenging for greens at the edge of the forest found the body of Don Babbuinu. What drew them to it, they said, was the spiral of vultures winging the air. The villagers' versions of what they saw expand in detail from one telling to the next, but on three facts all witnesses agree. The *gabbillotu*'s corpse was lying belly-down on a rock, his throat slit from ear to ear. Both of his hands had been chopped off. Around his head had been placed a donkey's harness.

Later that day we heard word that inside the baron's mansion Don Cani had shot and killed his two friends, one of whom apparently attacked him with a knife. In the bloody struggle Don Cani had died, too.

It took a few more days for the remainder of the story to take shape. Soon everyone believed that Don Cani and his two friends had stolen the baron's gold and livestock, then fought over how the bounty would be divided, murdering one another in the process. The proof was that a bag of the baron's missing gold was found hidden in Don Cani's belongings, and nearly all the stolen livestock was found in the forest not too far away in makeshift pens. An inked map to these pens was discovered in Don Cani's pocket.

Of course I told no one what I knew.

A month later the baron's first son journeyed to our village from Roma and declared Don Babbuinu a great hero. The baron's son had us gather one noon out in the hot sun to listen to him recite a speech, though his northern dialect was so strange and weak we could hardly comprehend a word of what he said.

What the men around that night's fire pieced together was that

Babbuinu had uncovered Cani's plot and as a result been murdered by Cani and his vicious partners, who in their greed over the baron's riches then turned on one another.

The baron's son also announced that as a result of the tragic incident he was hereby increasing his share of the year's harvest as a tithe toward the construction of a statue which would be erected in Babbuinu's honor. The new *gabbillotu* translated this portion of the speech in a dialect so clear and masculine that we each understood that we had no alternative but to suffer yet another new tax.

Three days later, as the wolf had promised, my dear father was set free.

OVER TIME I came to believe the villagers' story. I accepted the possibility that in my distress over my father's imprisonment I must have dreamed up the story of the wolf who knocked down the mansion door and rescued me. But since we all knew and despised Don Babbuinu, how could a tale about his murder be told in anything less than heroic light?

With each retelling, Don Cani's actions grew more honorable in the storyteller's eyes. Soon the stories told around the fire suggested that the wicked Babbuinu was in conspiracy with the two traitorous dogs, who'd plotted against and tried to deceive Cani, their trusting, noble friend, who would have befriended the peasants and taken their side, as the gentle Don Gattu had, if only given the chance.

And just as the baron's son promised, a statue of Don Babbuinu was erected on the mansion's grounds.

Again all the peasants of our village had to stand in the noon sun and endure an incomprehensible speech before the peacock from Roma pulled a rope that lifted a huge veil and revealed to all eyes the statue.

The statue's legs stood apart, one arm thrust toward the sky, the other crooked out at the elbow and back to the waist, which was girlishly thin and nothing at all like Babbuinu's ample girth. The statue wore shoes instead of boots, and a pair of fine pantaloons rather than a *gabbillotu*'s rough britches. We circled the statue looking for Babbuinu's long whip, which he was never in his life seen without, and which even the midwives claimed he was born holding, and which he used on his mother whenever she was slow in pulling down her blouse or when her breasts did not supply him with milk in his desired temperature and quantity, but on the statue there was no whip. As for the face, it resembled no one we had ever seen.

Indeed, the likeness was so crude and our hatred of Don Babbuinu so severe that among ourselves we referred to it only as the statue, then a year or so later as Don Cani's statue. After all, we observed, hadn't Don Cani's waist been nearly as thin as a girl's? Didn't he wear pantaloons from Roma? Weren't those buckled shoes on both of his hind paws?

By the following spring it was not uncommon to hear mothers tell their sons to be as true when they grew up as the martyred Don Cani. Indeed some went so far as to pray to the statue, leaving it offerings of flowers and herbs, candles and trinkets and lockets of their sick children's hair, believing in their hearts that the Almighty had turned the noble, martyred dog into a holy saint.

I WAS NEARLY EIGHTEEN years and on the verge of accepting these beliefs when early one evening as we sipped our modest soup of onions and wild greens I heard the sound of approaching hooves, then a shout.

"Mother of Ciccina," a voice yelled, "kindly hear me!"

My heart stopped still in my chest.

"Being both friend and stranger to your family," the voice continued, "and lacking a mother nearby to give voice to my deepest hopes, please allow me to propose a question."

By now Mamma stood at the doorway. "It's Babbuinu's dappled horse!" she cried. Immediately she made a horn of her fingers, spat, and pointed the horn out the door.

"Mother of Ciccina," the voice shouted as the speaker dismounted and took a step toward our door, "if a boy from a nearby village, the second son of a man named Santuzzu from the province they call Girgenti, came calling with his sweet mother Adriana, and you learned that he'd worked as a stableboy and sometimes as a cook, and now he was on his way with his sister Carla across the wide sea to the Promised Land they call *La Merica,* and if Adriana told you that years ago her son had also made soup for Nonna Nedda and stirred it with the little finger of his hand, and that he'd been of secret aid to your family that same season while in disguise, and these were secrets that could not easily be given voice to but were true in God the Father's sight and in Jesù Cristu's most holy Name, and true as well before the gentle eyes of Mari, his holy mother, as well as all of the saints and spirits who walk unseen across this land, then what would you say if she asked if you preferred a pie whose crust was knit with sixteen strips of dough or a pie topped only by nine?"

Before I could stop him Papa grabbed my mother's cap, put a finger to his lips, then slipped out the back window.

"Mother of Ciccina," said the voice a third time, "kindly answer me and at the wedding feast I'll steam just for you a big pot of couscous, and I'll roast for your whole family one of Don Ricci's finest lambs!"

"*Sìdici!*" I cried. I couldn't wait a moment longer for my dumb mother to speak. She stood as still and as silent as the statue on the mansion grounds. I dared not wait for my father in disguise to interfere.

"*Sìdici!*" I shouted again as loudly as I could. I was eighteen and sure that I could make my own match. In the doorway I now stood taller than my own mother, whom I was easily able to step past.

"*Sì!*" I cried, walking toward the dappled horse to meet the man who'd come to call on me. "*Sì, sì, sìdici!*"

Thus Nonna Nedda's bold prophecy came true.
I wed Luigi of Girgenti, second son of Santuzzu.

Salvatore, third brother, now solicits your ear.
His is a sad story that will make your eye tear.

In the City of the Greased Palm

ℰ Salvatore Girgenti

O<small>NCE THERE WAS</small> a poor but honest man, *un'omu di segretu,* a man of secrecy, who stayed behind in the desolate country of his ancestors' birth, caring for his aging mother and father. He remained behind, a faithful servant of his parents' needs, at a time when two out of every five *cristiani* bundled all they could carry on their backs and headed north. He did this far longer than either of his carefree brothers, who were like dandelion seeds flying in the wind first this way and then that way, only to settle down and sink their long claws into the earth where they would turn against and revile their younger brother, the one who'd stayed behind.

But I'm letting the donkey get ahead of the cart. I should start where the road north begins, back when the family was intact.

Even as a boy, this man of secrets had immense respect for, if not an outright fear of, omens. He knew of several men in the village who drew numbers in the dirt to ward off evil. Some carved designs over their doorways or on the handles of their hoes. He knew that some shapes combined into a truly powerful omen known as the *alfabetu.* Strung together in some impossible order, the bizarre symbols of the *alfabetu* could become so powerful that they could make people disappear and even negate the supreme authority of *destinu.*

This sorcery most often appeared inked on paper, though at times the magic's various symbols could be seen in the wrinkles of clouds in the sky or in the creases of dried ridges on the hills beyond the village or even in the branches of trees. Of course the boy was unable to make the slightest sense of these signs. He knew only that they were around him, lurking everywhere. His inability to decipher these charms made them seem even more mighty.

Every notable occurrence in the boy's life was preceded by some group of these symbols. How someone's will could be compressed into signs on scraps of paper was a great mystery to him. The boy believed that if God the Father were not an ancient man sitting in the golden chair of judgment on the highest cloud in Paradise above, as the priests in their buckled shoes vigorously asserted he was, God would be a thick bundle of papers covered top to bottom with an infinite number of dark and indecipherable scratches, lines, curlicues, wrinkles, whorls, spirals, arcs, loops, and every other twisting deviation of shape and form.

The boy's first encounter with this sorcery occurred on the day before his oldest brother disappeared. The boy was playing with an Italian army cap discovered years before on the head of the family's donkey, Gabriella. Indeed, the cap was a most frightful omen, for it suggested that someone eventually would be taken from them. The boy knew that no sooner would an Italian cap appear in the village than one son or many sons would disappear. As a result the boy's mother, Adriana, took the cap from the foolish donkey and tossed it away. But since the family was poor and never threw anything away, she only hid the cap deep beneath the straw where they slept.

One morning the boy's idle fingers uncovered the cap. Since he was alone and had nothing to play with, he put it on his head and marched about pretending to be part of the Italian army. The boy pretended to find sons who were hiding inside wells, atop roofs, under stacks of hay, behind secret doors, until something inside the cap scraped the top of his ear.

Expecting to find a burr, the boy turned the cap inside out

only to discover stuck in the lining the torn stub of some sort of ticket cursed with a dark swirl of letters and numbers. The boy's heart raced. He realized that the symbols foretold something great about to happen in their lives. Since calamity visited their village more often than good fortune, the boy feared that by bringing the stub out into the light of day he'd awakened some horrible portent of misfortune.

Then, just like in a bad dream when time grows as heavy as sand and slows to such an extent that the dreamer sees the grain of each passing moment and knows in his bones each horrible thing about to occur a full moment before it takes place, the boy's mother walked into the hut and saw the cap on his head and screamed, and the next morning the boy's oldest brother kissed Mamma and Papa good-bye, then marched away to the north like one of the stolen sons, never to set foot in the village again.

THE BOY'S SECOND encounter with omens took place years later, on the day a letter alleged to signify the absent brother took sudden form in the village. Now, while some here might have you believe that the document dropped from the mouth of a flying fish, I'll attest that in simple truth the letter arrived inside a black leather pouch strapped to the back of powerful winged donkey.

My brother Luigi and I stood in the village scribe's shack after being summoned from the fields. The scribe withdrew a slip of paper from the satchel, then wrapped his face with the magical glass spectacles that would enable his eyes to still the manuscript's dizzy marks.

By the way that Luigi growled at the leather bag I could tell that the paper made him uneasy. "Are you sure this is really intended for me?" he asked.

The man who could read and write looked down his long nose and nodded.

"But how can you be certain?" Luigi snapped.

The penman pointed at the message's peculiarly slanted symbols. "Look here," he said with a smile, "I'll show you your name. Here. See? This says *Luigi Second Son of Santuzzu of Girgenti.* See?" The scribe's finger ran across several dark curlicues on the paper. "Your brother Gaetanu paid a notary in New York in *La Merica* to write this. See? *Luigi.* That's your name."

My brother stepped back as if struck, then let out a deep and profound breath. For several moments he pawed the top of his head, as if he were trying to rub the sense of the man's words into his brain.

I leaned over Luigi's shoulder, squinting my eyes, turning my head first to one side, then the other. The scribbling was narrow and slanted and looked nothing at all like the rounder form of my brother.

"Of course that's my name," Luigi said after a while. He cleared his throat and stretched himself taller. I knew he had no idea what the writing meant but didn't want to reveal this to the penman. "Now," Luigi continued, "would you be so kind as to reveal what is inside."

"Whoa!" I said. I had a thousand and one questions. "Not so fast! Tell me, how did this piece of paper come into being, here of all places in the world?"

The scribe leaned out the doorway, withdrew his *cosa,* and relieved himself, punctuating his efforts with occasional muttering and a string of high-pitched sighs. He wiped his hands on his shirtfront and pointed toward a rather unimpressive donkey tethered in the shade outside the shack.

Luigi snorted. "You must think we're fools. Don't tell me you'd have us believe that dilapidated beast swam all the way here from the opposite end of the world?"

I laughed heartily. "Brother, he must take us for two rubes."

The writer's eyes grew wide. "Rubes?" he cried, tossing both hands into the air in exaggerated concern. "A pair of refined and intelligent men like you?" He rubbed his spectacles between a fold in his shirttail, then held the magic glasses up to the light. "Ahh, I can tell that the two of you are a couple of foxes! But of course my donkey didn't swim across the ocean! With the aid of his mighty yet invisible wings, he galloped here across the top of the waves!"

THAT LETTER LED to Luigi and Carla's departure. Several years after my brother and sister turned into a pair of black dots disappearing on the northern horizon, the penman's donkey clattered again across the waves. This time the learned fellow interpreted the scrapes and claw marks in the message to indicate that it was my turn to escape the *miseria*. Moreover, I was directed to lead my father and three remaining sisters across the ocean to New York of the New World. By then inked messages from those gone before were not so rare.

By then it was common for sons and sometimes entire families to begin walking the trail north. And by then I'd married sweet Rosa Dolci. We were flesh to each other's flesh, the stressed and unstressed syllables of love's most ardent heartbeat. In my mind there was no question whatsoever that Rosa would not come with us, too. So I gathered her and my three sisters and told them to prepare to depart, then went to talk with Papa Santuzzu about precisely when we all should leave.

"Leave as you like," Papa said with a nod. "Choose whatever day most suits you."

"Most suits me?" I said. "What do you mean? Of course you're coming, too."

"Absolutely not," he said, stomping a foot so hard on the ground that a flock of birds startled and took dark wing from a nearby tree. By now Papa's eyes had puddled over with ricotta. Gabriella's coat was snow white, too.

"But you must come with us," I said. "It says so on the paper that flew across the sea. The penman told me. It's written here. See?" I held the document up to his eyes. "You have no choice in the matter."

"That drunkard doesn't speak for me."

"He wasn't speaking for you," I said. "He was only reading and interpreting the inked signs."

"Here's a sign he can interpret," Papa said. He grabbed his forearm and thrust his fist in the air.

I laughed. "You'll need that spice for the long trip ahead of us."

"Clean the wax from your ears," Papa said. "I'm going to stay right where I am. This is where I live and where someday I'll die." He shot a hand forward and pinched my cheek so hard I screamed. "Don't be a fool. Obey your father or I'll give you the back of my hand."

"I am being obedient," I said. "This letter says you're going with us to New York."

He pulled the letter from my hands. "Here, let's see what this noisy scrap of onion peel has to say after I feed it to Gabriella."

I screamed and grabbed the sheet before he could do harm to it. "But paper foretells whatever is to come!" I told him about the army cap and the ticket stub that made Gaetanu go away, and how the letter borne by the penman's donkey had caused Luigi and Carla to disappear, how similar letters all across the province were doing exactly the same. I told him that like many others I fervently believed that the right combination of characters and numbers written over a doorway could have indelible effects on a person's or family's destiny.

"Fine, fine," he said as I explained my beliefs. For a while we walked in the sun, then sat in a patch of shade. "Yes, yes," he said. "Sure, sure. Of course. I agree. Fine. Yes. All that may well be true."

"So you'll come with us?" I said after I finished my speech.

His face softened. He placed one of my hands on the letter, the other on his chest and replied, "Tell me *figghiu miu,* what you feel. Which has the beating heart?"

I sighed a long sigh. "Of course you do, Papa."

"Then why heed what you can't hear?"

"Because of *destinu*," I said, growing frustrated. "*E u destinu*. Are you so stubborn you can't see?" I unfolded the paper and pointed at its scribbles. "See? It's written here, or perhaps here or here, or maybe here, and whatever is written in such powerful black ink cannot be denied!"

"I can deny it," he said.

"But Papa," I shouted, "consider what will happen. Once we leave, you'll be here all alone."

He laughed. "Alone? Me? What's gotten into you? Where's your sense? I'm never alone. Adriana!" He pointed to a space on the ground a few paces behind me. "Look, your poor mother's standing right here. Adriana, give this *babbu* Giufà a crack on the head for forgetting you!"

Old habits being hard to break, even though I could see nothing I still ducked. I swear I felt something brush the top of my hair. After the coast seemed clear I said, "But Papa, you *must* come with us. It's God's will."

"God's will," he said, "God's will." With one hand he made as if he were shooing away flies. "Do you really think God has the time to care about a measly little mouse like me? Do you understand what I mean? I think sometimes that God is so old and feeble that his eyes close and he falls asleep, and then as is true with any sleeping cat, the mice are free to get into any trouble that they want."

"Perhaps," I said, "but even his closed eyes see."

"No," he said, "when God is asleep he sees nothing." He gritted the few teeth he had left in his head and pounded his fist on his palm. "Of this I am completely certain. God lost his sight years and years and years ago! How else could he be so blind to our *miseria*? No decent father would allow his children to suffer as we do here." Papa nodded for several moments. "God is asleep! Do you understand? For all God knows, my firstborn son grows tall and ripe right beside me. And where's Tannu now? Eh?"

"Be calm," I said, "before you blaspheme."

"Don't talk like a priest. The *miseria* in this cursed land is the greater blasphemy."

I tossed up my hands. "Who can judge?"

"I can!" my father shouted. His finger thumped his chest. "I can judge! After all, who sent Tannu away from this place? Tell me, you who dares to argue with me about *destinu*! What had God willed for *my* children?" He took a deep breath. "I'll tell you his plan!" Triangles of foam formed in the corners of his mouth. His quick tongue licked them away. "God's plan was that my children would work every day of their miserable lives for the unfeeling *baruni,* fall into bed every night hungry, then die a hopeless and disconsolate death knowing that their children will have no better! Do you see why I say he's asleep? God's either asleep or he's one cruel bastard! If he can hear me now, let him strike me down dead! He's one cruel son of a bitch for what he's done to us! Or else he has an empty head!" He stared sightless up at the sky. "Empty head! Do you hear me up there? Strike me dead!" He looked back at me. "Tell me, what had he willed for Tannu, Luigi, and Carla had they remained here?"

"Papa," I said, "calm down. Be calm." I feared that his blasphemy truly would cause the earth to open up and swallow us.

"Is your head empty, too?" Papa screamed. "Answer me. What had God willed for my children?"

I resigned my argument to his. "The same of the same," I responded.

"Only if they were lucky," he told me. "It's more likely that had they stayed here they'd get even less."

"The crops have been bad this year," I said, "but maybe next year—"

"You agree with me, so shut your mouth." He gripped my shoulders and shook me hard, then with the flat of his palm slapped my chest. "Can't you comprehend what I did? *I sent away my children!* All of them! All of them!" He thumped his chest seven times. "First one, then two more, now the four that remain! I sent them away! I did! All seven! God sent away only one!"

"Papa," I said.

"Seven against one," he said. "I guess we both know which is more." His hands grabbed the letter and crumpled it.

"No," I said, "don't do that." I pulled the paper from him and immediately began smoothing its many creases.

"Even if that letter was marked by the hand of God himself," Papa shouted, "and even if it bore the picture of Jesù's face and three drops of his sacred blood, there are some things here on earth, here on the ground that we walk, in this air that we breathe, in the lives that we live, that are more sacred!"

He gummed the air for several moments, reached out and cuffed my cheek, then knocked his knuckles so hard against the side of my head that I fell right down and saw stars. "*Babbu,* you should be old enough now to understand."

"PLEASE COME WITH us, Papa," I said again the next day, then the next, for the next thousand days.

Papa put his arm around my shoulders and shook his head no. "Keep in mind," he told me during our arguments on one of those days, "that God began the beginning of time as the old man he still is. The Almighty Father never had the chance to be a little boy. He didn't have a mother and father to love, to respect, to honor. He never took a wife. He never laid a loved one in the ground and covered her face with stones. When his own son died he couldn't even grieve three full days before he brought him back to life. So how could God possibly begin to understand the bond that ties me to my Adriana, as well as those that bind me to my dear mother, to my father, my brothers and sisters, my *cumpari,* to all the dead whose bodies lie in rest here, whose spirits still walk this most cursed and beautiful of all lands?"

• • •

"I want to show you something," Papa Santuzzu said to me early on the morning that we intended to leave. "Follow me, *figghiu miu.*"

Together we walked from our hut to the fields. Old Gabriella trailed us, head down, out of habit.

"Papa, would it do any good if I asked you again to reconsider?" I said. "If I insisted once again that you come with us?"

He said nothing, walking ahead of me as sure-footed as any goat, leading me up a slight rise toward the base of a hill, which we ascended, and which I knew overlooked the far western portion of the estate owner's fields. I didn't know why he was taking me to this place. I knew there was nothing here to see. As the third-born son and the last to get to do anything, I was eager to start out on the road north. I feared that by the time I got to the New World, there would be nothing new left.

Once we neared the top of the hill, Papa Santuzzu told me to cover my eyes and walk the rest of the way like him, blind.

"Why, Papa?" I felt I had no time for games. "I already know what's up here."

"You may think you know, *babbu,* but you don't."

So I did as I was told, climbing as slowly and carefully as old Gabriella. "What's up here, Papa?" I asked again after we'd reached the top of the peak.

He put his hands on my shoulders and pointed me away from the rising sun. "Open your eyes," he said. "Regard my garden."

I blinked madly in the bright morning light and saw only the same wild, untended fields that my eyes had beheld a thousand times before. The fields were cruelly studded with unmovable boulders and the broken and shattered remnants of various ruins— the eroded columns of ancient temples, the fallen sections of what were probably once immense statues—now all useless slabs of miserable rock, making it impossible to plow furrows in anything resembling a straight line. Here and there areas of field were sprinkled over with piles of crushed rock. The hard clay soil lay baking in the heat, in spots stripped bare by winter's rain and summer's wind, save for patches of bramble and the dark trunks and twisted branches of an occasional gnarled tree.

"You don't see them?" Papa Santuzzu said. "There!" He pointed. "There! And there!"

"Who, Papa?" I said.

He laughed at me, disbelieving. "Rub the sleep from your eyes! Look at that pair dancing there in the field! They're celebrating the morning sun. Can't you hear the pipes?"

I looked but saw only rock and weed. I listened but heard only the wind.

Papa stood beside me, milk-white eyes open, a smile cracking his face, both arms out and raised, dancing a twisted little dance. Gabriella stood a pace behind him, patiently suffering the first of the day's thousand and one flies.

"From up here," Papa said, "you can see them all best, particularly when they wake up and dance. Look at that group over there, prancing in a circle with joined hands!" He grinned and gave the air a little leap. His right hand kept time as he swayed back and forth. "What joy! How they greet each new morning!" He turned to me. "They like me to dance with them down in the field, but most mornings I prefer to watch them from over here."

"Who, Papa?" I said.

His hand waved my words away. "In the field you can feel them better. I'll go down there later, after you and Rosa, the twins, and Assunta have gone. You have to go slow because some still frighten easily. They've not been there long. Others, the ones who've been dead the longest, are more bold."

"Papa," I said, "you should stay out of the sun."

"The boldest ones trust me enough now to talk to me. We sit in the shade of the ruins. Sometimes they feed me. And it's like I'm a young man, and Adriana is young, too, and there beside me, and all of the fallen rocks are standing straight up, back where they once stood, and the roofs of the temples glisten so brilliantly in the sun you have to hold up the flat of your hand over your eyes. You know with your whole being that this is a sacred land where the gods walk."

"Those gods are dead," I said. "The *baruni* and *gabbilloti* rule this land now."

"You disappoint me," Papa said. "I expected you, more than any of the others, to be able to understand this. The third son is supposed to be the special one. He should be wiser, more sensitive."

"I am wiser," I said. "That's why I continue to ask you to come with us on our journey to the New World. Papa, truly there's nothing here but ruins and death."

"Just yesterday I was reminding your mother that was why we gave you the name Salvatore, so that you'd be our rescuer, the family's savior."

I sighed and looked past the ruins to the blue line of the horizon shimmering beyond my long shadow in the rising heat. The line beckoned to me, inviting me to explore it while at the same time threatening to swallow me in its dark abyss if I made even the slightest mistake. What in the world should I do? My desire to leave the cursed land was stronger than even the orange ball of sun blazing on the horizon behind me. What could I do or say to convince my father to come with us?

"Look," Papa said, pointing again down into the valley. "Can you make out the orchards and flower gardens? They're all there, all of them, even the ones who have left. Dunce of a son, look where I'm pointing before I knock you in the head! See, way over there Tannu and Carla lie sleeping in the shade of that tree in our garden, and now Luigi sits up beside them, awake, reaching up for a fat fig."

"What will you do," I asked, "if I really do leave you behind?"

Papa turned to me, the sharp beak of his nose filling his lungs with air, the ends of his moustache drooping down nearly to his chin, a fierce smile beaming from his face. "Why, pass all my time with them in the valley below. Why else do you think I brought you here? I wanted to show you that I won't be alone, that I'll be well taken care of, here with all the old ones and your mother and Carla and your brothers, and soon here with your sisters and Rosa and you."

I looked back down into the valley. "If Tannu and Carla and Luigi are here and you can see them, does that mean that now they're dead?"

"No one dies. Not here in this valley, in our garden."

"But in *La Merica*," I said, "are they alive? If I and the others go there, will we find them all still alive?"

"I think that's a question you'll have to answer yourself," he said. "What do I know of *La Merica* except that as of tomorrow I will have sent all seven of my children there? May each of them beget seven more, and may each seven beget again seven, until the earth is full."

"You truly want to remain here," I said.

He smiled and took my hands in his. "Yes, *figghiu miu,* just as strongly as you desire to leave."

"WHAT DO YOU MEAN, you didn't bring Papa?" my two brothers yelled once we arrived in the tumultuous chaos of New York, after we'd made our way to the Mulberry District where Gaetanu and Teresa Pantaluna, Luigi and Ciccina Agneddina, Carla and Gerlando Cavadduzzo as well as Teresa's first dozen or so kids shared a tiny flat on the top floor. Within a moment everyone was shouting at once.

"He didn't bring Papa? Go on, he's dunking his bread!"

"*Mischinu!* He's joking! Open the door wider. I bet Papa's just behind him, standing outside on the landing."

"Papa's probably down the hall trying to figure out how to work the toilet."

"Or else he's in line waiting to use it!"

"I can't believe it! Salvatore says he didn't bring Papa."

"No, Papa probably got turned around and walked into the wrong building. I do it myself all the time. These buildings, they all look alike."

"Papa must still be down on the street."

"Sure, Papa's climbing the stairs."

"He says he didn't bring Papa."

"You're delirious. Of course Salvatore brought Papa. By now the man must be feeble and most likely blind and lame."

"Perhaps, but with a strong heart."

"He must be as helpless as a newborn."

"Salvatore says he didn't bring Papa."

"No one with any compassion could leave an old man like that alone."

"How could he possibly not bring Papa? We sent him coins for five."

"Papa's probably down on the next street corner, listening to the organ grinder."

"Of course, Papa's playing with the monkey!"

"Coins for five, that's right. There's Salvatore—"

"Papa's probably standing alongside the street listening to the many wagons, hoping someone will offer him a ride."

"Maybe he stepped off the curbstone and stopped to clean the horse droppings from his shoes."

"—Assunta—"

"The streets are so filthy, sometimes I can't believe it!"

"No, I bet someone on the street has given Papa a big chunk of ice. Papa can't get over it, how at the same time it both freezes and burns!"

"—Rosaria—"

"It's a miracle! One minute it's like rock, the next minute water."

"—Livicedda—"

"Papa's probably admiring all the fine horses, praying that one of their owners will bet him one in a game of tresette!"

"That's all we need up here!"

"With no room as it is, who would notice?"

"—and Rosa Dolci. He brought her instead! Oh Jesù and Mari, no!"

"That's right, Salvatore didn't bring Papa. What am I, talking to the walls?"

"Lord, have mercy on us."

"You didn't bring Papa. You must have a heart made of stone."

"With no one to care for him."

"Lord, have mercy."

"No one to feed him!"

"No one to kiss him!"

"No one to wash him!"

"No one to close his eyes the day he dies!"

"Dear merciful Lord!"

"No one to bury him!"

"No one to grieve for him!"

"Oh, motherless son!"

"A deed like this could be done only by the one with the tail!"

"Bring the bucket of water. She's passed out!"

"All so he could bring his new wife in Papa's place."

"Slap her wrists hard. It gets the blood moving again."

"Oh, you've made us all orphans!"

"That's right, splash some in her face."

"All alone for the rest of time! Unthinkable! For this you're sure to burn!"

"Don't drown her. She's sputtering like a whale."

"Oh, darkest of days!"

"How could you possibly leave Papa all alone?"

"Most ungrateful of sons!"

"Demon!"

"Ingrate!"

"Unbelievable!"

As LONG AS you have ears and I have breath, I'll cut their litany of insults short and continue my tale. No one here has yet mentioned one of the more indelicate indignities we suffered while living under the *baruni*'s rule, that of the estate owner's presumed right of the first night. As the wedding festivities come to their end, and the food has been eaten and the jars of wine emptied and all the celebrants are making their way back to their huts, the groom is expected to leave his bride at the *baruni*'s mansion, where she'll be made to pass the next few hours or the whole night.

The wounds left by this violence are normally wrapped in silence and vociferous denial. As for the stained bedsheets proudly displayed the next day by the bride's and groom's relations, they're mainly a show. Know that the couple likely took advantage of the blood of one of the hens scratching the dirt floor of their hut.

So when the rock from my sling landed beside Rosa, as I'd hoped it would from the days when we were children together, I dreaded surmounting the difficulty of the estate owner's right of the first night. Like my father and grandfather, and perhaps each of the men in my line who came before them, after deciding to marry I headed for the forest in search of someone whose powers could help me.

I knew that in the forest I might find the *banditi,* whose brute strength could persuade the *baruni* to be absent from the village on my marriage night. I also knew that in the forest I might meet the *mavaza,* whose potions and spells could transform the baron into any one of the lower animals, or paralyze his arms and legs, or put him into a sleep that would last days or even months. Walking in the forest the month before I was to wed Rosa, I felt safe and content, as if both my true parents were waiting to meet me. Deep in the woods waiting was the masked strength of Papa Banditu. Deep in the woods waiting was the cunning of Mamma Mavaza. I'd leave the rest to *destinu,* inked in the *alfabetu*'s twisting variations scrawled on the countless pages that make up God's empty head.

ONCE THERE WAS a poor but honest man, *un'omu d'amuri,* a man of love, who journeyed to the forest in search of one of the two powers who might help him keep his beloved safe from the *baruni*'s evil. To aid these powers in finding him, as he walked through the forest he sang a song:

> *"Third son of Santuzzu and fair Adriana,*
> *I search the forest for someone strong.*
> *Be you bold* banditu *or sly* mavaza
> *Help me fashion right from wrong."*

I walked for a day, two, three, singing my song to everyone and everything I met in the forest. I sang my song to the crow, the fox, and the rabbit. I sang to the mouse and the wolf, the dove and the ox, the turkey and the lizard and the fly. I sang to the old toad who sat croaking in the marsh. I sang to the whiskered fish who swam in the river. I sang to the bee and the boar and the ghost of the great forest's bygone lion, who roared and roared with terrible sorrow at me. "Oh, woe!" the lion roared, "it is so lonely to be no more!" I sang to the widowed spider, who spun the words of my song into her web.

I sang until a bright-eyed, short-faced dog with a smooth coat and curly tail appeared on the path before me. Since the dog wore a black mask over his muzzle, I immediately guessed he was a *banditu*. I raised my open hands to eye level and said, "Please don't attack. I'll give you all I have, whatever you want."

"If that's your manner of giving," the dog replied, "you'll find no acceptance from me, since I also wander the forest in need."

I lowered my hands and opened my pack. "Then you're welcome to share all I have," I said. In my pack were a few hard crusts of bread. We stopped and gnawed on the crusts for a while, though the bread was so old it was nearly hard as bone.

As we ate we exchanged stories. The dog told me that he roamed the forest in search of his mistress, whom he lost track of one day while she was gathering herbs. "I came to one spot," the dog said, "where the odors hovering over the trail were so overwhelming that they turned into colors. The colors were so luminous and varied that I had little choice but to follow them to their ends. I chased the dazzling ribbons of smell until I felt like rolling over and over on the ground, and then I chased them some more! But by then it was dark, and the odors grew faint, and now my mistress is nowhere to be found."

I told him that my love for Rosa sometimes made me feel like rolling over and over on the ground. He asked me why I had never surrendered to the temptation. So we rolled on the ground until we were dizzy. While he chased things I couldn't see, I described how I left my hoe standing in the fields and ran off to the forest because the image of the baron touching Rosa so infuriated me I feared I'd go insane.

"Roll in the dirt some more," he said, "and the pain will go away."

I told him I didn't want to roll in the dirt anymore.

"Snap your teeth in the air, like this," he said, snapping his teeth as he ran about in tight circles. He explained that the air was full of mischievous spirits that greatly relished being snapped at.

I told him I didn't want to snap my teeth. I didn't want to chase my tail. I didn't want to roll about or dig holes and sleep for hours in a patch of sun. All I wanted was to sink my fingertips into the master's soft neck until his lungs ceased pumping and his face turned as dark as a plum.

I sang my song to a thick cloud of mosquitoes, who sipped me as if I were a garden of flowers. I sang my song to the stars and the darkness that softly spanned the sky. As the night grew colder and the new day began to break, I sang my song to the falling dew.

That morning while the dog was sleeping, I found a bush full of berries beside a tree whose limbs were heavy with nuts. Rather than devour the abundance myself I took off my shirt and gathered all I was able to reach, then shared the sweet harvest with the masked dog.

Again at noon he took a nap, and in my wanderings I came across a rabbit roasting on a spit. I turned the spit once and called out to all who might hear me that the rabbit appeared ready to eat. I turned the spit a second time and called out that the rabbit was beginning to burn. I turned the spit a third time and called out that before the rabbit turned black as a cinder I'd take it, out of respect for its soul, and share its flesh with the dog.

That evening while the dog again slept I found a pot of *babbaluci* boiling over a fire. The water had been generously spiced with fennel and garlic. "You don't want to cook these snails too long," I shouted to whoever might hear me, adding a few greens to the pot, which I then stirred three times. By the time I carried it to where the masked dog was sleeping, the broth was cool enough to sip, which we did after we sucked each morsel of sweet snail meat out of each dark shell.

On the third day the dog led me to the *mavaza*'s house. She sat at her table in her black dress, thin as a gnarled olive branch, mashing something in her mortar. I sang her my song, then dropped to my knees.

She gestured at me with her pestle. "Three times you were tested and three times you were generous with my bounty, so I'll be generous in kind and grant your request. But first understand that my potions are strong, much more potent than you can possibly imagine. Are you willing to be tested again?"

"Yes," I said.

"Is your heart pure?" She stared into my eyes. "If it isn't, you'll be destroyed, too."

"Yes," I answered, "my heart is pure."

"Then make a figure of the man whose unwarranted desires you wish to thwart." She pointed at a pile of twigs and vines and bark, then at a rising mound of dough.

And so I fashioned a crude likeness of the baron, using twigs for his bones and wrapping them with dough for his flesh. From the paper-thin bark I made a sort of shirt and pair of pants, which I tied around the figure's waist with vine.

The *mavaza* took the figure from me and sprinkled it generously with the powder she'd ground in her mortar. "Are you sure your heart is pure?" she asked me a second time.

"Yes," I replied.

We walked outside, where the dog had built a pyre. "Flare bright, ardent fire," recited the *mavaza*. "Quell all false desire for the woman this man claims to love."

She had me put the likeness on the pyre, which leapt at the figure in blazing, hissing anger. The figure's paper clothing flared orange and then curled and withered into ash as the rest of the body slowly burned. After the fire cooled, she brushed the ashes into a pile and then into a leather pouch. "Are you certain your heart is pure?" she asked again.

I nodded.

"Then I mark these ashes with your name, Salvatore. Now, sprinkle some of this ash in each jar of wine served at your wedding banquet, while saying the words I said before."

"May the Lord bless you," I said.

"And wear this disguise," she said, passing her hand across my face so swiftly that even if I had tried to stop her I wouldn't have been able to. Her hand was quicker than a beat of the hawk's wings. No sooner had the flutter passed my eyes than the masked dog stood behind her unmasked, his face still clearly a dog's though his body now just as clearly had transformed itself in every other way into a man's.

He tied the pouch of ashes around my neck, and I started back. I didn't understand what the *mavaza* had done to my face until I reached the village. The villagers treated me as if I were a stranger until they heard my voice and noted my gestures and manner of walk. Then one of them had the mercy to tell me that my face was hideously discolored by a black patch that stretched over my eyes and nose like a mask. Whatever were you eating? they asked me. Your face looks as if it's been splashed with wine!

"It resembles a birthmark," someone said.

"But he's a grown man. Why does it wait to appear now?"

"Perhaps because he's about to marry ugly Rosa."

"He's just returned from the forest, hasn't he?"

"He must have done something evil there and been cursed!"

Suspicious and frightened, they shied away from me. And even though I washed my face with lemon juice and olive oil and then scoured the flesh until it bled, I couldn't remove the shadow that covered me.

"His true nature's showing," the villagers said. "Even Rosa the Harelip won't want him now."

"No woman would want him."

"His homely mug nearly makes hers beautiful!"

"What a ridiculous pair!"

"Look at his dark countenance, splashed as if with tar."

"Surely he's been cursed for having committed some horrible deed."

"Of course. That's the only sensible explanation. His mark is the stain of some past sin."

They kept pregnant women from me, for fear that if the women's impressionable eyes fell on me, the children swelling within their wombs would be born discolored, too. The village priest told me that I'd bear the mark until I fully confessed and atoned for whatever evil I had done. Everyone but Papa Santuzzu, my sisters, and Rosa shied away from me. Even the songbirds in the trees grew silent and fled from my sight.

To go about my work in the fields, I wore a sack over my head. The twins, Livicedda and Rosaria, cut holes in the sack for my eyes, and another for my nose and mouth so I'd be able to breathe and eat.

I told Rosa that I understood if she no longer desired me. After all, I said, only a fool buys a donkey that's gone lame. She told me that I was the fool, and that a melon can still be sweet even if its rind is a variety of shades.

Thus we were wed on the day we'd planned, at the hour when the priest was sober. None of the villagers attended, out of fear. Only Papa Santuzzu and Gabriella, the twins, and Assunta joined Rosa and me around the table for the wedding feast. I'd nearly forgotten about the ashes in the pouch around my neck until Rosa insisted that I unhood.

"Flare bright, ardent fire, quell all false desire," I said as I sprinkled the ash marked with my name into our three jars of wine.

We made the sign of the Cross and broke bread, and then a pair on horseback rode toward us across the fields.

It was the baron and one of his henchmen. Papa raised his nose and sneered, then muttered a string of curses in the general direction from which the men approached.

"What a charming gathering," the baron said as he neared our table. "What an amusing assemblage of curiosities. Do you realize that all you're missing is a dwarf in foolscap?" The fat *gabbillotu* laughed heartily at the master's joke. "Here we have a harelipped bride and her masked groom," the baron continued, "a toothless old blind man and his useless donkey, a rag-sucking red-eyed little girl and a pair of twins so simpleminded that if they aren't ordered hourly to shut their mouths they'd drown in the sea of their own drool. How kind of you freaks to invite me to this feast." He nodded at me, then sat across from Rosa.

I poured him a cup of wine. "Drink to us, master," I said.

"What the devil happened to your face?" he asked.

"Never mind me," I said. "Drink, master."

"To your union," he said, tipping back his glass.

"Again, master," I said, pouring him a second cup of wine.

He laughed. "To the health of all present."

"Once more, master," I said, filling his cup a third time.

"To the pleasures of this night," he said, draining his cup.

I drank three glasses of wine, too. By this time a servant driving a wagon approached from across the fields. He led Rosa to the wagon. Within a moment the baron and his *gabbillotu* galloped away on their horses, and the wagon bearing Rosa raced after them in the night. I took a deep breath, then kissed Papa and my sisters and bid them God bless before I began the long hike across the baron's fields, all the while reciting the *mavaza*'s words, "Flare bright, ardent fire. Quell all false desire."

· · ·

At the mansion Rosa stood waiting for me by a window. The window was above an arched trellis, which I climbed. On the floor of the room lay the body of the *baruni,* curled like a snail's shell.

"Is the beast dead?" I said.

"No," Rosa said, "though for the last hour that's all he's been praying for."

"And you?" I said, studying her face.

She smiled. "I am just as I left you, untouched."

She then recounted all that had taken place. No sooner had the servant escorted her up to the room and the baron reached for her hand than he bent over clutching his midsection, complaining that he felt a sudden pain. The master fell to the floor, hands at his sides. The room smelled sweet, she said, like berries and roasted almonds. Three servants hurried into the room, but even their six hands couldn't stop the man's rigid body from spinning peculiarly on the floor, as if he were impaled on a spit. All the while the baron shouted to his servants to extinguish the flames that were engulfing him, though no one could see any flames. Indeed, Rosa said, the air smelled suddenly of cooking meat. The servants rushed from the room and returned with three pots of water which they began pouring over the baron's body, causing him to shriek so hideously that they doused him with three pots three times more, until the air grew so thick with steam that no one could see and everyone could smell fennel and garlic. After the air cleared, the master still writhed and twitched on the floor, his body coiled in a tortured spiral, praying that he were dead.

"May Jesù and Mari grant his prayers," I said.

At that moment the *gabbillotu* walked into the room. "Grab him!" he shouted to the servants, pointing to me. "He's responsible for this. He poisoned the master."

"Tell me how," I said, raising my hands.

"You poured him three glasses of tainted wine."

"Didn't you see me drink three glasses as well?" I said. "How could the wine be poisoned if I drank it, too?" When the *gabbillotu* didn't answer me I said, "No, this is the baron's own doing, not mine. Leave me be. Whatever is torturing the baron comes from inside his soul. You know what he was about to do this night." I took Rosa's hand. "In the name of Jesù and Mari, you know that I'm not wrong."

As Rosa and I walked freely from the mansion I realized that I too would be tested. "Whatever happens to me," I said, "remember how I felt for you from first sight, when we were children together working in the fields." I smiled at her sweet face. "Oh, Rosa! How I love you! May my desire for you be pure."

Must I state the obvious, that as we kissed I passed the test?

Waiting for us in the shadows of the trees was my friend from the forest, the masked dog. He put his head down between his front paws, then charged us happily, running three circles around us. "The mark," Rosa said suddenly, pointing at my face in the moonlight. "If only you could see yourself, Salvatore! It's fading!"

> *Then the dog proclaimed: "Rosa, need you ask*
> *Why your groom no longer wears the mask?*
> *Since your bride's veil wasn't wrongly torn,*
> *His face is restored! He's spared the horn!"*

NONE WHO STOOD judging me in the flat that night in New York knew this story. God alone comprehends the scribbled symbols that outline my destiny. Which leads me to the peculiarities that happened next.

I kissed Rosa's cheek and whispered that in due time I'd return, then nodded good-bye to my brothers and sisters, stepped quietly out the door, down the stairway, and out onto the New World's terrifying streets, which I walked for three days and nights without rest.

Everywhere I looked I searched for a sign, some indication of the direction my fate intended me to follow. Truly, I was now in a land where signs were everywhere! Nearly every building was numbered in an attempt to ward off evil. In nearly every shop window were letters saying God only knows what. Later, when I could make out a few of them, I thought that since nearly every street sign said "Ave" *La Merica* must be a wonderfully holy place!

I saw that on most street corners boys in knickerbockers and caps waved sheafs of folded papers high over their heads, exchanging these for coins from men in fine suits. Coins tumbled from their vest pockets with such frequency that one piece of silver leapt off a man's palm, bounced on the pavement, and rolled to my feet. I kept to my own business and, as no one else saw or seemed to care, scooped up the coin and placed it in my empty pocket. Indeed, I thought, this was a sign from the Almighty! Men continued to purchase these papers with such eagerness that I was certain the symbols inked on their sheets must be God's own utterances and the very reason why the men were rich.

"Tell me, please," I said to whoever would pause long enough to listen to me, "what's written on these folds of papers?"

Most shrugged or answered me in a language that made no sense to my green ears.

Finally a familiar tongue called out to me. "Hey *paesanu,*" a man shouted, "what do you know?" The man said he was from Vizzini, had been here for nearly two years, and did I need any help because he knew all the ropes.

I looked about the pavement for ropes but saw none. "In Napuli I once met a man from Vizzini," I said. "For his living he sold prickly pears."

"Ahh," nodded the man, smacking his lips, "how I'd love to eat one now!"

I asked him my question about what was inked on the papers.

"What do you think?" he answered. "News."

"News," I said. This was a foreign concept to me.

"Sure," said the man. "Those are newspapers."

"Newspapers," I said. "The paper part I understand. But what exactly is this news?"

"How can I explain?" said the man from Vizzini. "Think of the Old World, how the same things happen over and over, again and again. Here in the New World there are other happenings. That's news. News is the word of change."

"The word of change," I said. Another strange concept.

"Sure," said the man. "People want to read all about it."

"Read all about it," I said. "But now don't tell me that they're willing to trade their coins for paper?" The very thought was both intriguing and absurd.

"Sure," said the man. "Each and every day."

I could hardly imagine that they'd do it every day. "What," I said, "does the paper fall apart? Why don't they just look at the one they bought yesterday?"

The man from Vizzini laughed. "Because every day there's new news."

"Go on!" I said, slapping my forehead. "They exchange coins for paper every day? What a ridiculous idea!" And what a way for a poor man to become rich! In my mind I imagined a huge mound of silver coins.

By then we were walking together along the street. "Your reminding me of prickly pears makes me hungry," the man from Vizzini said. "By chance have you got a nickel for a beer? I'll teach you how to eat a good meal here."

I showed him the coin I had in my pocket.

"How fortunate," he said. "That's a dime. Ten cents. Enough for us both."

"Ten cents," I said.

We went into a saloon where my new friend called out to a man in an apron for two beers. "Don't drink it," he told me as I started to raise the heavy glass to my lips. "It's bitter as horse piss. But buying one lets us eat all we can push down our throats." The man from Vizzini gestured toward a spread of food set out for those who purchased beer.

Eat all that I could push down my throat? Now *that* was a new and foreign concept! I was beginning to like this country, where the rich gave the poor silver for paper, where money for bread and boiled chicken eggs and slices of meat and cheese bounced toward the hungry on the sidewalk!

As we stepped from the saloon door an hour or so later—my belly so delightfully bulging that for the first time in my life I could not eat another bite—a cool gust of wind blew a torn sheet of newspaper flat against my chest. I peeled it from me and nearly threw it back to the breeze before I understood that this event was yet another sign from the Almighty.

"What does this paper say?" I asked my friend from Vizzini.

"How do I know?" he answered. "I can't read."

Of course, I thought, his eyes weren't wearing magic spectacles. "Please, let's go back inside and find someone who can."

"It's a story about Chicago," said a man in the saloon who could both read and speak our tongue. "Something about a man rescuing a baby from a terrible fire."

"A rescuer!" I said. Another sure sign! I thought of the meaning behind my name. "This Chicago," I said. "Where is it? Which direction is it? Can I walk there tonight?"

"You don't want to go to Chicago," said the man from Vizzini. "It's an awfully rough place way out on the prairies, full of the worst scoundrels and thieves."

"It's hundreds of miles away," said the man who could read, "and inhabited by thugs, though I hear it's less crowded than here, with many new opportunities."

"Opportunities," I said. Now my mind held more foreign concepts than I could ever hope to keep straight.

"Employment," replied the man who could read. "Job, the great god under whose cruel and exacting boot the proletariat kneel."

"Amen to that," said the man from Vizzini.

"What," I said, "you mean here in *La Merica* there's a different God?"

The man who could read nodded. "You bet. Here, everyone is made to kneel down before Big Business and its creator, Capitalism."

"What he means," said the man from Vizzini, "is that here the rich owners are encouraged to plunder the poor. And most of the time the poor stand in line outside the factory gates, caps in their hands, more than willing to be plundered!"

Then the man who could read began to sing.

> *Conditions they are bad,*
> *And some of you are sad;*
> *You cannot see your enemy,*
> *The class that lives in luxury.*
> *You workingmen are poor—*
> *Will be so evermore—*
> *As long as you permit the few*
> *To guide your destiny.*

"Now the chorus," shouted the man from Vizzini.

> *Shall we still be slaves and work for wages?*
> *It is outrageous—has been for ages;*
> *This earth by right belongs to toilers,*
> *And not to spoilers of liberty.*

Soon others in the saloon circled around us and joined in.

> *The master class is small,*
> *But they have lots of gall.*
> *When we unite to gain our right,*
> *If they resist we'll use our might;*
> *There is no middle ground,*
> *This fight must be one round,*
> *To victory, for liberty,*
> *Our class is marching on!*

Everyone sang the chorus again, and then the man who could read sang the third and final verse.

> *Workingmen, unite!*
> *We must put up a fight,*
> *To make us free from slavery*
> *And capitalistic tyranny.*
> *This fight is not in vain,*
> *We've got a world to gain!*
> *Will you be a fool, a capitalist tool?*
> *And serve your enemy?*

"All that may very well be true," I said, "but if my family's hungry I have no choice but to work so that they may eat."

"He's still seasick and dizzy from the boat," the man from Vizzini told the man who could read.

"Give the poor fellow time," said the man who could read. "Not too long ago our gills were green from the boat, too."

"So," I said, "are there jobs here in New York or not?"

The man who could read pointed out the saloon window at a wooden pole. On it hung a handbill of daily wages, which he read aloud.

> *COMMON LABOR, WHITE $1.50 TO $1.75*
> *COMMON LABOR, COLORED $1.30 TO $1.50*
> *COMMON LABOR, ITALIAN $1.15 TO $1.30*

"So how can I get to be white?" I asked.

Both of my new friends shook their heads and laughed.

"Being white isn't something you can get to be," said the man who could read. "You either are white or you are not. We're not, so forget about even trying."

The man from Vizzini said, "The *Americani* think of us as dirty sewer rats pouring out the garbage holds of each new ship that docks in the harbor."

"Sewer rats?" I cried, incredulous.

"Even worse," said the man who could read. "They think that by our nature we're evil. They call us assassins, anarchists, kidnappers, blackmailers. They think we're all bandits, black-eyed and swarthy, with rings in our ears and stilettos in our pockets, ready to steal their purses and slit their pale white throats. In the newspapers they say we're lawless and care nothing for our children, whom we'd sell into slavery just as easily as we'd wink, and that we have a natural and inborn inclination toward criminality. They think we're all ignorant peasants, dirty fleas reeking of garlic, hardly fit to blacken their boots."

"How can they say that?" I said. "They've never met me or my family."

"Nor mine," said the man from Vizzini.

"Nor mine," said the man who could read. "Still, they're more than willing to let us do the jobs their soft hands have grown too grand for."

"We should be grateful to them," said the man from Vizzini. "Job puts bread on the table."

"Remember that your labor fills the boss's breadbasket first," said the man who could read, "as well as his soup and salad bowls along with his meat platter."

"You forgot his dessert tray and cigar box," said the man from Vizzini. "You forgot his three glasses of wine."

"Well," I said, looking back at the sign, "how can I get to be colored?"

My new friends shook their heads again.

"On one job I said I was colored," the man from Vizzini said, "but the foreman laughed and told me my accent was all wrong and my skin wasn't dark enough."

"We're darker than some, lighter than others," said the man who could read. "We come in all shades. I know a *Siciliana* as white and blonde as the whitest white woman. I know a *Sicilianu* as black as the blackest colored man."

I looked at the back of my hands. I wanted to say I was white, too, but I have my father's skin and in truth am more the color of an olive that's been soaking for a very long time in a barrel of brine.

"We're caught somewhere in the middle," said the man from Vizzini, sucking his teeth.

"We're neither white nor black. We're like a *macchiatu,* coffee splashed by milk."

"Amen to that," said the man who could read.

"Do you see that boy?" I said a few moments later, pointing out the saloon window at the newspaper seller on the corner. "Do you think I could get a job doing what he does?"

"Sure," said the man from Vizzini, "but why would you want to? His boss pockets most of the profit."

My mind pictured the boss's fat pockets. "So how can I get to be his boss?" I asked.

"I believe they stopped accepting applications for that job last week," the man from Vizzini said and laughed.

"He's right," said the man who could read. "Besides, by now all the good street corners in this city are taken."

"That's true for more than just street corners," said the man from Vizzini. "Sometimes I fear our boats touched these shores too late."

"No," said the man who could read, "we arrived at precisely the right time, at the moment of a vital historical imperative. Without wanting to sound like an anarchist, let me say that we're nearing the dawn of a new social order. Someday soon we'll witness the birth of a society run fairly by all the workers of the world."

"Someday soon doesn't pay the butcher or the landlord," said the man from Vizzini. "Someday soon doesn't buy a pair of shoes when your feet are bare."

They continued talking while I stared at the newspaper story about the rescuer in Chicago until an idea sparked a fire that burned inside my brain.

• • •

"WE'RE LEAVING AT once and going to Chicago," I told Rosa after I bid my saloon friends farewell and made my way back to my brothers' top-floor apartment.

Immediately Assunta said she preferred to come with us. Then the twins said they wanted to accompany us, too. I looked expectantly at Luigi and Gaetanu. Carla proclaimed that as oldest of the sisters she'd go wherever the others went. Besides, she said, her husband Gerlando was complaining about the moss that was beginning to grow between his toes.

I smiled. That's often the way it is with *la famigghia*. Everyone can be content sitting inside the house doing the same things until someone announces that he's going to take a walk out in the morning sunlight, and then if the first to respond doesn't try to talk him out of it, everyone will soon agree that it's a fine idea, and in no time the five-minute walk out in the sun will turn into an afternoon picnic to which everyone will be invited, even the lame and the infirm, and to which baskets of food will be taken as well as coats and umbrellas in case of cold weather or rain.

Only Teresa stood her ground, wearing her dark pantaloons, a sea of children washing her legs. "Go if you'd like," she said, "and may God bless you, but our home's here."

Gaetanu sat on a stool near a window, coughing into his sleeve, his thin shoulders hunched over as if he were about to break in two. Behind him a tattered clothesline strung heavy with wash stretched to the next building. "You left Papa behind," he said, "so you might as well leave us behind, too. Teresa and I are content to stay here."

"Go on," Luigi said from the table, "abandon me as well." He gave a look to Ciccina, who cast her eyes to the floor as if to say that it was his decision, not hers. "Abandon us just as you abandoned Papa."

"But we seven can't live apart," Carla said, shaking her head. "No, no. I won't have it. It's not right."

"We've lived apart the past twelve or so years," Gaetanu said. He stuck out both hands, fingers spread, hesitated, then tapped one foot twice.

"Brother," said Rosaria, "can't go against brother," said Livicedda.

"Just as son can't go against father," Luigi said. "I tell you, I never would have come here if I knew that you were going to leave Papa behind."

"You're no one to talk," I said to Luigi. "You were the first to leave us, after the *banditi* enlisted you. Have you any idea how worried and sick Mamma was for all those years you were missing? She didn't know if you were dead or alive."

"I did it for the rest of you," Luigi said, "so there would be more food in your bowl."

"That's false," I said. "You did it for yourself."

"Stop," said Gaetanu. "I won't have this talk in my house."

"And you," I said to my oldest brother, "you could have returned, as so many sons who'd left did. Don't think that Mamma and Papa didn't notice some of the others coming back, a few like Arabian sultans, with jangling pockets and wooden chests full of riches. You abandoned them every year that you didn't return."

"Enough," said Gaetanu.

"Don't you dare sit in judgment of me," I shouted. "Any of you." I turned to Luigi. "You too, don't you dare have the gall to judge me. Mamma gave birth to three sons and only one was at her side, holding her hand, soothing her brow, giving her a last sip of cool water, during the hour that she died."

"Please stop," said Assunta.

"Only one of her sons was there to lower her body into the ground," I said. "Only one of her sons covered her face with stones."

"No more!" screamed Livicedda.

"Brother against brother!" screamed Rosaria.

"*Matruzza mia,* forgive me!" cried Carla, falling to her knees and covering her face with her hands.

"Don't you see?" said Luigi, raising a flat hand like a knife. "This is what happens to a family when you cut off its head."

"If so," I said, "the blood's on your hands, not mine."

"Enough!" shouted Gaetanu, coughing into his arm. "There's been enough talk under this roof for one night!"

Thus Rosa, my four sisters, and Gerlando Cavadduzzo journeyed with me to Chicago, where we settled on the North Side, near Cleveland and Elm, in the Italian parish of Saint Philip Benizi. There we lived more or less happily until the *paesani* were scattered like a great tree's many leaves in the wind and the magnificent brick church was tearfully torn down.

And it was there that I fulfilled my *destinu* by selling newspapers, first in Grant Park and then in the Loop of downtown Chicago, in the city of the greased palm, so named because no action can be considered, yet alone approved, without a thousand and one outstretched palms first receiving a little lubrication.

As they say, some butter always sticks to the wrapper.

I greased the palms of the newspapers' distributors, who each day sold me the papers I labored to sell. I greased the drivers who delivered the bundles of papers to me. I greased the policeman who walked the local beat. I greased the merchants whose stores stood near my stand. I greased the merchants' neighbors. The policeman who rode by on his horse every day asked me for a little grease. Then the cop who walked the beat told me I had to have a permit. I said, didn't I just grease you yesterday? He said sure, I'm greased good, but don't think for a minute you can get away with not greasing City Hall.

Way down in the basement of Chicago's City Hall is a gigantic wheel so big that it takes a thousand and one hands to turn it. This wheel is studded with countless metal teeth, each of which meshes with even more teeth on smaller wheels, which in turn mesh with still other gears, and so on and so on. Each and every gear must rotate smoothly in order for even the slightest action to be accomplished. As anyone who's ever worked with machinery knows, in order for the wheel to rotate every gear needs to be oiled. If you want the wheel to turn, you have to supply the grease!

I greased the man whose office issued the application for a permit. I greased the man whose pen filled out the empty spaces on the application form. The man who received the application required grease to move the piece of paper off his desk. He sent out an inspector to investigate the spot I'd chosen. I greased the inspector, who told me my application needed to be notarized. Back in City Hall I greased the notary. Then the man who received the notarized applications informed me his desk was covered with quicksand, and I'd have to construct a bridge of grease so that my application could slide its way across.

I built that bridge, then greased the official who issued me a temporary permit. I greased his boss, who drove by the next day with an open hand to say hello. The beat cop's sergeant came out as well to meet me. After I greased him he told me that within the next few months I'd need a regular permit to replace the preliminary one, and the cycle began all over again. All of this took years.

They say that God created the world in six days, and that on the seventh he rested. Let me assure you that he didn't create the world while living in Chicago! Even if the Almighty had worked at lightning speed, in the City of the Greased Palm getting just the permits would have taken him a century!

Don't think for a moment that I'm complaining. I'm grinning wider than *babbu* Giufà because one happy day, after years and years of work, all the hands that could be greased were greased and that first newsstand was officially mine!

Mine, all mine! Nowhere else but in *La Merica*!

Newspaper and fire brought my family west
After the mavaza's *pyre baked my wedding guest.*

Now Assunta, born last, extends these twelve tales
With one of vast love and how sometimes it fails.

The Botanist's Assistant

ℚ Assunta Girgenti

THE PEOPLE HERE in this village of Evanston, Illinois, are blessed to live beneath so many trees. There are wide-spreading elms, maples, poplars, and oaks so majestic they must have been saplings back in the time of Christopher Columbus. There are cedars, black walnuts, sycamores, white pine, sweet gum. They say *La Merica* is the New World, but by the size of some of her trees you can see that she's an ancient place. You can understand why she's called the Golden Land each autumn when the maples and oaks turn color, and the wind shimmers the vibrant leaves and makes the treeline appear as if it is flaming, and the yellows and oranges and reds tremble and flutter in the crisp air. On days like these I truly feel that each tree is alive. The colors are so bright, sometimes they hurt my eyes. I have to cover my eyes to prevent them from tearing. I have to cover my mouth to prevent it from screaming in delight. The leaves float like big, lazy boats down through the air to the browning fields. There they gather in waves and tumble and spill across the wind-blown grasses, crackling and whispering like the sea.

I like to stand at the edge of a field, pretending to be the shore, and feel the leaves beat against my legs. Sometimes I kneel amidst the leaves and whisper a prayer for the wild plants, trodden weeds, and forgotten greens that still prosper in the black, fertile soil of this quiet village resting by the shore of the great lake.

Many sow in their front fields a flat green grass that sheep or perhaps horses or donkeys would eat, if given the opportunity. But despite this availability of food there are few sheep around, and the horses here are kept in fenced corrals, and not once have I seen in this village a goat or grazing mule or donkey. Mostly in the fields there are dogs and cats. Sneaky things, the cats stalk and kill the songbirds that fill the trees. In the grasses each morning you can see the birds' bright feathers, quills stained red with their blood. The dogs rush out at you, all paw and bravado, coughing *hunhf hunhf hunhf*. Sometimes the dogs are chained to a post or fence.

In the summer, colored men push machines with wheels and whirling blades up and down the fields, back and forth and then back again, chopping the green grasses and everything wild that tries to grow with them, gathering it all in metal baskets hanging behind their machines. They harvest the grasses in this manner every week, only to immediately waste them, dumping their metal baskets in yellowing piles behind the houses at the edge of the fields between the trees.

The colored men ride the streetcar on Clark Street each day from the city along with me. We board a good hour before dawn, with the sky's fading stars, when the air is still cold and wet. We seldom, if ever, talk. We remain on the car until it arrives at the last stop and the driver shouts, "OK, wake up! Look alive! End of the line! Everybody off!"

I walk along the concrete pathways behind the men with the other women on their way to work. We arrive in the village each morning with the rising sun. The women scratch the sleep from their eyes and yawn into their shiny palms. Their palms look like finely varnished wood ranging in shade from the softest yellows to the richest browns. The only sounds come from the march of our thudding shoes on the pavement, the wind rustling the leaves in the many trees, and the sweet trills and whistles of the songbirds joyous to have survived another night, to be able to stretch their wings in the rising sun.

DID I SAY HOUSES? Really, many of the buildings here are mansions made of sturdy red bricks, set beautifully beside graceful pockets of woods. Other mansions are made of handsome planks of painted wood. I especially like the shaded porches that line the front of the planked houses. It would be pleasant to sit on such a porch some summer evening, I think.

Where the houses stand in sight of one another, the fields are often enclosed by wooden fences. Sometimes these fences are painted white. Once a forest stood on this land beside the great lake. By the size of some of the tree stumps that still remain, you can see that it was an ancient, mighty forest. Now nearly all of it has been cleared and fenced. In its place the mansions' owners have planted shrubs and flowering trees beneath their windows.

Walking about, I sometimes imagine that I live in this village, that the second-floor room in which I sleep looks out over one of these pleasant groves of elms, that on summer nights when I am most restless the white embroidered curtains on my windows toss their skirts gently toward me in the cool breeze.

Unable to sleep I reach out my hand and touch the curtains. The daring breeze caresses my cheek.

Most owners who pass me on the street think I am a servant. They conclude this by my clothing and the wicker basket which I always carry beneath my arm. I wear a long wool skirt, cinched tightly at the waist, durable enough to withstand my foraging and explorations. I wear a long-sleeved blouse, which I carefully wash out in the sink each evening before I fall to sleep. I wear a shawl and wide-brimmed hat, which protects my head from the sun. I am always polite. I smile whenever one of the village's old masters speaks to me. I gaze directly into the man's eyes and repeat whatever he says to me, even though I often do not know what his words mean, mirroring his manner as I make my mouth match the lilt and tilt of his sentences.

"Hello," they say, "how are *you*?"

"Hello," I answer, "how are *you*?"

"I'm feeling quite *fine* today," they say and smile.

"I'm feeling quite *fine* today," I respond and smile.

Sometimes they talk at length to me. "Are you here alone today?" they ask. "Are you searching for something? Are you lost? Tell me, please, I'm rather curious, are you colored or Italian?"

"I am here alone today," I respond. "I am searching for something lost. I am rather curious and Italian."

Though in truth I am a *cristiana* from Girgenti, the province for which all seven of the children in my family who journeyed here to *La Merica* were named, and where my dear father—may God bless his soul—perhaps still stumbles about blindly, alone save for his white donkey, and where my mother and her parents and my father's parents and many who lived before them lie sleeping in the rocky ground. I have lived now in *La Merica,* in the city of Chicago, for ten years.

"Why are you here walking on this private property?" they ask. "Tell me, please, what is your business? What do you have in your basket?"

"I am here walking on this private property," I say. "My business is my business. In my basket are the greens I have found."

I open my basket and show the master whatever I've found that day, perhaps some wild asparagus, some pigweed, fennel, borage, wild cabbage, usually a bit of chicory, and of course dandelion, which grows everywhere here among the useless grasses the colored men are ordered to mow.

I repeat whatever the old masters of the great mansions say, responding like a songbird in a tree, until their masters' mouths empty of questions and their eyes stop narrowing and instead smile or glance down or away, as if sad or distracted, and I understand that I am free then to fly away, free to continue my exploration and foraging.

. . .

ONE DAY I encountered a handsome young master who asked
me if I was connected with the university nearby. When I told
him I was connected with the university nearby, the master asked
if I was a botanist, so I answered, "I am a botanist." We have a
similar word in Sicilian, *butanica*. By his smile I knew that he very
much wanted me to agree.

But you can't already be a botany professor, the master said.
You're hardly old enough. You must be only a botanist's assistant.
He laughed in a way that made me step toward him. I saw that
he was my age, and not yet closed to life. Sun sparkled on his big
front teeth. He had fair skin and what appeared to be soft, freshly
washed hair. Unlike the older masters, he did not wear a hat.
When he held out his hands to me, I could see smooth white
moons at the base of his fingernails. On his wrist there was a
timepiece strapped with golden braids.

"Yes," I said, "I can't already be a botany professor. I am hardly
old enough. I am only a botanist's assistant."

I could see that my answers pleased him. I could see in his
soft eyes that he wanted to take my arm and walk with me, lead
me beside an old oak tree deep in the cool shadows, stroke my
cheek with his clean fingertips, and kiss my lips. I considered for
a moment whether I would allow him to do that. I decided then
that I would because his smile seemed sincere, and his hands were
so smooth and clean.

Ever since I was a child, I have been able to see in my mind
visions that others are not able to see in theirs. I could see that he
was a gentle man, the youngest son of one of the wealthy masters.
I could see that his heart desired only love. Just as I walked about
each day searching for greens, he walked about in search of someone who might be kind to him and offer him her love. I smiled
and offered him my arm. But then his mind grew cloudy, thinking
of his father and remembering that he had once loved before and
been hurt, and so he hid his eyes from me, and then all at once
he nodded and stepped back, then hurried away.

The visions come once or twice a day, and then usually I will see nothing for several days, and then the darkness in my mind will explode with another flurry of visions.

I FIRST SAW these fields in the eyes of Ziu Griddu.

Ziu Griddu was born near Trapani, on Sicily's dazzling northwest coast. Like many who are fortunate enough to be born near the sea, Ziu Griddu was a natural explorer. There is something about an expanse of water that draws the ear and eye to it and then makes the heart ache to see what lies across it on the opposite shore. But rather than gaze out at the sea longingly, the exceptionally tall and thin figure of Ziu Griddu stared down at the shore. He spent so much time squatting, his buttocks nearly scraping the ground, his long legs bent at the knees, walking in this manner inspecting the earth and whatever sprouted from it, that the men of his village came to call him *griddu,* which means cricket. In our neighborhood in Chicago, near the church of Saint Philip Benizi, Ziu Griddu is more famous than even Columbus. This is the story of how Ziu Griddu came to discover Evanston.

ONCE THERE WAS a man named Ziu Griddu, a poor but honest man, who worked the whole day—day after day—in the unrelenting heat of the blazing sun, even though like nearly every other man in the city during these hard times he had no actual work. As a result, Ziu Griddu made the discovery of work his occupation. Like a miner scratching a mountain's stony face for ore, Ziu Griddu searched all over Chicago for a job, or what all the men in our neighborhood came to call a *gioba.*

At home, Ziu Griddu had a lot of hungry mouths to feed. Each day before dawn he tied the piece of rope that held up his pants and donned his jacket and put on his cap, then smoothed his drooping black moustache and ventured out with his knife and empty sack, looking for anything that he could bring back that evening to feed his family. No frog or snail, no snake or worm or slug, was too small.

Since most of the other men in our neighborhood were busy doing the same, you can imagine that the city's North Side was picked pretty clean. Hardly a weed or blade of grass could poke the green tip of its head out from a crack in the sidewalk without two hands and two knives diving toward it. Hardly a crumb of bread could fall to the floor. The pickings were so meager that any mice or rats desperate enough to venture out from the cracks in our walls took a spicy swim in our soup pots, and even *caca-rocchi* grew scarce.

Well, one day Ziu Griddu found a coin in the gutter. His first thought, after thanking the merciful Almighty, was to use it to purchase food for his children. Then he paused and thought that perhaps he should test his good fortune so as to determine just how far it might extend. A streetcar clanked toward him at that moment, sounding its horn, heading north.

Ziu Griddu felt a sudden, overwhelming temptation. He waved his coin and touched the brim of his cap. The streetcar stopped. Stepping aboard, the shrewd explorer decided to see how far the wheeled machine would take him, what new shore he would be deposited upon after the vehicle arrived at the end of its course.

Ziu Griddu rode the streetcar until it stopped at the southern edge of Evanston. The driver jerked his thumb for Ziu Griddu to get off. By the air's thick and complex smell Ziu Griddu could tell he was out in the countryside. He decided to roam about until he could scavenge something for his family to eat, even if that meant walking all the way to the North Pole! Smelling water, he headed toward it, then kept the lake over his right shoulder so as not to become lost. He slung his empty sack over his back. The day was as beautiful as it was promising. Ziu Griddu wandered north for perhaps an hour.

Then he saw something that made his heart leap. Tears of elation squirted out from his eyes! There just ahead was a field spotted with a good half-sack of wild *carduni*!

Now, you know that the cardoon is a relative of the artichoke, though in appearance *carduni* more closely resemble young rhubarb or celery. It's twice as delicious, particularly when simmered in a bit of butter or oil. Pull out the tough strings with a knife, then cut the stalks into pieces. I like to boil my *carduni* first in water and the juice of a lemon when I can get one. Then I fry the *carduni* in oil along with some sliced onion, topping it all off with grated *pecurinu*. Oh, how my mouth waters just saying the words!

Well, lucky day, Ziu Griddu could hardly believe his eyes after they'd stopped squirting with tears of jubilation. He ran to the field, drew out his knife, and quickly began harvesting the tender plants, carefully cutting above the root crown. If you cut wild *carduni* too deeply, you kill it. A sensitive creature, *carduni* cut too close to the roots shrivels up and refuses to grow back. The plant is forever ruined. But Ziu Griddu was a most considerate soul. He thought of the next hungry forager to come across the field, so he harvested the stalks with great care. What beautiful *carduni*! he thought as he hurried to fill his empty sack.

At that moment the front door of the mansion flew open, and a snarling dog sprinted toward him. A woman's voice from the doorway shrilly shouted, "Hey, you there in the field! Stop!"

Ziu Griddu knew that he was as good as dead. He threw his knife to the ground, dropped his sack, and slowly raised his hands high over his head in surrender while the fierce dog growled and barked and snapped at the air near Ziu Griddu's ankles.

"What are you doing?" the mansion's owner shouted as she neared.

Ziu Griddu decided that the best course was the truth. Now, there's no dishonor in stealing food when your family is hungry, but one doesn't go about admitting it to the masters or their men. Ziu Griddu took off his cap and held it humbly in his hands. "Madam," he said, staring sadly at the ground, "as you might be able to tell, I was cutting down a few of these weeds."

"I can very well see that!" said the mansion's owner.

Ziu Griddu nodded, wringing his cap.

"And then," the owner said, "I see that you were putting the weeds in your sack!"

There was no denying it. On the ground beside him lay the bulging sack. "Yes," Ziu Griddu admitted.

"Whatever for?" the woman asked.

Ziu Griddu was too embarrassed to answer. Let him be taken to jail for stealing, he thought, but he'd be hung by the neck and left for the vultures and flies before he would allow himself to be additionally humiliated by having to describe to anyone his family's *miseria*. So he looked into the woman's eyes and said, "I'm putting them in my sack to feed my horse." Of course Ziu Griddu didn't own a horse or else long ago his family and all their neighbors would have eaten it.

"Your horse likes these weeds?" the woman of the mansion asked.

Ziu Griddu nodded, picturing his family sitting around the table feasting on the wild *carduni*. "Oh yes, so very much," he said, with a woeful tremolo in his voice. "My horse likes to eat them so much you wouldn't believe it, and most of all he likes them when they're young and tender, just like this."

"Then take them all, please," the woman of the house said. "And if your horse can eat even more—" She motioned with one hand for Ziu Griddu to follow her. They walked around to the back of the mansion.

There in the mid-morning sunlight stretched an immense field just bursting with young *carduni*!

"Chop all these weeds down and I'll give you a dollar," the woman of the mansion said. "Please, cut it all and take it all away! In my garage I have as many extra sacks as you'll need."

As his eyes again glistened with tears of joy, Ziu Griddu gave thanks to the Madonna and all the saints of Trapani for his day's exquisite fortune.

That night everyone in the neighborhood, all the *Siciliani* who knew Ziu Griddu or who knew someone who knew Ziu Griddu or who knew someone who knew someone who knew Ziu Griddu, or even those who didn't know anybody at all but who, down on the street outside the public housing where we all lived, could smell the aroma of it simmering in our pans, feasted on wild *carduni*!

Such eating! Such bliss! Ziu Griddu had indeed walked to the North Pole! He became a Santa Claus, passing out handfuls of delicious *carduni* to everyone from his bulging sacks!

And each spring up until the year that he died he returned to the secret *carduni* field that lay hidden behind the great mansion. To this day whenever anyone in our neighborhood mentions *carduni* we smile and tell the story of Ziu Griddu.

> *I walk around praying for the Virgin's sweet grace,*
> *Searching the ground in Ziu Griddu's place.*

IN OUR VILLAGE in Girgenti, the people thought me strange. As a young girl, I often had visions of things as they occurred. I saw a young boy tumble into a well. I saw two lovers sneak off together to the forest. Sometimes I knew what the women would talk about even before they did.

Listening to the women gossip, I could give them details from the visions I had seen. The women would play a game with me in which one would hide a knife and I'd have to tell them where it was. Sometimes I couldn't see the knife at all, but other times I could see it right away.

Once a woman tried to trick me. Laughing, she told the others that she'd have her husband hide the knife that night as soon as it grew dark. See, it was a clever trick. The next day when she asked me where he'd hidden it, I pointed to between her legs and told her that the real knife was still on the shelf.

One day I heard a voice, as plain and clear as any human voice I'd ever heard, saying, "Go to her, Assunta! Now!" So I ran from the fields back to the village, where a young girl lay sick in bed with fever. The old woman who kept the leeches had already placed four on the girl's chest. The leeches were growing as fat as sausages. The girl burned like a hot coal.

I laid my hands on her, flat, palms down, gently enough so as to feel the heat of the ember blazing inside her. No one told me how to do it. In my mind I simply saw an image of my hands on her, so that's what I did with my hands. Then I closed my eyes and saw a darkened meadow in the forest, an old tree spotted with lichen, and in a nearby clearing some mosses and herbs.

I ran and gathered the lichen, the mosses, and the herbs and pounded them in a mortar. With a bit of clay this mixture produced a paste, which I fed to the fevered girl after I pulled off the disgusting leeches. In maybe three hours her fever broke. She sat up and smiled, then reached for the bowl of paste and eagerly stuffed her mouth with all that remained. She even licked the mortar clean. Then she slept for two days and was well again.

After that, people came to respect me. Even the men gave me the distance of respect, despite the fact that I carried everywhere with me an old rag and I sucked my thumb and cried much of the time for my dead mamma. I was only a baby, only six or maybe seven years of age. In those days everyone called me Assunta Red Eyes.

"That's why she has the visions," the women said. "Because she looks so hard for things. She gets those red eyes from searching so hard for her mamma's soul."

"She has red eyes because she rubs them all the time with that filthy rag," some other women said. They wrestled the rag away from me and scrubbed it in lye. That same day, our donkey Gabriella's coat turned completely white. My rag remained just as dirty as ever.

The women left me alone after that.

Whenever someone fell sick they called to me. "Assunta! Assunta! Ahh-sooon-taa!" Like *friscaletti* they crooned my name, so

that I might lay hands on someone sick and then prepare a cup
of boiled herbs or a bowl of paste.

It's really quite a simple thing. I just follow the images that
appear now and then before my eyes. You lay your hands on the
abdomen or head, careful not to press too hard, and feel for the
light inside the person's body. When it tingles your palms just
right you know you have it. Then you close your eyes and stare
into the darkness until you see the pictures. Then you walk into
the pictures you've just seen.

I WAS READY TO walk into that second-floor bedroom, the one
with the dainty white lace curtains overlooking the grove of elm
trees. Tom, the wealthy master's son, was ready, too. Each morning he waited for me to stroll past his window, his thoughts throbbing with the words his tongue was too weak and timid to let
loose into the air. I could hear his mind clearly rehearsing the
words that would lead me into the shadows beneath the trees
where he would hold my waist and kiss me and then ask to marry
me, the botanist's assistant.

He was certain that I worked for the university, and said that
he had told his father about me and that he'd even visited my
laboratory. He said he told his father that in the laboratory I used
a microscope and wore a long white coat. Tom further claimed
that I played the piano and that I'd emigrated from Italy's proper
and acceptable north, that I was the daughter of an old aristocratic
family that lived in a mansion much like their own, at the foot of
the Alps. I laughed at all of that. As he held me, he assured me
that his father would never discover the truth.

Tom painted the lies so vividly that his feelings grew entwined
in them, like the tangled grapevines that twisted through and covered the latticework of the arbor on the southern edge of his
property. I told Tom the ancient story of the spider who told the
passing flies so many falsehoods that he lost his immunity to the

stickiness of his own web. In time the spider grew so enmeshed in his web that he could not move, and so he starved.

Early each evening Tom slammed the mansion's thick wooden door and rushed out to walk with me, asking me to show him the herbs and greens in my basket. He'd been reading a book about herbs, he told me, and had memorized several Latin names. As I showed him what I had gathered that day, he would recite each scientific name, extremely pleased with himself, and then I'd say the herb's name in my own tongue, and he'd brush his hand against mine and kiss me.

At first his kisses were shy and tentative, like those a lonely girl who grows up without a mother might give the back of her hand. They were more the idea of a kiss than the actual press of lips or mouth. I waited patiently, watching him, to learn what he was made of.

I had no visions of what was to come with him. As we fell further in love and Tom grew more bold, my body began changing. Then my visions of things fell away, too. Only rarely now could I see things before they occurred. My ability to speak English improved. Tom grew more sure of himself, more confident and daring. We met each evening beneath the arbor circled by a grove of magnificent trees, then hurried inside the small house built for servants set deeper in the woods.

Those evenings are jewels I still hold inside my heart.

One night as we lay together Tom asked me what I knew of men and women, and I told him the story of Elena and Stefanu.

ONCE THERE WAS a poor but honest woman, what we call *una bona fimmina,* a woman of true goodness, whose full heart burned with love for anything injured or sick. Her eyes were the color of almonds, her lips as red as autumn's ripest apples and as full as the noon sun. She was known over all Sicily for her many abilities as a healer.

Some said she was from Taurmina, where she derived her

powers from electrical charges in the volcanic air. Others claimed she was born in Siracusa by the sea, or on the rolling plains near Caltagiruni, or in Ragusa's craggy hills. Myths rose up around her, that she possessed many great and unimaginable powers even as she lay curled inside her mother's womb, once having cured a cripple whose crutch accidentally knocked against her mother's bulging abdomen. Not only did the lame man walk but the crutch sprouted leaves and soft blue flowers! She was known only by her first name, Elena. She was a breech birth, born in a caul, with a full cap of hair and a complete set of teeth.

Shortly after her birth she arrived in Girgenti, some say on the back of a raven, others on the edge of a summer breeze, still others in the saddlebag of a winged donkey. As a child she played mainly with the animals. Wolf and dove alike lay peacefully at her feet. Any injured animal from the forest could come to her and be healed. In time the villagers began bringing her their ailing livestock. After she laid her hands on the animals and stared into their eyes and mouths, she described weeds and greens the *campagnoli* should feed their beasts. All brought before her left cured.

How she learned about herbs I won't reveal quite yet, but everyone in our village believed that she was born with the wisdom. That was why, they said, she had kept her eyes closed for three full months after her birth, so that the visions she'd seen in her mother's womb wouldn't spill out of her eyes and into the air and so that she'd have time to fully memorize all that the womb had taught her.

In my family I was the youngest of seven and the third daughter of four girls. If that sounds like a contradiction I should explain that a pair of my older sisters, Rosaria and Livicedda, are twins and are so entwined in personality that everyone who meets them comes to think of them as a single individual. No one hurried me to grow. A mother has the most patience with her last baby, the women say. I was given time to watch and learn everything. My mamma died before I could reach two full years of age, while I still hungered for milk at her breast.

She lay beside me in the straw as I suckled, my mouth pulling in the last drops of her milk while her mouth drew on the air, as if she too were trying to drink. Then she coughed suddenly very hard, and the light that was within her spilled out into her hand. The light was blue and at the same time gold. Her hand then fell beside me as her head slumped into the straw. Her light grew more radiant, relieved of her body's gnawing *miseria*.

I reached out toward the light, but one of my arms was pinned beneath hers while the other was not quite long enough to reach it. Then the light pulsed and spread, and I was able to grab some of it and pull it into my mouth. I wanted to push my mouth into the light's center and drink it all in, but the weight of my dead mother's arm held me tight, and the light grew diffuse and stretched upwards like a vapor, hovering like blue and gold smoke just beyond my reach. Then it flew out the gap in the roof toward the dim sliver of a moon.

I suckled the last of her milk and continued suckling long after the breast on which my head rested grew cold, until my brother Salvatore's hot tears bathed me as he moaned deeply in unspeakable sorrow, rocking her body as well as mine, after he heard me whimpering and raced up the ladder to discover me lying with my mother's corpse up in the straw.

After she left us, I turned not to my older sisters, the twins, who have their own kind of intelligence and often talked in a language no one else could understand, but to Elena. We seldom spoke. Elena wasn't the kind of woman to put much trust in words. Each day I trailed after her, fiercely sucking my thumb and holding tightly onto my rag, as she left the village to gather herbs in the forest. The boys working the fields hailed us with nicknames: Elena the Virgin and Assunta Red Eyes. They called her the Virgin because they knew she was forever beyond their reach.

One day when I was four or five Elena and I came to a clearing, where she found a plant I had never before seen. It had no flowers, only leaves shaped like the fingers of a closed hand. I asked Elena if the plant was some kind of yucca or cactus. She gave me no answer and simply knelt beside it, eyes closed, fingers pressing her temples, as if she were trying to remember something she had learned back in that womb that could cause a crippled man's crutch to flower.

I stood at her side, my hands imitating the shape of the peculiar plant. Each day after that we returned to the clearing. Elena bathed the plant's broad leaves with water she carried from the village well, then wet its hard and thirsty crown, all the while crooning soothing tones, not so much speaking to it as singing, as you would to a frightened animal or lonely child. The leaves thickened beneath her touch and stretched upward and open like a dozen *baionetti,* like long knives.

One day Elena played her *friscalettu* to the plant. It was a sunny day. The sun reflected off the flute, which she held to her lips. In my bare feet I danced. I wore a ring of rosemary in my hair. Around my neck hung a necklace of chicory. The sweet blue flowers had just opened their eager mouths to the air.

Then from the plant's center stepped a man, Stefanu.

"Assunta," he said to me, "follow the green vine and see what you can find. In an hour or two, when the sun is lower, return to us."

At my feet I saw a green vine. I followed it into the forest, finding all the herbs I knew and was able to name. It took me the whole two hours to gather them in my basket. When I returned to the clearing, Elena and Stefanu were embracing. Then in the wink of one eye he stepped back into his plant.

Each day Elena and I returned to the clearing, where I followed the green vine. As I learned more about various herbs and their powers, I noticed a change coming over Elena. Her belly began to swell. Her breasts filled her blouse. Everyone in the village observed the change in her, too. Now the boys in the fields called her *disgraziata* as she and I made our way each morning to the clearing. Elena's three older brothers noted the change, too.

One morning we discovered that in our absence something horrible had happened to Stefanu's plant. Its leaves had been slashed and broken. Its wounds oozed a thick, nearly clear fluid that hardened like sticky amber in the air. At once Elena reached into her basket for her *friscalettu*. It wasn't there. Frantic, we retraced our steps through the forest and past the fields. The boys were silent. We raced back to the village and searched Elena's house.

There we found the flute lying beneath three blood-stained shirts. Elena's breath tripped in her throat. The shirts belonged to her brothers. We rushed back to the clearing. Trembling, Elena brought the *friscalettu* to her lips.

I can hardly describe how battered Stefanu appeared as he stepped out from the center of his shattered plant. Imagine a thousand and one slashes on a man's face and neck, arms and chest and back, buttocks and thighs and legs, each cut brimming with bright beads of blood. It was as if the clothing of his skin were now a bright red suit of slashes. Stefanu held his arms tightly around his chest, as if he were trying to keep himself from falling apart.

I was only a child who still sucked her thumb, who peed each night in the straw up in the loft in which we all slept, who carried a piece of her dead mother's shirtwaist everywhere she went, praying that the smell of her dear mother in the ragged cloth would never fade, and her soul would never leave me. Can anyone here blame me for becoming so frightened that I ran away screaming? I ran back to the fields, all the way shouting for my father and brother.

"*Aiutu!*" I shouted. "*Papa! Salvatore! Aiutu!*"

My cries were answered only by Elena's brothers. In a field the three men stood tall and bare-chested, leaning against their hoes, laughing, full and proud of themselves, telling me not to hurry in the hot sun.

"Be careful," they shouted, "or you'll get sunstroke."

"Go with Satan," I whispered to the three. In my mind I suddenly saw their futures, the three of them bent, twisted, sizzling like grubs thrown onto a pan over a fire, writhing in an endless dying, their skins crackling with bubbling sores.

I hid then beside some thistle, and after my heart grew calm I returned to the clearing. Somehow Stefanu's plant had mended. All of its wounds had healed. It stood as healthy as ever, as if it had just been watered. Indeed, the earth around it was dark, as if wet. Near the plant's crown lay Elena's *friscalettu,* which I quickly put to my mouth and played.

As he stepped from the plant Stefanu was surprised to see me and not Elena. His wounds had been entirely cured. He whirled around with a puzzled look, calling her name.

He whirled a second time, then a third. Then he ran toward a nearby tree. A dark trail led from his plant to behind the trunk of the tree. There lay Elena's body, both arms gashed open from elbow to wrist.

You can fill in the gaps yourself. Elena understood that the only cure for Stefanu's wounds was a sacrifice of blood. She knew there was not enough time to return to the village for a goat or lamb. So she used, quite literally, the only blood she had at hand.

Stefanu trembled in sorrow and rage, and the earth began to shake.

"Fools!" he shouted. "Such foolish men! Why did they have to interfere? In another month she would have given birth, and the spell that has entrapped me would have been broken. We could have walked arm in arm to the village and been married. Ahead of us both lay a long and happy life."

He cradled Elena's body in his arms. "Once I too worked in the fields," he said, "until my wife of one month fell sick. The healer's chants and leeches were no help. I searched in the forest for herbs so I might save her. There I met a *mavaza* and with her made a pact, her knowledge for my freedom. My wife was saved, but I was condemned to live inside this plant until my seed could bear a child."

He paused and stared dolefully at me. "Assunta, I have been waiting in this clearing for over a thousand years! Finally I had the idea that I could send a piece of my desires through the air and the seed of that need might lure someone to me, like some plants lure insects to care for them. Eighteen years ago I released my scent into the hot sirocco, knowing it might blow north and east, to Caltagiruni or Taurmina, or perhaps drift south, toward Ragusa or Siracusa by the sea. Wherever the hot winds of Africa sent the seed, Elena's mother inhaled it. I knew that the knowledge in the smell would eventually lead the child to me. I had a one in two chance it would be a girl. I prayed that she'd be *una bona fimmina*. But I didn't count on her three brothers."

"I'll have your baby," I told him. "That will break the curse."

"No," said Stefanu. "You have brothers, too."

"Two have disappeared," I said, "having fallen off the end of the earth into the mouth of a hungry monster. The one who remains, Salvatore, is most gentle and kind. In my heart I know he would never harm you."

"A girl's brother is still a brother," Stefanu said. Then he ordered me to leave the clearing. "I can remain outside my plant for only an hour each day if I am to live. This afternoon I'll spend that hour digging a marriage bed deep enough for two."

Elena's brothers searched the forest for her the following day, after she failed to return to the village. They found nothing. They searched the next day, then the next and the next. That third morning was when I heard her voice calling me to the bed of the fevered girl.

In time, everyone in the province came to believe that Elena had been carried away by wolves. Memory sweetens even the most bitter wine. As the people of the village recounted her story, they remembered all the animals she'd cured and again called her Elena the Virgin.

Only I know the whereabouts of the grave because I concealed the bodies with grasses and stones and briars and weeds and so many tangled and thorny branches that each spring, from that year to the end of time, all the songbirds of Girgenti flock to that place for twigs to build their nests, filling the sweet air with love songs.

• • •

IN THIS NEW land the assassins of love deliver speeches, using their tongues instead of knives.

Of course Tom's father objected as soon as he learned of his son's intention to marry me. He ordered Tom and me to accompany him to the university. There, he said, we would receive an education. Tom said he had nothing to hide and would certainly welcome any truth.

At the university we met a man who called himself the Dean, and who informed us that he had no knowledge of me, no knowledge of any Milanese aristocrat's daughter who worked for him or for anyone at the university as a botanist's assistant.

The dean sat behind a big empty table, like a king with nothing to eat. He questioned me in some northern dialect, which was so fine and dry I could barely understand him.

"Look at this little charlatan," the dean said. "She can't even speak proper Italian." He wriggled his fingers in the air. His white fingers were as pale as worms, as fat as leeches ready to be milked of the blood they'd just sucked. "She's so stupid she comes from a country and can't even speak its language."

"You're so stupid you can't even speak," I said. By then I knew what I was saying.

The white worms of his hands waved my words away. "You must never again impersonate a university employee, do you understand me?" he shouted. He made a fist. For a moment I thought he was going to hit me. "You must never again lie about working here, *capisci*? Or else I'll be forced to call the police, and they'll arrest you and toss you in jail with the others of your kind, all the socialists and anarchists, all the murderers and thieves, and if you choose to continue this kind of behavior you'll be deported and get what's coming to you, won't you, *signorina*? Won't you?"

"I won't," I said. "I won't, sir."

"Yes, you will," he said, "in the name of American justice." He slapped his palm against his table. "Your anarchist *paesani*

Sacco and Vanzetti are going to get what they have coming to them, aren't they?" He grinned. "They're not sitting in Death Row cells as we speak for being altar boys. They'll fry like bacon in a skillet one of these days, mark my words. Or are you too ignorant to read the newspapers?"

"You are too ignorant to read the newspapers," I said.

"Did someone tell you to lie and say you work here?" he asked.

"Someone lied and said you work here," I answered.

"These Mediterraneans," the dean said, laughing along with Tom's father, "they're an amusing people, aren't they? We certainly let them pour out of their boats for a while, didn't we?" He looked directly at Tom. "They spilled onto our clean, white shores like vermin, like steerage rats, the garbage and scum of southern Europe, and our great nation stupidly accepted them. But that doesn't mean we want to marry them. We have our standards to uphold!" He nodded vigorously.

"Tell me, Tom," the dean continued, "are you familiar with Madison Grant's fine book, *The Passing of the Great Race,* which proves beyond the slightest doubt the biological inferiority of Mediterraneans? See, just look at her, she's nodding her head now just like a monkey."

I was not nodding my head. I had only bowed my head so that my tears might fall unnoticed.

"Listen to me, Tom. Statistics bear this out. Italians rank the lowest of all groups in their ability to speak English, the lowest in proportion of having children in school, and the highest in proportion of children forced to work. Nearly all Italians are socialists, anarchists, and thieves. As a race they have weak chins, low foreheads, little or no intellect, are short in stature, volatile, unstable, and lacking in any morality. We've opened up our arms to them and in response they've given us the Mafia and the Black Hand. They're a race of criminals! Look in her basket right now and I'll bet you'll find a knife!"

Tom's father opened my basket, then showed the dean my knife.

"Ha!" the dean said. "Living proof! Stripes on the zebra!"

"Don't forget the poem," Tom's father said.

The dean nodded behind his shining table. "Yes, yes, I haven't forgotten. Tom, I wanted to show you a humorous poem I found a few years ago in *Life* magazine." The dean pulled the magazine from a drawer beside his legs. "The poem is titled 'A Wop.'"

The dean cleared his throat and began reading:

"A Wop

"A pound of spaghett' and a red-a bandan'
A stilet' and a corduroy suit;
Add garlic wat make for him stronga da mus'
And a talent for black-a da boot!"

Tom's father applauded, then laughed so hard that his face turned red. Then he began to cough without control. He rolled his fingers into a tube and coughed into it, *hunhf hunhf hunhf,* jerking his shoulders and neck up and down just like a marionette in Sicily's puppet theater, the miserable comic wretch Mischinu, from the famous *Orlando* cycle of plays, set at a time when Palermu was the capital of a mighty empire that stretched from England to Jerusalem. Tom's foolish father tapped out with his shiny shoes a spastic dance on the wooden floor as wave after wave of coughing spewed from his chest, until he bent to one knee, holding his chest with one hand, and wheezed.

The boys of any village would have cheered his performance.

I could have touched him and tried to look for the vision that might have cured him of his illness, but I was too numb to move. Tears fell from my eyes of their own accord.

My Tom, well, something in what the dean said turned him into a puppet, too. He became made of wood, like a dead dry tree drained of all sap. His eyes stared vacantly, as if they were holes. Woodpeckers and termites would soon make a home in him.

Tom's father wiped his mouth with a handkerchief and tried

to catch his fleeing breath. The dean slid the magazine back into its drawer, then intertwined his fingers and stretched his arms forward, twisting his hands backward as he stretched. The sound he made with his knuckles was like crushed stone. The dean then stared at his fingernails until Tom's father reached inside his suit jacket and drew out a fat envelope, which he quickly handed to the dean.

"On behalf of the botany lab," the dean said with a smile, "you have our heartfelt thanks." He placed the envelope into the drawer with the poem. Then he reached across his shining table to shake my hand.

Of course I would not touch him.

It took great effort for me to resist spitting in his face, to not utter the dark curse he and all of his kind the world over deserve.

LOVE IS LIKE any plant you find growing wild. Discovering it is always special and rare. It's best to harvest it as soon as it is ripe, to share it with others if it grows in abundance, to enjoy it for as long as it is tender and fresh, to nurture it so that it may continue growing for the next to come along.

The machines with the whirling blades discovered Ziu Griddu's *carduni* field just as I did. I stumbled onto it that same afternoon. I was still weeping, walking wherever my feet took me. The workers had set their blades so low to the ground that they cut easily below the plants' crowns. I could hear the wild *carduni,* which had been growing on the land since before the time of the wide-spreading elms and oaks and maples, scream out in anguish and pain.

The colored men helped me walk to the shade of a large walnut tree near the mansion. They handed me a jug of water. "Drink," they told me. So I drank. They gave me a bandanna to wipe my brow.

"Hey," they said after I had stopped crying, "we know you." They gathered around me. "Sure, in the mornings we ride the same streetcar. You're the lady with the basket of plants."

"Yes," I said, "I'm the lady with the basket of plants."

Drops of sweat glistened on their skin like jewels.

"If you don't mind me saying," one of the men said, "in this heat a woman in your condition needs to be more careful."

I nodded, looking down at my abdomen that was obviously swelling, my breasts that were beginning to fill my blouse.

The *carduni* stopped screaming. It lay chopped in useless pieces all over the field.

"It will never grow back," I said, pointing to the field.

Already I could see the grasses that would be planted there, that would choke everything wild, the weeds and forgotten greens, the mosses and lichens, and that would be kept high enough to hide the cats lying in wait to kill the songbirds. The vision was so strong I had to squeeze my eyes shut.

Now you know why I have such a heavy heart.
I've watched love die, I've felt it torn apart.

Cavadduzzo the baker wants to share his sweet feast.
The proud pastry-maker has a tale about yeast.

Cavadduzzo's of Cicero

ℒ Gerlando Cavadduzzo

We use only the finest ingredients, everything top of the line. No short cuts. Nothing fake or artificial, imitation or second-rate. Our sugar is only the purest granulated. Our salt is the very best from the sea. You can sift through any barrel of our flour and see not one single gnat! Hey, there's a shop I won't name two blocks south of here they use a flour so full of flies the customers think the bread is poppy seed! Another shop I know cuts its flour with sawdust. In the name of Saint Rosalie, it's true.

Our flour is pure, one hundred percent wheat. Our milk and cream only yesterday were still part of the cow. That's one of the reasons why we moved out here to Cicero from the city, to be closer to the farmer. Our honeys—both dark and light—are so sweet that the beehives that produced them don't *zzzzz,* they *mmmmm.*

Our almonds—the taste floats on the tip of the tongue! Now, you don't want an almond that bites the tongue back. An almond should caress the mouth delicately, like a breeze swaying a new leaf on a tree. The same is true of cinnamon. There you aim for an elegant pungency, a somewhat sharper taste that also arouses the nose. A nut, bark, or bean should persuade and seduce the taste buds, never dominate or overwhelm. We select all our spices and flavorings with the utmost care. My Carla and I search constantly for new combinations. If only the mouth had time enough to sample them all!

Our vanilla is so silky that just its smell makes you think you're floating away on a cloud. Our cocoa bursts warmly across the tongue with an assurance as complete as an embrace. You know the three wise men who brought baby Jesù gold, frankincense, and myrrh? I think much better gifts would have been vanilla and almond, cinnamon and cocoa. What else, other than the Madonna's most sweet and holy milk, could have given the Child more delight?

We use only the purest butter, never oleo or lard. Even a goat's tongue can tell the difference. Butter lends a lightness to the dough that its greasy impersonators can't possibly match. We spare no expense.

Our eggs, they're so fresh we crack them when they're still warm from the hen. And clean! I scrub each egg with a little brush until its shell is so shiny it hurts my heart to have to break it. Of course, with food you can never be too sanitary. You're right, we could eat off the floor we're standing on. And your kitchen floor, too, I bet.

Here, have a taste. *Biscotti,* just five minutes out of the oven. Yes, yes, of course it's free. Free taste, the *Americani* way. Try it and believe me. You like? Isn't that one of the most delicious things you ever put in your mouth?

A dozen? Sure. Or maybe you'd like two dozen? This bag can hold two dozen, easy. Our *biscotti* never go stale, though your family will eat them up too fast to find that out.

Two dozen it is, and for your hard-working husband I'll throw in two extra. No husband? Go on! Not married? A knock-out like you? I can't believe it! You're pulling my leg!

THESE DAYS, IT pays to advertise. I talk to everybody who walks in, though the *mugghieri* don't let me go on a tenth as long. They know me well and have heard it all before.

"Cavadduzzo, Cavadduzzo," they say with a laugh, "you allow your tongue to gallop around too many words."

It's a joke on my name. I laugh along with them.

"If I wanted to hear a sermon," they tell me, "I'd go to church. For a speech I'd visit the alderman or drop by Bughouse Square!"

They're entitled to a smile after working all day: the women at home with their kids doing the cooking and washing and ironing, the men shoulder to shoulder in the factories, operating the complex machines of American industry.

Factory, home, shop—the difference is small. Work is work. Every shoulder drags a cross. Each head bleeds beneath its own crown of thorns. Everyone labors on one type of assembly line or another, doing the same things over and over every day, all day long, sunrise to sunset, day after day after day.

I remind myself of this whenever I grow weary, when it's four in the morning in the dead of winter and I want to remain curled in bed beside Carla's dark warmth, when it's summer—ninety-five degrees—and the temperature of my kitchen becomes so high I swear I'm baking, too, when I see a shortcut in a recipe and the devil whispers, hey, Cavadduzzo, listen to me, I know an easier way, no one will ever know, Cavadduzzo. In these moments when I'm tempted to make not the best loaf of bread I can but something merely passable, something the mouth will not too strenuously object to, I think of what it means that working people eat and depend on me. I pretend that my dear mother and father will break the next loaf, and then I think the same of their parents, then their parents. And when I'm so tired that even my great-grandmother Crucifissa's face doesn't encourage me, I make believe I've been selected as the baker for the Last Supper, and Jesù Cristu will hold my bread up in his hands.

"Mangiate," he'll say to the apostles.

Taking his example, I draw the next breath and continue.

.   .   .

STILL, MOST PEOPLE don't know quality unless you smack them with it in the face. They don't know what they want until you convince them that they want it. A man doesn't crave his own candle before God has suggested that he can be a saint. For the sake of the bacon, sometimes you have to tickle the pig's ass.

During our first months here we kept the front door open so as to lure any passers-by with the smell of our bread. I waited patiently by the cash register and watched. The people of Cicero walked down the street, head down, most of them fast, like busy people with a purpose, intent on getting where they wanted to go. You could see that their heads were full of this and that. Some mouths would mumble a steady intonation to the sidewalk. Other mouths would smile or frown, as if remembering better times. Then they'd get a whiff of my bread and hesitate, head whirling about, nose unconsciously sniffing the air. The nose would then compel the brain to order the feet to turn into Cavadduzzo's bakery, *now*.

Then they'd walk through our doorway, and even if they'd just left the evening table their mouth couldn't help but begin to water. Usually they'd overhear me talking to somebody as if the person was my best friend—and how will people ever become my friend if I don't treat them as one?—and then I'd see the stranger's mouth drooling and I'd offer the tempted soul a free taste, a sweet piece of whatever just came out of the oven, and three times out of five they'd walk out with not just a loaf of bread but a bag full of *biscotti* or perhaps a cake or pie or both.

People make a habit of buying from our shop. They learn the times of day when our breads emerge hot from our ovens. They assume a fresh loaf will always be waiting for them. In this business, timing is everything. You don't tell a woman with three kids at her ankles and a fourth in her arms rushing home to cook her husband's supper to wait. We strive to match supply to their demand. By day's end when we've guessed right we have five or six loaves remaining, just like Jesù Cristu with the loaves and fishes. As you know, after his sermon in the desert the apostles gathered up twelve baskets of leftovers. Not too bad when feeding thousands. The wise baker always ends his day with a little left over, and never disappoints by selling out.

After a while many form a favorite weakness, something special, for their sweet tooth, whenever they have an extra nickel. For many it's our *cannoli,* which I make two or three times a week.

Everybody wants me to tell them its secret.

"Cavadduzzo, Cavadduzzo," they implore, "every Christmas, Easter, and Saint Joseph's Day my dear wife makes *cannoli,* but hers are never quite this good. Do you have any hints for her?"

"Tell her not to go to all the trouble," I answer, "when she can always find them here."

"Cavadduzzo, Cavadduzzo," others continue, "you know I respect your privacy and in my wildest of dreams would never intrude, but please, tell me one thing. What sweetener do you use? And how much sugar and bitter chocolate do you blend into the cream?"

"Precisely the right amounts," I respond.

Sometimes they plead, wringing their hands. They fall down before me on their knees. They kiss my hands, feet, the hem of my apron. "Cavadduzzo, Cavadduzzo, trust me! I'll do anything on earth for you, please! I'll even name you godfather to my firstborn son! Just tell me the sweet secret to your *cannoli!*"

I make a big show of looking around, shushing them quiet with a finger to my lips, shutting the light, locking the front door, bringing them back into my kitchen by my ovens, clearing my throat, sipping a glass of cool water so as to facilitate movement of my vocal cords as well as lubricate my powers of memory, and then I have them place one hand over their heart as they swear never to tell anyone what I am about to say.

"My secret," I then whisper into their ear, "is use only fresh."

One man told me that as his great-uncle Federico lay on his deathbed he waved away the monsignor and in the delirium of his fever asked instead for my *cannoli*. No sooner had word of this request reached my ears than I had a boy in the neighborhood deliver to the unfortunate man a dozen of our finest *cannoli* in a paper box. The next morning I was informed by the grieving nephew that as the angels came down for the old man's soul he was polishing off the eighth *cannoli* and had bitten into a ninth!

Here was a priest offering a dying man Holy Communion, and he wanted instead just one more taste of the creamy sweetness that comes only from the kitchen of Cavadduzzo!

Perhaps I blaspheme. May God forgive me. But between you and me, the pews at Sunday Mass would be infinitely more crowded if the Pope used a crispier wafer and a sweet ricotta filling!

LET ME TELL you how Cavadduzzo's of Cicero began.

One day in our former shop, down on Chicago Avenue just west of Hudson Street, near Saint Philip Benizi's in Chicago's Little Italy, a man stopping by for a loaf of bread told me that he was moving to Cicero to work at a new factory being built there, Western Electric. Line work, he said, acceptable pay, assembling the earpieces of telephones.

Make mine loud, I said. The one we got here on the wall—I pointed to our shop's pay telephone—its receiver is way too low. Oh, he said, I can fix that easy. As I made change for his coin, he unscrewed all our phone's screws and was disconnecting the various different wires inside the piece you hold up to your ear. Of course we never heard one sound out of that telephone again, but in passing the man did say how much he'd miss eating our bread.

So I said, don't they have bakeries where you're going? And he said, what do you think, there's a Sicilian bakery on every street corner in *La Merica*? I said, perhaps not Sicilian but maybe Neapolitan. And he said, what do you think, there's a Neapolitan bakery on every corner? So I said, perhaps not Neapolitan but maybe Genovese. And he said, do you think there's even a Genovese bakery on every corner? Even every other corner? So I said, well, perhaps not Genovese, but maybe Tuscan. I hear the Toscani don't make too bad a loaf of bread. But not sweet, he said, with a sad shake of his head, not sweet like your Sicilian bread.

In truth there's no bread on earth as good or sweet as Sicilian, no higher compliment you can pay a person—living or dead—than to say that he or she's as good as bread.

I reached for a loaf and gave it a kiss as he again said, you know, I'll really miss this. Here, my friend, I said, breaking off the loaf's end, breaking off a piece for me, then pouring two glasses of chianti.

Any crust of bread, I said, is good if nourishment you lack. He knocked back his glass and said, maybe if you're sick or cold and dead, but since I'm still alive and hot I'll say there are some breads I would not want to put too near my face, and so I said, in this new place is there really no good bread? Go on, I said, you're pulling my leg.

He said, I beg you, listen, there's not even a Tuscan bakery there, and I said that the Toscani bake their share of decent bread. But not fair, he said, not rich and sweet like this!

God blessed this wheat himself!

Eat, I said, breaking off another piece.

At least today, he said, I'll feast and end up full. He pulled my sleeve and said, I grieve to think of the thousand and one *cristiani* just like me who'll work all day long in the hot factory in Cicero and trudge home to a table empty of good bread.

> He sighed, then with his fingertip wiped away a tear.
> "What I eat today," he cried, "may I eat next year!"

LATER IT BECAME clear to me that he was no ordinary man. Undoubtedly he was a messenger from God himself, most likely an angel or archangel whose earthly assignment was to get my feet moving down the path of my destiny. So of course I concluded that I had no choice but to journey to Cicero.

Then all at once the place's name hit me. "Cicero!" I shouted.

I threw my apron to the floor. With the heel of my hand, I gave my forehead a loud whack. The name itself seemed like a sign from God. I ran to the back of the shop to find Carla, who sat beside our warm ovens, sewing. "Can you believe it," I shouted, "here in the prairies of *La Merica* there's a town named for the famous Roman orator, statesman, and philosopher Marcus Tullius Cicero!"

Carla looked up calmly from her needle and thread. "Living all these years with you, Gerlando, I've come to believe even in green mice."

I paid her no mind. "Cicero!" I cried. "Known the world over for the rhythm and cadence of his sentences, his elegant diction, his skillful balance of antithesis, and several other oratorical qualities too numerous to recount or remember!" I'd always been a firm believer in the powers of oration, so I was careful to enunciate each of my consonants and vowels, creating a firm yet flexible hollow of my mouth, pushing breath up from my diaphragm while simultaneously gesturing with both hands and arms.

"See-sah-rro!" I sang, a cappella. Like cookie dough in sugar, my tongue happily rolled the *r*. "Carrr-lah," I crooned, "too-morrr-ow we jourrr-nee to See-sah-rrro!"

WEARING OUR FINEST clothes, we began at the Hawthorne Works gate and walked wherever our feet carried us, finding one less than adequate Czechoslovakian bakery and a pair of general groceries run respectively by a German and a Pole with rheumy eyes. None of these storekeepers comprehended the melodious tongue of Marcus Tullius nor any of its more muscular southern dialects. Ergo, Carla and I returned to the main plant, where we waited outside the gates until a squadron of whistles shrieked a somewhat less than ceremonious ending to the day shift. Then we let our ears be our guide, listening for the least scrap of Italian, until we found and then followed a pack of several young *cristiani* smoking twisted black cigars as they trudged home.

The men entered their doorways breadless, having stopped along the way home at no bakeries.

I asked Carla for her thoughts. She said she was still quite displeased that the angelic visitor had broken our telephone, and at the same time happy that this morning she'd thought to wear comfortable shoes.

"No," I said, "I mean about this place."

"I'd forgotten just how bad those cheap cigars stink," she replied. She waved a hand before her nose. "Gerlando, I'm so very glad you don't smoke."

"I leave that for my ovens," I said with a wink.

Once again we traced our steps back to the factory. In the meadows alongside the road, a hundred thousand grasshoppers soliloquized noisily, clinging to the swaying blades of wild grasses and weeds. "No bread," the chorus of grasshoppers sang. "No bread, no bread, no bread!"

"Maybe the broken telephone is a sign, too," I said. "Taken literally, it suggests that we should make no more calls from that box. At least here in the village of Marcus Tullius Cicero"—I pointed to Western Electric's huge Hawthorne Works complex—"if our telephone ever breaks again we'll know where to get it fixed!"

In the end Carla had to admit that the angel had been right about one thing. There was no place anywhere, no matter what direction you walked in, for the workers to buy a decent loaf of bread.

That is, until Cavadduzzo rode to the rescue!

SICILIANS ARE NOT too unlike the place from which they come. Being an island, Sicilia gives birth to people who often are islands themselves. As a people Sicilians tend to be withdrawn, generally looking inward rather than out at others and the world. Living on an island teaches you that everything useful and worthwhile and certain is inland rather than beyond and out on the dark, strange, forbidding sea.

After enduring endless centuries of plunder and humiliation from whatever exploiter was mighty enough to anchor its ships offshore, Sicilians grew to strongly suspect anyone they didn't know. Some say that our dialect, which those from the mainland find nearly unintelligible, came about as a form of defense or protection against outsiders. Even today it's not uncommon for a stranger asking directions from a Sicilian villager to be told that no such place exists, even though the village in question may be in plain view in the valley below, and the man from that very village.

Why trust the unknown when for thousand of years it's brought you mainly suffering and pain? You don't want to be on this side of the grave the day a foreign vessel drops sail off your shoreline. Its crew is anxious to commit the very actions that haunt your worst nightmares. The brutes are sure to rape your wife and daughters, kill or enslave your husband and sons, and steal whatever else they might desire, even food from the fists of the tiniest children. Avert your eyes if you like. These aren't pretty pictures. Truth seldom wears a ribbon in her hair.

We Sicilians feel our own isolation. We open our hearts only to our closest friends and families. Since Sicily is the Mediterranean's biggest island, perhaps you'll understand my belief that we have the region's biggest hearts. Our hearts cannot help but explode with a mixture of emotions just as Mungibeddu, or Mount Etna, Europe's only living volcano, creases the sky with lava and smoke. We have such fierce pride coupled with great sadness because *bedda Sicilia* is such a beautiful land, the land of our parents and ancestors, and yet our lives there were so harsh that we left it! Understand that only the most desperate of people do such a thing!

Hear me! We Sicilians here in *La Merica* are all a bit desperate, all a little crazy in the head, all the time going in at least a couple of directions, all proud and happy and eager to work and to please others and yet private and sad and split and confused, all in the same moment. Our feelings are like a *minestra,* the soup that we eat each day, made up of water and a pinch of salt and whatever else we can scrounge or find.

We resemble a *minestra,* too. In Sicily you can see hair of every texture and shade, skin color ranging from the darkest to the most fair, all evidence of the island's many invaders. Since the beginning of time Sicily has fed countless millions of people—from the Phoenicians and the Greeks, the Carthaginians and Romans, the Vandals and Goths, the Byzantines, the mighty Arabs who ruled for three centuries, to the Normans, the French, the Germans, the Austrians, and the Spanish.

Mark this. Whatever power ruled Sicily, ruled the world!

We Sicilians have outlasted and endured over two thousand years of foreign occupation, plunder, and slavery until we've become what we are now: a triangular bowl of rising dough routinely splashed by a miscellany of foreign seed.

You MAY HAVE noticed that I've yet to talk about seed, or about yeast, the curious organism that permits dough to swell and rise. Well, put the children and the priests and nuns to bed. I'll begin with the tale of how I got my name.

It began innocently enough back in Palermu, where my father owned the finest bakery on the Via Duca della Verdura—the Duke of Vegetable Street. As apprentice to my father, I worked all day long in the kitchen beside the hot ovens, responsible for maintaining the fires and keeping a watchful eye on whatever at the moment happened to be baking. My main duty was to avoid falling asleep. My favorite task was to put the loaves in the oven as I recited the benediction of the bread.

> *Bread, grow*
> *As the Madonna's belly swelled with baby Jesù!*
> *Grow, bread in the oven, grow*
> *As God's love expands throughout the world!*
> *May each crumb be healthy and nourishing,*

As pure as Saint Joseph!
May each crust be fragrant and full of flavor,
As generous as Saint Anna!
May each loaf be wholesome and sweet,
As inviting as Saint Francis!
May each slice be a tonic to those who eat it,
Just as the most merciful Saint Rosalie
Put an end to our plague!
Grow big, dough,
Big and long as the Holy Father's staff!
Saint Nicholas,
Let this bread swell and come out well!

One day I must have recited the prayer too loudly, or perhaps the Holy Father or Saint Nicholas got his aim wrong. Anyway, that morning more than just bread began to expand in the oven's stifling heat. So I went outside to douse the fire in my pants with a bucket of water. Watching me beside their baskets of fruit and vegetables were the men of Via Duca della Verdura.

"What are you doing there, young Gerlandu?" one of the dukes called out. "Giving your bean a spring bath?"

"No," said another, "he's only washing his little mushroom."

"It looks as if he's holding a cherry pepper," responded a third.

"No," said a fourth, "it looks more like a young eggplant, only not quite as dark."

"Eggplant?" the first duke cried. "Look at its size. The head's as fat as a peach!"

"No," said the second, "it's as broad as an artichoke!"

The third agreed. "It's some sort of squash or pumpkin attached to a thick vine!"

"And that's only the tip," said the fourth. "Look, I can't believe he's taking out more!"

"I never imagined such a melon!"

"Step back! The water's making it breathe!"

"There's no end to it! It's taller than he is!"

"It could knock down a church!"

"It's an oak tree, I swear!"

"See how it blocks out the sun!"

"If he leaned over a bit, I bet he could lick it like a cat!"

"No, that would be a grave sin."

"Yet one worth risking Hell for!"

"He'll need a second bucket if he wants to wash it all around!"

"There's not enough water in the sea!"

"What a door-knocker!"

"It will take a week to dry!"

"Look how he's able to push it back."

"Amazing! It collapses back inside his pants just like a concertina!"

"What music that instrument could play on a wedding night!"

"His bride would never want to stop dancing."

"It would take away her breath and more!"

"She'd never want to leave the sheets!"

"It would put even the mightiest horse to shame!"

At that moment a passing horse, hearing its name, *cavaddu,* whinnied long and loudly. And because I was a boy, only fourteen or fifteen, from that day on the men of the Duke of Vegetable Street called me Cavadduzzu, or little horse. They pounded my back and smiled whenever they saw me, in all ways treating me as their equal.

FOR EVERY BLESSING there's a curse.

God the Father must get bored all day long sitting on his throne up in Heaven hearing the archangels chant his praises. He must get restless every day eating his dry and tasteless wafers of flat bread. His boundless mind must be tempted to play tricks on his most pathetic of creations, man, the talking monkey who struts about the earth so falsely inflated with self-importance it's as if he doesn't have a stinking *culu* in his pants. What other explanation beyond an ironical disposition can there be for God's decisions regarding our fates? Why else would he mock me with such an imposing tool only to render its output ineffective?

Be sure that the men of Via Duca della Verdura took me to the most forbidden parts of Palermu, where the right coin could be exchanged for ecstasy beyond Christian imagination. At the century's turn Palermu was a pretty desperate place, thronging with people trying to put two twigs together and end up with a bundle. For the right price there was someone willing to do just about anything. I cast no stones. I make no judgments. I call no woman or man a whore. That's God's job. And that's why we have priests, to hear our confession and grant us absolution after we've wrestled all night long with mortal sin.

Sinning's a gamble, sure. Just before dawn, as soon as the last tingle is over, it's wise to pull up your pants and begin the search for a priest, hoping the devil and death don't find you first.

I was just a colt, not quite sixteen, but I grazed long and hard in those fields of pleasure, savoring each and every moment, until one night a droplet or two of my seed bounced off the wall or ceiling, somehow landing on the tongue of the sweet angel who lay beneath me calling out my name.

"Ca—" she cried, then all at once stopped. "Cavadduzzu, God made you with sugar instead of salt!"

I confessed I didn't understand.

"Taste," she said, smearing my mouth with some of the milk I'd puddled on her belly. "See? It's sweet. It's supposed to be salty, more like the paste of anchovies."

"Like anchovies?" I said, tasting my seed, quite amazed.

"Sure, men and women both. It's said we taste of salt and the sea because that's where we once came from."

"From the sea?" I said. "Go on. You're pulling my leg."

"If this is a leg," she said, "where is its shoe? Believe me, I know my business."

"As do I," I said. I then told her of my work in my father's bakery.

"Well, that explains it," she said. "As a youth you must have eaten too much sugar and honey."

"No," I told her. "I'm not permitted. My father would have beaten me senseless with his fists and belt and a dozen sticks if he had ever caught my fingers in the honey. I tended mainly to the ovens, making sure they were hot, then sliding in the bread, reciting the benediction, then pulling the bread out."

"From what I can tell," she said with a smile, "you've more than mastered *that* lesson. Believe me, Cavadduzzu, when it comes to delivering the loaf you're no apprentice."

Again I confessed I didn't understand.

"Ahh!" she said suddenly, slapping her forehead with her hand. "I know the answer! Of course! The heat from the ovens must have cooked and sweetened your seed!"

"Go on," I said.

"No, really," she said. "Believe me. The ovens cooked you."

"But I'm not made of bread," I protested.

"And yet like a loaf you rise and swell."

"A man is not bread," I argued.

"And yet during the Last Supper," she said, "when Jesù Cristu told the apostles to take and eat his body, he didn't hand out cheese."

"True," I agreed.

"He gave them bread. Bread was his body."

I nodded my head.

"Bread is sacred," she said, "as is the body."

Again I nodded.

"Without bread," she declared, "neither man nor woman could live."

I nodded a third time.

"And without a body," she said as she wiped the luxuriant length of her own with the bedsheet, "the soul would float away like smoke in the air."

"True," I agreed.

"So where would the body be without bread?"

"In the grave?" I guessed.

"Correct," she said. "And what would happen if you were to bury a piece of bread?"

"It would grow green with mold," I answered.

"Correct again," she said. "And what would happen after it grew green with mold?"

"Worms would crawl all over it and eat it."

"And what happens to the body in the grave?"

"It grows green with mold," I responded sadly, "and then the worms that sleep inside our guts wake and crawl out and eat us."

I wept for several moments into the soft folds of a pillow. The logic was complete and inescapable. My body was made of bread, and somehow I'd cooked it!

Then an even more fearful thought crept from my brain onto my tongue. "With seed sweet rather than salty," I said, "what temperament of children do you imagine I'll produce?"

"For that," she said, laughing and pulling the sheet between us, "you're mounting the wrong mare. You'll have to marry *una bona fimmina* to find the answer to that question."

So CARLA AND I married, of course after first finding each other agreeable. That she was passing through Palermu with her brother Luigi and his new wife, Ciccina, made our getting together infinitely simpler than having to endure the innumerable stages of courtship in her backwater village in Girgenti. One day the three appeared strolling down the Via Duca della Verdura just as I was taking a batch of *biscotti* from the oven for the second time. The smell proved irresistible to Luigi's long nose. Soon the three stood in my father's shop, each holding a plate of my warm *biscotti*. After several minutes Luigi was telling us that he used to steam couscous and bake bread for his companions in the hills, and as Carla and I exchanged glances, Luigi and my father discussed the difficulties higher altitudes present to yeast.

"Yeast is a most temperamental animal," Luigi proclaimed

with a smile. Already I could tell that he was the type of man who thought himself an expert on life. From the many lines around his eyes I imagined he'd seen his share of Hell, but from his deep laugh I guessed that he hadn't forgotten there was also a Heaven. He was a man who knew what it was to live, how to suck the juice from each moment and spit out what doesn't agree. So I nodded in assent at all he said, every now and then giving Carla a smile, then offered the trio coffee and a platter of my finest *cannoli*.

Carla did not immediately pull her hand away as mine brushed against hers when I set the platter down on the table. Again our eyes met and smiled. After Luigi ate the first *cannoli* and reached for a second and moments later a third, I knew his fair sister would be my wife. At that moment outside on the street, the salt-seller was singing.

> *"Sa-li a-iu! Sa-li!*
> *Cu vo-liu' sa-li?"*

> *Salt have I! Salt!*
> *Who wants salt?*

Knowing what I know now about my sweet seed, I should have run out onto the street. "Me!" I should have cried. "I want salt! Me! Me!"

ALL WENT WELL between Carla and me until the wedding night.

We knelt beside the bed, reciting our prayers. Afterward I stood, took her fair hands in mine and kissed her cheeks and lips, and then as was my habit proudly pulled off my nightshirt and with a flourish threw it to the floor.

"Aiieee!" shrieked Carla, stepping back.

"Don't shrink from me or hide your eyes," I said. "It's only a loaf of bread."

"Get away from me!" she screamed.

"As you like," I whispered, slipping my shirt back over my head and shoulders and down past my hips, "but, believe me, there's nothing here for you to fear."

"But your *cosa*!" she said, pointing.

"Remember that we are each made in God's image and likeness."

"Not the God that I kneel down before!" She made the sign of the Cross, then held her breastbone so as to catch her breath. "Mother of God, I thought the name Cavadduzzu was only a joke!"

"Don't tremble so," I said, sitting down on the bed beside her. "In matters of love God did not create anything forbidden or wrong, just as long as the heart is pure and both agree fully on the practice."

She shook her head. "I'm married to a horse!"

"If that's what you think, then I'll leave you and go sleep in the stables." I stroked the backs of her hands, kissed the soft insides of her arms, then walked to the door.

"Show me your feet," she demanded.

I lifted my nightshirt. "Don't fear me," I said. "See, my feet aren't cloven. I have five toes on each foot, just like you."

"Now your backside," she ordered.

"See," I said, pulling my nightshirt up further, "no tail."

I turned and bent before her so that she could inspect the crown of my head. "See, no horns. I'm human just as you are, though hardly half as divine, not a quarter as lovely as your gentle fingertips, as inviting as your alabaster arms, your luminous smile, almond eyes, rosy cheeks, raven hair, supple neck." I thought of a different adjective for each part of her body, slowly and lightly kissing each feature as I gave it praise, until Carla fluttered like a little bird within my arms.

"The hour's late," I whispered.

"I'll never lie with you," she sighed.

"Then we'll just sit together here on the bed," I said. I ran my lips again down her neck. "I'm a patient man. All good things in time. If not tonight, tomorrow. If not tomorrow, the next day."

"You'll never touch me," she said. "Never."

Her body was like wax, slowly melting. "No matter, my darling," I said. "If not the next day, then the day after the next day. There's no rush, Carla. If not the day after the next day, then the day after the day after the next. If not the day after the day after the day after—" Then I could no longer speak, for she was pressing her moist lips upon mine.

We fell back together on the bed as I kissed the throbbing stretch of her white throat, then stroked her dark and suddenly wild hair.

A BAKER HAS real cause to worry when the bread fails to rise.

After our first year together, Carla's belly was still as flat as any maiden's. We were living then in a third-floor apartment in New York's Mulberry District with Luigi and Ciccina, Gaetanu and Teresa, after having passed through Ellis Island, where they changed my name's ending *u*'s to *o*'s. Carla went to church and made novena after novena to the Madonna. I recited countless prayers to the saints. Now, the best thing about the saints is that there are so many of them. If one's no good you just move on to another. Carla worked the Madonna, and I worked the saints, going so far as to drop in on different churches at various hours in the day in the chance that perhaps their hearing might be better in one place than the next.

After we came to Chicago with Salvatore and Rosa, we told Assunta about our situation, and she agreed to try to help us. She rested her hands on Carla's belly, then on mine, then with her mortar and pestle prepared for us a gamut of cures mixed in clay. Carla and I pinched our noses and swallowed all that Assunta had to offer us. Several weeks later Carla sprouted a new set of molars, and I now have to shave twenty times a day.

Month after month passed, each without event. Nothing but anticipation grew in the garden of Carla's sweet womb.

"I've been thinking," I said one night to my beloved as we stood after kneeling together on the floor beside our bed reciting our prayers. "Maybe God is denying us children because of the manner in which we perform the act itself. Perhaps we each draw from it a bit too much enjoyment. It's possible that we've inadvertently given insult and as a result made the Madonna and the saints jealous."

"That's it!" Carla cried. "Of course the Madonna and the saints are jealous! Nearly all of them were virgins!"

"So from now on let's be like them, virgins," I suggested, though after several moments of thinking it over we recognized the obvious contradiction in that plan.

"Well," Carla said as we climbed into bed, "I still believe that's the solution. Perhaps it's our pleasure the saints object to. So let's try to perform the act from now on in a very holy and saintly way. Let's derive no pleasure from it."

I agreed with her fully. "No pleasure," I said.

"None at all," she concurred.

We shook hands on it, then put out the light and held each other in our arms and lay down together, embraced, and kissed.

"I'm deriving no pleasure from this," I said after a while. I had to grit my teeth to speak. "Absolutely none! None! None! None! None!"

"Nor am I," she cried, writhing beneath me in my arms. "Nor am I! Nor am I! Nor am *aiieee!*"

FINALLY I BECAME so desperate that I took the most extreme and reckless step any mortal man may in this life take. I went to see a doctor.

Now, my belief about doctors is simple. If you're sick you can stay home in bed sipping a bowl of soup, and you'll feel better in two weeks. Or you can go to a doctor and pay him for his time and a bottle of pills that, taken with soup and plenty of bed rest, if you're lucky will make you feel better in fourteen days.

Most of the time while the doctor's figuring out what's wrong, the patient turns green and dies. And while the dead man starts to stink and rot, the doctor runs out of fingers adding up the bill!

This doctor asked me to put some of my seed into a small cup. I told him if he waited until tomorrow I could bring him a whole jarful, but he said no, he needed a dollop while it was still fresh and warm. While my seed was still fresh, he separated some into six or seven glass tubes and added drops of this and that to make the liquid change color. Of course I knew this display was only a circus for my benefit, a show designed to convince me that he was an expert at his job. He wanted me to think he was earning my money. But then he put a droplet of my seed on a rectangle of glass and inspected it beneath his microscope.

He explained that inside each seed there exists the whole baby, perfectly formed, though extremely small and curled up and hungry. Each seed comes equipped with a tail that enables the baby to swim toward the mother's egg, he explained. The mother's egg is like a big omelet, the doctor said, feeding the baby and lasting for nine months, during which time the child grows. When the entire omelet's eaten, the thirsty baby claws its way out of the womb in search of some milk.

"Hey," I said, "what do you make me out to be, a rube fresh off the boat? Tell me something I don't know."

He viewed my droplet of seed, noisily sucking his front teeth for the longest time, then turned to me and let out a long sigh.

"You don't have any swimmers," he announced.

The room suddenly drained itself of air.

"You are most certainly wrong," I told him. I pushed out my chest and stood tall. "You must be mistaken. I am Gerlando Cavadduzzo, from the Via Duca della Verdura in Palermu." I stood on my tiptoes and thumped my chest. "I know for a fact that my seeds swim with the very best."

"Perhaps your seeds once did," he told me, "and perhaps one day they will again, but they don't now. Look for yourself." He gestured toward the microscope. "I've never seen a case quite so bad," he continued. "It's like a little cemetery down there. Your seeds are as still as tombstones."

I put my eye to the tiny hole of light at the top of the tube and saw at the other end a bluish sea scattered with what looked like tiny, motionless ships. Their smashed and broken hulls floated silently in the water. After the doctor showed me how to reposition the glass slide, I explored the ocean below, searching vainly for anything that might show the slightest sign of being alive.

I found an island, triangular in shape, surrounded by a thousand and one invading ships. "That's only a bubble of air," the doctor told me when I showed it to him, though when I looked at it again I could see clearly that he was wrong. I was able to make out the tip of San Vito Lu Capu, Marsala, Sciacca, the long coast of Agrigentu, Gela, Puzzallu, Pachinu, Siracusa, Catania, Taurmina, Messina, Milazzu, Sant'Agata di Militellu, Cefalù, Bagheria, and Suluntu.

Then I sighted my hometown, Palermu. A cascade of tears blurred and tumbled from my eyes. I adjusted the focus and after a few moments saw the Duke of Vegetable Street and my father's bakery. Outside on the street stood overflowing baskets of fresh mushrooms and cherry peppers, eggplants and squash and watermelons. I waved a hand to my old friends.

Then again my eye searched the sea. My eye moved past the long-dead ships of the Phoenicians, Greeks, Carthaginians, Romans, Goths, Vandals, Byzantines, Arabs, Normans, French, Germans, Austrians, Spaniards. Their crippled hulls cluttered the unhappy waters around my island.

Finally, all by itself out in the middle of the gray Atlantic, steaming its way hungrily toward the promise of the Golden Land, I spied a lone ship gamely wriggling its little head.

"Figghiu miu!" I cried.

Then the rotten piece of meat with eyes who dared to call himself a doctor examined it and said it was as dead as stone, that its apparent motion was due entirely to the fearful trembling of my hands.

• • •

SHOULDERS SAGGING, I dragged my carcass home, where my dear Carla was pacing the wax off the kitchen floor. As usual she'd mixed the dough for the afternoon loaves, but for some reason today the dough failed to rise. Good Lord, I thought, this is the last thing I need. Around her lay a dozen trays of flat, barren dough.

"I don't know what I did wrong," she said, holding back her tears. "Please don't be angry with me."

I took a deep breath, then smiled at her and kissed both her hands. "My dearest Carla," I said, "only a fool could be angry at a saint."

"But today's business—" she said. "It's a Friday. You know how well we sell on Fridays. We're hours and hours behind! You were gone so long at the doctor's! Gerlando, look at the clock! The three o'clock whistle's about to blow!"

"The hour's of no importance," I replied. "Did I ever tell you how grateful I am to you for being my wife all these years and putting up with me and my many faults, and for devoting so much of your time to our business?"

She sniffed my breath. "If you're not drunk you must have been walking too long in the sun. What do you mean, the hour's unimportant? For a bakery, timing's everything! Open your eyes! Look at all I've ruined."

"My darling," I said, "my eyes are wide open. I see clearly probably for the first time in my whole life. Believe me, you've ruined nothing."

She shook her head. "I can't for the life of me think what I did wrong."

"You did nothing wrong," I said. "You're not at fault here, Carla."

"I must have offended the saints," she said, turning from me and twisting her apron in her hands. "That's the only logical explanation I can come up with. You know how I sometimes get all those couplets of the bread prayer confused. Maybe I rushed through the benediction or recited a few of the words out of order."

"No, my jewel, my treasure, my long-suffering companion." I took her hands in mine and again kissed them. "Please understand what I'm saying. There's nothing wrong with you. It's my fault, not yours. You never gave the saints offense."

She pushed me away. "How can you remain so calm? Can't you hear what I'm saying? It's Friday! Today the workers are paid!"

"Then they'll take their rich pockets to the Czechoslovakian. Or they'll go without." I looked at my Carla, then at the empty ovens, then back at Carla. The flesh of my heart began to break. "Please," I said, "if you don't mind, leave me alone for a little while. I must be by myself for a few moments. Please go into the shop and care for the customers."

I locked the door, then shut the lights and fell to my knees, sobbing. My tears dripped saltily down my cheeks and into my mouth. For a dark moment I wondered if I should take my life so Carla could be free to have children by some other, more virile man. I looked around for a long knife I might use to stab myself with and then slice out my beating heart. At that moment there was a sharp banging on the door.

"Gerlando," Carla cried, "the workers say they'll wait!"

"Tell them there's nothing to wait for," I shouted back. "Tell them the tragic news. The seed is all dead."

"Don't talk crazy," Carla shouted back. "Already the workers are standing in line."

"You don't understand! There's nothing I can do! My seeds are like tombstones in a cemetery!"

"Don't talk nonsense!" she screamed. "You've never failed before! Have faith. Say the prayers. Through all the years we've been together, your bread has always risen!"

"But Carla, I'm not talking about bread! I'm talking about you and me!"

"I'm talking about you and me, too, Gerlando!" she shouted. "Don't give up hope! You know how to do it! Start with a clean, warm bowl. Measure the flour. Recite the prayers. Try again!"

So I lit the candles that flanked my statue of Saint Joseph and started from scratch, measuring the flour and the water, and so on. I mixed the ingredients and then kneaded the dough carefully, reciting every prayer my father ever taught me. I gently separated the dough into graceful mounds. These I carefully covered with warm towels as I repeated my prayers.

It was to no avail. Clearly a curse had fallen on my kitchen. The toweled dough drooped as flat as sewer lids.

I unlocked the door to the shop. A crowd waited patiently before the counter, stretching like a serpent out the door and onto the sidewalk. I raised my hands for their silence.

"My dear friends and neighbors," I began, "I am exceedingly sorry to inform you that this humble bakery, Cavadduzzo's of Cicero, which has had the supreme and unsurpassed pleasure of serving you and your loyal families for lo these many years, is hereby and henceforth, from this day forward, closed. Please return to your homes. Due to tragic circumstances, there will be no bread today."

"No bread today?" they said, shocked and disbelieving.

"My ears deceive me! What did he say?"

"Mother of God, no! No bread?"

"I am grievously sorry," I said, "to be such a bitter disappointment and so grave and absolute a failure to those I so deeply and dearly love." I looked at my Carla's face until a wash of tears obliterated my sight.

I knew the crowd witnessed my tears, which soon grew to thunderous sobs, but I was unashamed.

"We're sorry," they told me as they left. "We're so sorry. So sorry. Whatever the situation, you have our sympathies, our sympathies."

The crowd fell into a hush as they exited, and then I could hear them talking outside on the sidewalk.

"Did you see him cry? What a display!"

"I've never heard a man issue such moans and wails. He could make a fortune as a hired mourner!"

"He wept as copiously as Niagara Falls! I saw it once! They make you wear a raincoat to get near it!"

"He must be in great shock. His face was as white as a nun's bedsheet."

"Of course, he must be grieving for someone he loved."

"That's it! There's no bread today because somebody in his family died."

"His wife has family living back in the city, in the projects near Saint Philip Benizi."

"That's it! There must have been a terrible accident! They must all be dead!"

"No, he's not rushing out to grieve over them. He went back inside. That means that someone back in Sicily must have died!"

"I kept hearing a telephone ringing as I stood there waiting in line. I knew it wasn't just in my ears!"

"That's it! He must have received a telephone call."

"Yes, it was a member of his family."

"Somebody back in Palermu."

"A brother, sure. Somebody said his brother."

"His twin brother, of course."

"He's closing the shop for the funeral, out of respect."

"Did you hear? Cavadduzzo's brother is dead!"

"Oh, darkest of days!"

"Oh, woe and despair!"

"Better him than me!"

"Touch iron!"

"The saints have mercy! Did you hear the news? Cavadduzzo's twin brother has departed and is no more!"

"I know already. I heard it this afternoon. The entire Via Duca della Verdura in Palermu is draped tonight in black."

"Gerlando's poor heart must be broken into two."

"Of course, Cavadduzzo's of Cicero will be closed for three days, out of respect."

• • •

THAT DARK NIGHT I held Carla in my arms until I could hear her soft snores, and then I went down the stairs and locked myself in the kitchen. All that night I grieved, weeping so profusely that my tears washed clean the floor. A pod of blue whales could have drowned in my tears, I shed so many. There are not more drops in all of the Mediterranean Sea.

At four o'clock the next morning, my eyes popped open out of habit. I found myself sleeping on a table in the kitchen, which without the heat of my ovens felt as cold and damp as a grave. Curse or no curse, I arose and fired up my ovens and began as usual to make bread, measuring the flour and mixing the et cetera, separating the dough into et cetera, reciting et cetera to Saint Et Cetera.

The morning dough remained as flat as the earth before the voyages of Columbus.

Don't panic, I cautioned myself. What distinguishes man from the lower animals is that man has the potential to think even when he has to itch his ass. So I devoted the rest of the morning to scratching my cranium for some idea that might spark my yeast into a bubbling froth.

I had no doubt whatsoever that the problem concerned my yeast. Like most bakers I kept a variety of yeasts in stock in the event one should become temperamental or go bad. These I tested with some warm water and a bit of sugar. Each yeast foamed up just fine.

Now, you know that yeast is just like an old man with a sweet tooth. If you offer him only flour and water, he'll do nothing but sit in the shade and snore. But if you want him to get up and plow a field or draw water from the well or pick tomatoes for the evening sauce, you have to coax him with something extra. You slip him some grains of sugar or a few drops of honey or molasses. Then after he's started eating the sweets, he can't help himself and begins feeding so happily on the wheat flour that he begins belching, which in turn causes the dough around him to expand and grow.

All afternoon I worked, coaxing the yeast, mixing it with various sweeteners. Every time I added the flour—*phhttt,* like a flat tire. I worked all Saturday evening, into the early hours of the night. No bowl I owned went unfilled.

I tried sugar (granulated, powdered, brown), honey (every shade from dark to light), molasses, corn syrup, maple syrup. Each dough remained as lifeless as Lazarus.

AGAIN I SLEPT on the hard slab of my table, until just before four on Sunday morning, when I had a most peculiar dream.

I dreamed I was a boy again, out on the town with all of the dukes of Vegetable Street. Everything was the same, except that Palermu had somehow sunk beneath the sea. It made sense in the dream. We all had to swim by wriggling our tails. In my dream the dukes and I and everybody were having a great race.

They swam far ahead of me, laughing, coaxing me to catch up with them. I knew somehow that if I lagged behind all would be lost and I'd be forgotten and dead. So I wiggled as fast as I could, slipping farther and farther behind until they disappeared in the darkness, and then I began to fall into a terrifying void that I somehow understood would be without end.

In my dream I tried to scream, but then a beautiful lady with dark hair and eyes and graceful white wings like a butterfly caught me. She caressed me, telling me not to worry. The dukes' race isn't important, the beautiful lady said. She held my face to her breasts and said swimming was not to be my destiny.

"Lie still," she whispered to me. "Don't wiggle your tail or try to move. Allow yourself to listen to your own silence. Be who you are. Accept your true fate, which is to lie still and be surrounded by water. Be like an island." She sketched a three-sided island in the air. "Try to be like the egg that calmly remains in place rather than like the restless, ever-wandering seed."

"But kids," I said. "I want sons and daughters. Carla and I—"

She bared one of her breasts and placed its nipple into my mouth to silence me.

"Gerlando," she said, with a voice I knew was my dear mother's, "your kids are all those who eat of your bread."

THEN THE ANGEL transformed into Carla, who in the darkness hovered over me saying it was perfectly all right if we didn't have any children, she loved me just as I was, at the same time stroking me in my dream or actual life or perhaps only in God's wildest imagination, causing the little horse for which I was named to rise up on his hind legs and with a shudder whinny furiously, causing the Mungibeddu on my island to erupt, shooting into the air a dozen arcs of seed which I could hear splash on the floor as well as into one bowl which held a portion of yeast cake, which within moments began to bubble. Somehow, in my excitement and confusion over awakening in so unorthodox a manner, I accidentally knocked this bowl over into a larger bowl containing flour, water, and salt. These ingredients I then mixed together without thought after I put on the kitchen light and lit my morning candles to Saint Joseph.

Though I could hardly trust my eyes, the morning dough appeared to rise.

As was my habit I then kneaded and separated the dough into loaves, then with a sharp knife scored each with three crosses.

> In the name of the Father,
> and of the Son,
> and of the Holy Ghost.

I ran then from the kitchen, leaving the dough to fall flat or to rise again, according to its destiny.

I UNLOCKED THE door and left my shop, walking about the dark streets of Cicero. Other than me, only the songbirds were awake. My tale might be better if I said I stopped by a church and bowed my head and prayed, but in truth I attend Mass only twice a year, on Christmas and Easter morning. Still, it felt a bit like Easter morning, with the promise of spring in the chill air. I listened to the chirping birds and the sound my shoes made on the roadway, thinking of my father's shop in Palermu and how I should put my shop up for sale now that I'd lost my ability to be a baker. I'll go to the Hawthorne Works tomorrow, I decided, and ask for a job of any kind. Perhaps my future was in telephones.

My feet took me in a circle, like a pair of old horses eager to return to the barn. After an hour or so I found myself at the start of my street.

Something's wrong, I thought. The front door of my shop was open! Somebody had broken in! Thieves! Murderers! Oh dear God, I thought, somebody's stolen the cashbox and murdered Carla in her bed!

Instead she'd simply opened up the shop for the day. When she saw me she shouted, "It's risen! It's a miracle! Alleluia! It has risen! Bread!"

ALL THAT SUNDAY my customers poured my ears full of praise, saying that my loaves had never before been quite as sweet and delicious.

"I don't know what you did," they told me, "but this new bread, it has a peculiar richness—"

"A delicate flavor—"

"No, it's more of an integrity—"

"A wholesomeness—"

"A certain fullness of texture—"

"It isn't a sourdough, is it?"

"No, it's more of a sweet undertaste—"

"A quite abundant flavor—"

"My widowed aunt ate an entire loaf by herself!"

Over the next week business in my shop doubled, then like a dough rising doubled once again. "This new bread's a dream!"

everyone told me. "Whatever you do, Cavadduzzo, don't go back to your old recipe!"

Of course in time I returned to more conventional means of feeding my yeasts, though maybe every other year, on the most special occasions. . . .

Isn't the body—plant or animal—the source of all food? Doesn't the mother feed her children with secretions from her breast? Isn't honey the saliva and regurgitation of countless thousands of bees? What is an egg if not a cleverly packaged menstruation?

How can the male body offer another life? If we can happily chew a tasty nut, which in truth is nothing less than a form of a tree's seed, why not a man's?

Why shouldn't a man imitate Jesù, who at the Holy Supper gave bread to his friends saying, "This is my body, take ye and eat"?

> *Knowing God sweetened my seed to help my bread grow*
> *Gives me all I need: Cavadduzzo's of Cicero.*

> *Now Ciccina's girl Anna recites her dark story*
> *Of how the black Madonna came to her in all glory.*

Caesura

✿ Rosa Dolci

THEY SAY THAT sometimes on nights like this, with a newly waxing moon, the dead souls rise from their graves and join us here around the fire. Don't be afraid, unless you have done one great harm. The dead are to be remembered, not feared. As long as we keep them in mind and repeat their names, they retain the ability to live among us if and when they choose. On nights like this they're free to mingle with us, sometimes taking form: the distant echo of a laugh or cry, a passing shadow, a once-familiar odor drifting through the night air. Sometimes you'll hear a dead soul faintly call your name, as if you were a child being summoned in from play. Or a dead soul might make its presence known through a persistent image or dream. After my mamma died, I dreamed on consecutive nights that she wanted a drink of water. For seven days I carried a full bucket from the village well to her grave.

If you think of memory as a field of vision, the dead stand just at the edge of view. You can avoid looking at them if you like. You can live your life like a bull with a single purpose, to charge forward into what can be plainly seen. There's no law that says you can't be a dunce. But if you're bright you learn to look at what can't be clearly seen. So cross yourself and say some prayers for all you know who are dead. Forgive them every trespass. Remember something pleasant about their life, and share the story with your children so that it, and they, may live. Bid the dead comfort and rest. And if you're a real saint, add a prayer for those who are forgotten.

See, the dead are not that different from you and me, once you really start to think about it. What makes someone a person? It can't be only that they have a body. Am I not the same person if you cut off my hand? Both hands? Cut off both my legs, too, and take my eyes, ears, nose, my imperfect lip. You can whittle me down to a nub and I'll still be Rosa. It's the same for the dead. The mere act of dying doesn't negate their having been a living person with worries and concerns, wants and needs.

Sometimes a soul dies too fast and gets caught between dying and finishing a thing. I know of a woman who dropped dead while making linguini and could not rest in peace until each strand was boiled and eaten. I know of a man who tumbled off the roof of his house and walked uneasily through it until his grandchildren climbed up there and hammered down the last row of nails he had set.

These ruins here in the valley, they attract the dead from all across the province. They're a magnet. The ruins are powerful enough to lure even the drowned from the sea. The dead find the ground of a church or temple, anywhere that has once been the site of prayer, especially comforting. Prayers don't just float up into the sky, into God's ears, like noisy smoke. No, prayers sink into the earth as well, into the soil and rocks and stones. Stone holds prayer particularly well, much better than water or fire or air. That's why we put stone on graves, because it endures, and because it can hear our prayers and hold them. Stone is exceptionally good at holding things in. You can crack a plain rock and find inside it the most splendid crystals. At night when the air is cool, you can turn over the most humble stone and feel some of the day's warmth emanating from within. And if you hold a stone up to your ear and listen carefully enough, you can hear everything that the stone has ever heard said.

That's why the moon is more special than the sun, because the moon is a stone that has seen and heard everything that has ever happened on earth. The moon has witnessed each being's birth and death, and all that has occurred in between. She knows every event and secret. That's why she keeps facing the earth the same way. She's a mother who will not turn her head away from her children. And that's why she changes her face and each month disappears only to wax again new, as she does now. It's to show us that even though a thing sometimes can't be seen, nevertheless it may still and always be with us.

As I will still be with you, even after the hour of my death.

As you will still be with your children, after your hour.

The Black Madonna

ℒ Anna Girgenti

I'M TOLD THAT in old Palermo during the year or so before my parents made the journey to America, my mother, Ciccina Agneddina, was fond of frequenting a marketplace known as the Capo. After winding her way along Palermo's twisting streets and narrow alleyways, she could find herself inside a square facing the Panificio Morello storefront upon which remains to this day the most breathtaking Art Nouveau mosaic in the known world.

The mosaic depicts a woman in a layered, multicolored dress, its hem studded with squares of gold. The woman stands barefooted, left arm raised, head sideways, right arm cocked at the elbow, palm up, giving the appearance that she's setting into motion a series of orbs that nearly encircle her. The expression on her face is cool and inviting. Her hair is dark and stylishly clipped. Though I have only several photographs scissored from magazines, the pictures are clear enough to present the piece's intention: an image of woman as creator.

Now that I'm older, let me confess that my life's main regret is that I never traveled to Palermo to see the mosaic for myself. I never recited a rosary in memory of my dear mother at the cathedral across the square. I never prayed to its statue of Saint

Anna. I never walked the ground my mother walked at this dark century's bright and hopeful beginning. I've long imagined how it would feel to genuflect in precisely the spot that my mother once genuflected. I know I'd recognize that she'd been there. I've long imagined how the mosaic's quiet beauty must stand in contrast with the noisy, vulgar life teeming in the square. Many nights as I lie in bed unwilling to sleep, praying with a burning urgency so that the Madonna's predictions of worldwide cataclysm might be forestalled, my fingers drop my beads and reach out to touch the image of her that hovers before me. I picture the image she imprinted on Mother Superior's closet wall, and then my imagination transforms it to the one cemented to the bakery's facade. Then, as if I'm somehow outside my body looking down on someone else, I see myself kneeling before the mosaic in old Palermo.

I observe a young woman with dark eyes and clipped hair as she stands and reaches forward to touch the mosaic's cool surface. Now, instead of me, the figure is my mother, Ciccina. She presses her palm against the figure's heart, then kisses her thumb and makes the sign of the Cross. Then she bends and kisses the figure's feet. Then that image fades and I see myself kneeling in the rear pew of the orphanage chapel at the feet of the *Madonna nera,* the black Madonna, who revealed herself to me seven times over a span of seven days decades ago when I was fourteen years of age.

They say that at age eighteen my mother visited the mosaic each day as the tiles were laid. According to these stories, told to me in bits and pieces by my aunts, my young mother influenced the artist so greatly that in the middle of the project he altered his design and gave the figure the likeness of my mother's face. This so enraged my father that he threatened to smash the tesserae with a length of pipe until the artist was able to prove that his relationship with my mother was pure, his intentions benign and honorable.

One version of the story claims that since the artist was one of the cathedral's castrati he sang the "Ave Maria" and then displayed to my father his hairless face and chest. Another account has my father pursuing the singer into a shop where the man proved he was *un castratu* by singing notes so high they cracked the glass of seven crystal goblets. In another story the artist proves his innocence by running into a nearby alleyway, unceremoniously dropping his trousers, and displaying to my father the absence of what enraged him.

They say that during the confrontation my mother waited across the square in the Cathedral of Sant'Anna. They say that each day for fourteen days she knelt beneath the statue of Saint Anna, begging the Virgin's blessed mother to intercede on her behalf. The stories claim that my mother made a vow to Saint Anna that if the artist and his mosaic were kept from all harm, my mother would baptize her firstborn daughter in the generous saint's honor.

Thus, these tales claim, the mosaic was saved and I was named.

SOMETIMES I DECIDE that cracked goblets and lengths of pipe, the artist and my jealous father, have nothing whatsoever to do with my mother's story. Can't there be stories in which men are absent or do nothing? Consider all the tales in which the woman's main contribution is to wait idly by a window, hold a broom and sweep, stir a pot of sauce, say "I do," or weep in sorrow for a man. After all, isn't the main point of the Blessed Virgin Mary's story that woman doesn't necessarily require a man? That all by herself, without a man, *immaculately,* woman is able to create and birth a perfect thing?

I've been told that the mosaic's tiles were already set onto the storefront's wall and that my mother's face was imprinted on the design as a sign to sinners to repent. That's one of the reasons why she makes so many visitations on earth, so that we who stumble so blindly about this dimension of our existence don't forget her.

I mean the Madonna, the third of God's three faces, not my mother, whose lovely face can still be seen today in the tiles in

Palermo's Capo Square, where it's possible that some visitor at the very moment you hear these words is remarking, "Just look at her! What an absolutely beautiful face! How utterly calm and serene!"

But I'm getting ahead of my story.

I SHOULD BEGIN in New York City, in the flat we shared with Ziu Tannu and Zia Teresa and their countless children. Zia Teresa used to say that all Tannu had to do was hang his pants on the nail on the back of their bedroom door and in a week she'd drop twins or triplets. Ziu Tannu would laugh and say that as long as the oven was hot it only made sense to bake two or three loaves at a time. Twins ran in his family, he said. He claimed to have inherited the double-headed seed. Tannu had been a twin, though his poor infant brother tangled his neck in the birth cord and lived barely long enough to feel the trickle of baptismal water on his forehead. Papa Santuzzu, who sired my twin aunts, Rosaria and Livicedda, had been a twin, too, his brother also dying at birth.

Ziu Tannu had weak lungs, though Zia Teresa claimed he was once as mighty as the fiercest bull before he was taken away to fight the Great War and repeatedly exposed to mustard gas. That was on top of their years of work at the mills in Lawrence. Whatever the cause, it was clear to anyone that Ziu Tannu's lungs sucked in barely enough air to keep a goldfish alive. His mouth gasped like a swimmer's at the water's surface. Periodically a spasm of coughs would rattle his frame, and he'd wheeze and pant like a dog left out in the July sun. After a while nobody else in the house could breathe right. Soon all his kids were imitating him, choking wetly into their fists. During the years I lived with them, I covered my mouth and nose with a kerchief like a bandit and kept my distance from everybody.

Ziu Tannu grew so skinny inside his clothes that from behind sometimes you thought he was one of the children until he turned around and you saw his puckered old man's face. Zia Teresa pulled on his trousers and went out looking for work each day in his place. That put an end to the annual tide of twins and triplets. Then a man from some governmental agency said that Ziu Tannu had to be taken upstate to a tuberculosis sanatorium, and half of their kids would have to go along with him, so Teresa and her river of coughing doubles surged out the door, and my father and I were left in the flat all alone. This was during the years people called the hard times.

I remember I was always hungry. I remember I was always unhappy and cold. The flat was so cold that first winter alone that my breath hovered in the air before my face like a persistent ghost. Even the inside walls iced over. The far corner of the front room, where I burned a candle before my mother's shrine, flickered so brightly with frozen ice that it resembled the shiny wet inside of a cave.

We had no electricity so we lit the place with a couple of lamps—that is, when we had oil. To cook and to warm the place we used a coal stove. I'd feed the stove little pieces of coal, praying to each lump to last for all eternity before I offered them to the flames.

> *Oh blackest coal, burn long and slow!*
> *Warm my poor body with your red glow!*

I'd pretend each bit of coal was a sinner, and I was the saint in charge of sending their souls to Hell. I'd line up their sin-stained spirits in the shape of a cross on the shovel I used to scoop their ashes, then swing the stove's grate open and cast the evildoers to their just fate.

> *I bid thee, devils, go to Hell!*
> *Heat God's good angels long and well!*

I'd bang the side of the soup pot with my mother's wooden spoon, demanding that the empty pot fill itself up at once. When the pot didn't obey me, I'd throw myself on the floor and kick my feet and pound my fists and scream until the misery I was causing myself was greater than the grief that throbbed within me. I'd cry, "Mamma, Mamma," over and over again until my cry became a single endless groan. I'd do it until my head was aching and the floorboards beneath me would float and I'd forget who and where I was.

Sometimes my father would try to hold or comfort me, but I'd punch and kick him away. I'd scratch his cheeks and claw his eyes until I heard a string of dark curses rise beneath his breath. Then he'd do what I wanted him to do, or what I most desperately didn't want, which was to grab his jacket and rush out the room, slamming the door as loudly as he could when he left. He'd always return some time later—whether it was a few hours or several days later I can't remember—with a couple of turnips or onions, a bunch of carrots, some celery, a few soft potatoes or old tomatoes, whatever was cheapest or what he could scrounge or perhaps steal. Then I'd make the floor stop floating and see if there were any more sinners I could banish to Hell while he filled the pot with water for soup. I'd get the knife and chop the vegetables, praying to them to last a long time.

Food, I command thee, fill up this pot!
Remain brimming till we're hungry not!

For supper that night we would eat only the clear broth, saving the vegetables for the next day when we'd add more water and then again eat only the broth, saving the vegetables for the third day when we'd add water and again eat only the broth, and so on, for as long as something that resembled soup lasted, adding more and more water until nothing but the memory of soup remained.

I was a scrawny thing then, with long tangled hair the color of coal and legs like two lead pencils sticking out from the bottom of my gown. Inside I was tough, a thick elastic band, as fierce as any alley cat. Sometimes when my father was out scrounging for food I'd pretend I was an alley cat and crouch beside an open window, yowling. I'd scratch my fur with my front paws, then pounce on my shadow that leapt on the icy walls. Sometimes I grew in power and became a lion. I'd roar and roar and roar and roar until my voice was hoarse.

That was how I discovered the first tasty spot. One day like a cat I licked my hand, then out of thirst the ice on the wall, and then the icy wall again and again and again until the paint on the wall disappeared and the grayish plaster beneath began to soften. It was very easy to allow my nails to scratch out the first real taste. Soon I had no difficulty whittling out entire spoonfuls of wall.

In the beginning I ate wall only until my stomach tightened with cramps. Then I sat by my window, howling happily with pain. I didn't mind the pain. The pain made me feel alive. The pain was my friend and companion. The pain was my sister. Later I allowed myself only one mouthful of wall at a time, usually at night when it was dark and no one could see me, and only after my father was sleeping.

I crunched the wall slowly, in rhythm with my father's resonant snores, relishing each delicious morsel of grit. Then I'd sit again by my window smacking my lips and sucking my cat teeth, contented.

Though I was often tempted, I never ate from the wall on which hung my mother's shrine. I was afraid that if I did, the wall might fall down and my mother's soul would tumble into Hell like the unlucky coals. I knew that my mother was in Heaven and that Heaven was never-ending, for always and ever with never an end: a sweet pear that couldn't be reduced to its core no matter how many bites were taken, a pot forever full of vegetables and noodles and even fat pieces of meat.

The shrine held my mother's picture and a lock of her hair mixed with a few strands of my baby brother Petru's hair, which

was as black as india ink and finer than eyelash. Beneath the
picture there was a crucifix and the next several beads of a broken
rosary, still bound by the tight links of their chain. Beside the
beads there was a blue cloth flower I found on the street, and a
painted plaster likeness of the Virgin Mary from a set of Nativity
figures I once saw scattered on a dime store shelf. When no one
in the dime store was looking, the Virgin stuck fast to my palm
and wouldn't let go no matter how hard I tried to shake her from
my hand. Then she climbed up my wrist into the fold of my sleeve
so as to allow me to walk out of the store empty-handed. It was
my sacred duty to dust the ledge on which these tokens rested
and to tend to the shrine's candle, which I vowed to the Holy
Mother would burn uninterrupted in my mother's honor and
memory for ten years.

In truth the candle burned only a few hours each evening, a
few evenings each week, and only when there was sufficient wax
and wick to light it. Most of the time my mother's shrine remained
as dark as the soul of one who's forsaken all hope. This was right
after my mother died, when I was only about seven years of age,
barely old enough to understand.

I understood that she was no longer there. That her voice
would no longer sing me any songs. That I could no longer hug
her. This was after her skin grew cold and Zi'Assunta had washed
her, and for a day or two she lay near a window, all alone in a
box, and we knelt around her and cried. Then some men I'd never
seen before came and took her away after wrapping her so tightly
in a sheet that I worried that even though she was dead she
wouldn't ever be able to breathe again.

I knew enough even then to attend Mass each day. I liked
sitting with all the other people in church where it was warm,
where the sweet smell of incense and the softer scent of melting
beeswax mixed with the sharper odors of moth balls and wet coats
and the sour-milk smell of people's breaths. I liked the bright
lights hanging overhead, the impressively sturdy pillars that rose
to the ceiling's row of domes, the various tales suggested by the

pictures in the stained-glass windows. When I sat back on the pew with the others, their shoulders would press on each side against my own, and I wouldn't feel quite so alone. Then from up in the loft behind us the organ would play, and it would sound like the voice of God. Whenever it stopped at least one baby would start crying. What song! What joy! How I still love the fresh, red sound of crying babies!

I knew that the painted altar was only a larger variation of my mother's shrine, and that we were all praying to someone just like her, someone holy and dead. I knew you had to be dead to be holy. The priest would sing from his book, and the altar boys in their black dresses would carry the book from one side of the shrine to the next. The altar boys would ring bells and wash the priest's fingertips and pour something into his grand gold cup for him to drink, and later he'd give everyone a small, nearly tasteless cookie. He'd eat the biggest one himself, after first showing it to the hideously tortured man nailed on the cross above the golden jeweled box where a domed goblet of the cookies was stored.

The Virgin had her own altar, off to one side. Even though it was smaller and less colorful, I immensely preferred it to the altar of the tortured man. I'd grow weary of staring at the priest's back during Mass and would rise from my pew to kneel before the statue of the Madonna. I liked that she stared me in the face. Her face was so pure and trusting that I felt I could whisper my most secret thoughts to her.

I'd ask the Madonna if she knew my mother and if at night when my mother went to bed did she have pains in her belly from hunger, too? I'd tell the Virgin all about my being a wildcat and about my prayer to the coals and our empty soup pot and my eating spoonfuls of our walls. I'd tell her the story of Petru's birth and death.

One Sunday I got the Blessed Virgin and my mother confused. I cried and asked her why she had left me and Papa and turned to silent, painted stone.

"Answer me!" I shouted, unaware it was in the middle of High Mass. "Mamma, what's the matter with you? Why do you stay here in church instead of coming home with me?"

One of the old priests rushed out from the sacristy and hissed at me and clamped his soft, perfumed hand across my mouth.

That's when I learned that the best prayers were silent. You could say anything you wanted to in silence, before the altar of privacy inside your own mind. There, no one but you and the Virgin would know what you prayed.

As soon as I began silently mouthing my conversations, the soft-palmed old priest nodded and smiled at me. Sometimes after Mass he'd sit with me in a pew and teach me things about the Madonna. He let me borrow his rosary, which was unbroken and whole, with all fifty-nine beads. After he was through with his lessons we'd walk to one of the founts where I'd kneel before him, the rosary laced between my fingers. I had a special way to lace it, a special way to hold my hands. I had a special way to genuflect and hesitate when I crossed myself. I had a special way to kneel and remain still. The priest would sprinkle me with holy water, inscribing the sign of the Cross in the air over my head.

I noticed that just beside her altar the Madonna owned several tiers of squat, white candles in clear glass cups. There were so many candles and cups that it was beyond my ability to count them. One Sunday at Mass a thought occurred to me. I gazed up at the Blessed Virgin and asked her if I might borrow a cup and candle for my mother's shrine.

Her unmoving eyes said nothing.

"Madonna," I whispered in my mind, "please look down on me, your servant and child."

Still her eyes did not move, though I sensed I had her attention.

"Madonna," I asked, "tell me if there would be too great a difference if one burned here or at my mother's altar?"

She gave me no answer.

"Madonna," I said, "isn't it true as the old priest has told me that these candles exist for your honor and glory?"

She said nothing in response.

"Madonna, isn't it true that you're honored and glorified whenever another mother, particularly one dead, is honored, too?"

She remained still, trying her best not to move.

"Madonna, isn't it also true that you sent the old priest to me, as he said, to educate me in religious ways?"

I thought she nodded though in the light I couldn't be quite certain.

"Madonna, please shake your head no if taking one or two of your candles to my mamma's shrine would be a sin."

Her head remained as still as stone.

"And after the candles have burned down, Madonna, please shake your head no if it would be a sin for me to replenish them."

She stayed as still as a statue.

"Madonna, I am eternally grateful to you for your kind generosity."

From then on my mother's shrine flickered night and day with light, at least until the sunless afternoon when my father gave me away.

I WAS WORKING in the house, talking as usual to my mother. I carried on endlessly long conversations with her, speaking to her sometimes as if she were a girl my age, occasionally mumbling whole sentences out loud. That day I was explaining to her how to wash a floor. My father was out, as usual, looking for work. As I scrubbed the floor near the stove, I felt something sticky seeping down my legs.

"Aiutu, Mamma!" I shouted after examining myself. "Mamma, help me, I'm bleeding!"

My main thought was that I'd somehow swallowed the broken-off tip of a knife and that the tip had lodged itself deep down inside me where I make water.

By now blood oozed thickly down the insides of both my legs. My guts cramped and ached so bad I walked doubled-over. I searched the drawer where we kept our knife to see if its tip was broken. It wasn't. Still, I was certain that just like my mother I was about to die.

Papa entered the flat at that moment, his face empty and drawn. Taking off his long coat, he saw the blood staining my nightgown and let out a scream. Then he called me the devil's own slut and pushed past me to strangle the good-for-nothing fellow he roared must be taking refuge beneath my bed. In a frenzy he tore my bedsheets from the mattress. A few feathers from an old pillow fell silently in the air as he raged.

"Where is he?" he shouted. "I'll kill him! Then I'll kill you!" He pulled my hair, which at the time I wore unbraided, like a warm cape around my shoulders and back. He slapped me hard across the face. He ripped my bedsheets in long strips and threw my mattress across the room, the rope-like veins on his forehead and neck red and throbbing, his mouth frothing with white spit like an angry dog.

"You see what happens when I leave you alone?" he howled. Like a dog in a vacant lot he growled and snapped his teeth. "You filthy slut, where are you hiding him? I'll tear the son of a bitch apart! He'll regret that the sun ever rose on the day he came here to see you!"

I held my stomach, the knife from the kitchen drawer still clutched in my hand, and watched as the wild dog's snarling muzzle grew a pair of upward-pointing tusks, and the animal before me transformed into a boar. Now his words were only snorts and squeals.

I could still feel my blood dripping down the inside of my legs. If the wild pig charges me, I thought, I'll have no choice but to try to stab him in the heart. Then I'll chop his flesh into pieces and cook him in the soup pot on the stove. Sure enough, the boar lowered his snout and lunged at me. Both hands on the knife's hilt, I thrust the blade's sharp tip up and toward his heart.

"Let me die!" I screamed as I shoved the blade forward. "Mamma, take me!"

The knife stuck the beast's belly, then sliced a line up his gut nearly to his throat. All at once the room stopped spinning. The boar curled his front legs across his belly, then fell to the floor, amazed. He sucked in a deep breath, changed into a dog, then back to my father, at once paling and wincing at the sight of his broken flesh.

In all of his many battles, he said, he'd never been cut. He hadn't even been wounded during the Great War, not even scratched or nicked. As I helped him unbutton his bloody shirt he talked about his experiences during war, how in truth looking back he'd genuinely enjoyed marching through the forests of France, helmet strapped tightly on top of his head, rifle and bayonet in hand, how it was both frightening and truly quite thrilling to observe that while many men around him died he remained alive and whole, untouched, due to the Creator's divine and holy will or the whim of destiny he didn't know, though he was certain not every man could have survived the life he'd led, going off into the hills as a youth and joining the brave brigands and their fight against the aristocracy who heartlessly plundered the *cuntadini* at every turn, who fattened themselves on the stolen grain and fruit of the common people's labor. Oh, he said, how he detested the thieving barons and brutal overseers and all the contemptible others of their ilk: the parasites, the leeches and bloodsuckers, the toadies and bootlickers, the men who willingly carried out the orders of the powerful against the weak, the class of vile, loathsome beasts for whom the insufferably hot fires of Hell were created. How he knew down to the marrow in his bones that the battle against them was ethical and right but how, peculiarly, *the fight itself* rather than the principle behind it was what excited him, was what thrilled him beyond any innocent's imagination, how the fight grew hypnotic, narcotic, mesmerizing, how marvelous it was to be young and reckless and alive, and once as a young man even heroic—he told me that before he and my mother were married he'd rescued her from three men who were about to ravage her, how killing them was the most exhilarating and complete deed he'd ever committed in his life, how later he had thanked God for placing such obvious and undeniable evil in his path, for blessing him with the opportunity to kill, how evil is seldom so pure or obvious, more often than not diluting itself by wrapping its essence around something good, like a poisonous snake vined around the trunk of a sweet fruit tree, making the choice to strike the snake down with your hoe all the more complex lest you kill the tree in the process—until one dark day all the blood and gore he'd seen congealed in his heart and made him so sick that he went to a priest to confess his wrongdoings, but the priest denied him absolution, and so for a while, until the Great War, he lost his stomach for fighting.

His wound bled freely. He washed it, then bound it tightly with several strips of the bedsheet. Watching him, I bound myself with a strip of sheet, too.

It was convenient that he'd torn up the sheet. God works out all of these details in advance, I thought. Now that we needed them, we had bandages. It was convenient that I'd been washing the floor because now I didn't have to get the bucket from the closet or draw water from the pipes. I got down on my knees and began washing up from the floorboards the blood—my father's blood mixed with my own—as he tightened the compress around his chest and kneeled next to me.

"What have I done to you?" he said, a tear shimmering in his eye. "Forgive me, my jewel, please, for having insinuated . . ." He hesitated. "For impugning your honor, insulting you, pulling your hair, and striking you. Forgive me, *figghia mia,* for being so cruelly and desperately wrong."

Perhaps I only imagined my father reciting this apology. Like a knife's sheath, memory protects those who carry it. Perhaps the tears dripping down his cheeks were only water I'd accidentally splashed up at him as I scrubbed the blood that stained the floor.

"I can't do this any longer," he whispered to me. "Not alone.

Not by myself. You must understand this, please! You need a mother to take care of you. You need a woman's hand, not mine. I'm not a woman. I'm no good as a mother. *Figghia mia,* there are so many things I don't know."

"I have my mother," I said, gesturing toward the shrine. There squatted a half dozen candles flickering in their smudged glass cups, the dark beads of the old priest's rosary hanging over a corner of the frame holding my mother's photograph.

My eyes were as dry as two stones. "I have all I need," I said.

"REALLY, IT'S THE best decision for both of us," he told me a moment later, or was it the next day, or perhaps the day after that, after someone had stitched closed the wound I'd slashed in his belly. The gash was deep enough to require stitching. I remember only that once again I was down on my knees.

Was I washing the floor? Was I praying before my mother's shrine? "It's only temporary," he told me. "Only for a couple of years. Believe me. It will be just until you're a bit older."

"What?" I said. Inside my soul, something that I thought had been full was now collapsing. A hot flush of fear washed over my heart.

"They'll feed you there," he told me. "They said that all the girls there get three meals each day. What do you think of that? They said they'll teach you how to read and write and how to count numbers. That's more than I can do. The Sisters told me there are plenty of other girls there. With everyone around you won't feel quite so all alone."

My lungs had stopped doing their work. For the life of me I could not draw the next breath.

"Don't you see," he said, "this is for your own good. I can't do any more for you. I can't even put enough food on the table for myself. Now that Tannu and Teresa are gone, I can't pay the landlord the rent due him. I'm tired of walking door to door, asking for work, a handout. I'm tired of searching garbage buckets for scraps." He squeezed the hollow of his eyes, then put his hands on mine.

"They say there's work out west, in a place called California, picking fruit from trees. They say there's so much fruit in California that it rots on the ground. Can you believe it, so much food that it's going to rot! You're so young I can't possibly bring you with me. Maybe if you were a boy I could toughen you up and you could string along beside me, but you're a girl and in need of a woman's hand. They say that in California they need workers like me, men willing to move from job to job, men with a strong back."

My next breath was a brick that would not fit into my mouth.

"Your mother would have wanted it this way, believe me. Look at me, how I react. I slapped you so hard that you fell to the floor. The side of your face is still all black and blue. Beneath your eye there's a welt as fat as a walnut. I'm no good for you, I'm telling you. I'm never here. I worry all the time about you. This way I won't have to. You know, you talk out loud to yourself nearly all the time now. You have nobody to keep you company. It's better for you this way, to live for a few years with the nuns. At least this way you'll be fed."

His jaw kept on flapping, open and then shut, like a door with a broken latch in a windstorm, a banging door in an empty house where nobody lived. I didn't listen to another word he said. Instead I watched as his face turned from something familiar—that of my father's, a face I'd never questioned—into that of a stranger's, the face of an animal, a despicable animal, a reprehensible brute. His face was so close to mine that I could count the whiskers on his cheeks and jaw and neck, and then a moment later his grizzled face was far away, at the other end of the earth. I never before realized how truly ugly my father was. At once I felt that the blood that pumped through my veins was no longer of his. I understood what Jesù Cristu must have felt when the false apostle kissed his cheek in the garden.

Without a word I stood and swallowed the brick lodged in my

mouth. I walked to my mother's shrine, genuflected, and then began blowing out the candles.

OUT OF DEATH comes life is one lesson this cruel world has to teach us.

Everyone called my mother the Little Lamb because she was kind and pure, critical of no one, trusting of all. Jesù, too, is a lamb we eat each Easter, after we slaughter him each Good Friday on the cross. Because of his death the gates of Heaven have been opened to us, and through his death the Father offers us the possibility of eternal life.

The week that my mother was due, Zi'Assunta came to serve as midwife. I was seven years old then. Zi'Assunta arrived from Chicago on a train, carrying in her arms a surprise, her daughter, Rosalie. This was the first we in New York had heard of the baby. Though Rosalie was barely one year old, we could see at once that she was Zi'Assunta's child by her serene and detached expression and the way her big dark eyes examined and followed everyone and everything in the room.

That afternoon, out of the women's earshot, the men gathered to talk. Ziu Tannu remarked that while out in the forest searching for herbs Assunta must have found the child beneath the cap of a mushroom.

"Only after its stem grew long and thick!" laughed my father, thrusting his forearm into the air. He added that the child was further proof that Salvatore was weak and careless.

"He and Gerlando must have been in the house fingering their pitch pipes," Ziu Tannu said with a wink, "while Assunta was outside buying a big bass drum."

My father nodded, then recited a rhyming joke. A child hears *boom-a, boom-a, boom-a, boom-a* and shouts, Papa, Papa, what's that big sound? Come to the window, I hear a drum in a parade! Papa answers, Ninu, Ninu, that's no big drum! Come away from the window, there's no parade! That's just your mamma, she's a-scratching her belly!

Ziu Tannu laughed and coughed and then grew serious and said, "It would never in the world have happened if she'd stayed here with us."

"Of course not," agreed my father.

"She'd be wearing a wedding ring," said Ziu Tannu.

"Or widow's black," said Luigi.

"Li figghi nun su parenti, su vudeddu di la ventri," recited Ziu Tannu. Our children are not our relatives, they are the guts from our womb.

MY MOTHER'S WOMB was still, a fact that caused Zi'Assunta grave concern. She said the delivery must be that day, at once. She ordered everyone out and scrubbed down the back room while my mother sipped an herb tea Zi'Assunta prepared. Since Zi'Assunta wanted to keep an eye on Rosalie, and the child was content to sleep in my arms, I was permitted to remain in a corner of the room where on a low, narrow bed my mother lay.

Zi'Assunta held her hands out in the air, then placed them on my mother's belly. "Tell me if this hurts," Zi'Assunta said. Her face grew dark, and her eyebrows edged down toward her nose.

"I don't feel anything," my mother said.

"I should have seen this before, when I delivered Anna," Zi'-Assunta said. "All this time I should have had you eating a paste."

"Such foolishness," my mother said. "Years ago in Sicilia an old fortune-teller told me that twice a week I should eat a spoonful of dirt."

Zi'Assunta nodded, eyes closed, the flat of her hands running over my mother's body. "You should have listened to her. Her eyes saw better than did mine."

"She also said I could eat some of the wall," my mother said.

"Sure," Zi'Assunta said, "for the minerals and grit. The minerals build up your bones, and the grit scrapes your insides clean. You know that our insides are full of worms that uncurl when we're sick. Grit pushes them out. Grit is also very good for the bones."

"My bones feel fine," said my mother.

"Tomorrow I'll make a paste for you, for the babies yet to come. There will be many, believe me. The paste will make them stronger and help their bones to knit. I'll show you how to prepare it when I'm gone."

"But this child—" my mother began.

"Hush," said Zi'Assunta. Her hands molded my mother's belly as if it were dough. "What's made is made. What's done is done. Now, let me get the children out of here so I can deliver this child." Her hands moved down between my mother's legs. I could see Zi'Assunta was doing something.

"My waters!" cried my mother in sudden pain. "They're breaking!"

Zi'Assunta told me to wait outside with Rosalie. I kissed my mother's forehead and lips and did as I was told. I was overjoyed to be needed. The hour was late, the beginning of night's dark fullness. I sat just outside the door. I think for a while I fell asleep.

Then Rosalie began to fuss and I woke up. The child writhed in my arms, clawing me, wanting to nurse.

I didn't know what to do. Everyone else, even Zia Teresa, had cleared out. No one else was in the flat. The room where my mother lay was strangely silent. Rosalie was whimpering and sucking the dry fabric of my gown. I didn't know what else to do so I stood and pushed open the door.

Zi'Assunta crouched between my mother's knees, helping her to deliver the birth sack. With one hand Zi'Assunta pressed and massaged my mother's abdomen while the other gently tugged the cord dangling from between her legs. The front of Zi'Assunta's blouse was smeared with blood. She was speaking to my mother in a low, soothing voice. As I stepped into the room I could hear my mother moaning.

It was then that I saw something curled in a shallow pan at Zi'Assunta's feet. It looked enough like a baby to have once been one, though if someone had said it was the offspring of some animal, from the distance where I stood I would have believed it. It was late at night, and the light from the oil lamps in the room was low, but I could clearly see that whatever it was it was dead and, worse, that it had been dead for some period of time and was already decomposing, rotting away like all dead things rot away, its edges beginning to blur and become indistinct, the sharpness of its features already crumbling away.

Then as I stepped nearer I saw its true beauty: the fine silk of its hair, the even row of dark lashes on the perfect lids of its closed eyes, my father's nose—both nostrils plugged with something that resembled wax—my mother's full lips gracing the blue mouth set in a fierce grimace. It had my father's chest. Both of the infant's fists were raised, as if in the womb it had been fighting something.

Beside it lay a length of the birth cord, coiled in such tight loops that I imagined it twisted around the child's neck. Already I could hear my father praising the infant, he was so unmistakably a boy! His *cosa* and sack were so huge that his chubby thighs were parted wide, like my mother's, as if to give them room.

Zi'Assunta took Rosalie and scooted me away at once into a corner where I could no longer stare at my brother. With a finger to her lips, Zi'Assunta told me to hush. She opened her blouse and dropped her undershirt, allowing Rosalie to nurse. The healthy child suckled with zeal.

I squatted against the wall, sucking my thumb, as I skirted the wall until I could see everything again. Zi'Assunta crouched between my mother's legs, kneading her belly, coaxing out the birth sack, crooning a soothing song, while one child fed noisily at her swollen breast, and another lay silent and dead in a pan at her feet, fists raised, fighting the invisible and terrible air.

•　•　•

WHAT I REMEMBER next is the sound of Zia Teresa weeping, the women gathered around my mother, who lay sweating on the narrow bed. Someone had changed the sheets. In a basket on a table beside her lay the baby, swaddled and bathed and as still as a stone.

"I did everything in my power," Zi'Assunta was saying. "But in the end his tiny heart gave out and he stopped breathing." She turned to me. "Anna, you were there, remember? You heard his bright cries!"

Zia Teresa held back a sob. "Thank God there was enough time to baptize him."

"My son!" my mother cried.

"Of course," Zi'Assunta said. "I did so while he was still breathing. I sprinkled water over his forehead."

"My son!" screamed my mother.

"At least he's spared this cruel world's misery," said Zia Teresa. "He lives in Heaven now, a saint."

"My dear son!" my mother wailed. "Oh, darkest day!"

"I did everything I could," Zi'Assunta assured her.

"At least now the child's with God," Zia Teresa told my mother.

"God, take me in his place!" my mother wailed.

"Be calm," Zi'Assunta said, "or he will anyway."

Zia Teresa put her arm around my waist and drew me to her, then with the tips of her fingers brushed my hair. Zi'Assunta made my mother another cup of tea. For a few hours it put her to sleep.

I knew that unbaptized babies spent eternity in Limbo, a region that existed on the border of Hell as the everlasting abode of all souls barred from Heaven through no fault of their own. Limbo is a neutral place of cloud and endless waiting, a middle world made up of unfeeling neglect, a place of oblivion, of neither pleasure nor pain, neither reward nor punishment, something like being suspended blindfolded and unhearing inside a room packed horribly with cotton that cannot be smelled or tasted or touched.

I might also have rested as my mother slept. The events of

that long night and day flicker dimly. I know that I was allowed to hold my brother in my arms for a few minutes before someone took him away. It was as if he were empty, as if his body had no real weight. I remember that at one point Zi'Assunta tried to comfort me. I pushed her away and screamed with all my might until she let me go.

I knew that my mother was sick even though no one else chose to acknowledge it. I blamed Zi'Assunta for everything even though I knew that my brother's death was not her fault. I knew that she'd felt his stillness the moment she laid her hands on my mother's belly. I knew that his body was full of the worms that crawl out and start to eat us after we're dead. I knew that while in the womb he had strangled himself with the cord. Moments before, my mother must have smelled some strange, enticing odor that worked its way down into her birth waters where my brother smelled it, too, and in his excitement twisted around and around, desiring it. That's why they say it's best to keep pregnant women away from strong odors. My father taught me. He said that anything, good or bad, a pregnant woman could see or hear and smell or taste or touch would end up in the womb.

I knew that a pregnant woman could look at an ugly thing and the ugliness could stamp itself on the child. That's why you keep pregnant women away from dogs. The mother could be frightened by a dog, and the child could be born with a dog's muzzle. If she sees a demon, even for a split second, her baby could be born with horns and a tail. There were old stories about babies being born with tails. The midwives cut them off. The ones with horns they left out in the forest for the wolves. My mind tried to remember all the precautions and stories I'd heard my father tell me. In the next room Ziu Tannu and some men from the neighborhood held my father as he wailed.

After they took my brother's body away I stayed with my mother, wiping her forehead with a cool cloth, stroking her cheeks with my fingertips, watching the sweat puddle in the dark, olive hollows beneath her eyes.

"I love you, Mamma," I said again and again.

Her skin was yellowing and growing hot with fever. She asked Zi'Assunta to again tell her everything that had happened. So Zi'Assunta told her the story of my brother's birth, baptism, and death.

My mother smiled and kissed Zi'Assunta's hand. "Thank God," she said, "that you were able to bless him in time! You don't know what a relief it is to me. This past week and a half, when I no longer could feel him moving, I feared he was dead."

"You remember hearing him cry, don't you?" said Zi'Assunta.

My mother shook her head.

"Sure," said Zi'Assunta. "His cries were real strong. After I cut the cord I brought him to you, remember?"

My mother nodded. "Maybe. If I think hard I think I remember."

"You were very brave," Zi'Assunta said, "and in great pain, but you smiled and held him for few moments, and his clear dark eyes held you, and then you kissed his lips. It was for only a moment. You remember that, don't you?"

"Yes," said my mother. "Now I do. Thank God, yes."

"Then you slept," said Zi'Assunta, "and I baptized him."

"You baptized him in time," my mother said.

"Of course," Zi'Assunta said, "while he was screaming."

"And what name did you give him?" my mother asked.

"Why, the name you told me," said Zi'Assunta.

"I told you a name?" my mother said.

"Yes. Don't you remember?" She changed the cloth on my mother's forehead. "I'm sure you do. Tell me that you remember."

My mother bit her bottom lip, then nodded. "I thought I'd kept it to myself. I was certain I told no one. But I always wanted a boy named Petru. If it was a boy I wanted to name him Petru."

"Of course," Zi'Assunta said, "that's precisely what you said as you held him and kissed him. So of course I did just as you wanted. I baptized him Petru, just as you said."

"In time?" my mother asked again. "You're sure?"

"Of course I'm sure."

"But I don't remember any cries," my mother said. "Are you sure you heard his cries?"

"As certain as I stand here," said Zi'Assunta. "Ask Anna. She heard them, too."

"You heard them?" my mother said.

I could say nothing. I could only cry.

"Tell me again," said my mother to Zi'Assunta.

OVER THE NEXT several hours Zi'Assunta told the story of Petru's birth and death again and again, allowing my mother the opportunity to shape its details however she wished. In one version the child reached out for my mother, as if to caress her cheek. In another version he suckled her breast. Each time Zi'Assunta ended her story with the words of the baptism: "Petru, son of Ciccina and Luigi, I baptize you in the name of the Father. Petru, I baptize you in the name of the Son. Petru, I baptize you in the name of the Holy Ghost."

My mother's fever burned hot and ever hotter, and in the next hours she spilled all of the guts of her womb into a pan, and late that night when she had no more blood to bleed and no more sweat to give the sheets she died.

Her eyes opened wide and held me, and then her mouth gave out a long breath. *"Phewwwww,"* she said. It was the sound a woman makes after she's scrubbed a floor or a washtub full of clothes. It was the sound a woman makes after she's hung a heavy basket of clothes out on the clothesline. It was the sound a woman makes after she's walked a great distance while carrying a heavy load. You expect her to wipe her brow and stand up and empty her bucket. You expect her to put a last clothespin on the line to secure the cord. You expect her to put down her load and sit on the ground and rest her tired feet.

Then it was finished. My mother's dying was finished, and the room slowly emptied itself of the sound she'd made. Her hand grew cool in mine. There was no sound in the room. She was finally still. Dead.

My life was only beginning.

In the orphanage, when I was not in the chapel praying or in class learning to read and write and count, I was made to scrub floors. The orphanage had endless miles of floor, all tile, and each and every single square needed to be scoured and polished until the floor looked as wet as the sea. The tiles were dark green like the sea. With the exception of the few hours each day given to classes, it seemed as if I was always on my knees.

Sometimes I was asked to peel potatoes, so many that I filled deep buckets and wide bowls. Potatoes and bread, and often beans, were mainly what we were given to eat. We were lucky to have them, the Sisters told us whenever we complained. All across the rest of the country, the Sisters reminded us, there were people without beans, without potatoes, without even an old hard scrap of bread.

They told us a story about a poor family boiling their last bit of macaroni in some water on the stove. This was the store-bought kind of macaroni that came in a paper box. The family fueled their stove with their last few lumps of coal. They stood around the stove complaining about how poor and unhappy they felt and how tired they were of eating macaroni when they heard a sudden knock upon their door. They opened it to allow inside a ragged stranger, who begged their forgiveness for his intrusion and said he had just been walking by when he smelled their macaroni. Then he asked what were they planning on doing with the water the macaroni was cooking in. If they were going to throw it away, he said, could he please have it to take to his starving, pregnant wife?

They liked to tell us stories like that just before the evening meal. Sometimes the more sensitive girls would cry over their bowls, no longer wanting to eat. They'd ask that their food be given to the neediest ones in the stories.

But I never cried. The sight of Petru in the pan on the floor, and the knowledge that he was trapped forever in Limbo, dried all my tears. The nuns' stories just made me hungrier. I told every crying girl that I'd be happy to eat her share if she was too weepy to want it.

WHEN I FIRST arrived at the orphanage, they stripped me naked and cut off my long hair. They sprayed me with foul-smelling poison to kill any insects or disease I might be carrying on my skin. They scrubbed me with a brush that made my skin raw, rinsed and soaped me, then rinsed and soaped and rinsed me again, all the while reciting the orphanage's rules, which I was made to repeat until I could do so backwards. From the window I could see them in the courtyard below burning my clothes. The smoke from the fire twisted in the air like a vine, like the cord that had connected my brother's corpse to my mother's living body.

I certainly wasn't the only child in the orphanage with a parent who was still alive. Some girls from big families had both parents living. Some families grew so big that they were forced to give up two, three, or more of their daughters.

The girls with living parents were fond of telling one another that maybe today their parents would come and take them home. I didn't like that game. I never played it. I'd always shrug and say something like, "Sure, my father will come and get me as soon as green mice dance," or "Sure, he'll be here when monkeys grow wings and learn to fly."

I didn't know what any of that meant. It didn't mean anything. It was just something silly and unlikely. To one girl who seldom washed I said, "Sure, as soon as gold mushrooms sprout from your ears!" The other girls laughed and said that with her it was very likely.

Still, we considered ourselves blessed. We knew that outside the orphanage walls many were starving. These were hard times. We knew there was *miseria* everywhere.

The Sisters took in as many girls as there were beds. Sometimes we slept two to a bed. Sometimes new girls slept on blankets on the floor. They slept in classrooms, in the hallways, wherever there was space and a body could lie down.

Once, in winter, in the middle of a lesson on multiplication, with all the girls sniffling and coughing into their hands, and the fierce wind howling through the cracks in the windows, and a snowstorm raging so angrily that the white windowpanes throbbed, and pebbles of hail tinkling on the glass like a thousand tiny drums, the old Sister teaching us suddenly turned from her calculations and snapped her piece of chalk in half and said what in the name of God was this great nation coming to? Why had our parents dragged us all the way across the ocean only to give us up?

I stood and said, "Sister, nobody brought me over. I was born here just like you."

Sister looked at me strangely, then called me to the front of the class and slapped my face so hard my head banged off the blackboard. Talking without permission was against one of the orphanage's most sacred rules, nearly as bad as speaking in a tongue other than American. I was sent then to the chapel to beg the Lord's forgiveness for my insolence. This incident started my habit of praying in the chapel each afternoon.

My American wasn't very good, though I was an attentive listener. Sometimes when the Sisters thought I was praying I was really going over in my mouth the various American phrases I'd heard spoken that day. I'd keep my mouth shut until I was sure of the new words.

Words, they're like slippery stairs. You can climb them nearly to the top and make one mistake and end up flat on your face, back at the bottom again. I was silent for so long that some of the Sisters thought I had a damaged brain. I spoke only now and then, and didn't cry even when they hit me. But then I experienced the seven visions.

Then even the archbishop couldn't shut me up.

•   •   •

PEOPLE WONDER ABOUT visions, how they begin, how they end. They expect you to say that the Madonna appeared while you were kneeling on nails reciting your ten thousandth novena. They expect you to tell them that out of the blue you smelled roses or heard the first movement of a Vivaldi concerto or some aria by Verdi. Perhaps for some whom the holy Madonna chooses to visit these details are true. For me, her first visit was not quite so dramatic.

One Friday afternoon I was kneeling in the back pew of the chapel, as was my habit, going over my growing list of American phrases. I enjoyed kneeling in the chapel because it was so quiet and because at least one candle always burned there. Burning candles made me feel closer to my mother. Even now there is something about the smell of melting wax that makes me feel content.

Halfway up the outer edge of the main altar's right wall was a candle enclosed inside a red glass dome. It burned day and night, seven days a week, to signify that God is physically present in the form of the consecrated Hosts stored in the tabernacle. I greatly appreciated the reliability of that candle. It assured me God was near. I admired the stillness of the chapel's statues, and the way footfalls echoed sharply when anyone neared.

I'd like to say that I was reciting the Hail Mary when the Madonna first appeared, but in truth I was going over the words to the Pledge of Allegiance, which we were made to recite daily in class after our prayers. I was stumbling over the phrase, "one nation, indivisible," always confusing it with "invisible," which made no sense, when all at once I had the overwhelming feeling that someone else was in the room with me even though I hadn't heard a soul enter. So I raised my eyes cautiously and looked about.

There in the side aisle beside me stood a dark and beautiful woman with a big-eyed child in her arms. By the fancy cut of her robe I knew at once that she hadn't just walked in from the street. She was elegant, like a figure etched in a cathedral's stained-glass window. She had dark, deep-set eyes the color of shelled almonds and seemed about twenty years of age—maybe somebody's maid, I thought, until I noticed that the child she held was dark, too, thick-lipped like his mother, with a head full of shiny and tightly curled hair. The child's eyes were peculiar, the eyes of an old man. Her eyes looked brand-new. Her robe was blue, the color of a midday summer sky, and like the sky curiously alive and gently shifting in hue. She stared at me as if she had always been beside me and had been patiently waiting for me to look over my shoulder and notice her.

Her free hand reached out toward me, but she'd appeared so suddenly and silently that I was afraid, and so at once I ran away.

I RETURNED TO the chapel at the same hour the next day, clutching in my hands the beads of my mother's broken rosary. This time I'm sure I said the Hail Mary. I recited it word for word, in perfect American, about twelve or fifteen times, until I again sensed that I was in the presence of something far beyond my measure or scope.

If you bite down so hard with your back teeth that your jaw and neck shake and then multiply that feeling by a thousand and spread it throughout your body, you'll have some understanding of how I felt as I sensed the Virgin's nearness in the chapel that second day. The feeling was a vibrant aching deep down in my bones. It lasted so long that after several moments I didn't think I could bear it. Then it sharpened to a tingle in the center of my soul and stretched into a yearning that arced in rippling yellow circles throbbing through my body. I believe I gasped out loud. I was terrified to turn my head and look, but finally I couldn't resist.

This time the dark-faced woman stood in the aisle beside me without her baby.

"It's you," I said stupidly.

"Anna," the lady said, "your mother asked that I give you her love and greetings."

"You know my mother?" I said.

The lady nodded.

"Where is she?" I asked, looking about.

"Here," the lady said, smiling and pressing her palm on her breastbone. "With me."

I think that was when I first realized she was the Madonna because where else could my mamma be other than within the Holy Mother's heart? I fell out of the pew and into the aisle, pressing myself to the floor near her feet like the lowest cockroach. I called her all the holy names I could think of: Blessed Mother, Queen of the Angels, Mother of Good Counsel, Tower of Ivory, Ark of the Covenant, Queen of Virgins, Seat of Wisdom, Mirror of Justice, Mother of Perpetual Help, Queen of Peace, Singular Vessel of Devotion, Mother of Mercy, Mystical Rose.

She silenced me by saying she didn't come to me to be praised. She said my mother was concerned about me, fearing that I felt alone and abandoned. My mother was with me always, the Madonna said, every second of the night and day, as were she and all of the holy angels and saints.

I peeled myself up off the floor then and knelt in the pew as the Blessed Virgin told me how pleased she had been that my mother had named me in honor of her mother, Saint Anna. I responded by saying that, as the old stories I'd heard go, my mother had so admired a tile mosaic on a storefront in old Palermo that she frequented the area and afterwards liked to stop to say a few prayers in the cathedral across the square.

The Madonna listened, then told me the version she'd heard was different. She asked me if I wanted to hear it.

"Yes, Holy Mother," I said.

The Madonna told me her version. Rather than go to the square to see the mosaic or meet with its artist as my father feared, my mother's goal was the cathedral, where she prayed each day for the redemption of my father's soul. My mother had a series of dreams in which my father stood in diverse settings tortured and in agony: at the foot of their bed, on the edge of the forest, deep in the hills in the company of wolves, at the gateway to the valley of Hell, his body writhing in indescribable pain, hands and chest dripping with fire and blood. My mother understood that only the intercession of mothers could save him. So Ciccina prayed to all the dead mothers in Heaven, who advised her to pray to the Virgin's mother every day for seven months so that the blood on Luigi's hands might be washed away and his penchant for violence might release him from its hold.

My father fiercely resisted this intercession. Satan's hold on him was powerful and tenacious. Soon Luigi became enraged with jealousy, certain that each day his wife slipped away to the cathedral she was secretly meeting with some lover. To catch her in the act and thus expose her deceit, Luigi followed her six times through the maze of alleyways and streets of ancient Palermo, each day becoming impossibly lost. On the seventh day he trailed her all the way to the cathedral, where from the shadows he could overhear her prayers begging Saint Anna to intercede on behalf of the salvation of his eternal soul.

He waited for his young wife across the square, where he argued that she had no right to interfere with his life. She shouldn't meddle with his business, he said, or with any of the other affairs of men. A wife should know her place, he maintained.

"Just as the *baruni* and *gabbilloti* were certain that you should know yours," she replied. She then told him about her visions.

"If these apparitions of me as tortured and damned are true," he said, "have the Holy Mother of All Dreams give me a sign." He stood facing the mosaic.

At that moment the figure's tiled face changed into that of my mother's.

I nodded, understanding. "And was he saved?" I asked.

The Madonna smiled, her face revealing nothing.

"When my father dies," I said, "will he go to Heaven or to Hell?"

"He's still deciding," she said. "Pray for him. Pray every day.

Recite the rosary for him, and for all the others in the world like him. Make room in your life for the daily recitation of the rosary. And come back here tomorrow at this time."

HER THIRD VISIT was less formal than the others. Not only did she wear a plain brown cloak but the curls of her hair had relaxed and hung freely and unbound to her shoulders, like any common girl. I said that her hair looked a lot looser than her son's, and she said it was true, her hair was finer. She sat down in the pew beside me and asked me about my life in the orphanage.

I told her I was happy to have something to eat every day, and that I was grateful to lead a life of work and prayer, that it gave me a sense of peace.

"And what feelings lie beneath these?" she asked.

I didn't want to say. My other feelings were insignificant and petty. Still, it was impossible for me not to tell her the whole truth. So I admitted that I often found myself aching for my mother.

"What makes you ache?" she said.

"That she isn't here with me," I answered, though at once I knew that wasn't the whole truth. "That I can't hold her in my arms."

"And what else?" she said.

I was afraid to say it. Admitting it made me appear so childish and weak. I hung my head. "That there's no one left to hold me," I said finally.

The Madonna wrapped her arms around me then and rocked me just as my mother used to.

Then she put her hand inside my chest and caressed my heart. I really can't describe it more clearly than that. She didn't make me bleed or anything. It wasn't like a surgical operation. Her hand simply slipped through my blouse and inside my skin. She did it as quick as that. Quicker. No words passed between us. And as her fingers closed around the center of me I cried out in such joy that I thought the whole world would hear me. Then I wept until I became empty, all the while without thinking my fingers braiding her long, loose hair.

When it was time for me to leave she said I should return tomorrow at the same time, then added that she'd protect and defend me.

I said, "Blessed Mother, against what?"

The Mother of Christ smiled. "Fear and doubt."

ON THE FOURTH day she was back in her sky-blue robe, her hair hidden beneath her long veil. She emanated a warm and radiant light that was more soothing than the sun at daybreak. I fell to my knees and recited the Hail Mary so loudly that one of the Sisters passing by came into the chapel and told me to hush. I continued praying as the Sister came forward to admonish me, but just as she reached for me she fell to her knees. At once her hands clasped themselves together in prayer.

"Hail Mary, full of grace!" the Sister and I exclaimed. "The Lord is with thee! Blessed art thou among women, and blessed is the fruit of thy womb, Jesus! Holy Mary, Mother of God, pray for us sinners, now and at the hour of our death!"

Our shouts drew the attention of more of the Sisters, each of whom reached for me as if to make me stop, then fell to her knees, as if pushed or thrown, the palms of her hands pressed together in prayer. Soon every nun in the convent was reciting the rosary along with me.

Then we heard the children, their voices singing out in sudden and ecstatic freedom. With none of the Sisters left to tend them, the girls were free to do as they pleased. Their footfalls thundered joyously up and down the hallways until one child pushed open the chapel door, and the crowd of girls out in the vestibule fell in a hush. Soon the chapel overflowed with all the girls of the orphanage praying in honor of the Madonna.

"Hail, Holy Queen, Mother of Mercy," we cried. "Hail, our

life, our sweetness, and our hope! To thee do we cry, poor banished children of Eve; to thee do we send up our sighs, mourning
and weeping in this vale of tears! Turn, then, most gracious advocate, thine eyes of mercy toward us; and after this our exile,
show unto us the blessed fruit of thy womb, Jesus! Oh loving, Oh
sweet Virgin Mary!"

THAT EVENING MOTHER Superior called me into her office. She
told me to sit and tell her every single thing that had taken place.
I did, starting with the slap that first sent me to the chapel.

Mother Superior sighed heavily as she listened to me. She said
that she'd have to report the incidents to the archbishop of the
diocese. Then she took my hand and told me that since Satan has
the power to take on a variety of forms, we both had to be extremely careful. I told her I was certain that the woman who'd
appeared to me was the Madonna.

"To be more safe," Mother Superior said, "I'm going to give
you a vial of holy water that I'd like you to keep with you on
your person at all times." She opened a drawer and withdrew a
light-blue vial of water, then poured some on my forehead and
with the water made three signs of the Cross. I knelt at her knees
and crossed myself three times, too. She blessed me with holy
water on my eyes, my ears, my nose, my mouth, and both of my
hands, then placed a cross on a chain around my neck and smiled.

"My child," she said, "may God bless and be with you in the
coming days! Now, if the vision appears again tomorrow, sprinkle
some of this holy water on her, saying, 'Stay if indeed you are the
Blessed Virgin, but in the name of Jesus Christ if you are anything
else, begone!' "

"Yes, Mother Superior," I said.

At the appointed time the next afternoon I returned to the
chapel, followed by Mother Superior and several of the Sisters.
Seven or eight priests were gathered near the pulpit, milling about
like chickens scratching for seed in a yard. As I entered the chapel

the priests stood motionless and watched me, each eye trained on my slightest move. I knelt in my usual spot, near the side aisle in the back pew, fingering the beads of my mother's broken rosary. "Hail Mary, full of grace!" I said in a loud, clear voice. "The Lord is with thee! Blessed art thou among women!"

She appeared before me then, wearing her blue robe as well as a gold, multipointed crown. I completed my prayer and stood, then sprinkled her with the vial of holy water as I recited the words I'd been told to say. "Stay if indeed you are the Blessed Virgin, but in the name of Jesus Christ if you are anything else, begone!"

She smiled patiently. The holy water I splashed on her gown sparkled like jewels.

"You didn't doubt me, Anna, did you?" she said.

"No, Mother," I said. "Not for one moment."

"Then put the vial away and do as I say. Have the smallest children brought here to me at once."

I turned and repeated her words to Mother Superior. She glanced toward the priests, who edged closer down the center aisle, then nodded at several of the other Sisters. Soon the orphanage's youngest children were gathered around me, sitting or standing at my side or cradled in the arms of the older Sisters who cared for them.

Most of the children saw her, though the Sisters apparently did not. The children smiled and reached their arms up toward her. How I still can remember the sweet sound of their bright cries!

The Madonna moved among the infants, blessing them and soothing them until all were content. Some gurgled with glee. Some cooed. Others fell back in their baskets, sound asleep.

One of the older Sisters who was too feeble to do much of anything sat among the babies, weeping openly and twitching, as she always did, with palsy. The Madonna touched the old nun's forehead, and the woman's body grew still and at peace.

Then a blind girl about three or four years of age gazed suddenly around the chapel. Her fingers tore at her eyes as she shouted incoherently, then grew calm and laughed and stood up on the pew, stretching her hand toward the ceiling as if she might touch one of the dangling lights. Then the twisted legs of a six-year-old crippled girl relaxed in their braces and straightened. A young girl with a face so frightfully disfigured that she usually hid behind her hand screamed as the Madonna gently drew the girl's hand down from her face and folded it with her other hand in prayer. Mary then pressed the flat of her palm against the girl's forehead, and the girl's deformity melted as her face grew radiant and beautiful.

There was so much rapture around me I could hardly think. By now the priests from the diocese had rushed forward in alarm. One Sister's clear voice began singing "Ave Maria."

The Madonna stood before me then, her face as dark as a womb. She said I must tell all who would listen that she wanted to announce the beginning of a new order.

There are three orders of time through which the world must pass before its end, the Virgin told me. These orders of time correspond to the three faces of God: the Father, the Son, and Holy Ghost. During the first order of time, she said, the world was created and governed by the Father. During the second, it was redeemed by the Son. The world was now entering the cusp of its third and final order, to be perfected and ruled by her.

"And not the bird?" I asked. Please understand that then I was only a child, used to thinking of the Holy Ghost as it was usually depicted, as a bird.

She laughed at me. "If you need to think of me as a bird, then for you I'll be a bird." She transformed herself then into a dove, gracefully flapping her wings, then allowed them to grow darker as she turned into something that more resembled a raven or crow.

"But I thought you were Jesù's mother," I said.

"I am," she said, folding her dark wings into her robe and once again resuming her human form, "as well as his sister, as well as his spouse, as well as the third face of God known to you as the Holy Ghost. I am all of these things, all at the same time. Jesù and I are twin souls, and one with God the Father."

LATER THAT NIGHT, as we sat around the head table in the orphanage's dining hall, the priests asked me to recount all that had occurred. Joining us was the archbishop and his personal aide.

After I described the three orders of time and told them the prediction of the Virgin's rule, a priest with narrow eyes and white, bushy hair leaned forward and said the apparition was likely an ignorant schoolgirl's hysterical hallucination. He spoke to the others at the table as if I weren't there.

"Look at her," he said. "Look at her hands and how she's gnawed her nails down to the quick. Look at her dirty face and uncombed hair. Why would the Holy Mother reveal her most sacred personage to someone like this?"

The priest sitting next to me lifted one of my hands and showed my chewed nails to the others, as if I were a thing on display.

"And even if there were an apparition," the white-haired priest continued, "it proved itself to be evil by its heretical words." It was sheer and utter heresy, he went on to say, for anyone to suggest that the Virgin was equal to Christ. Thus, even if a spirit had appeared in the chapel, by holy doctrine it had to be Satan's doing rather than God's.

The others looked at one another and nodded.

A dark young priest smiled at me and raised a finger in the air. "For the sake of discussion," he said, "consider the many similarities between Jesus and Mary. In all of the Master's creation, only Jesus and Mary were conceived without sin. Both led lives of absolute goodness and undeniable purity. Both were assumed bodily—that is, literally and physically taken—into the sky and beyond, to Heaven."

"But Mary is not God," the white-haired priest said.

"Her divinity may be the very issue we're discussing," said the dark priest. "My initial point is that she shares more in common with Jesus Christ than with any mortal, including the holiest of saints."

There was a moment's silence, during which no one disagreed.

"As for the question of heresy," the dark priest continued, "let's think for a moment of God's revelations as existing on a continuum. History teaches us that God has revealed his divine nature to us incrementally, through a series of prophets, rather than entirely or at once. Consider, for example, how heretical Christ's teachings must have sounded to the Jews."

"But we're not Jews," said a third priest.

"For the sake of argument," the dark priest countered, "let's pretend for the moment that we are. For argument's sake, let's imagine ourselves in Jerusalem two thousand years ago. Who among us hasn't thought that if he were alive then and so privileged as to hear Christ's message and witness his miracles, he'd have the courage to follow him?"

"We have all chosen to follow him," said the white priest. "I fail to see your point."

"We follow God," said the dark priest, "whose workings lie beyond the scope of our comprehension, and whose face is infinite and changing."

"Preposterous!" said the priest who'd displayed my hands.

"Mary didn't die on the cross," a fourth priest said.

"True," said my dark advocate, "but it's every bit as true that God the Father didn't ask her to. What he in his wisdom requested of her was to accept Christ without the physical stain of man, and to be Christ's mother and to raise him. Jesus was asked to suffer on the cross for three hours after leading a public life of three years. The assignment given Mary cannot be said to be any less, since it lasted thirty years plus three, and then years beyond."

"I won't stand for this!" shouted the third priest. "This is blasphemy!"

"This is merely an intellectual discussion," said the advocate.

"Even if what you say is true," the fourth priest said, "we

should consider how Mary failed to lead a public life and as a result left behind no teachings."

"What is the life of example," said the advocate, "but teaching in its highest form?"

"Yet none of it is recorded," said the second priest.

"At least not officially," said the advocate. "Your argument becomes circular and thereby null once you admit that the only documents that we're officially allowed to accept are those that record the teachings of Christ."

"Are you suggesting we give credence to the apocryphal gospels?" the white priest said.

"I can't speak for His Holiness," said the advocate.

"And therefore it's most inappropriate for you to speculate on what in his wisdom the Pope has declared apocryphal," said the archbishop's aide.

"I heartily agree," said the white priest, "and, if you'd be so kind, allow me to add an obvious point. Mary can hardly be thought of as equal to Jesus since she was born a mere woman."

"But in God's eyes both women and men are equal," said the advocate.

"Then why didn't Christ choose any female apostles?" said the white priest. "Your point is dubious at best."

"We also have the girl's testimony that the apparition changed from human form to animal," said the fourth priest, "as well as from white to black, specifically"—the man paused and ran his finger down his page of notes—"from a white dove to a crow or raven. Such can only be the work of Satan!"

"Indeed," said the fifth priest, "the girl further claims that the spirit's face was colored! She herself called it a black Madonna!"

"A colored Madonna?" the second priest said.

"She'd have us believe the Blessed Virgin was colored?" the third priest said with a laugh. "A Negro?"

"Precisely my point!" said the fifth priest, slapping the table with his hand.

"The very idea is ridiculous!" said the second priest.

"Absurd!" said the third priest.

"It's worse than that," said the fourth priest. "It's heresy!"

"It's incontrovertible proof that the spirit is Satan!" said the third priest, bouncing like a nervous child on his chair.

"Forgive me," my advocate said, "but there is more than ample research to suggest that both Christ and Mary were of dark complexion. Further, there's a well-documented history of black Madonnas in Italy's Mezzogiorno region as well as on the islands of Sardinia, Malta, and the girl's native Sicily. We should remember that, at least geographically, the island of Sicily is closer to Africa than it is to Rome."

"I've toured southern Italy," said the archbishop, leaning forward and speaking for the first time. "This was several years ago, shortly after I'd taken the holy orders, while I was studying at the Vatican. I grew a bit weary of Rome's decorum and civilities and wanted to see a bit of the countryside. I tell you, it was like stepping down from the carriage and into the mud."

The priests around him laughed.

"In Calabria," the archbishop continued, "I met a local priest who made it his business to uncover statues of this so-called black-faced Madonna and have them repainted white."

"As they should be," said the third priest.

"Others took an even stronger stand," said the archbishop, "and had the false idols destroyed. They themselves smashed the figures to bits against the ground, then threw the broken pieces into the sea."

"Meaning?" said my advocate.

"Meaning," the archbishop's aide interrupted, "that His Excellency sees no reason why we shouldn't follow their prudent example."

"But what about the miracles?" my advocate replied. "A crippled girl walks tonight because of this black Madonna. A blind girl sees the delighted faces of others for the first time. Another child's disfigured face is now beautiful and whole. A nun's nervous disorder is now cured. Surely you can't deny these four miracles!"

"There are any number of explanations," the white priest said.

"Hallucination," said the second priest.

"Hysteria," said the third priest. "Delirium. Madness."

"Miracles?" the archbishop said, unpeeling the curled arms of his eyeglasses from behind his ears and then pinching the base of his eyes. "This afternoon in the chapel I didn't observe any miracles. Did any of you?" He rubbed his spectacles' lenses with a white handkerchief, then held them up to the room's light.

With the exception of the dark priest, who stood and walked angrily from the room, one by one the others said, not me, I saw nothing, that's right, nothing, who me, I saw nothing, not one single thing.

THE NEXT AFTERNOON I was forbidden to return to the chapel. It was to be repainted, I was told, on orders of His Excellency, the archbishop.

The Sister charged with carrying this news to me genuflected before me and kissed my hand, then looked up at me with sad eyes. "Forgive me," she said. "They told me to tell you that the apparitions must stop at once. I've followed their orders for so long that I don't know how not to obey them. On the archbishop's orders you're to scrub the floor each afternoon until the visions come to an end."

I got my bucket and scrub brush, my soap and water and rags, and started as usual in the front lobby near the entrance, where the floor was always the dirtiest. After a few minutes the sad-eyed Sister knelt a few yards away from me with a bucket of soapy water and a brush. She folded up the long sleeves of her black habit and began scrubbing. The nun whose palsy had been healed soon joined her, then a third and fourth.

Then Mother Superior walked over to where I was washing the floor. She nodded to the others, then lay prone in the dirty water at my knees. Taking the brush from my hands, she instructed me to pray. Behind her stood all the other Sisters, each carrying a bucket and scrub brush! My throat gave out a tiny cry. Behind the nuns stood all of the orphanage's girls. Mother Superior began scrubbing the floor in my place, and everyone else took out their rosaries and knelt and made the sign of the Cross, and I began the Apostles' Creed.

We went through three rosaries before the Madonna appeared there in the lobby, barefoot and somber, wearing a peasant's apron over a simple gray gown the color of an autumn storm. After blessing the infants and then the girls and the good Sisters, she told me that I must carry her message out into every corner of the world.

She told me I must tell everyone who would listen that the world must immediately stop all warfare, all violence, and all attraction to violence of any kind. If warfare was not stopped, she warned, the world would soon experience a cataclysm beyond imagination. She said that fire would fall from the sky, and the ground would shake and rip itself open, and the walls of the city would crumble like dirt spilling into a newly dug grave. The flesh of the living would melt and drip like beeswax, and Satan would rejoice with this victory over the Prince of Peace, and all the living responsible would be coupled for all eternity to their deeds. This was the main message of the world's third order, of which she was the herald as well as the determiner of whether the world would continue or would be destroyed.

"Dearest Mother," I said, "please forgive me for asking you this, but how can we possibly stop the world's wars and violence when we can't even prevent a dozen priests from repainting the chapel?"

"By doing three things," the Madonna responded, "the first of which is prayer. Each day you must pray a minimum of seven Our Fathers, seven Hail Marys, and seven Glory Bes along with the Apostles' Creed. It would be better still if you were to recite the rosary. Make room for the rosary in your life! Make prayer a daily habit. Pray devoutly and without distraction so that you strengthen your soul to do the next two things."

"And the second thing?" I asked.

"The second thing you must do is bear witness, by which I mean that you must observe, question, and speak out in a clear voice against any and all acts of violence. The eyes that witness acts of violence, along with the ears that hear of violence, possess the power to end it only if they speak out. Make absolutely no threat while doing so. Say simply what you've seen or heard, then firmly request that the violence be ended. Say the same the next day, for the next hundred days. Ask a hundred other voices to join yours. If after a hundred days the violence continues, speak out for a hundred days more. When one tongue is joined by ten others, ten tongues by a hundred, a hundred tongues by a thousand, even the cruelest master will put down the whip."

She said this included violence of any kind but particularly violence against the world's women and children, violence against the old and sick, violence against the weak and helpless, against the animals and plants, against even the earth and its water, its soil, its fire, and its air.

"And the third thing?" I asked.

"The third thing is conversion, which follows from prayer and social witness. You must work to convert all those attracted to violence and its various forms and manifestations to a love of peace. When you hear a man say that he is thrilled by fighting, take his hand and kneel with him and pray. Begin with a single Hail Mary, Our Father, Glory Be. Recite with him the Creed. Conversion begins with prayer. If he will not pray with you, say that you will pray for him, then kneel down in his presence and pray. Ask him again, every day, to join you. At no time should you make any threat against him. Pray for him, then pray with him, then ask him to join you as you bear witness against the world's violence. Teach him the methods of conversion. If over the course of a life you convert one man and he converts another, and the other converts a third, and so on, over time you will have converted the world, and it will be spared the horrible cataclysm that awaits it."

She took leave then, after turning the dirty water in our buckets into a liquid so lucid and transparent that we saw every good thing we'd ever desired or found lovely reflected in it. I saw the glowing face of my mother holding me in her arms, then nursing a wide-eyed and pink-cheeked Petru!

Hearing our shouts of delight, a pair of priests came out of the locked chapel. Seeing us all down on our knees, they demanded that we stand at once.

In frustration one of the priests kicked the side of Mother Superior's bucket, causing it to bleed. Deep red blood rushed copiously from the side of the metal bucket. Then the blood thinned, and water ran from the wound. One of the girls then pointed and shouted, "Look!"

The crucifix over the chapel doorway was bleeding from each of Christ's five sacred wounds. As we crowded around to see it, one girl noticed that inside the chapel the towering crucifix over the altar had also started bleeding. There were droplets of blood on each crucifix above the wooden carvings depicting the stations of the cross. Blood ran from the images of Christ in the chapel's stained-glass windows. There was hardly a place in the church that wasn't bright with blood. Each representation of Christ in the chapel dripped deep-red blood.

One of the priests rushed up the altar steps to the tabernacle, genuflected before it, and unlocked it in an attempt to rescue the consecrated Hosts stored there. As proof that these were sacred rather than evil signs, the gold ciborium holding the Hosts immediately overflowed with blood.

The blood spilled out from beneath the ciborium's lid, over the priest's fingers and wrists, and down the three steps of the altar. The blood took the form of a scarlet ribbon about an inch or two wide. It flowed past the communion rail, where it pooled in a graceful coil, then turned and ran parallel with the first pew toward the side aisle, where it turned ninety degrees down the aisle and ran to the spot where I was standing, by the back pew where I'd knelt when the Madonna had first appeared to me five days before. The blood stopped at my feet.

"In the name of the Father," I shouted, "and of the Son, and of the Holy Ghost." Everyone, even the priests, then joined me in the recitation of the rosary. As we finished the rosary's final decade and I began the closing prayer, the blood in the chapel and the hallway began to fade and then disappeared altogether.

I walked to the main altar, stepped up to the pulpit, and in a voice so calm and unflinching it seemed to me not to be my own announced all that the Madonna had told me about the evil attractions to violence and war and the world's horrible ending as a result, how the Blessed Virgin was the herald of the third order, and how we must pray, bear witness, and convert others to prayer and social witness if we hoped that the world might be saved.

On orders of the archbishop, I was confined to a closet in Mother Superior's office on the seventh and final day.

The older girls were told that they'd be taken with the Sisters to a picnic at the zoo. They were promised baskets full of fruit, sandwiches made of meat and cheese, and chocolates wrapped in shining paper. You should have heard the girls' cries as the parade of motorcars arrived, sounding their bright horns. For many girls it was the first time they would sit and ride inside a motorcar. For many it would be the first time they'd see a wild animal.

Mother Superior's closet was just wide enough for a prie-dieu on which I could kneel without discomfort just as long as I didn't try to stretch my legs all the way back. Convinced that the visitations were the work of Satan, the archbishop sprinkled the closet with holy water and drew crosses on each of its four walls. Then he pushed me inside the closet and down onto the prie-dieu.

Meanwhile, his aide spooned sweet-smelling incense onto a hot white coal inside a silver censer. The archbishop took the smoking censer and swung it back and forth over my head inside the closet, blessing the cubicle with so much smoke that I could hardly breathe. Then he splashed me with holy water, and with his thumb inscribed a cross on my forehead and the backs of both of my hands with oil, and then he drew over the three crosses with his dark marker. Then he forced my mouth open and stuck his thick thumb between my lips, rubbing another oily cross on my tongue and marking it with his pen, saying that he'd slap me if I tried to spit out the bitter ink or oil.

"When the black Prince of Evil comes calling for his little slut," the archbishop said, pushing me again down onto the prie-dieu and back into the narrow closet's far corner, "show him these signs and tell him that you belong to me." He shut and locked the door then, and I fell into the darkness.

I was not discontent to kneel there in silent prayer, though my jaw ached from the struggle with the archbishop, and after the first few hours the air in the cubicle grew dank and stale and I could hear the orphanage's rats scuttling inside the walls. The rats ran across our legs sometimes when we were asleep. I recited a dozen rosaries, then grew weary and tried to stretch my legs. That only caused the rats in the walls around me to become more noisy.

I was thirsty and hungry and searched the floor with my hands for a stone or pebble on which to suck. One of the baseboards was loose, and after a while with my fingertips I was able to pry it off its nails. The plaster beneath the baseboard was crumbly and soft. With my fingernails I scraped some of the plaster into the palm of my other hand, and soon I had enough for a good mouthful.

There was something very soothing about listening to the rats, about eating wall again, after all those years. In the darkness I imagined myself back in the cold tenement flat where I'd lived with my father, and before that with his brother and wife and their family, and I remembered how in winter a thickening glaze of ice would glisten on our walls, and how I'd sit by the window and yowl and pretend to be a cat. I swallowed the grit and licked my palm like a cat. Then I licked my arm up to my elbow, and then I licked my other palm and arm. Soon I grew so lonely and sad that tears fell freely from my eyes on their own accord.

I wondered why the Madonna hadn't yet visited me. Had I

rushed through the rosary I'd recited as I stood before the ribbon of blood? Had I spoken too loudly or vainly from the pulpit while conveying her messages? Or had she found out from God that perhaps all this time she'd made a mistake visiting me because in truth I was so sinful? Maybe everything the archbishop said about me was true, I thought. Maybe I really was the devil's slut, and she no longer found me worthy.

Then I saw clearly that what had filled my heart the day before was pride, humanity's main failing.

I was sinfully vain that it was me the Madonna had chosen rather than another girl. My heart was selfishly giddy with the idea that all of these exciting events were occurring because of me, the ragged little dark-eyed girl the nuns first thought was fresh off the boat from Italy. I remembered how much pleasure I felt when Mother Superior stretched out before me on the dirty, soapy floor. I remembered how happy I felt when she took away my brush and kissed my hand. I remembered how proud I became when the other Sisters knelt all around me.

I wept and pulled my hair and beat my chest. "Mother in Heaven," I said to the dark wall, "forgive me."

I wondered what I had done wrong to have made my mother die. I wondered why it was Petru, rather than me, who was destined to suffer the endless void of Limbo. I knew that both events were somehow my fault, that I never should have left my mother's room the night she gave birth to my brother, that I shouldn't have been weak and become sleepy but instead been stronger and kept Rosalie quiet and brought my mother a cool cup of water or somehow soothed her or stroked her hand. I should have said a prayer for her, I thought. Maybe that would have been the difference. I wondered if when my brother was born there might have been one or two moments that busy, tired Zi'Assunta missed, some fierce fraction of a second when he was really alive, and in that slit of an instant if only I'd been more aware I might have been able to baptize him and save him from an eternity of numbing nothingness.

How I hated Zi'Assunta for lying to everyone! I thought that if I were God I'd surely damn her to Hell. I wished that her precious Rosalie was in Limbo in Petru's place. That was only fair, I thought. I damned her patron, Saint Rosalie, for having saved Palermo centuries ago from an ancient plague. Maybe it would have been better if everyone in Palermo had died, I thought. Then my parents would never have gone there since there would have been no place to go, and there would have been no mosaic of a lady on a wall and no Cathedral of Sant'Anna, and my parents wouldn't have married and journeyed here and conceived and given birth to me and Petru, and my brother wouldn't be stuck in Limbo, and I wouldn't be locked in an orphanage's dark and suffocating closet with an aching jaw and bitter balm still burning my tongue while all the other girls were out riding in fancy motorcars and having a merry time at the zoo.

"Why are you feeling so sorry for yourself?" the Madonna said to me as she appeared.

She hovered on the wall before my prie-dieu. I didn't know what to say to her—I felt so upset and ashamed and unworthy—so I said nothing and for several minutes only sniffled and cried.

"You're worried that everybody else is having fun," she said. "You don't know that right now they're kneeling in the park saying the rosary for you. You don't know that right now your mother and brother Petru are rejoicing at your courage, and that both are one with me in Heaven."

"How can that be?" I said, hot and angry. "Zi'Assunta lied. Petru's not in Heaven. I saw his dead body with my own eyes."

"Be calm," the Madonna said.

"She didn't baptize him!" I shouted. "I saw his body on the floor in a pan."

"And do you think that your Zi'Assunta was the only one who could perform a baptism?" said the Madonna.

I didn't know what to say, so I shrugged.

"Do you think Zi'Assunta is the world's only midwife?"

I shrugged again.

"Do you think that for all these centuries I could be in Heaven content to sit by idly while all the world's unbaptized babies were sentenced to Limbo? What kind of woman do you think I am! What kind of mother would possibly do that to her children? Limbo is so empty it's void even of emptiness! Compared to Limbo this narrow closet is Paradise itself! Oh, Anna, I tell you, since the first moment of human time I've baptized them all! I've fed each unborn child the milk from my breasts, I've washed each with my tears, I've swaddled each with cloth from my robes, I've cradled each in my arms, I've kissed each with my lips, I've soothed each with my song to blissful sleep."

"Holiest Mother!" I cried.

"After Eve and Adam's fall, it was determined that the part of God known as Jesù would redeem the living, and the part of God known as Mari would redeem the unborn."

"Jesù e Mari!" I screamed.

"Trust me, my child. Only the purest of souls are those taken into Heaven before their first year! Each has a special place beside me! And each woman who does the sacred work of midwifery shares a special place beside me upon her death! Why else do you think I made my own mother, Anna, patron saint of women in labor? Why else do you think I was conceived without sin, as well as able to give Jesus a virgin birth? It was to show the living that birth is the most sacred and blessed act anyone may commit or attend."

She told me that during the time she walked the earth, ever since the child Jesus was old enough to accompany her, she had served others as a midwife. She said it was the most sincere form of compassion, rather than deceit, for midwives who delivered dead babies to assure the families that the child had been baptized in time.

She didn't have to say in so many words that it was her last visit to me. After a while she grew silent, and I understood that she had nothing more to say. Like old friends we gazed into each other's eyes for a while. As I became aware of the silence between us, the figure on the wall before me gradually became still and fixed. I reached out my hand to touch the hem of her gown but her image was flat and unmoving, imprinted as if painted on the closet wall.

Both the image and my prie-dieu remain there to this day, in what was originally Mother Superior's office, on the site of the old orphanage. Now on any given day you can see scores of pregnant women gathered around the shrine reciting the rosary. Sick and invalid children, as well as women carrying babies with known birth defects, kneel at or touch the prie-dieu in the hope of being cured. The chapel has become such a popular place for baptisms that the cardinal has had five baptismal founts built there. The Church unofficially acknowledges reports of over three hundred miracles.

The Vatican has yet to acknowledge her. Politics, I'm told. The Church calls her Our Lady of the Orphanage, though because of the image she left behind, the people of the neighborhood call her *Madonna nera* or the black Madonna.

Not even the Pope will be able to paint her face white.

I TOOK THE VOWS when I was eighteen, then spent several years in east Africa performing missionary work, tending mainly to sick and pregnant women and orphaned children. More than once I saw the Madonna in the face of the beautiful Eritrean people for whom it was my blessing to care. I was forced to return to the United States after the outbreak of the Second World War, after America added its name to the long list of powers to invade the shores of Sicily and sweep in power across the island.

As they say, he who rules Sicily rules the world.

Now I live a fully cloistered life, a life of silence and prayer and fasting. But back then, before the war, sometimes I'd stand on the Eritrean shore and try to see across the water. I'd look out at the expanse of the Red Sea, imagining that my mind was a boat able to paddle its length. I'd pass through the Suez Canal and head west and north for Crete, then follow the sea-lanes the ancient Greeks traveled until I set foot on the ground of the Sicilian province of Agrigento, then Girgenti, from which my father's family received its name.

I've often dreamed of visiting the village of my mother's birth and then following the road she took at the century's beginning, north to Palermo and the sea. There I would wind my way up and down the twisting streets and narrow alleyways of the old city and view the mosaic on the storefront of the Panificio Morello, then pray a rosary at the Cathedral of Sant'Anna. I like to think that as I entered the church I'd recognize the pew where it was my mother's habit to kneel and pray. I'd kneel in that spot and pray, too. In this way I'd be joined to her.

I'll be joined to her by praying the prayer she prayed every day for seven months, that men abandon violence in all of its forms and manifestations. I'll pray for the day when the world's gaze changes from a focus on Christ's death and resurrection to a worship of the female and all of life. I'll pray for the day when veneration of the crucified male shifts to adoration of the living female and the true miracle of virgin birth. It will be as fundamental a transformation as the world has ever witnessed. On that day churches the world over will replace the two blunt lines of the cross with a round image of the pregnant womb.

On that day the Virgin Mother will be given her full glory, and violence against women and children will begin to end, and the world will escape the cataclysm looming before it. That day will mark the beginning of God's third order, two thousand years of rule by the black Madonna, the Holy Ghost and third face of God.

In the name of the Mother, all who hear me, pray!
Have no other goal than prayer this and every day.

Now the twins of Girgenti ask if you're able
To join their Lenten feast at Saint Joseph's table.

At the Table of Saint Joseph

ℰRosaria and Livicedda Girgenti

OUR DOOR IS always open. Always open to the hungry. We know. No other way. There is always a pot on the stove. A pot of *sucu* or *zuppa*. Fresh *lasagni* we put in some water and boil. We make the *lasagni* fresh every day. Mix the flour the egg the spoonful of oil. Roll the dough flat out on the table. Cut the dough in thin strips with a knife. Lay the *lasagni* out on the bed to dry. With the knife we cut a piece of bread. For whatever mouth comes to our door hungry. Even in the middle of night we feed any mouth a bowl of hot *zuppa*. Some *lasagni cu sucu* if we have it. Piece of bread. Cup of coffee *cicoria*. Whatever we have. All that we have. And all we ask in return. Before they leave they bow their head say a prayer. For our special intentions. A prayer to Saint Joseph. Whom we beg with bent knee. To intercede with God on our behalf.

Our door is open. To whatever mouth knocks on it hungry. Ever since we followed Salvatore. Here to this new place. Elm and Cleveland streets. Chicago.

We follow Salvatore. Up the long road to the sea. The road it goes on for days and days. Endless days everlasting. The sea it stretches out into the air. The sea touches the hem of the faraway sky. The sea rages beyond the far reach of our eye. The long road it finally comes to an end. At the edge of the desperate water. A mighty boat lurches back and forth in the water. Thick ropes straining. So eager is the boat to depart from the land!

The water leaps at our feet. Foaming and hissing at us to stay. Salvatore he says don't walk in the water. We don't walk in the water. Don't pull up your dress. We don't pull up our dress. Stop making those sounds. We stop making those sounds. Follow me. We follow him. So many people climbing up on the boat. So many people leaving!

Up on the boat so many people. So many faces sick from the sea. Our mouth it has no air to breathe. The other people they breathe all the good air. We breathe all the bad air. The bad air it's all that's left. We follow Salvatore. Up on the dizzy deck. The boat sways this way and that way. That way and this way. To one side and the next. Way up and way down. There is so much sea. Between us and the land.

Salvatore he says stay close to Rosa and Assunta. We stay close to Rosa and Assunta. Keep your eyes down. We keep our eyes down. Wipe your mouth's drool. We wipe our mouth's drool. Don't run all over the boat eyes fluttering flailing your hands. We don't run all over fluttering flailing. No *eeeyaah-eeeyaah*. No *eeeyaah-eeeyaah*. When we arrive on the shore do everything. Each and every single thing the strange men ask.

Breathe says the strange man on the shore. We breathe. He listens with a black tube. Stuck to his ears. Breathe some more that's a good girl in and out. In and out. Look at you two you're a couple of dwarfs. You could be in a circus sideshow. The way you've trained your actions to mirror the other's. You're like two figurines inside a music box. Now stop dancing. Show me your tongue say *laaa*. He pulls up our eyelids. With a shiny little hook. He smells our skin. His fat nose all full of dark hairs.

So many people everywhere in the great room. All the tongues talking at once. Shoes shuffling scraping pounding the floor. Babies crying screaming. One woman she holds her face in her hands and weeps. She weeps with her face she rocks it in her hands like a dying thing. All over her poor back is written. The evil signs of the chalk. I want to go *Eeeee!* I want to go *Yaaah!* So many agonies. Crashing together in waves in the furious air.

Do you have a job one man he says. A job we say. Did you sign any papers. Papers we say. Sign the man says. Sign we say. His hand he wiggles his fingers in the air. Like eels pulled from a barrel wiggling in the air. Did you sign his mouth says. Yes we say we sign. Our fingers. We wiggle our fingers in the air.

They sign nothing Assunta she says. Assunta she pushes herself in front to the man. She tells us hush. We hush. She takes the hands of the man in hers. The eels.

And who are you says the man. He puts the eels in his pocket. I am Assunta of Girgenti Assunta she says. These two women they are my older sisters. They are confused from the long voyage here. Oh so confused from the long voyage. They are a bit simple from the time of their birth. Oh so simple from the time of their birth. But at work believe me they are quite bright. Oh so bright. They are harmless and shy. Oh so harmless and shy. They are excellent workers. Oh so excellent. They sign nothing. Nothing.

We sign nothing Rosa she says. None of us. *Niente.* Nothing. And who are you the man he says. Rosa Dolci their brother's wife Rosa she says. She takes out from her apron pocket. A piece of folded paper. The letter from Gaetanu and Luigi. The letter one day it fell from the sky. And Salvatore he looked up at the sky. Salvatore he gave his forehead a hard smack. Salvatore he said thanks be to God I thought they forgot me! Smacking his head with the meat of his palm.

Rosa she opens up the folds of the paper. As if it is a fragile leaf the hot wind might blow away. Read Rosa she says to the man. He puts on his spectacles. See she says and points with her finger. She points to the *alfabetu* on the paper. We come to join our family they live in *Nova York*. Our family they live in *Nova York*.

The man he takes our hands. Into his. He rubs the soft tips of his fingers. Over and over our hardened palms. Excellent workers he asks to our hands. Beyond belief Assunta she says. You should see them clean. They can work for hours and hours without rest. And cook! They cook like two angels. Nobody quite understands why. They have a special way with food. It's one of God's gifts. No one had to teach them. Just give them a hot pan and a drop of olive oil. Oh give us a hot pan and a drop of olive oil. And with scraps you'd throw to a goat they'll make you a feast. Oh such a feast. And since they don't talk much. You never hear them complain.

If they never complain the man he says and laughs. Then they're the best kind of worker. His eyes they sink into Assunta's brown eyes. Into Assunta's soft smile. If only every boat to land here the man says. Had its hold packed with pairs like these.

> *Give these two hands some mortar and bricks,*
> *I'll build the New World.*

CHANTS A MAN out on the street. He chants in the old way of the salt sellers. In the way of the men who sell fish. Of the men who sell nuts and seeds. Of the men who sell watermelons. Of the men who sell ears of corn. Roasted chestnuts. Sweet potatoes. We follow Salvatore up the New World's streets. So many horses and wagons and carts. So many people their tongues all talking at once. Such big houses they stretch all the way up to the sky.

Such noise all around you want to cover your ears. We cover our ears. You want to cover your whole head. We cover our whole head. You want to curl into a ball and cry. We curl into a ball and cry. Mamma! we cry. Mamma! Salvatore he shouts stand up what are you two doing out here on the street get up off the ground! We stand up. Wipe your dress! We wipe our dress. Stop crying! We stop crying.

We follow Salvatore. To find our sister Carla. Behind a doorway way up at the top of a hill of wooden stairs. Carla she lives there with Gaetanu and Luigi. They kiss us our lips with their lips. They embrace us our shoulders with their arms. Pinch our cheeks. Kiss us again. Our arms they push everybody away. Look at them Gaetanu and Luigi they cry. They're not so small! Look how they've grown almost like grown women!

Then everybody they all shout at the same time. Where's Papa everybody they say. All the faces the mouths the frightened eyes. They grow as dark as the darkest of nights.

We cover our head. Thrash on the floor. Kicking as hard as all of the shouting. Everybody they shout at Salvatore.

We follow Salvatore. Down the steps to the angry streets to the train. So many sad whistles from that train. Like somebody is dead. The train is sad we are leaving again. We are again leaving. Our ghost brothers and their wives. The ghosts of brothers and wives.

Mamma she says to us my bread my wine. My smallest sunrise smallest sunset. Whatever happens follows Salvatore. Wherever he goes. Make of yourselves a shadow. To his every step. We make of our self. A shadow. Do all he tells you. We do everything he tells. Without doubt or question. Without thought or hesitation. You are two lost lambs in the world without him Mamma she says. We are two lost lambs in the world we say.

> *Though I may be poor and clothed in rags*
> *Something in me sings.*

MAMMA SHE TEACHES US. Everything all that we know. She teaches us how to eat with a spoon. Which end of the spoon to hold. How first to chew. Chew and then swallow. The mouth doesn't first swallow and then chew. Not swallow first and chew. She says that over and over as we choke. As we go red and blue gasping for God's sweet air.

She has to pound our back. Over and over hard with the flat of her hand. Have us raise our two hands. Up to the heavenly saints. She teaches us how to wash our face. Our neck our hands our ears. Our arms our legs. Feet. The place. In between our legs. She teaches us how to make the napkin. With a fold of cloth.

How to wash out the blood. Until the cloth is again clean. How to comb our hair. With the teeth side of the comb. The comb pulling. Ouch! No I feel it ouch! No I feel it! She teaches us how to put on the stockings. Only one stocking on each foot. She says that only one of us. Should talk at the same time. She says that we should use. A tongue her ears might understand.

We have our own tongue. Our tongue it lives inside our mouth. Our own tongue it lives inside our ears. Only we hear it only we understand it.

Our own tongue it's too fast and strange. Too much a jumble for Mamma's slow ears. Papa's ears. For Carla for Gaetanu. For Luigi who is all of the time not there. Luigi he is all of the time not. For even Salvatore who loves us more than. He loves us more than. For Assunta whose hands. For Rosa with the curled lip.

> *Not enough land for the sons,*
> *Not enough dowry for the daughters.*

MAMMA SHE TEACHES US. How to put our feet in our shoes. Feet and shoes they both like to live on the ground. Shoes live on the ground one for each foot. She teaches us to put on our dress. In our dress there are two holes. One for each arm. The first hole is for the first arm. The other hole is for the other arm. But which arm is the first. The two arms look so alike. Which hole is the first hole. The two holes. Look so alike.

Mamma she teaches us not to put both arms. Into the same hole. Even if both arms. Fit. Sometimes we put both arms. In one hole anyway. Such fun it is. Oh such fun! To run outside and scream. Running outside screaming. Both arms in one hole. With both holes on one arm! One hole and both arms raised. Up to the holy saints. We make believe the dream man. Chases us. He comes from inside our sleep. Oh how he chases us! He puts bumps down our arms. He puts bumps up our legs. We scream! Oh how we scream!

Over our dress Mamma she says. We wear our apron. The side

with the pocket is the outside side Mamma she says. She teaches us about buttons. How they become very lonely. Whenever one is left alone all by itself. Like a lost brother. Or sister. Whenever your fingers forget to push. The sweet button into her hole. The sides of the hole they're just like a pair of arms. Like two arms they hold the button tight. Mamma she holds out her arms to us. We are her little button. Pushing our head. Our button head up between her arms.

Mamma she kisses us. Oh how sweet she kisses us. She kisses our cheeks. She kisses our lips. She kisses our eyes. She kisses our eyelashes. She kisses the tip of our nose. She kisses our chin. She kisses our fingers. She says these are your fingers. She kisses the tips of our fingers. These are your fingertips she says. She kisses our hand. This is your hand. Your fingers they are on the end of your hand. Your hand it is on the end of your arm. This is your arm. Your arm it sticks out the end of your shoulder. This is your shoulder. This is your other shoulder. This is your neck. It sticks out between your two shoulders. Your head sticks out the end of your neck. She kisses the top of our head.

She says oh even when you want so bad. When you want so bad inside you ache! Even when you ache so bad Mamma she says oh my sweet darlings. My innocent darlings! Don't knock your head. Against the wall! Don't knock your head against the ground. Against the door. Against the almond tree. Against the lemon tree. Against the olive tree. Against the mossy stump. Against the rocks in the fields. Against the stones on the ground. Against the side of the well. Against the bricks of the priest's house. Against the mansion of the master. Against the hard and tired earth.

Mamma she says oh my special babies. Listen she says oh listen to me. Inside your head she says. There's a little brain. Inside your chest. There's a soul. Her fingers they pick up an almond. Asleep on the shaded ground. She shakes the sleeping almond next to our ear. Can you hear that she says.

We hear the little spirit. Who lives inside the shell. The spirit she taps with her little hammer. Trying to get out. Inside the shell is an almond Mamma she says. Your brain is the same as this almond. So sweet I wanted you to eat it. I wanted *you* to eat it. Mamma she kisses the top of our head. The broken top. Her lips they come away from the kiss. All bloody and red.

Your head is like this shell she says. Broken and cracked. This is your head she says. Our head. She strokes our hair with her fingers shiny with water. Washing away the red bleeding blood. She squeezes our cheeks tight. She holds us close.

Please she says. Please. Don't smash your head. Any more all bloody on the ground. She shows us. The bloody ground. Mamma we say why does the earth bleed so bloody and red. When we smash our head against it.

Mamma she puts one finger. She pushes one fingertip against our lips. *Shhh* she says my precious babies. I can't understand you. When you talk. That giddy tongue. When you both. Chatter like mad birds at once. Please use words. My poor ears can understand. Don't knock your head. Don't make the *eeeyaah*. Even when your souls. When inside you feel so bad you ache. At times like those there are two things you can do. Work and pray. Work and pray. Put your two hands to work. Join your mind with God's in prayer. It is why God gave us hands. Why God gave us a brain. Why God put a little almond of a soul inside the shell of our body. To learn how to join the separate things he has made. Into something greater.

So we learn to mix warm water with soap. And scrub a thing until it's clean. We learn to sweep the floor with a broom. Until even the dark cracks between the planks of wood are without dust. We learn to put heat beneath a pan. Mix the oil of olives with cut vegetable and onion. When there is no vegetable to cook. We fry slivers of garlic in the whispering oil. Not too long Mamma she teaches. You don't want the garlic to brown. Pour over *lasagni* along with some chopped parsley. Grate some *pecurinu* on top if we have it. All the while the voice inside us reciting in our special tongue a prayer. Making a prayer out of our labor instead of making the *eeeyaah*.

We like to make the *eeeyaah*. The *eeeyaah*. We like to loll our head. Lolling back and forth like this. Head down to one shoulder. Down to one shoulder like this. Then over to the other shoulder. Over to the other shoulder like this. From one side to the other. Very slowly. Slowly like this. Then growing more fast. All the while making a sound. Our mouth sounding. At first low. Low like a frightened bird in a tree. Then a bit more loud. Like many birds all the tree branches are full. Lolling our head. Back and forth as fast as we can. Until we are screaming. All the while screaming.

Eeeee! I like to scream. *Yaaah!* I like to scream. *Eeeee! Yaaah!* Loud! Louder! For hours. Hours and hours! Endless hours. Everlasting hours! Days. Days and days! Endless days. Endless days everlasting! Until the sun falls in the sky. To the faraway place at the end of the earth. We follow the falling sun to the fields. The sun in the sky falling. The fields ever baking beneath the sun and hot summer winds. The fiery breath of the winds blowing over the fields. The blue of air and sky purpling. Sky rusting into gold.

Workers they fill the fields as the sun falls. Singing in time with their labor. In the cooling air their arms swing their sharp blades. The air filling with the sound of their swinging blades. Their arms filling with sheafs of golden grain. Carrying the golden sheafs on their shoulders to the bundlers. Carrying the bundles on their shoulders to the wagons. The wagons hoping to grow so heavy that the wheels groan. So heavy that a dozen donkeys cannot pull them. So heavy that all hunger disappears even after the master's share is paid.

> *The month of grain gives me courage,*
> *I eat and don't complain.*

Across the parched earth broken with stones. The earth cracked open with crevices wider than the arms can stretch. The earth scorched with fiery light as if ablaze. The falling sun in the sky blazing.

Eeeee! Yaaah!

Sometimes here in the New World. In the golden light of

evening. In the sun's blazing light of fading. At the hour of our evening prayer. A lone worker he trudges up the street. His boots they know the way home. They march his way home from the factory. His shirt still damp with his sweat. Around his neck he wears his bandanna. In one hand he carries his lunch bucket. His other hand it smokes a twisted black cigar. The worker he chants a song as he tramps home. We listen to their songs. Chanting in the ancient way over and over.

> *What a fool I was ever to leave*
> *The place where my mother died.*

Our mouth sings. Giving air to our tongue. Like this our head lolling. Our head lolling like this. Tasting the sweet air in our mouth our mouth open. Head lolling. With our throat going *eee-yaah. Eeeeeyaaah!* Over. And over. Again. And again. For hours. And hours. Endless hours. Everlasting hours. Singing in the fading light. Singing this moment in the falling light. With the sun rolling down the rut that keeps it straight in the sky. This moment of fading sky. Lolling our head lolling. Singing *eeeyaah!*

> *Because if she does a thing in time with me.*
>   *(If she does a thing in time with me.)*
> *And I in time with her.*
>   *(And she in time with me.)*
> *In time together.*
>   *(Her me.)*
> *The frightening clamor of our thoughts slips away from my mind.*
>   *(The roar of her thoughts slips from my mind.)*
> *The screaming of* her *thoughts slips from* my *mind.*
>   *(Her screeching thoughts they slip from my mind.)*

The tumbling clamor inside me falls away. Fading like the golden sun. And my mind grows peaceful. *My mind* grows peaceful. Her thoughts fall away and disappear. Falling away her thoughts they disappear.

Sometimes the sound of her thoughts. Is so loud and maddening. So insistent and confusing that sometimes I just scream. I scream too. Then I scream louder. I always scream more loudly then. I scream even more loudly. I am the louder screamer. I scream until my head starts throbbing. I scream until bright sparks of pain shoot from my eyes. I scream until the sides of my head pound. My head pulsates so loudly it wants me to smash it against a wall. My head the maddening hornet's nest of her thoughts. My head throbs with the cacophony of *her* thoughts. Inside my pounding head her thoughts. Her thought inside my aching head.

Consider never really being able to finish. A thought. A whole idea. A complete and actual idea. All. By yourself. Without having her. Without having *her*. Without the other there inside you poking her sharp nose. Poking her words like a pointed stick into the middle of your thoughts.

The other there finishing the thought inside your head. Before you even have the chance to think it. Thinking more quickly than the other is able to think. Sometimes thinking even *before* the other has occasion to think. The other there completing the thought for you. Before you even have the chance to start to think it. Before Rosaria understands it. Before Livicedda even has the chance to understand.

I start to say a sentence. And my mouth ends up finishing it. I can sometimes say a thought all the way to its end. Sometimes I can too. Being older I'm better at starting. I can feel her mind as she begins each new thought. I feel her thoughts as her words complete mine. My words complete hers. It's as if I open the door. And I walk through it. With the start of her words my mind empties. My mind empties too like a jug overturned.

> *I am a stone no one has any use for,*
> *flung to the weeds by a hoe.*

. . .

MAMMA SHE SAYS once the thread is knotted. You can't undo the stitch.

What's done. Is done. The egg broken into the bowl. Doesn't crow the next dawn. He who is born round. Cannot be made square. A person eating. Must make crumbs. If you sleep with dogs. You wake up with fleas. You cannot have meat. Without the bone. From the fruit. You know the tree. Only a fool wastes his life. Trying to live the lives of others. Whoever gets a bargain. Praises the market. Beware of water. But make friends with wine. The wheel's weakest spoke. Is the one that talks the most. Eat as you like. But dress to please others. Whoever wants too much. Will end up with nothing. The hen makes the egg. While the rooster sings about it. A man who loves wine too much. Is not worth two cents. Don't speak about a thing. Unless you know something about it. The dog that barks loud. Does not bite much. Crooked wood. Is straightened by fire. Stretch your feet no further. Than the end of your bedsheet. Whoever loses his good reputation. Loses everything. Better to be a swine. Than a soldier. Better to struggle with a hundred thieves. Than with a single stupid man. The dog that welcomes everyone. Is of no use to anyone. Only a mother hears the troubles. Of those who are mute. To form and break a habit. Are both difficult. Old habits. Grow into laws. Always have the greatest respect. For the place where you are now. The ancient proverbs. Teach us the true way. The proverbs of the ancients. Are unfailing. The proverbs of the ancients. Never lie. *Lu muttu di l'anticu. Mai mintìu.*

Mamma she says my babies! Think before doing a thing! Why else did the Holy Mother. Give you a head. The Holy Mother gave you. Two heads. Splitting in half. What might have gone to one into two.

Mamma she says with God's mercy and grace. Between our two heads we might have the sense of one. Just as long as we stay forever and always. As we were once in her womb. One next to the other. The other next to the one. Forever and always. Together.

When you're as poor as I am,
You're always out of breath.

As a baby I came out first. She came out first. Then after a while. I stuck my head out too. Nobody expected her to make an appearance. Nobody expected me even to be there. They say Mamma was so long in our labor. She prayed a thousand rosaries. I was the firstborn. Named for all the rosaries Mamma she prayed.

Even as they wrapped me in cloth. Wiping the bloody ricotta from her face and chest. Nobody knew that still inside. Still inside I was waiting there unborn!

I felt lonely without you then. I felt lonely without *you* then.

The birth walls they convulsed. As if I were something being swallowed. Only backward. Swallowed backward toward the growing light. The walls pressed her further downward. Until a mighty tremor shoved me out into the horrible cold air.

They say that the midwife was drinking wine. Celebrating the birth eating olives and bread. Spitting the chewed pits into the cup of her hand. Dropping the chewed pits down on the floor. She was just another little olive so they named her Livicedda. The midwife she spat out another pit into her hand. Which caught her. Her hand caught me just as I fell.

She was so small that the midwife's fingers. Hadn't even felt me. Hiding deep inside the salty sling of Mamma's womb. For all those months I hid inside my sister's arms. She curled up nice and tiny inside my arms. I can remember how it felt being held.

They say that once we were. One. The same. Egg. The same. Person. Before we split. In two. They say that once all of us. Even you. Were one. The same person. Once. All of us were children inside the first egg. In the warm and salty womb of the first mother. Our true mother. The Holy Mother. Who covered us with ricotta as she gave birth to the world.

Then something happened. To separate us. Something evil happened. To separate us all. We fell asleep and the dream man. No not the dream man. His dark sister. She came and cut us with her knife in two. Such a sharp knife! To be able to cut souls in two.

I have my own soul. I have my own soul too. I grow weary of it. I grow so weary of it too. I want once again to be part of you. I want once again to be part of you too. I want to be part of the whole again. We each want to again be part of the whole. Once again one all of us everybody. As one and the same person. Such a burden being separate. Such a burden this having your own soul.

> *If I don't soon learn to speak English,*
> *I'll die here and no one will know.*

ONCE WHEN WE were babies. I fell headfirst into a bucket of water. I was the one whose lungs gagged for air! The water in the bucket looked so cool and inviting. I couldn't even draw in a breath. Before I knew it I was head down in the bucket. My mouth sputtered and tried to scream. I stayed down in the water and the dream man's sister she stepped out from between the shadows. Mamma she said what's the matter stop your noise her hand hit me. Owww! I shouted from inside the bucket. Mamma she said I'm so tired of the two of you and your games. You make me. Crazy. Her mind it didn't know that at that moment. I was drowning. No *I* was the one drowning. No me. Me. Only when my face turned blue. Did Mamma's eyes begin searching for the other. Mamma found her outside head-down in the water. My arm still hurting from when Mamma had hit her.

Whenever one of us eats. The other tastes it. If a swarm of mosquitoes bites me. It's my leg that begs to be scratched. If I burn a finger. Mine blisters. Whenever I drink a cup of cool water. It's my thirst that is quenched.

That's why we. Can never marry. Because the other. Would feel it. Imagine how confused our poor husband. Would become. If he kissed. Her. And I didn't feel a thing. While I was the one to close my eyes and say *mmmmm*.

So over time we learned to eat and drink. To do the same things. The very same things. At the very same time. In equal portions. Simultaneously. Reflection. To the reflected. Garlic. Onion. Each of us pretending that we're actually tasting. What we have inside our mouth. Relying on the other. To be true.

> *The stranger on the horizon*
> *Doesn't arrive bearing gifts.*

I USED TO WONDER why no one in our family. Talked in our tongue. I wondered why Gabriella. Had such a long nose. I wondered if our nose. Would grow as hairy and fat as hers. Her whiskers tickled us. Whenever she nuzzled our head. I wondered why Mamma. Was so tired that sometimes she'd collapse to the ground. I wondered why the light in Papa's eyes. Became so dim. Why the bowl that held our family's supper. Grew bigger and bigger. Making the food in it. Seem less. Each day less. The next day again even less.

Why Papa would say that the only good thing about each passing day. Was that we were a few paces closer to our graves. Why Gabriella walked home one afternoon. Wearing an army cap. Why Mamma shrieked and shrieked. Why at night Papa muttered to the stars. Why Gaetanu went away. Why Carla seldom smiled. Why Luigi disappeared too. We asked the goats where Luigi went. The one drying up only turned. And showed us her dirty *culu*.

Papa he killed the dirty *culu* goat. So we would have something to eat. He hung the goat upside-down her back feet tied together. Slitting open her neck with a knife until she bled. Her bumpy tongue dangled out sideways. From between her dead teeth.

Salvatore he closed Mamma's eyes after she fell asleep. Up in the loft in the straw. In the cool dampness of the deep shadows. In the winter when it was raining and the air smelled thick and dark. We wrapped her body inside a sheet. Laid her in a hole. Salvatore he dug in the ground. Papa he covered Mamma with a thousand and one stones. We knelt beside the stones. Tearing the sky to pieces. Even in Heaven. They could hear our screams.

> *If nobody hears me singing my song,*
> *How will they know I was ever alive?*

WE FOLLOW SALVATORE. Wherever he goes. Even when we were children. We would go wherever he went. To the well. To draw water. To the fields. To thresh grain. To see if the chicken. Made an egg in the night. I helped Salvatore carry rocks from the fields. I carried rocks from the fields too. So heavy. All the stone. We worked alongside our brother. His two shadows in the field of stone. Day after day. Day after endless day. The sun in the sky above. Like a hot coal baking us. As if we were pieces of meat. The dry earth at our feet drinking our sweat. Old Gabriella she always found a piece of shade. She would laugh at us when she wasn't sleeping beside Papa. The two of them always together. Snoring so loud with their long snouts in the shade.

Salvatore he said Papa oh my Papa. Papa what in God's name am I going to do. With. You. Look at your mouth. You've got maybe two teeth left in your whole head. Look at your eyes. They're as blind as two figs. They say you have to be fit and strong. To make the long trip. I'm going to have a difficult enough time. Bringing along the two idiots. I pray to God Rosa and Assunta. Will be able to keep them calm. They say that to get in you have to be healthy. Young. A good worker. With a strong chest and muscles. You can't be an old man with a slumped back. Hair white as a dandelion gone to seed. What other choice do I have. I wish to God there was some other way.

Oh sky above speak to me Salvatore he shouted. Give me a sign show me the way. Salvatore he talked plenty then. To the sun. To the air. To the walls. To his shadow. The ground. The roof. The door. The almond tree. The lemon tree. The olive tree. The gnarled stump covered all over with moss. The rocks in the fields. The briars between the rocks. The bucket beside the well. The stones covering Mamma's grave.

Each night he cried out. To the Madonna and the saints. So many saints. How can God keep them all straight. So many dead souls. Still walking the earth. At night Salvatore cried out to all the dead souls. Who gather each night outside in a circle. Telling one another their tales. And why do they tell their stories. Sing their songs. Night after night. Year after year. Why don't they shut their eyes. And go back to sleep in the ground.

Why does anyone. Do anything. They must still. Have some need. Some may have to tell another. They are sorry to have broken a promise. Some have to return. A borrowed or stolen thing. Some seek vengeance. Against another who has wronged them. Some are desperately searching. For something or someone they lost.

Many still search. For someone they lost. Someone they disappointed. Or forgot to care for. Someone they took for granted. Someone they left behind or all alone. Oh so many were abandoned! So many of the weak and old were left all alone. So many of the slow. So many of the stupid. Papa can you hear us. Can you hear us still today Papa. Even all the way from here such a strange place. Elm and Cleveland streets so far away.

So many left that place. Two out of every five. Stepping onto the ships. As if departing were nothing. Leaving behind on the shore. The old the blind the lame.

> *Weeping, the cracked jug*
> *Pleads not to be thrown down the well.*

WHY DID THE ROOSTER. Scratch his throat just before dawn. Only to pull the sun up from the darkness. And begin yet another day of hunger. Why didn't the weeds Gabriella pulled from the ground. Taste good to our mouth too. Why was the sun. So fierce each summer. Why were the rains. So hard each winter. Why was the bowl. Always so empty. Why was the ground. So useless and hard and dry.

Why did Salvatore. Tell us not to drink from the jar of wine he would pour for the *baruni*. Why were Assunta's eyes. Always so red and searching the sky. Why was Carla. So sad after Gaetanu left that she cut short her long hair. Why did Luigi. Disappear the night the air smelled so sweetly of lemons. Why did Gaetanu walk up the road. And not look back once and never ever not even once return.

Why does the oldest man in our village. Each morning roll the rock up the steep hill overlooking the valley of ruins. Only to watch the rock. Roll back again down the hill. Why does he roll the rock. Back up the hill again. Day after day. Year after year.

> *Why do they think I'm a gangster?*
> *Because I eat macaroni? Because of my name?*

MAMMA SHE TEACHES us God in the sky. In the blue sky above us. God he made the holy saints. In the whispering green of the grasses and trees. He made the saints to hear the prayers of the people like you and me. In the fields of grain turning to gold around us. He made the saints to hear the workers sing their songs. In the twinkling shadows of the hills and their green forests. He made the saints to give comfort to those in need. In the shining waters of the sea that leaps so freely and madly onto the shore. In the fields of stone where the *genti di campagna* labor. In the dark and narrow hollows of the mines that stretch so deep.

Mamma she said God told the holy saints. Stop sitting around Heaven useless get up and give me a hand. Help me care for the poor living souls. Most are so miserable they moan all day and night long. Pleading with me for whatever they want or think they need. Their prayers they sometimes give me a big headache. I could pull out all my hair. I could throw the stars through the sky and scream. Run away to the highest clouds. Turn my back on them. Put tomorrow in my pocket. And never return. Then who do they think would cook the night's *zuppa*. Who'd care for the sun and moon. It would be real easy for me to forget them and leave. I nearly killed them all once. I wanted to stomp on them with my foot. Like a thousand and one ants crawling all over the ground. Instead I made it rain for a thousand years. I wanted to drown them all. But out of my mercy and kindness I warned one poor family. I told them to build a big boat that would take them across the dizzy waves of the sea. To a New Land of promise. A new Golden Land of promise.

> *Give me a pick a shovel a wheelbarrow,*
> *I'll build a road to Paradise!*

YOU GOD SAID. Pointing to the nearest saint. In your life you were once a fisherman. You be the patron of all those who go to the sea and fish. You with the hoe. You help all those whose muscles till the earth. You care for women in their long hours of labor. You care for women with a suckling at her breast. You guide all those whose way has become lost. You care for the unfortunate children who are orphaned. You're the patron of hooved animals. You're the patron of children who die at birth. You're the patron of bakers. You guide those who lay on hands and heal and foretell things that are to come. You're the patron of barren women. You're the patron of fruit and vegetable pickers. You be the patron of textile workers. You be the patron of printers and those who work with and sell paper. You protect the industrial workers. You protect the orators who speak out in the cause of justice. You protect the wrongly accused. The most desperate and impossible of situations. God left to the last in line Saint Jude.

Whenever you lose a thing. It helps to say a little prayer.

> *Dear Saint Anthony, come around.*
> *Something's lost and can't be found.*

Mamma she said that's why people. Pray to the saints. You start by lighting a candle. To cast light upon the darkness. Praying to the saints takes a great deal of time. A great deal of patience. Time to the blessed and holy. Does not mean much. They have all of eternity. And then some.

You have to find the right saint. The one who fits your need. Mamma she said once the great city Palermu. Had a horrible plague. The people they prayed to one saint after the next. They tried a thousand and one different saints. Finally someone said a prayer to Saint Rosalie. Finally someone lit a candle to Saint Rosalie. Finally someone made a vow to Saint Rosalie. Finally someone carried Saint Rosalie's picture on a pole through the streets. Finally the people carried the bones of Saint Rosalie all the way to the bishop's palace. And at once the plague ended. Within a moment the sick were cured. The dying stood and danced. The living celebrated. Playing their horns. Beating their drums. Shooting fireworks into the sky. As four great horses pulled through the streets the saint's magnificent cart. Our eyes saw the cart as we passed through Palermu. The cart was as big. As the baron's house.

To this day each year in Palermu the people they give thanks. Until all the sand has run from the glass. Until God is so old that he forgets who he is. Until God thinks he's a rag seller riding through the alleys singing.

> *Rag-a-man! I buy what you got.*
> *Rag-a-man! You buy what I got.*

Calling out to all as one does now. An old white mare pulling his cart. The women they shout from their windows. Do you sharpen knives. And God laughs and says what rag seller doesn't. His toothless smile his leg pumping the big spinning wheel in his cart.

In the same way the morning after Luigi disappeared. Mamma she knelt and made a vow to Saint Joseph. If ever Luigi returns safe and alive Mamma prayed. I will make a table in your honor. If ever our family is once again whole. I make a table.

Then as a pledge of her good intentions. Mamma she made a table for Saint Joseph that first year. She made a table the next year. And the next year. Then after Luigi returned. In gratitude every year Mamma she made a table.

Each year March nineteenth we make a Saint Joseph table too. Just like Mamma. Because our family. Has been cut in half too. We pray to Saint Joseph. To make our family once again one.

Dearest Saint Joseph we pray. Bring us together again all in the same place. Gaetanu and his wife with the pants and their many children. Luigi and his sweetest little lamb. Carla and her Gerlando the baker of bread. Assunta and her darling Rosalie. Salvatore and his Rosa and their seven daughters and sons. Papa Santuzzu too. Who stands as we left him in the shadow of an almond tree. Weeping a sea as we make our good-byes.

Eeeee! Yaaah!

Part of us all died the night they strapped
the shoemaker and fish peddler in the chair.

PEOPLE THEY COME from all over. To our house. They knock on our door. For something to eat. A bowl of hot *zuppa*. A plate of *lasagni cu sucu*. Hot cup. Of coffee. Of course a nice piece of bread. To everyone who knocks on our door we give bread. We break bread with everyone the good saints lead to us. And after they eat we ask them bow their head to pray. Our door is always open. Always open to the hungry. We know. No other way.

Each day every day. Each night every night. We feed whoever comes. With hunger and need to our door. All the poor and starving. The pots on our stove they never grow empty or cool. Like a saint Gerlando he bakes for us the bread. And gives it to us free. On Saint Joseph's Day he bakes a special Saint Joseph's Day bread. Loaves shaped just like the staff Saint Joseph carried. We cook everything else all the special foods. Placing them on the three levels of the table. Just like the altar's three steps. Three for the faces of God.

We cook the Saint Joseph's Day *sucu*. It's a tomato sauce with fennel and anchovies. We sprinkle it with toasted bread crumbs. Grated to look just like Saint Joseph's sawdust. We cook Saint Joseph's Day eggs. Fried in a little oil. We cook vegetables and fish. We make noodles of every kind. Carla she comes to our kitchen to help. Assunta she comes to help. We all cook in our kitchen together. Sisters mingling together. Like spices in a *sucu*. Onion and garlic and *basilicu*.

We make *cucciddati* in a thousand and one shapes. We grate the figs. We chop the dates. We make cookies and sweets of every imaginable kind. Bones of the dead. Pine cones. We fry pieces of dough. Drizzling them with honey as sweet as the Virgin's grace.

> *What else can I do to belong to this land,*
> *To make it a home where I feel welcome?*

THE NIGHT BEFORE the big feast Salvatore he goes out into the streets. He finds for us the Holy Family. He searches the streets and alleyways for a poor hungry man to be our Saint Joseph. Salvatore he searches for a poor and hungry woman to be our Mary. He finds a needy child to be our Jesù. They make a knock on our door asking if we have room. We don't turn them away. We kneel before them. Kiss their hands. The hems of their ragged clothes. We thank them for blessing our house with their holy presence. We take off their shoes we wash their feet. We offer them three beds. Then we kneel and pray. Praying in thanks for their company through the long night.

The next day the Holy Family they sit on three special chairs. The seats of highest honor. All the people who come for the feast kneel. They ask the Holy Family for their blessing. Each food the Holy Family they have to taste before the food is shared. They have to take at least a bite of every single plate and dish! Then we kneel and say the rosary while everybody eats. We pray the rosary amidst the sounds of feasting the warmth of all the bodies crowded here in our house together in praise of God.

Some who come to the table of Saint Joseph. They leave a few coins in a bowl. A millionaire he pins a dollar bill to the tablecloth. The bowl fills with silver and copper coins. We give the money to the church for food for the poor. All the leftover food from the feast we give to the poor. All that remains we give to the poor. Even the smallest crumbs. What may be a crumb to one. Is a feast to another. This we do in honor of and petition to Saint Joseph. Who gave a life of labor and devotion to the Madonna and Child.

How happy are the people who come here to our house to eat! How their faces fill with light! We fill the poor man Saint Joseph his pockets with food. We fill the poor Mary's shawl and bags. The child Jesù eats until he's so stuffed he can't move his legs. Our feast puts some nice fat on Jesù's bones!

And in Heaven all the angels and saints. They look down on us and rejoice.

So many saints up in Heaven above! More saints in Heaven than stars in the sky. More saints than drops of water in the sea. More saints than branches and leaves on all the world's trees. Grains of sand on all the world's beaches. Specks of dirt on all the world's fields. So many saints praying in Heaven above! So many dead souls walking the earth! Telling their tales. Singing their songs. And who listens to them. The stars in the sky. The drops of water in the blue sea. Such a wide angry sea. Why did we cross it why did we ever come here. If it was our fate for our family to be apart.

Eeeee! Yaaah!

Saint Joseph. Hear our prayer.

> *Like Mamma before us we beg God to make whole*
> *What was torn in two and yet shares one soul.*

> *Now Carla the firstborn she waits until last*
> *To speak of the cursed land and the rest of our past.*

Easter Bread

℘ Carla Girgenti

As MUCH AS I appreciate the abundance and opportunity the New World provides, don't think for a moment that I don't know the price we paid. I know my way around the market. I wasn't born the day before yesterday. For every obvious gain, one surrenders some unseen loss. The day Papa Santuzzu played the round of tresette and was dealt the perfect run of cards that won him Gabriella and led to the rest of his high hopes and dreams—well, in a way that day marked our death sentence. Though we hardly suspected it at the time, that day brought on the true end of our family.

Even though Papa understood that part of the cost of our going to the Golden Land would be the separation of the seven children from their parents, I'm sure he had no doubt that in his absence we'd all get along and behave. He imagined we'd arrive in *La Merica* and live happily together inside one big house, every evening before supper our lips saying a prayer for the ones we left back in the old country who made our journey to this paradise possible. It would be like in a movie where in the end everybody gathers around a huge table and raises a glass of wine and sings. Papa believed that in the New World everything would be at least as good as before, and of course that we wouldn't be starving.

He couldn't have anticipated our squabbles and consequent scattering. He never could have guessed that his three sons would live as far apart from one another as they could. One son would lay claim to the East Coast and labor in its mills and factories. One son would disappear somewhere in the forests and mountains of the West. The youngest son would turn paper into coin in the middle of the country beside the shores of a great lake.

In the old stories whenever a king turns over his domain to his children, he thinks they'll all behave as civilly as the Dutch. He thinks his kingdom will stay united and strong. It's as if one consequence of his generosity is that his mind must crumble and grow feeble. After ruling his kingdom for so many years, his eyes turn blind to the actual workings of power. The king imagines that after he has surrendered his authority to his children they'll somehow continue to abide by it.

Sure, and there are cats who think that when they're gone from the house the mice remain terrified in their holes.

I'll tell you the truest version of the story. Once there was a poor but honest man, *un'omu di sonnari,* a man of dreams, whose wild and giddy imagination came to believe that his three sons and four daughters could be sent away to a faraway garden where so much fruit grew on the trees that it fell and rotted on the ground, and all a man had to do was to put in an honest day's labor in order for his pockets to grow fat, and there the dreamer's children would be eternally happy. Little did the man know that the garden was full of scorpions and snakes and spiders, and the three sons would quarrel like angry crows and rip everything in their paths apart, and then their dark wings would fly off in three different directions, leaving *la famigghia* to scatter like the thistle's bristly seeds.

At least that's what the realist inside me came to believe. Remember, even though in these tales I speak next to last, my nose was the first to dry in the air. People forget that I'm older than Tannu and his dead twin. They think a firstborn daughter is like the sound a man makes to clear his throat before uttering an answer. It proves the voice works but doesn't count for much. The firstborn daughter is the broom that leans in the room's farthest corner. You think of her mainly when you have some mess to clean. More often than not she goes unnoticed. At best, the girl grows into her tired and overworked mother's shadow and transforms herself into her mother's third arm. At worst, the girl becomes a real *maledizione,* something that eats and talks too much and that you pray to marry off before she goes gray. Romantic notions don't have much of a chance to take root inside the firstborn's heart.

Don't look for my story here. I could tell it if I wanted, beginning with the day that Tannu left for the New World, when in anger at not being the one to go I cut short my hair. I could describe the afternoon in Palermu when I decided that Gerlando would be my husband and leave his father's shop. I could put you in the back of our sweet bakery in Cicero on any summer evening and make you feel the heat. But, long hair or short, I'm my mother's daughter, and I've learned first and foremost to do the job in front of me, whatever's best for the family. And right now, with the hour growing late, what's best is to say the rest of our story. No one else can.

I've seen it all, from the evening when Papa Santuzzu hurried home with that swaybacked donkey, valuing the beast so much that he didn't even dare to ride her, to the afternoon when Salvatore and Rosa Dolci and the three sisters arrived in the New World without him, and all of us imagined Papa stumbling about the Sicilian countryside blind and terrified and alone. As sure as my voice speaks today, I've seen the beginning of Papa Santuzzu's dream as well as the end of it.

So perhaps you can imagine some of my surprise the Sunday morning I approached Livicedda and Rosaria's flat and saw them at their kitchen table preparing *pani di Pasqua* with a laughing man whose grizzled hair and warm brown eyes could belong to no one other than our long-lost brother Luigi.

·   ·   ·

HE WAS SITTING at the kitchen table shaping the Easter breads with his thumbs and drinking from a jug of red wine as the twins danced around him with striped towels coiled around their heads like a pair of fortune-tellers at a circus. As usual, a pot of soup for those on the bum simmered on the stove. I put down the bag of Gerlando's loaves I'd brought them as Rosaria slid a tray of Easter bread into the waiting oven. Livicedda cried something unintelligible, waving a red-tipped wooden spoon in the air. She was dyeing the eggs, which Luigi was wrapping with dough fashioned into a variety of shapes, a few of which resembled fans or, with some imagination, assorted birds in flight, each holding its red, hard-boiled egg fast to its belly with a strip or two of dough. Other breads looked like raised and defiant fists, with the thumb holding the egg fast to the palm.

"Isn't it a bit premature for *pupi cull'ovi*?" I said as Luigi turned to me. "Or has Jesù decided to rise a week early this year?" It was a full week before Easter. Indeed, that morning at Mass we'd been given the year's palms.

"Carla!" Luigi shouted, standing and rushing forward to embrace me.

"Fratellu!" I cried, kissing his cheeks and lips. "All we've shared these many years are farewells."

"Then allow me again to greet you!" he said, kissing me again a dozen times.

"You've grown thin and gray," I said, stepping back. "Life's put its scars on you."

Luigi nodded. "These hard times have tumbled me about," he said sadly. "But look at you. You seem to have done well. You're still as fresh and bright as a young girl."

"I see your tongue still wears its coat of honey." I kissed and hugged my two sisters, complimenting them on their head towels. Rosaria checked the oven as Livicedda made the sign of the Cross and then broke off and ate a piece of Gerlando's bread. "Yum," Rosaria said, smiling as she turned to accept a piece from Livicedda.

"You really shouldn't begin the *pani di Pasqua* until Good Friday," I told Luigi. "And since when have we started to decorate them?" The wings and midsections of several of the birds as well as the palms and wrists of the fists were red, sprinkled with dyed sugar.

"The old grows tiresome," Luigi answered. "This is something new, a new custom for a new place."

"To form and break a habit are both difficult," I said.

"The donkey gnaws on the dead vine," responded Luigi, "remembering the time when it was green."

I smiled. "And the others?" I said, in my ignorance looking about for Tannu and Teresa and the dark swarm of their countless children, each with dimpled cheeks, as well as for my brother's daughter, Anna, who I estimated would be nearly old enough by now to wed. Perhaps, I thought, Luigi has come here to announce his daughter's wedding. Surely everyone else was out taking a mid-morning stroll, or maybe hiding in the next room, waiting to jump out and surprise me. "Don't tell me you came all the way here without the others?" I said, playing along.

Luigi winced, then clenched his jaw, and then all at once he let out a great sob. "Sister of mine," he said, "I'm so deeply ashamed to tell you. May God cut out my tongue and leave me to rot! May he throw me still alive to the flames! I haven't seen or heard of the others for years."

"Bite your hand!" I cried, then bit my own.

"Eeeee!" went Rosaria. *"Yaaah!"* went Livicedda.

Then, as the pan of early Easter bread baked in the oven and the twins ran in circles and tore off their festive headrags and cried out, and another lost and hungry soul knocked on the back door and asked for a bowl of soup and a crust of bread, our prodigal brother poured himself a glass of red wine and let loose the details of his story.

WITH TANNU IN the sanatorium and Teresa drowning in the mad sea of her many children, Luigi thought that in the orphanage at least his daughter would be educated and clothed and fed, so just as Papa Santuzzu had done with us years before, Luigi gave up his daughter with the hope that she might thereby escape the *miseria* and rise above them. Luigi said that during the month before his decision he had a series of vivid dreams in which Ciccina appeared to him wearing a multicolored dress, her face so fiercely radiant that he had to shield his dream eyes with his arm.

"Why are you out walking?" Luigi shouted to Ciccina in his dream. "Go back to your eternal sleep."

A trio of dead dogs, throats slashed, chests torn open, lay at Ciccina's feet. The dogs were ancient enemies, Luigi explained. Each night they'd come back to life and attack him, and each night he would have to kill them, over and over again, sometimes with a knife, sometimes a shotgun, sometimes with his teeth and the nails of his bare hands.

One night as the dream-blood of the third slain dog cooled, Ciccina appeared to Luigi wordless and calm, her cocked arm indicating a roadway. She motioned to him to follow. The roadway led to the orphanage, Luigi said. Soon it was apparent that the soul of his dearly departed wife was suggesting he turn their wild, dark-haired daughter over to the good Sisters' care. Each night for seven nights Ciccina appeared in Luigi's sleep after he wrestled with the three dogs, and each night for seven nights she made him follow her down the roadway, until the afternoon of the eighth day when he obeyed.

Then he made his way west, riding the rails across the vast country to California, where he'd heard that a man with a strong back could find work and food. Of course a thousand and one other pairs of ears had heard the same story, and the one actual job that was available saw a cloud of dust rising over the horizon and heard the pounding hooves of the men's desperate stampede as they made their way toward it, each man screaming, "The job's mine! mine! No, mine!" until at once the job fainted from fright. Then the foreman lifted his lips momentarily from between the deep crack in the owner's *culu* and handed the job's carcass to his spineless nephew, who'd made a career of scabbing wherever there was a strike, and the destitute men realized that all they had accomplished by traveling west was that they'd transported their misery to a more temperate climate.

It was true, Luigi continued, that in California so much fruit grew on the trees that it fell and rotted on the ground. It was true that the mountainsides were studded with gold. But what the stories failed to reveal was that the orchards and mines were enclosed by fences of barbed wire, the lengths of which were patrolled by *gabbilloti*. These *gabbilloti* were known as the National Guard, sometimes Burns detectives, sometimes Pinkertons, known to all the workers as dicks and blockheads and scissorbills and finks and goons.

Those who opposed them were known as bindle stiffs. They hoboed their way back and forth across the country, buying jobs from men they called sharks, or begging for day work or scraps. The ones called snipes and jerries laid railroad tracks. The skinners drove mules. The splinter bellies did carpentry work. The muckers shoveled dirt and ore and rock. Pearl divers washed dishes. Sewer hogs dug trenches and ditches. Groundhogs worked in tunnels. Timber wolves cut trees. And each night these poor souls gathered around a blazing campfire in hobo camps they called jungles, where the newcomers brought wood for the fire and everyone would pool whatever food they'd earned or begged that day. And as the moon rose in the sky above they'd tell stories and sing songs from the little red songbook each man carried in his pocket. And the stiffs would gaze up at the heavens and see the three shining stars of the I.W.W., the Industrial Workers of the World.

The I.W.W. beckoned seductively to the West's loggers and miners and harvesters, promising that if only they would join hands and stand together, the masters would be forced to pay them a fairer share of their labor's gain. It was clear to anyone who could count on his fingers and toes that the workers left the masters' forests, mines, and fields barely richer than when they entered them. Luigi said that the harvesters worked long, back-breaking hours, starting their day before dawn and not finishing until after sunset, stopping only for a cup of water—if indeed any water was brought out to the fields—or a bowl of soup or a piece of bread, the price of which the masters deducted from the worker's pay. Even at night some of the harvest stiffs were forced to pay the owners for straw to sleep on. For some their only blanket against the cold night was the abject twinkling of the stars.

As for food, whatever the farmer didn't eat was given to the cow, and what the cow didn't eat was given to the dog. What the dog wouldn't eat was given to the pig, and what the pig refused to eat was offered each dinnertime to the harvesters.

At one farm an old sow had died the month before, and the workers dined on pork for a week. Then an old cow was found dead, and for the next month the workers ate beef. But when the farmer's grandmother died and visible scraps of meat again floated in the workers' bowls, Luigi and several others fled.

From his days long ago as a *banditu* in Sicilia, Luigi had an adequate understanding of the workings of power. He knew that with power came options and choice. Power meant having choice. True power meant that perhaps one had some influence over the unpredictable swings of destiny. Luigi recognized that while the *banditi's* exercise of intimidation and force was overt and active, the Wobblies' strategy of collective resistance was passive and based on the idea that withdrawal was also an assertive means of force. Luigi came to see that action and inaction were powerful brothers. Each was shadow in the other's light. Each invited the common people to unite.

> *When the unions' inspiration*
> *Through the worker's blood shall run,*
> *There can be no power greater*
> *Anywhere beneath the sun.*
> *Yet what force on earth is weaker*
> *Than the feeble strength of one?*
> *For the union makes us strong.*

Luigi labored for countless hours in the fields, following the tide of each harvest, moving across the vast stretches of the West as the crops in each garden ripened, until one day something inside of him burst or ruptured and he fell to the ground, twisting in pain. Strangely colored foam bubbled from his nostrils and lips. In the incessant heat of the sun he tried to stand, then buckled forward and vomited out a greenish froth so thick and noxious that the stray, rib-thin dogs trailing the harvesters howled pitifully and scampered away after barely sniffing the odious mound of his spew. Luigi slumped backward and collapsed, overcome by some curse or profound shift in the fundamental alchemy of his character, or perhaps as the result of all the powders and potions dusted on the many and various crops he had cut and picked.

> *It is we who ploughed the prairies,*
> *Built the cities where they trade,*
> *Dug the mines and built the workshops,*
> *Endless miles of railroad laid.*
> *Now we stand outcast and starving*
> *'Midst the wonders we have made.*
> *But the union makes us strong.*

Indeed, one method of New World farming involved sprinkling strange powders over the crops as they grew. It was hardly important to the farmer if the workers were dusted, too. To begin, the workers were the ones doing the dusting. What did it matter if some of the powder fell on a worker's brow, dissolved in his sweat, and seeped into his skin? What did it matter if powder coated a second worker's tongue, or outlined a third's nostrils, or mixed in with the workers' food? There was a crop to bring in. There was a thriving market back East awaiting it. The crop was all that mattered, and if the workers didn't like dusting the fields they could buy some other job. They could tie a bandanna across their faces and keep their fat mouths shut, particularly the ones with the red card of the I.W.W. sticking out of their back pockets! They could take all their slogans and demands and threats of the black cat and go back to where they came from. Especially the greenhorns fresh off the boat who could hardly speak English! They jabbered away in the fields like a gang of monkeys. You expected to see them swinging limb to limb in the trees. The black-catters who sabotaged tools and machinery you'd like to hang by the neck. Wesley Everest, Frank Little, and Joe Hill were only a start. Tools were more valuable than workers, and complained and demanded less! At least after you bought a tool, you could trust it to do the job you asked of it. With workers, you could never tell. The only good thing about workers was that they were replaceable. If one worker fell, there was always another— usually someone younger and stronger—willing to take the fallen one's place, and usually for a lower wage.

> *They have taken untold millions*
> *That they never toiled to earn,*
> *But without our brain and muscle*
> *Not a single wheel would turn.*
> *We can break their haughty power*
> *Gain our freedom when we learn*
> *That the union makes us strong.*

Luigi's vomiting continued, thinning in composition and shifting erratically in color from sorrel to aqua and then all the way to puce. Then the colors of his ejection settled into a more orderly and logical spectrum. The hues ranged from cream to banana, from apricot to tangerine, ocher to umber, lime to cypress, lilac to turquoise to indigo to cerulean.

> *In our hands is placed a power*
> *Greater than their hoarded gold,*
> *Greater than the might of armies*
> *Magnified a thousandfold.*

> *We can bring to birth a new world*
> *From the ashes of the old,*
> *For the union makes us strong.*

"What color is he today?" the workers who gathered outside his tent asked.

"They say he's still working his way through the blues. You know that yesterday morning he was stuck for several hours at robin's-egg, but at last report he'd hit something resembling lapis lazuli."

"The greens are next, I'll bet."

"God help him. But as for his next color, my money's on the reds."

"I say the purples."

"Believe me, he'll go back to the oranges and browns. I've seen this ailment before."

"As long as he stays away from black, he'll be OK."

"I knew a miner from San Cataldo whose vomit eventually turned pitch-black. It started out the color of ash, and over the span of a week grew progressively darker. In no time he heaved out his actual belly, then coughed out the length of his intestines, his liver and kidneys and spleen, then both of his lungs, piece by bloody piece, until everything that was inside of him was outside. If only he'd been able somehow to flip himself backward through his skin and guts he might have become whole again. As it was, it took him three long agonizing days to die."

"Poor soul. May he rest."

"Heaven's such a clean place, sometimes you have to turn yourself inside out before you're allowed in. They say that the man from San Cataldo had to get rid of all that dust from the mines so he wouldn't cough any on the lily-white cloth that covers the Madonna'a altar."

"This case is different," an old woman said. "You can tell by the smell." She sniffed the air. "What this man is vomiting out comes from the very center of his soul."

"*Phhheeuuu!* If that's what his soul smells like, his deeds before he came to these fields must have been most foul!"

"It smells damp and rotten, as if something has died."

"Yes, I smell the dampness, and with a dash of sulphur."

"Yes, and with the breath of a dead donkey."

"Yes, and with the worst of a bean-and-garlic eater's early morning farts."

"A fava-bean eater. Precisely! And with a tinge of eel and anchovy and sardine. Go on, sniff the air. You can smell the sea."

"It smells dark and salty, like the ink sacks of *calamari*."

"Yes, and with the scent of gnawed bone and marrow."

"Yes, and with the oily smell of silver coins. Thirty pieces of silver sliding together in a sack closed tight at the neck by a draw-string."

"Yes, and with the undeniable odor of betrayal. Isn't that the stench of Judas Iscariot's breath?"

"Yes indeed, and it's the foulest odor in the world: the repulsive stench of the disciple's breath the moment before he kissed Jesù's sweet cheek in the garden."

"The wretched odor's not his alone," said the old woman. "That's what all of us smell like, to a greater or lesser extent, at least on the inside. Fill your lungs with it! I tell you, that's the unmistakable odor of mortal sin!"

"If that's what our souls smell like, may the Father have mercy on us!"

"Likely, God *is* being extremely merciful," said the old woman. "He's allowing the sinner time to purge. Every time that poor soul vomits out another teaspoonful, he works off another century of burning agony in Hell."

> *Solidarity forever.*
> *Solidarity forever,*
> *Solidarity forever,*
> *For the union makes us strong.*

At that moment the reds set in, and Luigi disgorged crimson, scarlet, cochineal, vermilion, and every other shade of red known to fire and flame. Then the farmer insisted that Luigi be removed immediately from his land, lest Luigi's sickness infect the crops and harvest. And so my brother was put on the back of a wagon and taken to a clinic, where no one understood either his tongue or his malady. By then he was working his way through the purples. He was transferred to a second clinic and then to a third, in part so that he might be among his own people and his murmurs and groans might be comprehended, and in part so that they would be the ones to bear the cost of sprinkling his corpse with lime after he died.

Fortunately for Luigi, the last clinic was one founded by Francesca Xavier Cabrini, the great and holy woman known more simply as Mother Cabrini, founder of the Missionary Sisters of the Sacred Heart as well as countless orphanages and schools, convents and clinics and hospitals, each devoted to the care of the poor and needy, and particularly the immigrants from Italy.

ONCE THERE WAS a poor but honest woman, *una fimmina di misericordia,* a woman of mercy, who devoted her life to the service of others, particularly the impoverished and weak. Her name was Francesca Xavier Cabrini, later known as Mother Cabrini and the first citizen of the New Land to be recognized as a saint. Even as a young girl in northern Italy, Francesca Cabrini cared for the songbirds that fell from their nests in the southernmost trees and spiraled down to the hard ground, where their hollow bones shattered and they scrambled their brains, their blood growing black in dismal puddles as they expired.

"Easy," she'd say to each fallen bird as she comforted it in her hands.

"If only I'd been a bit stronger," the birds would mutter, "I might have lifted myself up into the bright stream of air that would have carried me all the way across the sea to the new garden."

"Well, why didn't you wait until you were stronger?" the young Mother Cabrini would ask the dying birds. She posed her question logically because she was a sensible woman who firmly believed in the powers of reason tempered by the dictates of a generous heart.

"There's no getting stronger here," the birds would reply. "It was either leap or starve."

"They say that in the new garden there's plenty of everything for anyone with an eye to take it," other birds told her.

"I didn't actually leap from the nest," other birds confessed. "Mamma and Papa pushed me out."

"They pushed you out?" said Mother Cabrini. "How on earth could they do something so unfeeling?"

"Unfeeling?" the birds answered. "Girl, wipe the sleep from your eyes! It was for our own sake. They pushed all the children out, and why not? The dead man has no say to those who are dressing him. Look around, child. Open your eyes! Let your feet touch the ground! Here there is no work or food."

"Then I'll grow food for you and feed you," said Mother Cabrini.

But at that moment a bird of passage returning from the New World landed at her feet. "Listen," the bird of passage said, "if you really want to help you should go to the New World, where the children of southern Italy are falling sick left and right, with no one to care for them or feed them. There is no one to nurse them after they've become ill. There is no one to teach them to count or how to read or write. There is no one to lead them in their own tongue in the recitation of the rosary. Their children live in tenements so dark and damp that the kids grow up not knowing the true touch of the sun, and each night rats crawl over their sleeping bodies and lick the sweat pooling in the sockets of their dreamless eyes as unseen swarms of pestilence and malady fly through the dank air, flower on the walls and ceilings, and crawl across the surface of every floor."

Then the Pope appeared in his miter and robes and told

Mother Cabrini, "Go to the New World and care for these children, and I will give you six nuns." So Mother Cabrini left immediately for New York's Mulberry District

> *and the six became sixty,*
> *and the sixty, six hundred,*
> *multiplying like Jesù's loaves and fishes,*

but still it was not enough. *La Merica* was such a vast place that it seemed endless and inexhaustible, stretching from the North Pole all the way down to Tierra del Fuego, and Italy's children had scattered themselves in every corner of its face. They worked in the New World's factories and mines, in its fields and on its logging camps, out on the water and the roads made of iron rails. So Mother Cabrini returned to Rome and reported these facts to the Pope, who in response gave her seven missionary Sisters

> *and the seven became seventy,*
> *and the seventy, seven hundred,*
> *multiplying like Jesù's loaves and fishes,*

but still even all of that was not enough to meet the needs of Italy's children. Even the many orphanages and schools founded by Mother Cabrini and her Sisters were not enough. So Mother Cabrini traveled to Italy a third time and trained Sisters there for an orphanage and school she began in Nicaragua

> *and the hundreds became thousands,*
> *and the thousands, tens of thousands,*
> *multiplying like Jesù's loaves and fishes,*

and from there her good work spread through Central and South America, wherever there were people who were needy or poor.

Meanwhile, she was back in New York helping Bishop Scalabrini run a hospital for southern Italians, who were all too often deprived care by other hospitals because Italians were seen as something less, a primitive race, inherently criminal, with no morals and little intellect, something closer to monkey than man. If Italians were to come to these shores, the Europeans already in the New World wanted mainly painters and opera singers and those able to squeak some Paganini from a violin.

So Mother Cabrini and her Sisters opened their own clinic for Italians, naming it Columbus Hospital after the mercenary *paesanu* who'd visited the same shores four hundred years before. Soon the good work of Mother Cabrini and the Missionary Sisters spread to Chicago, Newark, and New Orleans, and from there she opened missions in Colorado, Wyoming, Washington, and California. Her work in Nicaragua spread to Brazil and then throughout the expanse of the new southern continent, over all of the Americas, wherever there were Italians in the New World.

ONE DAY MOTHER Cabrini met with the three leading tyrants of American industry: Andrew Carnegie, John Jacob Astor, and John D. Rockefeller. The living saint met the three barons of steel, fur, and oil in a plush office in New York, in a room set so high up in the clouds that near a window someone had placed a shining telescope on a three-legged stand.

After the initial exchange of pleasantries, Mother Cabrini remarked on the telescope and the trio's apparent interest in the stars. She intended her conversation about stars to lead them to discuss Heaven, as preparation for her request of charitable donations to her clinics and hospitals, as well as better working conditions for the immigrants who labored in the barons' many factories and mines.

But the three barons of industry corrected Mother Cabrini and told her that instead of using the telescope to gaze up at the sky they preferred to look down on the people who scuttled below them on the streets.

"See how tiny they look from this distance," the moguls said. "Even with the aid of this powerful lens they're like creatures swimming in the eye of a microscope. They swarm like maggots. They're small as ants."

"In God's eyes," replied Mother Cabrini, "even the slightest among them is a giant beyond measure."

"His telescope must be much different than ours," replied one of the three magnates.

They gestured to four chairs positioned around a magnificent mahogany table, inlaid with diamond-shaped pieces of wood that came from every forest in the known world. The varnished surface of the table was so shiny that Mother Cabrini could see in it the reflected image of nearly everything inside the room. She remarked on the table and told the men that, in much the same manner as the table's surface, a man's deeds on this earth were a reflection of the true nature of his soul. She hoped that the men would agree with the analogy, and their agreement would be grounds from which they might consent to her requests.

But the three barons of industry corrected her and said that rather than serve as a reflection of the soul, the condition of the table's surface was a useful indicator of their servants' diligence.

"Sometimes we smudge the table deliberately to see if our servants are really working when we're not here," the moguls said. "We place the tiniest scraps of paper in the room's corners to ascertain how well they've swept the carpets. To test a new servant's honesty we leave a gold coin lying alongside the wall. If the coin isn't returned the following morning, the thief is in jail by nightfall."

"In God's eyes," responded Mother Cabrini, "even the thief who has repented has a place in Heaven."

"What God chooses to see is his own business," replied the three magnates. "Our business is ours."

They invited Mother Cabrini to sit down and then offered her tea from a china set so opulent and dainty that Mother Cabrini remarked on its transparency and told the men that just as they could see the outlines of their fingers and hands through the glass, so could the Almighty see through their riches and finery into the true nature of their souls. Rather than wait for their assent she then asked the three men if they might consider doing something charitable for the Italians living in America, or at the very least if they might consider improving the deplorable working conditions under which the Italians in the New World labored.

"Kind and most gentle sirs," said Mother Cabrini, "working for the three of you are hundreds of thousands of human beings, each with a divine soul created by God, and each enduring hardship and deprivation beyond imagination. I can describe hundreds of different injuries the workers have suffered as a result of unsafe working practices or machinery. I can introduce you to hundreds of children who have worked in your mills and mines and who now cough blood with every word they speak. Just this past winter, due to inadequate heating, even more thousands died in your factories."

The three barons of industry interrupted her and said that all who labored for them were fortunate to have jobs, regardless of the specific working conditions, and if this past winter some were cold they should warm themselves by working harder. If the Italians didn't want their children to work in the mines or the mills or factories, they should keep them at home or send them to school. Weren't Italians the foreigners with the lowest proportion of children in school, and the highest proportion of children in the American workplace? We don't force anyone to labor for us, the three barons said. In fact, for every worker who falls incapacitated beside his machine, there are over a hundred others willing to take the fallen one's place, often at a lower wage.

"You're still a bit green, fresh from the boat, still wet behind the ears," the rich men told Mother Cabrini. "You don't understand how this new nation works or what drives its operation. Don't rattle your beads and crucifix at us. We're not impressed by your mumbo jumbo. We'd just as soon leave matters of the soul to the men in black dresses just as long as they leave matters of the wallet to the men in suits and long pants!" the three said as they sipped their tea.

"Hours before dawn every day workers stand in long lines in freezing rain and snow," the men told Mother Cabrini, "just begging to gain entry to our factories and mines! They do this morning after morning, day after day after day. If they don't care whether a machine is safe or the workplace is heated, why should you?"

"I speak on their behalf," said the saint from Italy.

"We choose not to recognize you as their representative. Besides," the three continued, "this is a free nation. Let those with complaints raise their own capital and start their own factories, and if they so choose they can heat them hotter than ovens! In the meantime we'll run our work sites in whatever ways we see fit. And if the workers don't like it, they can take the next boat back to where they came from!"

Mother Cabrini took a deep breath and smiled. Had she not already been one of God's saints she would have informed the men that to listen to them their good mothers would have slapped their mouths. Instead she asked, "Have you any human feelings left in your souls, any at all?" Had Mother Cabrini known the tale of Don Gattu and the apprentice *gabbillotu,* she would have told it to the three barons.

"Madam," the tyrants answered, their patience now worn thinner than the hundred-dollar bills the white men of their class used to light their cigars, "you've grown quite tiresome and have more than outstayed your welcome. Perhaps you too should return to the place from where you came."

"My place is with the workers," she told the three barons. "My place is with all honest working men, women and children."

"Then join them," the moguls said, "by all means."

After Mother Cabrini took her leave, one of the men lit a cigar and asked if the others had heard the latest joke that was making the rounds. The joke had to do with the sound that *merde* makes when a clump of it falls to the floor. Because the man thought himself civilized, he used the French word, *merde*. The two others smiled in anticipation of the jest and said no, they didn't know what sound *merde* made when it fell to the floor.

"Wop!" the first man said and laughed. Now all three barons puffed happily on fat cigars. "The clumps of *merde* go wop, dago wop, dago wop."

"They go wop—dago wop—oh, that's rich!"

It was then that the first capitalist observed that the telescope standing by the window now pointed up to the sky and insisted on swinging back up to that position regardless of his attempts to direct its focus back down toward the street. Then the second capitalist noticed that his reflection in the table's polished surface bore a distinct pair of pointed horns, and when he showed this to the others they, too, recognized that their likenesses had grown horns. Then the third capitalist saw that the bottom of his teacup was stained with the miniature black impression of his hand, and the others also saw that their teacups were likewise marked with the sign of their black hands.

Of course they blamed Mother Cabrini for these apparitions, and rushed to inspect the bottom of the teacup she had used. They were certain they would find the black hand there, too. But the base of Mother Cabrini's cup bore the impression of the Madonna's sweet, glowing face circled by a bright halo of stars.

For several moments the three barons stood transfixed by the image's beauty, and one of them nearly crossed himself and genuflected before the portrait, which made all his worldly accumulations seem paltry and mean. But at that moment the Virgin's face grew too radiant for their eyes, and each was forced to look away. Then the three fought over the cup like the fiercest of alley dogs, spitting and snarling and biting, and in their struggles they smashed the telescope and overturned and scratched the fine table, and shattered Mother Cabrini's magnificent cup into a thousand shards against the wall.

At that moment each man thought of his mother and held the memory of her face in his mind, until he felt her hand slap his face. "Shame," said the three men simultaneously. Then the vision was over, and the barons picked themselves and their burning cigars up from the smoldering carpet and went their separate ways.

Only sweet Jesù, whose Sacred Heart bleeds,
Knows if these robber barons repented their greed.

LUIGI HAD HEARD this tale about Mother Cabrini, as well as dozens of others, as he lay recuperating in the clinic operated by the good Missionary Sisters of the Sacred Heart. The four of us sat around the table in the twins' kitchen, baking the remainder of the Easter bread they had made. After he regained his strength, Luigi told us, he made his way back east, once again riding the rails with his little red Wobbly card as ticket, using the hobo system of marking towns and areas as his guide.

Hobos chalked symbols on fences and signposts, indicating where vagrants were tolerated or arrested, where a day's work or a clean bed or some hot food might be had. Through stories told and retold on the rails and around the blazing campfires in the hobo jungles, Luigi learned about a pair of twins who lived in Chicago, a stone's throw from the doorway of a church. In some stories the twins were Polish or Greek, in others Irish or Serb or Ukrainian. Year round the back door of the twins' first-floor flat was said to be open to all who knocked. The women served soup and bread, kielbasa and beans, lamb covered in lemon sauce, stew so hearty that after you visited them you had no need to eat for a week. Like many twins, they were fond of finishing each other's sentences. Before they fed you they gave you soap and water with which to wash, and after your meal they invited you to kneel with them beside the table and pray on behalf of their special intentions. Luigi said that when he heard that the pair gave a beautiful Saint Joseph's Day table, he knew they had to be his sisters. And so he followed the hobo's signs across the prairies to their back door, where he'd knocked the night before.

Now he had to find his daughter, Anna, whom he had given up years before. He'd leave with the sun the next morning, he told us. To which Livicedda and Rosaria protested, and out of nowhere I heard myself say, "But Luigi, after all of this time, you can't travel back to New York alone."

And before anyone knew it Rosaria was packing Livicedda's things, and Livicedda, Rosaria's. I immediately walked to the street corner and telephoned Gerlando, who agreed that as eldest sister I should accompany my wayward brother east even though it was a busy time, the week before Easter, Holy week, and my assistance was needed in the bakery.

Then Assunta, now known in the neighborhood for her ability to cure various ailments as well as birth babies and set broken bones, stopped by and said that she and young Rosalie wanted more than anything to join us. Then Rosa caught wind of our plans and convinced Salvatore to have his helpers cover his newsstands for a few days, and by mid-afternoon she and Salvatore and their seven children—their sons Santo, Vito, and Nicolo, and daughters Narda, Gilorma, and the twins Lucia and Rigginedda— said that they would accompany us on the journey to New York, too. And then of course as soon as Gerlando heard that everyone else was going, he asked how in the world could the rest of us be so cruel and hardhearted as to even think of leaving him behind, and so he baked bread through the long night and got a friend to take his place at the bakery, and by ten o'clock the next morning all fifteen of us, the whole Girgenti family then living in and around Chicago, departed from Union Station with Luigi.

We didn't know what we would find back East. Our mood was reckless and festive. Our trip, a sort of celebration. Of course we brought along with us enough food to feed the whole train, and we nearly did, as all those who spoke our tongue greeted us warmly and, at our insistence, joined us. We remembered many of the old stories and retold them as the train charged through the day and the dark night toward the coming dawn.

Anyone observing us would have thought we were on our way to a christening or wedding, and certainly not to the unhappy funeral that awaited us.

ONCE THERE WAS a poor but honest man, a man of belly, *un'omu di panza,* whose destiny it was to travel back and forth between the worlds of darkness and light, between the forest and the village, between the open and often lonely domain of strangers and the tight and often constricting embrace of *la famigghia.* Perhaps while still an egg floating about the sea of his mother's womb he failed to stick properly to the walls and instead rolled back and forth, one moment connected, the next detached. Perhaps his dear saint of a mother happened one day to observe some long-legged creature leaping forth and back—perhaps a grasshopper or cicada bounding from one weed stalk to the next—and a piece of the grasshopper's leg or restless wing flew near her nose and she breathed it in, and the child inside the egg inhaled the fragment, and it formed his personality and character. Perhaps this was so as to be an example to the others, particularly the children, whose burden it would be to keep the stories alive in their minds and on their tongues lest the past turn to dust, and their ancestors to ghosts no longer seen. Though some ghosts may no longer be seen is no proof that they do not still exist and that they are not as present before our blind eyes as our own children. Listen to me! The past breathes even more distinctly than the present! Perhaps this man's life was to show the children how easy it is to slide from one world to the next, and how very difficult it is to keep one's feet firmly walking the path that stretches between the light and the darkness.

This man had two brothers who both walked about as near to the world of light as they could. As it often turns out, one brother prospered while the other failed.

The younger brother worked in the shadow of the lofty limestone-covered towers that dared to scrape the sky, hawking the latest editions of the masters' version of that day's events interspersed with advertisements for whatever useless things the masters happened that week to be selling. The younger brother was himself changing from a worker into a master, over time employing others and eventually making considerable profit off their muscle and sweat. He owned and operated three newsstands on three prime street corners in downtown Chicago, in the crowded darkness beneath the squealing wheels of the city's elevated line of electric trolley cars, where the routes converged and made a loop around the business section before making their return runs to points south and north and west. All the while he was greasing the countless extended palms of the various officials who would enable him over time to control more and then still more and more.

The older brother owned little more than the cracked mug he used each evening when he shaved. He labored each day and evening inside the pounding madness of any one of a dozen factories, moving from Albany to Lawrence, from Lawrence to the Mulberry District of New York, from Mulberry to Poughkeepsie and then down to the Bronx, and so on nearly endlessly, dragging his family from one job and crowded tenement to another and always thankful for the work, thankful for the lather that covered his chin and neck and jaw, thankful for the moment the back of his head touched the bedsheets and he slid into the dark deliverance of sleep. He might have remained like this, on the edge of happiness, had his lungs been stronger and had he not taken sick. After each release from the sanatorium he searched another town for whatever labor he could find, emptying his mind and welding his spirit and body to some machine or assembly line. Whenever he wasn't coughing or spotting his handkerchief with blood, the hard muscles of his arms and legs were stamping out the cogwheels and pinions of progress in a repetition so dull and endless that it would have made a stone insane.

All of his life it seemed to the older brother that he was a dollar short, a day late, that he'd fallen into a deep hole from which there was no escaping. By the time he earned a dime he owed eleven cents. Indeed he came to believe that he had been born inside a hole from which he could never escape no matter how hard he labored. And each night after work, after he washed his arms and face in a tub in the kitchen and then sat down at the table to a crust of bread and a bowl of soup or beans, after he was too exhausted to lift his spoon to his mouth another time, after he twirled the wet bristles of his brush in the mug that held his soap and he scraped his face clean, he fell in bed and closed his eyes. There he lay with his dark wife, whom he cherished tenderly and could not resist, wanting her constantly, to hold and to be held, moving with her toward that agonizing moment of release when for a heartbeat or two he would soar beyond the reach of angels. Then his seed and her egg would knit yet another soul, and the hard muscles of her womb would stamp out another child, nearly all of them daughters, until the world could bear no more children and was full.

THEY WERE KNEELING around his coffin, nearly ready to nail it shut and carry it down to the wagon waiting in the street, by the time we arrived. This was after we'd gone to the orphanage to claim Anna, who even then had a small following of admirers, mainly young women, most of them pregnant, with their hair cut severely in imitation of the visionary. The admirers knelt in the cold rain on the sidewalk below Teresa's windows reciting the rosary. Anna was upstairs with the others, leading them in their prayers.

At the orphanage the Sisters told us about Anna's visions and the miracles, and one old nun whose palsy had been miraculously stilled sat with us after bringing us bowls of soup. Only Rosalie and Rosa's children ate as the Sisters expressed their sincere sorrow over the news of Tannu's passing. Luigi and Salvatore were stunned beyond speech. The rest of us wept softly. Only Gerlando was able to follow the directions the robed women gave us, and even then Tannu and Teresa had moved so often from one place to the next that the Sisters argued over whether it was this town or that town to which the blessed Anna had gone. The nuns bowed their heads ever so slightly whenever they said Anna's name. She pretty much came and went as she pleased, the Sisters told us, often disappearing for days at a time after which she would be found in her cell, kneeling before a burning candle in a glass cup, rosary in hand, praying and fasting. It took us another full day before we finally came upon the circle of Anna's followers praying the rosary in the rain.

They were the sign that we could let loose some of the fuller weight of the grief that pressed down on us.

"*Eeeee!*" Rosaria shrieked as we clamored up the stairs. "*Yaaah!*" Livicedda crooned, like a stabbed bird. The twins fluttered their hands in the air, and on the third-story landing outside Teresa's door did a dance so agitated that all seven of Salvatore and Rosa's children imitated them, and a voice from below shouted for us to have mercy and shut up, and then the door to the flat opened and we saw a serene, younger version of Ciccina's fair face.

"Blood of my blood," shouted Luigi, "forgive me my dark sins!" He threw himself before his daughter's feet and kissed the hem of her long skirt, telling her he was not worthy even to look at her.

Anna looked beyond him at the dancing twins, who were spinning like a pair of Sufis, their *eeeyaahs* growing increasingly more shrill. Both were beginning by this time to froth at the mouth. I knew it was only a matter of time before they began banging their heads and thrashing. But Anna raised her hands and did something with her palms that quieted them, and after a few more turns their gyrations slowed into a spasm that seemed nearly normal. Then they mixed calmly with the sea of dark-haired children that filled the room that held their father's body lying at rest inside the coffin.

Luigi rose and knelt before the grieving figure of Teresa, who sat broken in a chair beside the box that held her husband. Salvatore stood beside Teresa, giving her his vow that she and her children would never again know even the slightest need as long as he had life and breath. Assunta and Anna were embracing, and then Teresa unleashed a sob that could have made even the most impenetrable slab of stone break apart and weep, and all of us at once commenced our grieving.

A STRANGER MIGHT think us Italians loud or crude, what with the way that we wail and scream when someone we love passes. Already I knew that we had come to a land that would stunt and shame and silence us. Our ways were too loud, filled with too much emotion and ardor. Already I could see that *La Merica* preferred that we tiptoe and whisper, and certainly that whenever we talked we tie our hands behind our backs. As anyone with sense knows, if your hands are made of wood you can't speak freely or openly from the heart. Speech is so much more than a mere set of sounds made by the tongue and mouth.

There's an old story about God, about how one day he and Jesù got into an argument. Their quarrel nearly split Heaven in two. God started things by complaining about how many of his commandments the living on earth were breaking every moment of each passing day, and how it was really making him sick, how in his infinite but steadily waning patience he was seriously considering sending down another forty days or so of fire and destruction, enough to roast most on earth and turn any nosy gawkers to pillars of salt, though as usual he'd spare a handful of the purest and more repressed and obedient souls, several wide-hipped young women and a few old men who could recite his laws by heart, enough to start the experiment over again, until Jesù interrupted the rant and said, "Hey, enough's enough."

The Son sighed deeply, then shook his head at the Heavenly Father. "Since you're God and it is and was and always will be your creation," said Jesù, "of course you may do whatever it is that you want, but in my opinion the cycle will only repeat itself, and in a couple thousand years we'll again be having this same conversation."

"This time will be different," said the Father. "I'll make the fire of retribution hotter. My children will learn their lesson. This time they'll behave."

"No, they won't," said Jesù Cristu. "This time won't be a bit different because you're no different."

"How could I be any different?" said God. "I'm everything that ever was or is or will be. I'm alpha and omega, the beginning and the end, and all that can ever be between. I'm perfect. I'm everything. I'm God."

"You're everything within your own nature," said Jesù. "You're each and every possibility and permutation within an extraordinarily vast but ultimately limited set. As for being perfect, your flaws are so obvious I could laugh."

"You think I have flaws?" roared God the Father.

"Does a lit candle have a flame?" said the Son. "Does burning incense have smoke? Yes, my Holy Father, you have flaws, the worst of which is your everpresent anger, which round the clock you keep at a steady, fully rolling boil. Your wrath is so volcanic that Vesuvius and Etna might as well be glaciers holding up the North and South poles. Now, please don't misunderstand my point. It's not so much that you become angry every time you're disobeyed, but that instead of letting your anger burn itself out as anger should, you let it fester and run like an untended sore."

For a moment God the Father stood speechless.

"Consider what you did with Adam and Eve," Jesù continued. "They didn't obey you and so you banished them from the garden and burdened them for all eternity with guilt and shame. I might agree with the banishment, but you never fully forgave them and still resent them so much that to this day you still consider the children of their children's children stained mortally with sin. You did much the same with the rebellious angels when you created Hell. When are you ever going to learn to ease up? I had to go down to earth myself and live there and die just to crack Heaven's doorway and shut down Limbo, where the dead souls were packed in so tight it was worse than the most evil slumlord's wildest dream."

"Watch your mouth when you talk to me," said God the Father.

"What?" Jesù said with his wisest smile. "And what will you do if I don't, crucify me?" He stretched out his arms in mock death and winked. "Listen to me, Father. What I'm telling you here and now is for your own good. Your unforgiving nature is, at the very least, extraordinarily difficult to live with. Now, it's perfectly OK to correct the contrary, but after a while the wiser course is to take a deep breath and bless and forgive. My advice to you is that when you feel something, feel it *completely* with your entire body, soul, and mind. I learned that as I knelt in Gethsemane, sweating drops of blood, as I accused you of forsaking me and cried out to you as I hung on the cross. Whatever you feel, feel it completely! Then be done with it once and for all! Be like the bell that tolls truly and fully when it's struck, then stills to a contented silence. Don't echo on and on, from one century to the next, punishing generation after generation. If and when you leave the flock of ninety-nine to go after the one who strayed, the poor errant sheep you rescue never hears the end of it. You punish it for the rest of its life, and you make its mate and children suffer, and their children suffer, and so on and so forth for a thousand and one years. If the wandering sheep baas out its contrition and means it sincerely, I forgive and wipe the slate clean and we both move on."

"You're too soft," God the Father told his Son. "That's precisely what's wrong with the world today, why it's growing more and more rotten by the second. You've grown soft on sin! Sin must never be tolerated or excused! It must always be punished, each and every single occasion, all sin, mortal or venial, whether by thought, desire, action, word, or omission, with no exceptions, alibis, or room for appeal." Bolts of lightning shot from the tips of the Father's fingers. He pounded his mighty fist in the palm of his eternal hand. "All that I gave them were ten commandments, so simple that even a dull child could put them to memory."

"And all that I gave them was hope," Jesù said. "Hope and forgiveness. Mercy and a chance for life after death. Heavenly Father, verily I say to you, you don't know what joy swells in my heart whenever a lifelong sinner repents at the last hour."

"That's why I made the fires of Purgatory every bit as hot as those that flow through Hell, for these so-called conversions at the end," said God the Father. "I'm nothing if not consistent and fair. I take the whole life into account. I reward the worker who labors for me from dawn to sunset over the one who comes to me five minutes before the moon is rising."

"Indeed," said Jesù Cristu, "that is precisely the difference between us. I'm nothing if not a forgiving master. I reward the workers who labor in my vineyard equally, regardless of what time in the day they come to me. I pay the one who comes to me a minute before nightfall the same as I pay the one who labors in my name the whole day."

"You're wrong," said Diu.

"No, you're wrong," responded Jesù.

Then the Blessed Virgin came upon the Father and Son and told them both to stop their shouting and go to bed, because the hour that was upon them now was hers.

. . .

AND SO I say to you who hear my words that the true way to express human feelings, particularly such severe and threatening emotions as anger and grief, is to allow them to purge and run their course! Don't fear them or avoid them, and don't fall in love with them either and hold them dear to your heart and end up rationing them out over a lifetime. Hold the feeling in your heart and allow it its full expression.

When you grieve, grieve as fully and completely as you are able. Shout out in sorrow. Scream. Tear your hair. Weep until your eyes and throat are red and raw.

Do everything you are able to do in front of the departed soul's body. Speak to your loved ones as well as to others. Pray. Laugh. Remember some of the old stories and songs, and sing and recite them. Eat, if you can, at least a little to keep up your strength. Drink so that your body at least may make more tears. At night, try to get a few moments of sleep. Doing all of these things in the dead's presence means that you know it's OK to go on living after the dead is in the ground. Doing these things tells the dead not to worry about you, to turn away and enter the world of the spirits. Believe me, if such things are not OK, the dead will sit up in their coffins and tell you!

Cry out with the pain of separation, if need be, from every cell that pulses in your body. Clothe yourself in black and weep copiously the next day, as well as on the third day, the fourth, the fifth. Then weep some more, until your sorrow has moved beyond tears and become as tangible and heavy as Jesù's cross.

Then drop the weight of the wood down on your shoulder and walk. Take the first step, then the next. Over time the weight of the cross will ease. Over time you will rejoice in the fact that you are still living. Live in honor of the departed. Take away nothing from the graveside but sorrow's weight and a handkerchief drenched a thousand and one times over with tears.

· · ·

KNEELING BESIDE MY brother's dead body, emaciated from the tuberculosis that wasted him away, I grieved for him and his wife and his family. I wondered how our lives would have been different if I, the firstborn, had been a boy. How would my character have worn the destiny Papa Santuzzu chose for him?

"Brother," I whispered, "I wish that I had been there with you, during the years you labored in Palermu. Brother, I wish that I could have kept you company whenever you were alone. I wish I could have stood beside you in the factories where you worked. I wish I could have held you during your long days and nights in the sanatorium."

From what we gathered from Teresa's stories, during Tannu's last years he was made to stay in the sanatorium the whole week and allowed to go home only every other weekend, and even then he had to keep to himself, and everything he touched had to be boiled. Later, after we'd all returned to Chicago, Teresa told us that Tannu would sit beside the window and cry because none of his children could hug or kiss him. He had to sleep by himself, too, then sterilize all his bedding before returning to the sanatorium for another fortnight.

"Brother," I whispered as I knelt beside the coffin that held his wasted body, "if only I had known, I would have been here with you. Sleep for now, brother. May Mamma cradle and rock you in her arms. May she kiss your brow and cheek." I stood and kissed my brother's brow.

"Brother, may you know that in a way you were father to all of us."

NO ONE WAS surprised when Teresa threw herself on Gaetanu's coffin just as the gravediggers were about to lower it into the cold ground. One gravedigger who was Italian had already given Teresa the flag sent by the government. Without hesitation Salvatore pulled Teresa away from the dark gash in the ground and back to the clutches of the living, at once and again accepting responsibility for her and her children.

Salvatore threw a clump of dirt down the hole onto the coffin, and the rest of us did likewise, and then the gravediggers and my brothers took up shovels and filled the grave until all that remained before us was a sullen mound of dirt. The gravediggers swung the shovels over their shoulders and left. The one who was Italian stayed with us. The wind whipped the bare black branches of a nearby tree, below which now stood three old women, and at once the gray sky whirled with a sudden snow.

Teresa threw herself down on the grave, and this time Salvatore let her remain there. *"Eeeee!"* cried Rosaria. *"Yaaah!"* cried Livicedda. Salvatore knelt beside Teresa and dropped his body down beside her, screaming out his grief not only for his brother but for Adriana and Santuzzu and all we had left behind. Then all of us grieved for our brother and for Adriana and Santuzzu, and all that we had left.

Now that we'd put our own brother—our own flesh—into the ground, now we truly belonged to this place. After Gaetanu's burial, America wasn't such a new world.

In the nearby tree, a trio of black crows squawked carelessly, callously. Our grief for Tannu welled up and spilled over, reminding us of all the others whom we'd lost. Rosa called out to her parents, Gnaziu and Francesca, as well as for her brothers and sisters who'd gone to Brazil and Argentina. Luigi grieved for Ciccina and Petru. Assunta wept in sorrow for Elena and Stefanu. Gerlando whispered a prayer for all those he'd left back in Palermu on the Via Duca della Verdura. Anna knelt, resplendent, reciting the rosary to the Blessed Virgin. Even the three strangers who watched us from a distance knelt at Tannu's graveside and grieved. The sound of their moans carried ours all the higher into the sky. And the twins cried out in sudden thanks to Saint Joseph for having answered their prayers. It was the table in his honor that had brought Luigi back to the rest of us, and the rest of us back together, into one another's arms, where we belonged.

. . .

LIFE TAKES ITS own turns, going first one way, then the next. Left to itself, life is like a river finding its own way through a valley, running not where others want it to go but where it chooses to run, entirely in its own manner and with its own force and strength.

Even though it was snowing, none of us wanted to leave Tannu's graveside. As if out of respect for us, the sun hid his face behind the clouds. The wind died down. The snow floated down in big, white, lazy flakes, much to the delight of the children, who were doing their best to behave and understand why we remained.

"You're fortunate the burial was today," said the Italian gravedigger, lighting his pipe. "You know, we can't bury over Easter weekend."

"Once we were all eggs," cried Rosaria, as if she had just discovered the idea. "Scrambled eggs," said Livicedda, "all stirred together inside Mamma's womb."

"The Church doesn't allow burials past Maundy Thursday," said the gravedigger. "None on Good Friday or Holy Saturday. Of course none on Easter Sunday itself. And yet the dead keep on dying." He took a draw from his pipe. "Come Monday morning you should see the piles."

"We were all piled together," said Rosaria. "Inside the Madonna's womb," said Livicedda. "Covered up all over with ricotta," said Rosaria. "Fresh ricotta and *basilicu* and a pinch of salt," said Livicedda, who then commenced, with Rosaria's assistance, to tell the gravedigger and the three mourners about the making of ravioli.

"It's not right," said the gravedigger. "It seems since we can't bury over the weekend, he might give death a reprieve."

"My sweet husband is dead!" Teresa cried and again fell forward on the mound of dirt, her sharp cries rising in yet another pitched frenzy.

I could already see some of the fear of our feelings in the eyes of our children, who I realized then were *menzi e menzi,* half and half, half like us, half the New Land. What had we done by coming here? I wondered. I felt my stomach for the eggs I knew were still within me but which would never grow fat because of my husband's cooked seed. For the thousandth time I grieved for my children that would never be.

"All that matters," continued the gravedigger, still speaking to the three strangers and the twins as if they were following the thread of his argument, "is that we are each going to die. Whether it's today or tomorrow, or next year or in twenty years, doesn't matter much. Whenever, it's too soon. Everything anybody needs to know stems from that fact."

The twins responded with something else about ricotta, and the children began asking for food, the smaller ones crying now in hungry complaint. We looked up from the dark ground through our hot tears into the falling snow.

"We're hungry," cried the children. They pointed to their open, empty mouths. "Feed us," cried the children.

"But we have nothing here to feed you with," Salvatore told them. He patted the pockets of his coat to show the children that he was hiding nothing.

"But we're starving," cried the children I never gave birth to. "Feed us." The smaller ones raised their little hands as if in petition to the sky.

Then the three old women joined the children in their request. The women stood and showed us their arms and legs, which were so thin they resembled sticks.

"But we have nothing with us to give you," Luigi told them, opening his arms. "Believe me. We brought only our hopes and sorrows and now our grief to this place."

Then Livicedda and Rosaria cried out as if something stepped on them. They opened a bag containing the Easter bread they'd cooked earlier that week with Luigi, and which we were saving until Easter. In light of the funeral, we had forgotten all about it. Rosaria and Livicedda gave each of the old women one of the *pupi cull'ovi,* a bird or hand clutching an egg, sprinkled all over with red sugar, and the strangers blessed and broke the bread and then blessed the twins and the children and Gaetanu and all the rest of us, and my twinned sisters handed out Easter bread to everyone there.

I didn't remember them baking so many. I remembered them baking at most three or four pans, but Rosaria and Livicedda gave the children dozens of *pani di Pasqua,* more than they could ever possibly eat! And since the twins' bag seemed full, they gave bread to the gravedigger and all the adults, and still their bag of Easter bread seemed as full as the snow that once again grew heavy and swirled blankly around us.

Then we heard a deep, low sound coming through th. snow toward us, the droning strains of a band of moaning horns, cymbals, and drums. Out of the whiteness toward us tramped an orchestra playing a slow and formal funeral dirge. Behind the musicians marched the group of Anna's followers. They stood at a respectful distance from Anna and shouted an apology. The trombone players and both clarinetists went to the wrong address, they said, and then they all became lost in the snow.

"You're lost no longer," Anna told them. "Here, pray with us."

Livicedda and Rosaria gave each of the followers one of the *pani di Pasqua.* The bread the twins now drew from their bag was in forms that I, wife of an expert baker, had only heard about but never actually seen. They handed my niece's followers Easter bread in the shape of baskets and church bells, water pitchers and candlestick holders, wine goblets and sacred hearts, rosaries and crosses and something resembling a crown of thorns. Anna gave each of the forms her blessing, and the followers ate the bread and eggs while the musicians reassembled and resumed playing.

The musicians played a dirge so beautiful and sad that the granite and limestone angels and saints topping the gravestones around us covered their faces with their hands and wept. The statues' tears shimmered down their stone faces and then froze like decades of a rosary into beaded lines of ice. Teresa's shoulders shook and her chest convulsed as the pool of her sorrow again tried to empty. She stood between Salvatore and Luigi, her brothers by blood, who held her up now in their arms.

One by one her and Tannu's children began crying out, "Papa! Papa! Papa!" and in an endless procession marched to the graveside and kissed their palms and then touched their kisses to the earth, which was being rapidly erased by the falling snow.

The musicians played on with sadness and a mourning edged with triumph, with dignity and an esteem fit for the highest king. Then Anna and her followers led us in the recitation of the rosary and the Litany for the Dead. And then for a third time the twins opened their bag of Easter bread and fed all who gathered around us as they grieved and prayed and gave honor to our brother, who lay buried beneath the earth and snow.

> *Now that Jesù's been eaten, the sun may ascend*
> *And our stories and songs may come to their end.*
>
> *Rosa, who began the round with the tale of Papa's fate,*
> *Returns us to true ground before the hour grows late.*

Tying the Knot

 *Rosa Dolci*

ONCE THERE WAS a poor but honest man, *un'omu d'onuri,* a man of honor, who worked the whole day—day after day—in the unrelenting heat of the blazing sun, scratching the pitiful dirt at his feet with a wooden hoe, coaxing the useless dust first this way and then that way, like a mother combing her feverish child's thin, dulled hair, urging the earth to release something he and his children and wife might eat, so that they might live to work beneath the scorching sun another day, and not starve. Thank God, *figghi di mi figghi,* daughters of my daughters, sons of my sons, that each of you is a stranger to real hunger. Do my arms squeeze you too tight? Ha! Imagine the slow and suffocating stranglehold of true starvation, like a snake slowly coiling itself around your belly and ribs, squeezing all breath and vitality from you. Each passing day you grow more weak. In the shadow of your hut you squat and chew straw.

The man's name was Papa Santuzzu. He was your great-grandfather, the father of your grandfather, Salvatore, may he rest.

No, I don't know exactly where the hut used to stand, but I think these were the *baruni*'s fields. May he burn forever and always, receiving for all of eternity what in his life he gave to those beneath him. These fields all look the same to me anyway, wild and untended as they are. You get the idea. The land is full of rocks and covered with thorns. That's prickly pear. We used to eat it whenever we could find some. Yes, Papa Santuzzu really owned a white donkey, Gabriella, whose trumpet was so mellifluous people would ask her to sing at weddings. Yes, Santuzzu really did win her in a game of cards. No, not pinochle. Not double pinochle either. Tresette. If you want, I'll teach you how to play back at the hotel.

Does it really matter that we find the precise site of the hut? Smell the air. This is the same air we breathed. Ahh, *bedda Sicilia!* I cannot live with you, nor can I live without you! Yes, this is just like the ground we walked and tended. Above is the sky to which we offered our hopes and prayers. Why do you feel the need to stand on the exact piece of dirt on which your grandfather was born? Here, where we stand, is where he was born!

Give me your hands. All of you. Your *nonnu* was born here. And here. Here. That's right, thump the flat of your hand against your chest. And I was born there, too. We were all born right there inside you, you understand? Inside your chest. What does it matter that we were ever alive if today we don't live inside your hearts, and inside the hearts of your children, and your children's children?

SIT WITH ME. That's right, all of us in a circle. Sure, later when it's dark we can build a fire. The story I want to tell you begins at dawn, on the day that your *nonnu* and I were destined to leave this place.

"I want to show you something," Santuzzu said to us as we awoke. Already he stood by the door. "Follow me, Salvatore," he said. "Rosa, follow me."

So together we walked from our hut to the fields, as we had done thousands of times before. Old Gabriella trailed us, as she always did, out of habit.

"What do you want to show us, Papa?" Salvatore said, pausing for a moment to look back at the hut. Though part of your *nonnu* was sad, another part of him wanted to chase his fate to see what the powers above had in store for him. Your grandfather thought there was nothing new to see here in this old place. He'd seen and explored everything within leagues. As the third-born son and therefore the last to get to do anything, he was more than eager to start out on his travels. As for me, I didn't much care. I loved him so dearly that I would have lived out my life with him even if he chose to live inside a cave.

Santuzzu said nothing. He scrambled up the hillside like a goat, walking sure-footed ahead of us even though he was nearly blind, leading us up a rise toward a hill, which the three of us climbed, and which we knew overlooked the far portion of the *baruni*'s fields. As we neared the top of the hill, Santuzzu said that in order to get there we had to cover our eyes and walk the rest of the way, like him, blind.

"Why do you ask this of us?" we said. "Papa, this is no time for games. We've been up here a thousand times."

"Ahh, you may think you know what's up here," Santuzzo said, "but in all truth you don't."

Still, we did as he instructed, climbing as slowly and carefully as old Gabriella so that we wouldn't trip. "What do you want us to see, Papa?" Salvatore asked again after we'd reached the peak.

Santuzzu put his hands on our shoulders and pointed us away from the rising sun. "Open your eyes," he said. "Regard my garden."

So we opened our eyes, blinking away the morning's fierce sunlight, and saw only the same untended fields that we'd seen a thousand times before. The ground was miserably spotted with boulder and bramble and the twisted black branches of gnarled trees. In the midst of the fields lay the shattered remnants of various ruins—the eroded columns and archways of ancient temples—now useless slabs of rock. The ground was stripped nearly bare of vegetation by the heavy winter rains and made up of a mix of broken rock and clay baked hard as stone in the unrelenting heat of the summer sun, then hammered by rain and baked again the next year, and so on, each time becoming twice as hard as before.

We said we didn't see anything that even remotely resembled a garden.

Santuzzu told us that we were both dunces. "You're not looking good enough," he said. "Look harder."

So we looked harder, past the fields, to where the blue line of the horizon shimmered in the morning heat. The blue horizon beckoned to Salvatore, who felt quite keenly that now was his time to be alive at last, that the possibility of change for him suddenly existed, that something not only was calling to him to explore the unknown region beyond the known and seen but was also simultaneously threatening to kill him if he dared make a mistake or perhaps even take one step beyond. Salvatore was like one of those ancient sailors who feared sailing too close to the horizon lest he be swallowed by sea monsters lurking just below the water's surface or lest his fragile boat fall off the sudden edge of the flat world into the dark abyss.

"Tell me what you see," Santuzzu said to us.

"Nothing," Salvatore said. "The same as always. The useless and the old."

Santuzzu laughed. "Rub the sleep from your eyes, *babbu,* and use them! Don't you see that pair frolicking down below in the field? They're my parents, Vincenzu and Gilorma. They celebrate the morning sun. Look at them kick up their heels! Can't you hear their flutes and bagpipes?" Yes, bagpipes. Their origins are from here, from Sicilia.

Your grandfather and I looked where Santuzzu pointed but we saw only ruin and weed. We listened but heard only the wind and Gabriella's impatient snorting as she suffered the morning's first swarm of thirsty flies.

Santuzzu stood beside us, his milk-white eyes open, a smile cracking his face, both arms outstretched, dancing a twisted little dance.

"From up here," Santuzzu said, "you can see them best, particularly when they wake up and play. Look at that group over there, prancing in a circle!"

We thought perhaps he was remembering something from some other time, some memory that had broken loose in his mind and drifted into the present, inviting him to again see and taste it. Even down in the village he often spoke to the vacant air, as if there were someone else in the room with him. At times he would mumble in confused loops that made little sense. Salvatore and I knew that we couldn't bring him with us, and yet we felt we couldn't wait for him to die. Do you recognize what I'm confessing? We left him, alone, to die.

Santuzzu told us that after we had gone he'd go down into the valley and join the others in the fields.

"Even though I still breathe," Santuzzu told us, "the boldest ones there trust me enough now to speak to me. We sit together in the shade of the ruins. They feed me bread, sometimes dried grasshoppers and honey. We drink a heady wine. And it's as if I'm a young man again, and Adriana is young, too, and sitting there beside me. All of the fallen rocks are standing straight up, back where they once stood, holding up the great temple, whose roof glistens so brilliantly in the sun that to look at it you have to shade your eyes with the flat of your hand. With your whole being you know then that this is, still and always, a sacred land where the gods walk."

"But Papa," Salvatore said, with all the confidence and virility of a young man yet to fully consider the reality of his own life and death, "those gods are dead."

"You disappoint me," said Santuzzu. "I expected you, more than any of the others, to be able to understand this. The third son is supposed to have special sight."

"But I have special sight," argued your grandfather. "In my mind I see a great new land, *La Merica,* just beyond the horizon. I see its three great cities: New York, Brazil, and Argentina. I see myself walking in those cities, my pockets bulging with so many coins that I jangle like a tambourine. I see Tannu and Luigi strolling arm-in-arm in the sun. I see our children, and our children's children, with so much food in their bowls that their mothers have to tell them to eat lest some of their food go to waste."

"You can see all that," Santuzzu said, "and yet your eyes remain sightless to the orchards and gardens below?"

Your grandfather looked down on the desolate fields owned by the family of the despised *baruni* who, happily for all, was safely dead and buried, having been turned into a snail by a generous *mavaza* and then boiled alive inside a pot overflowing with the juices of his own evil. "Other than you, Papa, I see nothing here," said your grandfather.

"Nothing at all?" said Santuzzu.

"Nothing good or worth desiring," Salvatore replied. He drew in a deep breath and looked back at the sun. "Nothing worth remaining here for, except of course you and the memory of my dear mother."

"Then there is nothing more to say," Santuzzu said. He turned, then nimbly started down the hill, with Gabriella at his heels.

LATER, WHILE SALVATORE was going over his instructions to Rosaria and Livicedda as to how to behave, and Assunta was inspecting the ground one last time and gathering a final basket of this weed and that, Santuzzu motioned to me and the two of us went for a walk, accompanied only by our lengthening shadows and old Gabriella.

"Tell me that you'll return," he said. "Not soon, perhaps not even while you are yet young, but someday before you are so old that you'll forget. Promise me that you'll tell your children about our lives here."

"Of course," I said. "Your grandchildren will love and respect you. I'll teach them all our ways. The new world will be just like here, only with more food and better work."

"I pray to the Father that it will be so," he said. "And I bless you, sweet Rosa. May you bear Salvatore seven children, and may each of them have seven children of their own, and each of them seven, and so on, down through all of time, until the day we are all together in Heaven above."

"And may you be safe and protected each and every moment while we are gone," I said. Must I say again that my heart was breaking? I took his hand in mine. "May the Holy Mother keep you forever in her palm." I pressed my fingers against his hand, then brought it up to my mouth and kissed the center of his hand.

"Don't worry about me," Santuzzu said with a laugh.

Then the mid-morning sun slipped behind the clouds, and for a moment or two in this other world, Sicilia, the land that time forgot, it seemed as dark as night. We had walked to the village's center, where on special nights those who stayed behind gathered against the darkness around a blazing fire talking about themselves and all those who'd left. Everyone was expected to bring some wood. As we squatted around the fire someone would beat out a tune or hum until a second would sing or take up some instrument and play, and as the moon slid higher in the sky toward the promise of the coming day a third would start a tale and, like a weaver with her yarn, stretch it out and let it spin

> *and end her story with a rhyme,*
> *and so the next soul with a tale would begin*
> *and all would pass the time*

bringing fresh wood to the fire, telling one story after the next, until we'd gone full circle and everyone who had wanted to had given breath to a song or story.

In that moment of darkness I watched Papa Santuzzu walk from me and join the circle around the fire, and there with him was Mamma Adriana and several babies who, I could only guess, were Salvatore's dead brothers and sisters. With them I saw my parents Gnaziu and Francesca, along with my brothers and sisters.

I saw Gaetanu and Giufà, Anna Lo Pizzo and Antuninu from Campufiuritu, Arturo Giovannitti, Joseph Ettor, Carlo Tresca, and Elizabeth Gurley Flynn. Beside Teresa Pantaluna sat Placidu and the sad-eyed ewe as well as Ducella and more dimpled, dark-haired baby girls than any division of mathematicians could ever count. There was Ciccina Agneddina and her parents and brothers and sisters alongside Luigi, Nonna Nedda, and Don Gattu, whose tears hissed as they trickled into the campfire's flames. There was the man from Vizzini and the stick-thin *mavaza,* on whose lap sat a cheerful dog wearing a black mask. There was Assunta and her daughter Rosalie, Ziu Griddu, Stefanu, and Elena the Virgin. There was Gerlando Cavadduzzo and Carla and all the merchants and whores from the Via Duca della Verdura. There was Anna and her infant brother, Petru, next to Anna's dark advocate and a host of children and nuns. There was Livicedda and Rosaria, Saint Joseph, Saint Rosalie, Saint Philip Benizi, Bishop Scalabrini, and Mother Cabrini. There was the miner from San Cataldo, Wesley Everest, Frank Little, Joe Hill. There was Nicola Sacco and Bartolomeo Vanzetti and all the others killed in the New World for being Italian. There was even the *Madonna nera,* Jesù, and their graying father, Diu, who held his head in his palm and seemed to be trying his best not to fall asleep. Papa Santuzzu stood before them all, clearing his throat in preparation of speaking the first words of the night's long story.

"Once there was a poor but honest man," began Papa Santuzzu, *"un'omu d'onuri,* a man of honor."

The vision lasted only for a moment, the moment when the sun was swallowed by the clouds. Then Salvatore called out to me, saying it was time for us to depart from this place, and the illusion faded.

Yet in my heart I have no doubt that what I saw was true. I saw them all, and more, gathered around a campfire. And I know that tonight, as the moon begins to rise in the sky and the sun again falls, all the dead souls will gather here in the center of this village, again, as will all of you, *figghi di mi figghi,* daughters of my daughters, sons of my sons, wherever on this bountiful earth you may be, for as long as we are able to sit together against the night and give voice to our true songs and stories.

If these rhymes and stories miss their aim or fail,
Cast blame on the teller and not on the tale.

And may the Holy Mother bless and heed most dear
All whose eyes read these words, all those gathered here.